ADULT BOOK

ADULT BOOK

MALCOLM KNOX

BLOOMSBURY

First published in Great Britain 2004
This paperback edition published 2005

A CIP catalogue record for this book
is available from the British Library

Bloomsbury Publishing Plc, 38 Soho Square, London W1D 3HB

ISBN 0 7475 7664 5
9780747576648

10 9 8 7 6 5 4 3 2 1

All papers used by Bloomsbury Publishing are natural,
recyclable products made from wood grown in well-managed forests.
The manufacturing processes conform to the
environmental regulations of the country of origin.

Printed by Clays Ltd, St Ives plc

www.bloomsbury.com/malcolmknox

For Wenona

Author's note

Although some real names have been included for context, the characters and events in this story are fictitious. On the other hand, the people who read and helped with various drafts are not. Thanks to Jane Gleeson-White, Antony Harwood, Fiona Inglis, Jane Palfreyman, Andrew Riemer, Zoe Walton and, most generously, Jon Casimir and Wenona Byrne. Acknowledgements also to Dr Procter for the consultations, Spencer Nadler's article 'A Woman with Breast Cancer' (*Harper's*, June 1997), and Luke Ford for shining a light around the bottom of the pit.

But if you are sympathetic, if you have the motivation, you can be in any town, any city, in the world, a stranger on your first day, and it will sing to you. Some people run from Grandma's house, they long for the bite of the wolf.

Louise Welsh, The Cutting Room

PART ONE

At 6.10 pm on the second Tuesday in November, Dr John Brand passed the entrance to the shop for a fourth time. He traversed one block, pivoted at the traffic light, and came back for a fifth pass. He paused at an automatic teller machine, pretending to examine the screen in the aluminium pod, using this apparent distraction to disguise another about-face and return past the doorway, his oscillations tightening.

Six.

He could find neither the courage to enter nor to go home.

An ordinary sixty-seven-year-old gentleman on ordinary business, Dr Brand was said to be a pillar of the community; though, as his wife occasionally remarked, if he was one of the pillars then someone should sue the builder. She meant it jokingly, a knowing quip crusted over by thirty-eight years of marriage to a husband dull enough to be beyond reproach. But then, Margaret thought he was working late tonight, half a city away.

It was a cool overcast evening. At this time of year, notion-ally springtime, days of winter and summer took turns, two seasons wrestling. Today winter had made its final counter-thrust, a last futile hurrah of low pressure, southerly gusts and mackerel skies. John preferred winter and welcomed days like this as a respite from the humidity. Nevertheless, a layer of nervous sweat tickled his forehead.

He tamped his brow with the flat of his hand, pretending to smooth his hair. Psychologically, John still had hair on his head. He still applied a comb and a swipe of Brylcreem to it each morning. Originally blond, then white, most of it had decamped, strand by strand; yet the aura upon his scalp still signified, to him, hair. So it gave him a start sometimes when he saw the shine of a bald man's pate in a closed-circuit monitor in, say, a bank or, as now, rather unnervingly, on a television screen on display in a hi-fi store.

John Brand looked up at the video camera, on sale, that was filming him. It was bracketed to a high shelf, well clear of the television. Things were arranged so he could look at one or the other – camera or television – but they were too far apart to enable him to see himself staring back out of the screen. Which was probably, he thought, for the best.

He was momentarily tempted to give a little wave, like those fans at sporting events who wave at the big screen instead of the camera. You can't have it both ways. It bemused him that people failed to grasp this principle.

He inspected himself in the screen, as if observing a stranger. His face was unremarkable in a blue-eyed way, less wrinkled than softened by age, marked by five prominent flesh-coloured moles distributed across his forehead and cheeks. He wore a lightweight, mid-grey suit, single-breasted, unfashionable. His toes flexed inside black brogues corrugated with four-year-old creases.

As John and Margaret seldom argued with words, their differences raged on other fronts, such as John's choice of clothes. His side – a stubborn unwillingness to spend one cent on himself, with cover from the high moral ground of self-effacement – was expressed in his old comfortable suit and old comfortable shoes. At his age, he supposed he could win the argument by running down the clock. Yet Margaret differed: he was still working, their

4

lives were full and active, this argument remained worth winning. Her side was represented by the shirts she bought him, Italian cotton with silk thread, which she forced him to wear by surreptitiously throwing the old ones out. Also, Margaret's mark could be seen in the asymmetric peaks of white cotton handkerchief poking from John's breast pocket, sharp triangles like the tips of the Opera House sails emerging from a grey fog. 'If you can't be a respectable man,' she liked to joke, 'you can at least dress like one.'

John stopped at the Vietnamese hole-in-the-wall restaurant next to the doorway. He feigned reading the window menu but couldn't focus. He fingered his tie, a point of compromise between himself and Margaret. She liked him to wear his club ties. The embroidery of the Royal Automobile Club, I Zingari, the Primary Club, the Royal Australian College of General Practitioners and so on spoke important words in the right places. But that, John countered silently, was precisely the point: *in the right places*. Here, in the great young black-haired tide of the western suburbs, where he was not meant to be, was the wrong place. So John had, before slipping out of his surgery an hour ago, replaced his RAC tie with an example of what Margaret derisively called 'Club David Jones', an inoffensive navy blue with diagonals in two reds.

Reason told him he was anonymous. Yet John felt as obvious as a colour figure in a black-and-white film. His armpits steamed. His heart laboured. He estimated his chances of being recognised – caught – in fantastic multiples. Panicking, he wondered if the video camera in the hi-fi shop had recorded his presence, could be used against him at a later date. A cab crawled past, the driver squinting out at John, who veered away and averted his face. Would the driver connect him with this door, would he wonder: *Him, I know him from where?*

John's panic rested not on probability but on consequences. Small risk, big stakes. It only took one pair of eyes.

In the next half-hour John passed the doorway more than twenty times.

Above the doorway, behind the first-floor window blackened by thick lead paint, a man watched Dr John Brand. This younger man, trimmer, more carved and alert, bore some resemblance to the grey-suited Brand on the street. His eyes were the same pale blue, the colour of the shallow end of a swimming pool. This second man wore a white suit of a material too pliable for polyester but too easy-iron for linen, and an open-necked mauve silk shirt. The suit's forearms bore concentric wrinkles, like an overtaxed accordion, having been worn repeatedly bunched to the elbows. As he crossed one sockless ankle over the other, tassels danced on his loafers. His hair's thickly breaking wave was set with a fragrant glue, insured against all disturbance short of hurricane and earthquake. It flowed down his neck like seaweed stiffened by a current. He had been browsing videotape spines for the past hour, sometimes giving front and back covers a quick glance before sliding the cassette back onto the shelf, much as in any video library. A regular of this shop, he was well known to the security guard perched downstairs with one eye on the quad-screen monitor and one on the *Daily Telegraph*.

The young man could afford to take his time, pause at the window to gaze dreamily outside. For privacy, the window had been blackened. But the lead paint membrane had shrunk back, splitting vertically, the edges curling, breaking the crossbar in the fluorescent second A of MARITAL, which the young man used as a peephole into the secrets outside.

The young watcher knew the history of this place better than the old man on the pavement ever could. For Dr John Brand these shops were too far out of the city to have histories. They were instant creations of his own need, without independent existence outside the matrix of his guilt and lust. For John Brand the west was a disposable idea, only useful in that it endowed him with anonymity. The young man on the first floor saw this as a kind of snobbery. He, by contrast, knew that this retail unit was once a flat that housed three families of clay-quarriers. Then for forty-seven years it belonged to a Polish-born tailor who mended suits while his wife raised a son who would build the shopping centres that put such lone artisans out of sight, out of business. When the retired tailor and his wife were shipped into a six-bedroom house on the North Shore to rattle around for a few decompressed months before perishing from luxury, the downstairs shop was bought by an organisation that used it as a front for an illegal casino. The economies of such casinos changed for the worse, and the organisation turned to buying and selling entertainment product.

The young man's eye lit on John Brand, who passed back and forth below like a tennis ball in a long rally. The back vents of the watcher's white jacket flinched like gills. His hand went out to the black paint to steady his balance.

John summoned one last resolution as sweat popped and fizzed on his paste-coloured forehead. He passed the doorway again, labouring against the oncoming pedestrians.

He shouldn't be so nervous, he told himself. He'd been here often enough. Yet it was always the same, this ritual of dithering. It was as if, in case he should ever be caught, he should have at the ready a Public John Brand who was uncertain, shocked, doing this for the first time. Public John Brand must be quick to protest his innocence. Meanwhile a Private John Brand mocked the silly old goat, the nervous nelly. Private John Brand, wise, cynical, an insider, winked and said: *We know what's happening here. We've calculated the odds. You can torture yourself, play your charade of being too scared to go inside. But only up to a point, my friend. There comes a time when you must go ahead and do what you have come for.*

7

Private John Brand had been here before and could see into the future. He would get what he wanted, take it back to his empty office and, taming his vibrant hands, unpick the sticky tape and slide the product from the plastic wrap. He would flick the pages fast, front to back, with the avidity of an heir going through an unloved father's will. Then he would suffer the angry disappointment, the bitter let-down, the realisation that the product was barely usable, a travesty of what was promised on the cover, and he would blanch at its shoddiness, its blatant trickery, his gullibility. But what could he do? Complain? Then – and this too was all ritual, anticipated and lived – he would take another moment, go through the pictures again, soberly digest the detail. The hurdle of his expectations lowered, he would begin to see less of what was missing and more of what was there. And so the enchantment would begin.

A lengthy survey had brought him here. Near his surgery in Kings Cross, opportunities overflowed but were poisoned by the threat of recognition. He felt safer taking a taxi to the west. He chose this particular store because its entrance was half-concealed in the portal of another bookshop, which, on the thirty-third pass, he entered. This ground-floor shop was one of those vaguely legal operations where new releases, best-sellers, true crime and compact discs sold at substantial discounts. John suspected criminality, but now, as he browsed the lower floor, he could not resist the urge to buy a new thirty-per-cent-off biography of Bernard Kouchner. He was a biography reader. It appeased his sense of propriety to buy a real book. Public John Brand could offer the biography as evidence: *I came here for a bargain.*

A jockey-sized teenager scuttled into the shop with a new consignment of plastic-wrapped magazines – flashes of skin clothed in shrink-wrap raincoats – similar to the kind of thing they had upstairs but which met the legal requirements to sell down here, as if obeying some physical law whereby the *hard* rise and the *soft* sink. A ripple widened among the browsers who had come into the downstairs section to warm up for a trip upstairs. John took his Kouchner to the desk. He handed his money to the beefy man with mature-age acne who set aside his *Telegraph* and turned heavily from the security monitor to wrap the biography in plain brown paper which, to John, lent it a slightly unsavoury air. He tucked it under his arm and came back out to the doorway, where he proposed, as if in an afterthought, to wheel around to the internal stairway that led upstairs. There, of course, he would not concern himself with discounts. For sinning, his pockets ran deep.

He glanced at the sign – *Some Material May Offend* – written in that genteel copperplate common to notices refusing credit and entreating silence.

Something about the sign gave him a shudder. The Kouchner biography felt tempting under his arm; he might just take it home and read it. The other, the *upstairs*, seemed too low, for him, just then. Yes! He'd go home, where Margaret would no doubt be on the phone to their grandchildren. John would find sanctuary, salvation as Grandpa-husband. He would stuff this expedition in some bottom drawer of his mind.

He made it to the first cross-street, choirs exalting in his ears. He was an idiot to have come here. All it would take was one pair of eyes, and he would be cooked. Was he mad? Did he want to be like that senator he had seen shuffling out of a Kings Cross doorway, neck shrunken into raised collar, acting with such conspicuous shame that anyone would wonder: *Who is that guilty-looking wanker?*

John gained the next cross-street, exhaling nerves. He had conquered the urge; he would go home. A spring entered his step. He didn't want to go into that shop anyway, and why bother, he asked himself, why tempt fate when he could get it on his computer, where sensible self-conscious men went for their bittersweet little deaths and disappointments?

He was bigger than it. He belonged to the healthy self-respecting world; he was not one of the men who went into those places; he belonged to his own world. He had the Kouchner biography as evidence. Yes, there had been a reason to come here: a bargain bookshop.

It was, ultimately, a matter of evidence, wasn't it? In the court of John's conscience, Margaret would lead a bench of judges. He couldn't imagine her sitting alone. She was too gregarious, too much a creature of committees – the school council, the P & C, the Gala Day, her charities, the God-knew-what-else of her life. Her laughter, her good cheer, her sharp tongue were gifts too social not to be shared. He'd heard her described as an 'infectious personality'. Yet what she was, really – unlike John and, surprisingly, unlike their boys – was popular. Margaret was a popular woman, in the best possible sense.

If she caught him she would turn to her fellow judges and say: 'It's not what he's done. It's the secrecy I object to. It's all this lurking about. Why couldn't he have told me?'

But that wouldn't be totally honest of her, would it? Oh, the secrecy and the lurking would hurt, but she was used to that. Furtiveness was John's nature. No, he thought, let's face it. What would shock her was the thing in itself. What he did. Margaret would cloak her real feelings by asking, 'Why didn't you tell me?' When of course he couldn't tell her! The whole point of this thing was that it was unconfessable. This was a pain that could never be shared, a pain that, if shared, would be doubled. Trebled.

Telling Margaret would be akin to turning oneself in and confessing to a crime without having been caught. He could tell her, plead guilty, relieve the secrecy, and take his punishment. Or he could hide it from her, avoid getting caught, play the innocent man.

John wanted to get away with it. There was no question of telling her.

And, if they were both to be honest, Margaret would have preferred it this way. For Margaret all consequences were of a social nature. If he told her, she would have her committees in mind. Keep it under the carpet, make do. In fact, he thought, Margaret would positively approve of keeping this a secret. If he had to do it, secrecy was best for all concerned: himself, Margaret, the boys, the family. Above all, the family.

From the first floor, the young man watched John Brand stride out onto the footpath, a thick hardback in the crook of his arm. It was 6.55 pm on the second Tuesday in November.

John Brand, like a gunslinger riding out of town after winning his duel.

But why does the victor need to leave? Did he not deserve a reward?

Now that he had stared it down?

For the young watcher in the white suit, this was the part he would love to remember, and remember with love.

Driving north from the Harbour Bridge, Davis Brand is thinking so hard he loses four suburbs between Cammeray and Chatswood. He comes to, driving twenty kilometres an hour and being honked from behind, arms hanging from the wheel like the cables of a suspension bridge, at a loss over the whereabouts of the last ten minutes.

That, he thinks, is the North Shore for you: hard to remember even while you're here. Driving home to Ma and Pa's is like a return to the primordial slime. The perpetual daydream, the natural state of things. Forgetting. Death. Consciousness is the exception. The rule is oblivion. Where Pa is now: returned to his own daydream.

The thought locks together too neatly to retain its grip on Davis for more than a flash. From here, it will be a long time before he can treat death as a subject for idle philosophy.

Davis blinks, opens and shuts his mouth and moves his jaw from side to side until it hurts. He snaps out of it. He speeds up to the traffic flow and sets his fingers on the wheel at the ten-to-two position. Or, he thinks, eight minutes past ten. Where watchmakers set their product for maximum attractiveness. Davis takes a breath, feels symmetrical at the wheel.

He turns east across the railway line at Killara. Two kinds

of suburbs define the North Shore. Close to the railway line are the double-brick mansions and bungalows, liver-brown and rhododendron-green, scented damply of rotting deciduous mulch, gas pipes, naphthalene and old ladies. Heading outwards, through a gully, the established suburbs give way to the native smells and khaki scrubland of the 1960s' new frontier, where families moved with their young for cut-price respectability, where near enough was good enough.

He passes from one period of local history into another, nostalgia to native fascination. The terrain slopes away from the ridge of the railway suburbs to sharper crests and canted blocks and lower values. On a hill he gets caught behind a burnt-red local coach wheezing black smoke. It leans precariously to the outside camber, crunching down to first. Slowing almost to a stall, Davis Brand matches each gear change. He remembers riding these buses to and from school, wondering if the driver, jiggling the metal rod furiously, would find the correct slot for the gearstick before the bus stalled and rolled backwards. Hollow, hard-seated, soot-stinking rattletraps, cranky and catarrhal, they enjoyed a monopoly thanks to the owner's good relations with the local council. Davis and his friends had stuffed bolt holes with chewy and Redskins – the full extent of their vandalism – while more daring boys from state schools ripped seats and slashed vinyl, pushed free the emergency rear window and drew dickfaces – balls as eyes, cock as nose – on the laminate panels.

Davis swings left into Warramunga Avenue. The street on which he grew up is as straight as only a surveyor's disregard for topography and flora could make it, boring through knolls and ridges like a skewer through kebab meat.

Warramunga Avenue is the type of street where people turn on their porch lights before dark. Davis has come every Friday night since he ceased living here. Equal parcels of land, divvied up by pencil and paper like some local councillors' postcolonial Africa, reconstitute the map of his childhood. When he was young, these houses held adventure – he knew who lived where, knew the secret passages behind houses, knew where you could smash bottles against a wall, where you could break into a building site, where you could find a cave or a burnt-out tree stump, where your dog liked to rush into a back-rubbing sprout of swordgrass, who were the weirdos and who had a sculpture on their roof and whose parents had divorced. Davis used to lead Hammett by the hand on journeys of revelation but inevitably little Hammett would disappear (the kid's greatest talent) leaving the teenaged Davis frantic with worry, unable to return home to tell his parents he'd lost his five-year-old brother. And then, in the nick of time, Hammett would resurface with an innocent expression that could only mean trouble.

What happened? Did every family recapitulate his own – raised children in the sixties and seventies, waved them off in the eighties, sat in front of the telly through the unencumbered nineties? This street – he used to sprint in his school shorts when he missed the bus, hoping to catch it on the next corner; he'd pounded the hills for fitness training; he'd trudged home in midafternoon from university lectures, uneasy at his outrageous freedom; and, with his first job, he'd walked in his father's heavy suit through the hot summer, stinking up the manmade fibres with his sweat until not even dry-cleaning could save it – this street is now empty of life. Automatic porch lights simulate comings and goings, but feebly. It seems he and his brothers were the last children to grow up here. He'd be as shocked to see a child as a kangaroo.

It's not that there aren't people. Warramunga Avenue is patrolled by a paramilitary of tracksuited men with dogs on leashes. But on closer inspection, the waistbands of the tracksuits are pulled too high, and the fabric bulges around the elastic in unparamilitary paunches. The dogs, like their owners, are greyer than they first appeared. Dog and man do share a common purpose: to go to the toilet as soon as possible. And so the owners' disposition to the dogs, who are freer in this quest, is not one of surveillance but of envy.

The Brand house is on a blind crest. Davis eases before turning, concentrating on the far side of the dip. He sees no cars coming, but he halts and whispers the four precautionary beats Pa taught him on his L-plates.

'*Solomon Grundy, born on a Mundy.*'

Ma, who had shared driving-instruction duties, contradicted Pa, arguing that if you hit the accelerator and darted in fast it wouldn't matter if a car was coming, you'd beat it through. It was simply a matter of commitment, Ma said. Davis alternated between Ma's daredevilry and Pa's prudence until, as his mother grew older and the years softened her decisiveness into a kind of fuzzy automatism, there came the day when, cruising across the road into the drive, she went within three inches of being smudged flat against a telegraph pole. Since then, Pa's caution has seemed more resistant to the weathering effects of age.

Davis wheels down the driveway. The house is a Cape Cod, an exotic novelty when Davis was a boy: something American and glamorous about it, with its red-brick walls, white-painted dormer windows and steep, blue-tiled roof. Adding to its odd appeal, the Brands' house isn't turned to the street. It faces off obliquely, giving the impression of an oversized A-frame. Depending on who told the story, his parents had the house built this way to maximise the view and northerly aspect (Ma) or to fit an overlarge structure onto the narrowish block (Pa).

Davis parks on the forecourt and tilts down the driver's mirror. He takes pride in not letting his considerable vanity be known to others. His obsessive mirror-checking is harnessed to an equally obsessive secrecy. He squeezes a pinhead pimple in the wing of his nose, his fingers working expertly despite the reversal of right and left in the mirror. He dabs the spot of blood-pus with a tissue, which he balls up and jams into an ashtray. Lips pressed in an inverted U, he touches up the arrangement of his thin pasta-coloured hair. Premature baldness is his vanity's curse. His brothers escaped it. Chris's hair marched back in his mid-twenties, but arrested itself in a still-respectable blond thatch he now wears bleached and modishly spiked. Hammett inherited the safely anchored dark mop of Ma's side – though anything could have happened recently. As for himself, Davis has been fighting this rogue baldness with increasingly desperate stratagems, the most recent of which is to centre-part it. But the tuft of hair on top has been isolated by the retreat off the back. The frontal mat has the symmetry and shape, he now notices, of a trilobite. Do others see it that way? Has the head finally conquered the hair, like a land mass rising at the end of an Ice Age? Is it time to shave?

Leaving his car unlocked, he lifts the Rolladoor. It stutters as it furls up, sounding like a flock of pigeons taking off in surprise.

Three cars line up in the garage, as if on the front row of a grid: Ma's snazzy VW Golf, Pa's contrarian dusty Morris, and the Toyota Camry belonging to Ian Bertrand. Davis gives a sniff and goes to the interior door linking the garage with the kitchen. The door is locked. Frowning, he takes out his keys.

Inside, the phone rings. Davis fiddles with the keys, working himself into a mild fluster as the phone keeps ringing like a trapped blowfly. There's no answering machine – Chris gave them one years ago and Pa had claimed it didn't work, though everybody knew the old man hadn't tried. Pa wouldn't leave a message on your own answering machine, preferring to leave a moment's silence then hang up, like a criminal on the run. But if Ma and Bertrand are home, why aren't they answering it?

Davis gets the door open but before he can decide whether to yank the keys out of the stiff lock, potentially damaging them, or leave them there and rush to the phone table, the ringing stops.

'Hello? Anyone home?'

Distantly he hears the television – or rather, feels it.

He treads down the dark corridor to the F-shaped space that

serves as kitchen, dining room and television room. Plates are stacked on the kitchen bar, crockery's transit lounge between dishwasher and shelves. Alongside them are yellow leaflets with a funeral parlour logo, offering information on Who To Tell, What To Do, How To Cope. The topmost is titled: 'It's All Right To Cry'.

'Davis, we didn't hear you come in.'

Ian Bertrand rises from an armchair with what seems to Davis a guilty half-smile. Bertrand moves quickly, to intercept Davis before he can reach the Reclin-A-Rocker in front of the television where his mother sits.

'Come.' Bertrand takes Davis's elbow, gently guiding him down the second corridor towards the stairs.

Once out of Ma's earshot, Davis says: 'I didn't expect you here, Ian.'

Bertrand's eyes widen slightly in recognition of his Christian name. Davis and Chris have called him 'Mr Bertrand' ever since he was their English teacher and housemaster, and although he became a family friend, a confidant, a de facto 'uncle', the men of this house refused to dignify him with his Christian name. Continuing to call him 'Mr Bertrand' into their thirties, Davis and Chris have been able to mock him while seeming to do the opposite. Just as Ma adopted Bertrand to somehow prolong the days when he was her boys' wonderful teacher, the boys have kept him in that place, recognising him as a teacher, not an adult. It's one of the few subjects on which Davis and Chris are united.

'I'm just doing what I can,' Bertrand says with a solemn authority Davis can't help wanting to lash out at.

'Wasn't that the phone ringing?'

'No. When?'

'Just then – you didn't hear it?'

'Ah.'

Bertrand pats Davis on the shoulder, somehow hoping this

sighing gesture will suffice. He has a State-of-Emergency look on his face, with all the Special Powers that implies.

'I'd have got it,' Davis says, 'except the door was locked. We never lock that door.'

'She's been locking the doors,' Bertrand smiles gently, apparently glad to be able to explain the non-answer of the phone by a concrete if irrelevant fact. Ma has taken to locking the doors. Therefore we didn't answer the phone.

'So how is she?' Davis has no stomach for investigation or argument about the phone. He moves to get past.

'She's watching Chris. They've just gone on. Minute's silence, the whole thing. You should have been here.'

'Yeah, caught in traffic. Anyway.'

Bertrand seems to want to detain him without actually blocking him. The teacher says, as if just discovering the fact: 'Hm, oh yes, that's probably why we didn't answer the phone. The minute's silence. It's been ringing off the hook. Er, Davis?'

Bertrand fixes Davis with a heavy-lidded warning look.

'I know, Ian.' Davis avoids the schoolteacher's eyes. 'I know.'

As Davis goes through the kitchen towards the lounge, he picks up snatches of commentary. Bill Lawry has taken the microphone for the beginning of the Test match. Davis catches the words 'brave show' and 'tragic circumstances' in the same tonal quiffs as 'even-looking wicket' and 'full house'. It must be a full house for them to be telecasting all day one of the local Test. Usually they hold back the telecast as a ransom against ticket purchases. For a second Davis thinks he hears Bill Lawry say 'very sad day for Australia', and he is about to vent some feeling – *What the hell does this goose mean, sad day for Australia?* – when it strikes him that Lawry is saying 'sad day for the Australians'. As in, the team. More bullshit. Davis wonders whether it is even a sad day for Chris, who is, like his teammates, wearing a black armband – electrical tape around the biceps – and moving to his position with a thoughtful and conceivably grief-stricken expression.

Davis bends to kiss his mother. Without taking her eyes off the cricket, she acknowledges her son by puckering her lips and pointing a finger to her cheek's web of gorged capillaries. He bends and hears the air smooched outside his ear.

Besides being slightly out of breath, Ma betrays little. She wears a Presbyterian mourning garment – a navy-blue sundress with fine white dots – and navy-blue flat shoes. Her silver hair is pinned into its neat bolster. Her hands cradle a mug of tea, a flag of steam curling up to catch the light. Davis notices the deepening of the two lines from the corners of her mouth to her jaw. She is pouring her entire soul into the picture on the screen.

He cautions himself against over-reading her expression. She is simply watching cricket. It is the first day of a Test, her son is on the field, and she is doing exactly what she would be doing on any such day. There is nothing wrong or unusual with her watching TV.

Yet – he can't help noticing – she has aged since he last saw her. Which was only the night before last, New Year's Eve. She'd put on a 'quiet soirée' for twenty-five in Chris's suite at the Australian team's hotel overlooking Circular Quay. All the family, Ian Bertrand, two members of the Cricket Board, a judge, the branch president of the party, a smattering of members of the local Lodge and Probis, the council of the boys' alma mater. All very relaxed, just a chance to watch the fireworks, yet, typically for Ma, loaded with agenda. She has been planning Chris's next move, sowing the seeds of influence for his life after sport. Which, in recent weeks, has taken on a sudden urgency.

But Ma is so adept at this, she manages such evenings so that they feel quite natural, a gathering of friends. On New Year's Eve, Davis watched her work the room. For such a large personality, a ship in full sail, Ma's great advantage was her petite stature. Her booming laugh and sharp tongue were offset by her tiny girlish frame, so that the men found her loudness delightful rather than intimidating. Before the nine o'clock fireworks, knowing some of the older guests might not last until midnight, she gave a welcoming speech. Instead of crassly trumpeting Chris – didn't his accomplishments speak for themselves? – she made some self-deprecating comments about her husband's lateness. 'I apologise for John,' she said, sipping her champagne. 'He's been in his rooms today, but it's my fault, I didn't screw his head on for him this morning so he's no doubt wandering around looking for it.' There were murmurs and chuckles from the old buffers. Davis made out an echo of the word 'screw'. Ma continued: 'He'll have forgotten what day it is, of course. I'll find him at home later and he'll be all innocence. I shall say, "Did you forget it was New Year's Eve?" And John will say, "I did hear a commotion in the distance. I thought the country must be being invaded, so I went back to my computer to finish my work."'

Davis remembers the laughter and looks now at the shell of the memory, his mother in front of the television. At the very time Ma was making jokes about him, Pa might have been lying on the floor here, crawling for the telephone. Davis wants to rush to her and say, 'Ma, he was always forgetting to turn up to functions, it wasn't your fault, you mustn't blame yourself for what you said.' But as he looks at her, something stops him. If the idea weren't too hard to acknowledge, he'd think she doesn't want him here.

'Do you want the radio on?' Davis asks, fossicking among the magazines on the coffee table for the TV remote. She usually watches the TV picture with the radio commentary. 'Ian,' Davis says to Bertrand, whose undertakerly walk is bringing him across the kitchen, 'seen the remote?'

'She wants the TV commentary today,' Bertrand says softly, as if Davis should have known.

Davis is about to say something, but holds back. Bertrand is neither old enough to be parent-like nor young enough to be a friend. Bertrand's narrow, pointed face is almost two-dimensional, as if designed in a wind tunnel. He can only be seen properly in profile, like a two-headed coin. He has a long nose and receding chin and forehead, so that his profile makes the shape of a piece of pie with the apex as his nose and the arc as the back of his head. He has a soft paunch, and a long upper lip that cries out for a moustache. Bertrand did have a moustache when he was Davis's English teacher, when he was striving to make himself look older than the boys. He removed it in his forties, but Davis has never been able to wipe the phantom moustache from the face.

Davis feels an unexpected rush of cruel pity for the man. Bertrand grew from child to grey middle-age in a boys' private school. He attended it for thirteen years, left for a six-month gap in Britain, came straight back as a boarding master, then teacher, and has never changed job, rising to Head of English. And today he is in their home.

'But Channel Nine!' Davis says crossly, his only way of expressing irritation at Bertrand and everything else.

His mother does not respond. Her tea mug rests on the remote control.

The other commentators must have deputed Lawry to take the opening minutes, because he's the only one who can do sincerity over the loss of Chris Brand's father. None of the cricket mafia has ever liked Chris. The others – Benaud, Chappell, Taylor, Greig – would have asked artless Lawry, the default guy, to carry out the dirty work of conveying sorrow. The camera tightens to a close-up of Chris, face shadowed by his hand visoring out the sun. Lawry musters words to match: 'His father would have wanted him to play.'

'Oh God.' Davis turns away from the television. Sanctimonious crap. There's not a lot about his famous brother that Davis admires, but one thing he's proud of is that Chris doesn't kiss arse, doesn't discriminate between high and low. A prick, but a prick to all. An equal-opportunity bastard. That's why the mafia dislike him – because he won't kowtow to them. He's never angled to join them in the box after his retirement, though with his record of achievement he could, and so they take offence that he will not. But that's Chris – he gets on with his own thing.

Davis leaves Ma in front of the set and crosses to the kitchen. Last week's Christmas decorations, green tinsel and miniature Santas, are sticky-taped across the window. A wreath hangs on the screen door, tied with gold-coated string. A plastic tree on the kitchen bar inclines sideways as if cocking an ear weighed down by polystyrene earrings. Beside 'It's All Right To Cry' is another leaflet with a checklist of funeral options: cremation, burial, hymns, readings, eulogy, pallbearers, surprising how far down the page the list runs. Some boxes are filled with Ian Bertrand's experienced tick, a pest that has insinuated itself from margins and markings and summary comments into their family life like an introduced weed.

Davis takes up a customary station over the mail. Whenever he comes to Ma and Pa's, he feels, he tends to avoid conversation, sorting through the letters that still arrive for him. He leaves the socialising for the women: Ma, Lucy, Suzie. He reads mail and plays with Chris and Suzie's kids. He mumbles a few words to his parents and can't wait to leave. And now that era is over. Never again will he enjoy the privilege of intolerance for the olds.

The newspaper is butterflied open at Deaths. Davis reads it, hoping it might have miraculously changed since this morning. Down the page are A people and B people dying in alphabetical order: Azzopardi, Beamish, Blair, Blanden, John Davis Brand. *Survived*, it says, *by two sons. Peacefully.* For the second time today, Davis feels like tearing the paper to shreds. *Two sons.*

Davis inhales his anger through his nose, catching a familiar scent. He crosses to the stove and unlids a saucepan. He reels back from the steam. He doesn't have to look. It's a meal his father would have cooked, the 'curry' – three teaspoons of Keen's transforming a heap of leftovers, the physical expression of Pa's waste-not-want-not fear of being struck into poverty by a vengeful

Depression-era god. Ma must have piled the scraps and curry powder into the pot, filling the kitchen with her husband's smell. Something, at least.

When Davis and Chris were young, Ma would go away now and then to help out on one of her father's campaigns. She was the unofficial electoral strategist for Grandpa Bernard Hammett, federal member for thirty-one years and one of those influential parliamentarians who never sought ministerial office, preferring to conduct his work for the PM as a 'close ally' or 'numbers man'. While Ma was away with Grandpa, Pa would look after the boys. They were wild weeks. He'd make his curry on the Monday and leave it in the pot, on the stove, until the Friday. Pa made withdrawals from the pot each night. By midweek he would bulk out what was left and call it 'fried rice'. By the Friday, with just a few chunks of meat floating in the bottom of the pot, Pa would toss in a few eggs, stir them around, and the curry-cum-fried rice would become a Spanish omelette. Once Chris, two years younger than Davis, was allowed to spend the entire week, day and night, in his favourite cricket shirt. The night of Ma's return, Davis said: 'Pa, shouldn't we give Chris a bath?' Pa blinked in surprise and replied: 'He's all right, he's been in the pool almost every day.' Davis said: 'He's had a runny nose all week. Shouldn't we wipe it before Ma comes home?' Pa looked at Chris for a moment and said: 'I had the impression he was enjoying the taste of it.'

'Hey Ma,' Davis says, making a spastic run at brightness, 'you can get rid of Bonnie and Clyde now.'

Bonnie and Clyde are the nicknames the Brands have given their cleaners, an affable couple whose real names have paled from memory. Since the mid-eighties Bonnie and Clyde have come twice a month to spend an hour or two sharing news, passing gossip, occasionally waving a dirty rag over the basins and pushing the vacuum cleaner in an asterisk in the centre of the living room. Ma has always said she needs to clean the place herself before and after their visits. She says archaeologists would have learned a lot more about Pompeii if its houses were cleaned by Bonnie and Clyde, and future researchers would learn much about the Brand family history from the records of their every daily movement – stains, scratches, dust, muck, food, filth, grot and mould – preserved in the spaces B & C miss.

But Bonnie and Clyde were Pa's gift to her, and he refused to lay them off, forever mistaking Ma's complaints as a martyrish offer to do the cleaning herself. 'Sweetie,' he'd admonish her when she'd get to work with the duster, 'relax. Why have a dog and bark yourself?'

It was typical of Davis's parents that they never stumbled across the commonsense solution: just get new cleaners. Instead their running argument had persisted. Davis sensed that Pa's real motive, beneath the bluffing, was middle-class guilt, and giving B & C their hundred dollars was a personal act of charity. But he'd never know for sure now. The time for honest reckoning had been less permanent than he'd supposed.

Unable to stand the sound of the cricket, he goes to the back patio. Under the awning, rolled-up and mildewy from disuse, crouches a banana chair, haunches half-folded. The clouds have blown off, leaving a midmorning ache of sun.

It's a long time since Davis has been here other than for a family gathering. Without Chris's kids running around jumping on everything, finding adventure in unexpected corners, without Chris's wife Suzie and Davis's Lucy to gossip fragrantly like a pair of polishing rags, the sheen is stripped off the house. He sees it as Pa must have seen it, in its decaying banality. The outdoor entertaining area is a relic from the mists of time, its centrepiece a Mutual Pool, kidney-shaped with pebblecrete surface. A waterfall rockery system feeds it at a bare dribble, long green Fu Manchu beards of algae flowing with the stream, once a freshet, now a seepage. Beside the pool is a trampoline, the mat yellow with a faded red cross, sagging under a dirty puddle into which mynahs dive and dip. A Totem Tennis pole, screwed into the ground since Davis was a kid, the ball hanging from the cord like a rotten but unyielding lemon, pins down the rest of the lawn.

The Totem Tennis pole forms an incidental headstone to the mossy patch that is the grave of Des, the Brands' dalmatian who died fourteen years ago. Every Christmas, the family tied a length of leftover ribbon around Des's neck so he could celebrate with them. They called him 'Christmas Des'. One Christmas, after tying the ribbon around Des's neck, they went to church and then lunch with Ma's side of the family. When they came back, Des had circled the jacaranda in a festive frenzy and managed to splint himself against the trunk. Each new effort to escape only tightened the Christmas ribbon's hold of his throat. They found him perfectly upright, warm but cooling, against the tree trunk. 'More like Easter Des,' Ma said before going inside. For some reason, she had taken a set against the dalmatian in his last years.

When Pa grabbed the dead dog's ribs to snip the ribbon, Des gave a wild twitch. It was hard to accept Pa's explanation of rigor mortis, so Des was buried with his head poking out of the ground, just in case. He stayed like that for a week, staring out of his plot at the Mutual Pool. When the currawongs came for his eyes, Pa gave him a Christian burial, the Totem Tennis pole marking his grave.

A bird feeder hangs off a liquidambar branch. Currawongs battle for the rim – only currawongs and magpies, never the king parrots, rosellas and lorikeets promised on the box. Beyond the back fence, the neighbourhood is silent. Sprawling avenues of houses, once ringing with the screams of brats, are now in grey hibernation, waiting fingers-crossed for grandchildren.

Davis goes inside, brushing past Ian Bertrand, who is perched on the arm of Pa's chair. The Test match has started. Ma will be feeding on every moment the ball goes near Chris.

Davis goes upstairs to his old bedroom which, despite Pa having converted it into a study, retains the porcelain plaque 'David Lives Here' on the door. The second 'd' used to be texta'd over with an 's' because no plaque ever had his real name. But the texta has faded and the plaque remains, as if testifying to a phantom David, a fourth son.

The computer squats like a stubborn house pet on the desk. Normally Pa's blobby fractal screen saver would be bouncing off the perimeters, but it has been switched off. Six removalists' boxes sit on the carpeted floor, gaping like chicks in a nest. Pa's papers have been swept up and plonked into the boxes with a haste that saddens Davis. He'd have liked to come in here and reflect, take one last look at Pa's life. The old man might even have died here, ergonomically in his office chair. Or outside, in the banana chair, his face masked by the comical Cancer Council sunglasses he always wore, the space-age wraparound types with extra square windows on the sides, which staid middle-aged people assume to be rather racy.

But Davis hasn't asked, isn't bold enough to flesh out his imagination with details that can only come from his mother. *Mercy*, he thinks. *Be merciful.*

He saw Pa in the hospital, yesterday. The wrinkles had run out of the old man's face. It made Davis think of a soul, wonder if Pa's soul was contained in the two vertical lines and three horizontals that had formed a tee above his brow, the apostrophes around his mouth, the spokes radiating from the corners of his eyes, the worry-lines and laugh-lines and frown-lines.

In death, the lines gone, Pa looked relieved.

Seeing Pa in the hospitasl like that touched Davis as rudely intimate, akin to seeing a stranger asleep. Was it an index of intimacy to view someone sleeping? Chris has Suzie and two daughters. He can watch them sleep as much as he likes. Ma and Pa had each other. Who can Davis watch sleep – Lucy, once a week?

The sight of Pa in the hospital brought back another kind of intimacy. About ten years ago, soon after Davis became a GP, Pa's longtime physician had died. Pa caught a flu, and asked Davis for a prescription. A year or so after that he asked Davis for a referral to an ear-nose-throat specialist. Some time later he asked, matter-of-factly, for a referral for a CT scan on his gall bladder. Around then, Davis realised with a shock that he had become, by unspoken agreement, by default, Pa's doctor.

With Pa's advancing age, Davis had grown terrified by the idea that he might have to examine his father's body more closely. Once, Pa needed a chest examination. Davis placed his stethoscope over forgotten landmarks – the scattered moles, the hairs on the chest, the patches of eczema – and remembered how, before adolescent modesty built its fences, he had so idolised this man, this body.

Through his fifties and sixties, Pa's health was remarkable. Davis wondered if it was the fear of giving himself over totally to his son that was keeping him strong. This fear silenced them both. Only once did they broach it, half-jokingly. John needed a referral for a bowel obstruction. Davis sat behind his desk, mutely wondering if he should examine his father – if that was what Pa expected. Pa read his mind, saying: 'I won't ask that of you, son.'

Davis said: 'You'll change GPs?'

John replied: 'I'll find a stranger.'

'That may not be the best way to have yourself treated.'

'In one sense, no, you're right. But in another sense, it would be for the best.'

The bowel obstruction was cleared up by the specialist, and things carried on until about a year ago. It wasn't that Pa made an announcement: 'Son, I won't be needing you as my doctor.' In fact, it ended as it had begun: tacitly. Some time passed before Davis realised he was no longer his father's doctor. Months elapsed, and John hadn't come by for a script or a referral. Either his father was in suspiciously perfect health, or he had found someone else. With the passing of time, Davis became certain that the latter had taken place.

He never mentioned it. He never said, 'Pa, have you found someone else?' In the hospital yesterday, looking down at his father, Davis cursed his reticence. Had Pa failed to get the right treatment? Had he been trawling around bulk-billers, effectively self-destructing on his own shyness? Davis looked at the body: all the answers, none speaking to him.

Davis goes downstairs to the kitchen. There is so little he can do here. He hears Bertrand murmuring to Ma 'private cremation and then the memorial service', and 'immediate family members', and 'the Crematorium will take care of that', and 'or perhaps go the quick funeral route', reading ugly copywriter words from a leaflet.

Bertrand is caught by surprise when Davis emerges. The teacher shifts abruptly away from Ma, like a salesman caught pushing product to the incompetent. He gets up, comes to Davis and folds the leaflet in among the other documents.

'Do you have a copy of the, um, the certificate?' Davis asks.

'The death certificate?' Bertrand whispers, shooting a look towards Ma.

No, Davis would like to say. *His birth certificate. The car registration certificate. The Blue Merit Certificate for Proficiency in English Fucking Composition.*

Instead, he nods.

'I don't know.' Bertrand shuffles aimlessly among the leaflets and mail.

'Who declared him, then?' Davis asks. It is dawning on him how much he does not know. He was at his apartment yesterday morning, sleeping off a New Year's hangover. His phone had been turned to silent. Bertrand left the message – 'Come to the hospital' – on the machine. Davis didn't get it until early afternoon, and by the time he got to the hospital no-one else from the family was there. He viewed Pa for a few minutes, then went home and drank half a bottle of Benedictine – all he had – on his own.

'I assume it was signed by Doctor Cobcroft,' Bertrand says.

James Cobcroft, Pa's partner in his practice.

'What, Cobcroft came here? It wasn't done at the hospital? I had the impression he . . .'

'Davis, now's not the time . . .'

'As far as I know, Jim Cobcroft wasn't Pa's doctor,' Davis says. 'He's not meant to sign a death certificate, and if he did he should have left a copy here . . .'

Davis scrabbles among the mail. Ian Bertrand leans close, hissing urgently. 'Please, boy – not like this.'

Davis looks up, follows Bertrand's eye to Ma. Davis takes a breath, straightens the mail lengthily. A minute and a half passes.

'I'm warning you,' Bertrand says, apparently struggling to contain his disappointment at Davis's tasteless behaviour, 'now is not the time. I don't know who signed the blessed thing.'

Davis looks at his mother. He feels pregnant with words too big to be born. But they're not far off, and they're going to hurt like hell when they force their way out. He wipes his eyes, which have begun to feel gritty and dry.

Outside, a gust tilts the bird feeder, spilt seed clicking onto the pebbly pool decking. It's the first week of January. The city is on holidays, watching cricket, easing itself off the festive season. The white noise of cicadas blows in on ash-scented air. It's a time for languor, beach, shorts and thongs. Davis, in suit trousers and a business shirt, feels as frosty as winter.

'He's fielding well,' Ma says. 'He's on his toes today.'

Davis is about to say something, but again holds himself back. Damn, the whole country knows Chris is on his last chance, how the selectors have run out of patience, how it's time for new blood, how the death of his father two days before this crucial Test match will likely break his resilience, how it was a mistake even to have let him insist on playing. But it's the last game of the series, and if Chris misses out here, he'll be dumped from the upcoming overseas tour, so – why can't anyone say this? – he's not playing because his father would have wanted it, he's playing because he doesn't want to be dropped.

But mercy.

'Better be off then,' Davis says.

He leans over his mother. Her eyes are fixed on the television. Her hand circles his wrist.

'He made a good save,' she says. Her voice is surprisingly strong – normal.

'I'll be at the surgery,' Davis whispers.

His mother doesn't seem to have heard him. Davis is about to repeat himself when Bertrand comes over, nodding gently to Ma, the TV screen, and Davis all at once – his head a universal joint of considerate nods – and escorts Davis along the corridor to the front door and out onto the porch.

'Go easy,' Bertrand says.

'Yeah? What hat are you wearing now? Are you the teacher, or the family friend, or the executor of the will, or the master of ceremonies? I'd like to know if *you're* an *immediate family member*.'

Bertrand risks a hand on Davis's sleeve. He looks into the distance, as if deciding whether to release more bad news. Across the road an old man is angrily dusting down an outdoor chair, his white chicken legs going at the knees.

'Please,' Bertrand says. 'What she's doing now – watching Chris, watching the cricket – it's her opiate, do you understand? Of course you do, you're a doctor. You understand shock. This Test match is going for five days, and then she has to wake up and look around her. Give her a break. That's why we've – she's decided to wait until after the Test to have the service. And she doesn't want to distract Chris.'

'She and Chris aren't the only ones hurting.'

Bertrand's hand pats Davis's forearm. Davis feels a sweat of confusion. He wants to hug the man, cry on his lapel, strangle him.

'It's understandable that you want more . . . details,' Bertrand says. 'But have you considered it might be too painful for you to, ah, know?'

'Have you considered how painful it might be for me *not* to know?'

Bertrand nods, sucking his long upper lip into his mouth. He puts on a face that implies he's really on Davis's side. A teacher face. Davis doesn't trust him. He knows what Bertrand is thinking: *If you'd answered your phone, if you hadn't disappeared yesterday, you could have known all you wanted.* Davis wants to push his stupid 2-D face in.

'Sometimes in the boarding house,' Bertrand says, 'we have boys who've lost a family member. It's almost always the same, what happens to the boy. He thinks he's meant to be crying, but he's not. He has few feelings. He feels normal and wants to do normal things. But no-one around will let him. We don't let him play sport, or go to classes. It's we who've changed, not the grieving boy. Not yet, in any case. And he starts to wonder why he's not feeling as upset and changed as everyone around him. So he becomes guilty. He asks himself why he's feeling so normal. He starts to think there's something wrong with himself. Do you see what I'm saying?'

'Frankly, no.' *You sententious git.*

'Davis. I respect your feelings, but my duty is to your mother. She is in a state of profound normality. She's doing what she always has done. Watching Chris is holding her together. Now, you can question why I'm here, and say I've got no right, but I think the best we can do is maintain this cushion for her. We don't need her to be questioning the *appropriateness* of her feelings and behaviour. There'll be plenty of time for . . . You know how it is – wounds only hurt when they start healing. That's when she's going to need you.'

'You think it's *normal*, that notice in the paper? I assume you're responsible for that?'

Bertrand gives him a hurt look, as if he can't understand what Davis could be angry at.

'The bit about the *two sons*,' Davis says. 'I take it that was part of your *cushion*?'

'Now's not the time, Davis. Think of your mother.'

Davis is about to jab the teacher with some insult when from behind Bertrand, like the blowfly waking, the phone rings.

He and Bertrand look at each other.

'That's our phone, Mr Bertrand.'

Davis moves to get to the door, but the older man holds up a stern hand and goes inside. He picks up the phone on the hall table. As he listens, his eyes are on Davis. He presses the phone too tightly to his ear, as if sealing its silence. He shuts the door on Davis, a full-stop. Davis gets into his car. Automatically, he looks in the mirror and is distracted by the disorganisation of his hair, which has ruffled up in a sucked-mango-seed tuft and exposed the freckled skin. Yes, he thinks, time to fucking shave it all off.

Davis's car, an expensively sealed pod of conditioned air, is the one place in the world where he permits himself to scream.

He scours the back of his throat, blood bursting in his face. He tastes the coppery gouge on his larynx. He breathes, in, out, in, out, and draws out another vowel. The handful of cubic decimetres moulded around wood and leather and chrome and synthetic curves is insufficient to contain Davis's screaming. His car cannot contain the vacant lot he's just seen occupying his mother's body in front of the television; the pomposity of Ian Bertrand's supervision and the weirdness of his behaviour with the phone; the absence of a death certificate; the idiocy of the near-miss Davis survived at the top of the driveway when, turning out of his parents' house (he mourned with a vow against thinking of it as 'Ma's house'), he failed to observe the Solomon Grundy routine and was nearly pasted by a souped-up Torana humming over the crest. Nor can his car contain the radio cricket commentary to which he listens with mounting frustration and fury. There is so much his car cannot contain.

He has exhausted his need to scream by the time he stalls in a queue for the Harbour Tunnel. In the next car three teenage girls are laughing at him. They saw him screaming. Face prickling, eyes wet, ears slightly deaf, he hands change to the toll basket.

He breathes, widening his ribcage. The cricket voices return to the car like a schizophrenic's familiars. He turns them off, then on again.

Slotting his phone into the hands-free brace, he tries to call Ma on the off-chance that Bertrand's protections might slacken for a second. But the number is engaged. He wonders why Bertrand acted so evasively with the phone. He wishes he had been more composed, and also more insistent over the funeral arrangements. He regrets not pursuing the broader unanswered question of exactly where, when and how Pa died. He wishes he could be more like eldest sons should be, probably are, in other families.

At a traffic light, he catches sight of himself in the rear-vision mirror. There's a white scab, some sort of sun damage, maybe a basal cell carcinoma, on his lower lip. He scratches it away, but it sends a warning jab of pain and he backs off. He flattens down his hair.

Davis is disappointed, he realises, in his mother. Perhaps he's more disappointed in himself, but from himself he expects no better. On the other hand, death is one of Ma's specialities. She is always going to funerals – for friends, friends' spouses, friends' parents, friends of friends. There are always last respects to be paid. When Davis asks her how so-and-so died, Ma has a shorthand intimacy with the language of death that he and his father, the medical men, have somehow failed to master. 'Oh, he had a primary in his lungs and secondaries everywhere,' Ma would say. Or breezily: 'Aneurysm at the golf club.' Or: 'Second stroke in six months.' From her years doing the funeral circuit, having her hair done, putting on a new outfit and what Chris calls her 'game face', Ma has been able to suburbanise death. Death be not proud? Death would not dare. Death, for Ma, is a social event.

Now, by capitulating, by retreating, she has, Davis cannot help feeling, let him down.

He tries Lucy's number, but for the fourth time today gets his wife's reassuring voicemail-voice. He tries to remember what

Lucy was doing today – what meetings and machinations she'd have told him about, to which he would have nodded understandingly and smilingly without taking in a word. She could be flying to Melbourne for all he can recall. He doesn't bother leaving a message. He knows her phone will tell her precisely how often and at what times he's called. Every lawyer and financier in town would be on holidays, up at the coastal beach house or skiing in Europe; but not Lucy. It's as if she's found a clique of fellow workaholics, the hairy-chests of corporate financing who are too tough to take summer holidays.

He drives into the inner city and pulls into the underground parking lot, out of the animal midsummer sun, near Pa's surgery.

He gets out of the car and leans into the grooved corduroy cement of the carpark ramp, emerging into the light of Fitzroy Gardens. The keys jingle in his hand. Nostrils senseless to Kings Cross's piss-spunk-falafel-disinfectant melange, he walks down Darlinghurst Road and pushes the warped aluminium frame of the surgery door, takes the stairs two at a time.

Claire Mullally is behind the reception desk, her face tilted down. Her button nose is chafed red. She hunches forward over the suggestion of a snivel. Davis freezes.

'Oh.' She looks at him through swollen eyes. The corners of a tissue poke through her clenched fist. 'Sorry.'

Davis Brand's heart restarts and he darts for Pa's room, slams the door.

He falls clammily into the patient's chair. His heart is flipping like a mattress being turned over. He lays his palm on his chest until it settles.

He gets up and eases into the standard grey office chair that still holds the ghost of his father's bum. He lays his hands palm-down on the desk, an easily wiped white laminate with four square-tube legs. The bookcase to his left is an Ikea kit, listing with the heavier texts and a MIMS pharmaceutical catalogue. Unusually for a doctor, Pa has no diplomas on his walls, no calendars or nature

35

posters, just a muscle chart, a paper towel dispenser and the light box for X-rays. Beneath the towel dispenser is a shelf of IV bottles, and in the corner a bed with a curtain, a washbasin and a needle disposal bin. Beside the sharps bin is a standard aluminium cupboard, about head-height. Pa placed no photographs of his children on his desk, no personal touches, no ornamentation. This is a room that can be hosed clean. No doubt it has been. Projectile vomiters, pustulators, weepers, pissers, shitters, pisser-shitters, leakers, cummers, all-comers. Ma thought him a saint. She would have preferred a cardiologist or neurosurgeon to a saint, or best of all a dermatologist – 'Nobody dies, dear, and nobody gets better!' – but a saint would have to do. How many times has Davis heard her sigh: 'You're a saint, John.' She has never meant it as a compliment.

Davis sorts through the papers stacked on Pa's desk. It strikes him that when he signs the documentation entitling himself to Pa's half-share in this practice, he will assume the position he might occupy for the rest of his life. Since he was a child, this was where he wanted to be. Before he wanted to be a doctor, Davis wanted to be his father. And now, here he is. The thought unnerves him. He gets out of the seat, tingling, as if he has tried on Pa's clothes. But he can't avoid it: at the age of thirty-five, he is doing what he can safely presume he will be doing for the rest of his working days. This is the practice he wanted, the poor-but-honourable social service his father and James Cobcroft gave birth to, here among the city's desperate. From those who have, much will be asked.

He dials into his email.

Claire Mullally is in the next room, seeing patients. Claire is the locum, called in during holidays and whenever Pa and Cobcroft need her. This year, she's put in a good four months here. Davis fires her a note – hello? – and waits.

He knows he can be a master of emotional disguise. Lucy didn't suspect his feelings when they met five years ago. He feared overwhelming her with the obviousness of his affection. So he assumes

Claire also doesn't know. Why should she? She's straight out of uni. He is successful, proper to a fault, and ready to take over his saintly father's saintly practice. He lives in the ideal relationship. Claire must know about Lucy. Pa loved to boast about Davis and never say a word about the famous Chris. Davis knows how proudly Pa will have described him, his integrity, the perfect union he enjoys with Lucy. He maintains an art deco apartment in Potts Point while Lucy lives in a contemporary waterfront unit across the water in Cremorne. They can almost signal each other over the pond. They'd met on holidays in Japan. Lucy was a successful commercial property lawyer, already a partner in a large city firm when she met Davis. Their romance, propelled by total frankness and candour, shot from meeting to cohabitation to discovering they got on better while living apart, all within four giddy months. On mutual agreement, they decided to maintain separate but equal lives. Once married, they continued the arrangement. After questioning such an odd notion of marriage, their friends grew accustomed to the idea and probably envy it. It's a wonderful way to string out the romance, Pa said; why rush into the humdrum of domesticity? Ma has kept an all-too-prim silence.

So he's safe, he's in shadow. As far as Claire knows, he has the perfect marriage.

Hi, Davis. Sorry about my state out there. You're not on duty today?

Davis regards the message for a moment. He types:

I'm on 1 wk compassionate leave

So how are you holding up?

b better if my brother wasnt on tv

Oh? I suppose it doesn't help, having everything in public like this.

He notes the punctuation. She takes care with her writing. What kind of a doctor does she think she is? But Davis, a spelling snob himself, likes her formality.

He copies her grammatical correctness, as if to be dressed compatibly for dinner.

It's not just that. I guess you know Chris and Pa didn't get on.

There is a long pause before Claire's reply.

And it's not just Chris and you.

He blinks.

Right. There's Ma.

His heart does the mattress-turn. He pulls the blood-pressure gear from the side of the desk, rolls up his sleeve, wraps the velcro tourniquet around his bicep, and works the hand pump.

They were making a big deal of it on TV?

Arm throbbing, he types his reply with one hand.

Radio too. But an hour into the day, they'd forgotten all about it. Not even talking about the armbands.

One hundred and ten over sixty-five. Way too low. He's got to get an ultrasound. Maybe he can ask Claire for a referral.

So you're angry because they're talking about your father on the radio, or because they're not?

He smiles.

Both. Don't they get it? When you lose your father, you don't just lose him for the first session of a Test match?

The wait is so long this time that he gets up and puts his head out the door. Claire is in James Cobcroft's room. There are voices behind the door. She must have a patient. Three more wait in reception. When Davis sits back down, she has replied.

We've all lost him. I can only imagine how it is for you.

No, he thinks. She cannot imagine how it is for me. She could not begin to comprehend what kind of man could, amidst his grief, be burning like a sixteen-year-old arranging a first date. Flirtation overrides grief, inhibits it, snuffs it out.

Something Ian Bertrand said comes back to him: 'A state of profound normality'. That could be it, Davis thinks. Ma has her cricket, I have this low-level campaign of flirting with Claire I've been conducting for most of the year. Ma and I think we're meant to be grieving, but our bodies just follow old habits.

It annoys him that Bertrand may be right about something.

He writes:

You looked upset.

Again, she makes him wait. He can't. He adds:

I mean that sincerely (no sarcasm in tone).

The instant he sends this addendum, he curses himself. Of course she was sincere. It's insulting to insinuate otherwise. She won't see that he's flirting – or worse: she will.

I am upset. He was a good man. He spoke so highly of you.

Davis drums the table. It often seems to him that the defining difference between himself and his brothers is their differing ways of expressing the hot male family blood. Davis shows nothing in public but screams in his car. Chris goes out in front of millions of people and belts taciturn centuries. And Hammett – well, Hammett.

He spoke highly of you too. He said you were exceptional.

Thank you, Davis, she replies quickly. That means a lot to me.

This one smells uncomfortably like a conversation-stopper. Davis ponders his next move. He types:

Jim's taking the day off?

He's up in Noosa.

Davis is about to type a response when something in the pile of documents on the desk catches his eye.

Death certificates, he thinks, have so little ceremony about them. Nobody wants a commemorative edition, bordered with gum leaves and coats of arms. There's not the same market as for birth certificates. Davis pulls out his father's death certificate pad, which is no more elaborate than a tradesman's billing pad, each sheet in triplicate.

New South Wales
Births, Deaths and Marriages Registration Act, 1995 (Section 39)
Medical Certificate of Causes of Death

He thumbs absently through recent entries, recognising none of the patients. He is about to put it back on the pile and type something to Claire when he catches a name.

First names of deceased: JOHN DAVIS.

The details are faint, this being the carbonised doctor's copy. The words are, unusually, typed. Pa's place of death is typed in as the suburb where he and Ma live. Under 'Date Last Seen Alive By Me' is December 31 – this time, handwritten. Further down, under 'Cause of Death (PLEASE PRINT CLEARLY. DO NOT ABBREVIATE)', the certificate is broken into several parts. Beside 'Disease Or Condition Directly Leading To Death' are typed the words:

HEART FAILURE.

Beside 'Antecedent Causes (morbid conditions, if any, giving rise to the abovementioned cause, stating the underlying condition last)' is typed:

SEVERE AORTIC STENOSIS.

Beside 'Other Significant Conditions', the space is empty. The medical practitioner signatory to the certificate is James Cobcroft, who certifies that he 'was responsible for the medical care of the abovenamed deceased immediately before death and/or I examined the body of the abovenamed deceased after death'.

Davis pinches his nostrils together and types:

When did Jim go up to Noosa?

Claire replies:

Today, I think. Why?

Davis types:

Oh, just that he didn't come to our New Year's Eve do. I had the idea he's been up in Noosa since Christmas.

Davis doesn't want to trick Claire, necessarily. But something doesn't seem quite right.

A message pops up:

I've been locuming since last week. But I don't know exactly what day he left.

Davis leans back in his father's chair, fingers steepled over his nose, examining Claire's email message. She is fudging, he thinks.

Davis types a businesslike summary of how he wants Claire to look after Pa's surgery in the next few days. He notes the need for certain office-related purchases and some medical supplies. Though it is a routine email from one doctor to a junior colleague, Davis takes particular care. Claire makes no addition to her last remark, perhaps considering their conversation over. Davis re-reads what he has written, checking for spelling and grammar as if squinting into a mirror in search of flakes of dried skin. He calms down before sending it, re-calibrating every word for its effect on her, trying to strike the right note of propriety, yet not wanting to sound unapproachable. He has no idea how she sees him – desirable but out of reach? Desirable and within reach? Undesirable? Another answer? Is he too distant, or not distant enough?

Then he curses himself for thinking, here, today, of making an impression.

But the power of the admonition – a kind of abstract moral headmaster – is no match for the wild life pulsing through his temples.

It is just as he hits the SEND button that his door opens and she is there. She wears a black turtleneck. Her beautiful pale face crinkles up in a smile, tilting to the left. There is a residual redness around her nose.

'I'm off now, Davis,' she smiles gently.

'I . . . I've just sent you an e . . . email,' he stammers, battalions of blood marching into formation on the parade ground of his face.

She pauses, as if monitoring his condition.

'Okay, Davis. I'll pop in and read it.'

As the door closes, Davis's face hits the desk.

It's All Right To Cry, he thinks.

An email pops onto his screen.

Davis. I'm too upset to do any work now.

No, he thinks. No. Nonononono. No.

I am, he thinks, a fucking turd.

The door shuts. She's gone out.

Davis hunches over the desk and mashes his fists into his eyes. A pulse of nausea rolls over him and for a moment he thinks he is going to throw up on his father's papers. He goes through the desk drawers for some Dramamine, but finds only stationery organised in neat piles. Nothing for nausea, no surreptitious painkillers, not even paracetamol. That was Pa: nothing for himself. Davis wonders if the old man was too straight for his own good.

And yet, something doesn't add up. As the nausea passes, Davis goes through the death certificate again. Parts typed, parts hand-written; aortic stenosis; Pa's pad. The date. Davis frowns at the copy, certain he could put his finger on the problem if only his mind could stay still.

He turns back to the computer. Claire's last message is on the screen. He clicks REPLY.

Whenever he's had a conversation with Claire, rare and brief as they have been, her words keep reverberating afterwards. Davis goes over and over each exchange, recalling and re-weighing every nuance. He's always left wanting more. This is the thing: he doesn't want to have an affair with her, because nothing of what he needs would be satisfied by sex; sex would be followed by farewell, and it is the separation that he cannot bear. He doesn't want a fling; he wants a friend. In a perfect world he and Claire would talk and talk until they collapse, and never say goodbye until they had talked away their loneliness. He would give anything to be fully known.

So, as he starts typing, it never strikes Davis as strange that he is confessing to his father's locum rather than his mother, say, or his wife, or Chris. It needs to be a new person, fresh eyes. His family can never know him, precisely because they think they already do.

Claire, he types.

Sorry if I was acting weird before. I'm just one big ball of anger at the moment. I'm angry at the whole cricket thing, angry at the obituary, angry at Chris, even angry at Ma. I guess I'm grieving and this is all normal, but I'm too angry to even think about my father for long.

But you know what? Maybe the whole function of this anger is to stop me thinking about Pa, because whenever I do it brings on something worse than feeling mad. When I think about Pa it's like my insides are being torn apart. So maybe the anger's holding me in one piece.

I try to think what I'd say to a patient in my situation. I guess I'd ask if they regret anything or feel they've left something important unsaid. If I had Pa back, just for a minute, would I tell him I loved him? Would I thank him? You know what, I can't imagine doing that. He knew I loved him and appreciated him. He was my hero. But we'd never say that aloud, and when I imagine saying it just because he's gone, it still embarrasses me and it'd embarrass him more than me. That's not our style. I honestly don't think I'm feeling so mad just because I never had the chance to speak the bleeding obvious.

You know who I'm most angry with? Me. I can't control what other people are doing, but I can control my own actions and I'm angriest because of what I did – or didn't do. The other night, I wasn't there for him. I was getting pissed on New Year's Eve when my Pa must have needed me most. Recently, I'd let him drift away from me. He used to be my patient, did you know that? But he stopped seeing me, and instead of being alarmed I was kind of relieved that I wouldn't have to deal with anything too serious. Maybe I could have helped him? I don't know – but I never tried to find out, and I don't think I can forgive myself for that.

But standing by and allowing things to happen is a speciality of ours – me and Pa, anyway. In our family, it's always been Ma and Chris who are the doers, and Pa and I are the peanut gallery, you know, the sceptical intelligentsia. When we'd go on family holidays when Chris and I were kids, Ma would stop the car if she saw a park cricket match. She'd get out and ask if Chris could join in. So our whole day would stop, in order that Chris could hop in and belt around some poor unsuspecting country bowlers. Ma was fiercely ambitious – she'd pack some whites for him, no matter where we were going. And Pa and I, we'd just watch and smirk at the two of them. We'd be superior, a little club. When I became a doctor, we'd have that to share, to tell ourselves we were above it all. But you know what, it was just another excuse for us to avoid taking action. Some really bad things happened in our family over the years, Claire – and when it mattered, Pa and I stood by and watched. It was Ma, mainly, but also Chris who were the engine of our family. Pa and I were the passengers.

Not that Ma didn't do what she thought best. She did. But see, it's only now that I see who I really am.

I've let things drift and let Pa down. That's why I'm so angry at myself. If I could say one thing to Pa, it'd be that I am going to do one last thing to honour him, and it's on that subject that I want to ask you, Claire, a favour.

I've come across a copy of Pa's death certificate. But it's quite irregular. For a start, it's on his pad, not Jim Cobcroft's, even though Cobcroft is the signatory. And then it mentions aortic stenosis. What's that about, and how would Jim know? Was he Pa's doctor? I didn't think he was. What I want to know is, do you know anything about the other night? Where was Pa, who called Jim, where did he actually see Pa, etc? I hope that this isn't awkward for you, but I need to know.

You might think I should be able to find this out from others – but that doesn't seem possible. Don't ask me why. Long story.

Sorry if this all seems, you know, melodramatic. But I have to put myself through this, not for me but for Pa.

Minutes pass while Davis sits before the screen, re-reading what he has written. He feels relieved, even reassured, to have put all of this down, but he hesitates before sending it. An awful doubt comes over him. He wonders if he can trust her. Claire is in her mid-twenties, ten years younger than Davis. Davis expects that when he takes over Pa's partnership in the surgery, once he negotiates a politic retreat from his registrar's position at St Vincent's, he might offer her a permanent position. She is an altruist, like Pa. Why else would an honours graduate want to locum on Darlinghurst Road?

But there remains the question of trust. He assumes Claire sees him principally, now, as her potential employer. She has to be careful of him. She's seen him around the surgery during the past year, dropping in, loitering, a harmless presence as Dr Brand's doctor son. But now Pa's gone, she must be calculating for her future. If there's a power struggle between Davis and Jim Cobcroft, whose side should she take? Where's her bread buttered?

Best she be directing her thoughts to politics, Davis thinks. Best she doesn't know what's really creeping about in my sick little head.

Half an hour later, Davis has still not sent the email, and Claire has not returned to the room next door. He tries to phone his mother. Engaged. He tries to phone Lucy. Voicemail. This time he leaves a message from which he cannot sieve out the petulance: 'I didn't know you'd be so busy today, Lucy. Call me when you get a minute.'

He is packing up when his mobile phone rings. The caller is unidentified: Private Number.

'Hello?'

'Davo.'

There is no mistaking it. The voice cancels out grief, stupidity, love, anger, a hand wiped across the whole shelf, sending all his wretched garbage smashing to the floor.

'Where did you get my number?'

'Nice way to greet your –'

'Sorry – it's just a shock to –'

'Yeah no. Yeah. Where are you?'

'I'm at the surgery. At Pa's, in the Cross. Where are you?'

'Good,' says the voice. 'You might be able to look up something for me.'

'What?'

'There are some things on the computer.' The voice issues some technical instructions on how to open files in Pa's computer. Davis copies them onto a pad. Then the voice requests a favour, something very specific; he phrases it slowly, so that Davis cannot misunderstand what he is being asked to do.

'You want me to do this now?' Davis asks.

'No. First, go to the cupboard by the sharps bin and look on the top shelf.'

'But, hey, how are you –'

'Later, Davo. Just go to the top shelf.'

Davis lays the phone on the desk and goes to the metal cupboard. It is unlocked. On the top shelf is a scrolled-up pair of light tan trousers he recognises as Pa's. He brings them back to the desk and unrolls them. A harsh staticky laugh from the phone bounces up off the desk. Davis holds the trousers up by the waistband. On the front, over the fly, is the imprint of a kiss: a pair of puckered lips in a bright, almost childish, pink lipstick.

When Davis picks up the phone, the line is dead. There is no callback number.

He pockets his phone, and without another glance at the pink kiss-print he bunches the trouses tightly and tucks them under his arm. Before leaving the room, he closes down Pa's computer. It asks if he wants to send the message still on screen, addressed to Claire. Davis clears his throat nervously. There's absolutely no question now. He slides the mouse over and clicks CANCEL.

At 6.59 pm on the second Tuesday in November, Dr John Brand, a gentleman in late middle-age with an unremarkable face and grey suit, came back up the hill with the sprung stride of the self-worthy and a biography under his arm. His brain was a powersurging mainframe of permutation and strategy, calculating when to approach the door, what angle of entry, how to hold his head at what precise angle, whether or not to meet other eyes, how to bear himself, how to hide the ever-so-soft tremble in his neck. Flushed with reward he came to the portal and, without hesitation, sure as a pastor entering his vestibule, he entered this shop that had no door. These establishments never had doors – the door was in a man's heart.

John's heart fibrillated the membrane of his Italian shirt. A trace of mercury crept into his legs up the stairway, but this time it felt a good, *living* kind of discombobulation, as if his nervous system were not jackknifing but dancing.

Nothing escaped him: neither the first thud of bass music, nor the first waft of antiseptic Magic-Mushroom-purple that met him from above, nor the wave of wellbeing reaching down the stairs and coddling him up. Safe safe safe from the streets. There was no door. He had disappeared through a stitch in time into this airlock, this womb. He paused again near the top of the stairs, brought

Bernard Kouchner out from his armpit and noticed that the brown paper was soaked quite wet: this, he felt, is what people mean when they discover, now and then, that they are alive.

He re-tucked Kouchner under his arm and lowered his hands into the clear – men who come into such places should keep their hands visible, as if under arrest. He was committed. Never again could he say he had not been in here. Outside on the street he had had his excuses – he was going somewhere else, a Vietnamese restaurant, a discount hi-fi store, the downstairs bookshop – but now he was stripped of lies. He and the others were all here for the same reason and they were more naked than the parts and penetrations, the membranous pink and glistening stretched invitation around them, which after all was only skin, whereas it was he, John, who stood there stripped.

Mentally he smoothed his lapels. Now: choices. Greet the counter assistant or not. Which section first. This door to the left – this . . . this *suckatorium* – give it a wide berth, yes, or would giving it *too* wide a berth expose him in some way? Look around and scan other customers, or keep eyes trained on the task? Was it better to know who was here and, if he saw an acquaintance, trap them in an eye-pact, or better to let them see him and steal his secret for themselves? Better to be compromised alone or in company? His forehead was filmed with something cold.

(Or then again, he might simply die here at the top of the stairs. Would his corpse look less guilty if it tumbled back to the ground floor?)

He steadied and entered on a resolution, head high. He decided, in the unthinkable event that he met an acquaintance, he would share the pleasant greetings of well-bred men.

'How are you?'

'How are you?'

'Come here often?'

'Haha, very good.'

'See you then.'

'All right, yes. See you.'

'Enjoy!'

When a man bore himself well, he could engineer a kind of safety.

He scanned. Two young surfer types; an office worker with a high brow and shiny knees; an Aboriginal man with an over-sedated girlfriend; four or five Asian men; a very tall, very heavy pinheaded man in the Teens section; and that was that. He was safe. Nobody he knew. The West is the Best. He proceeded.

Life relived, it still felt like the first time, a good thing for Public John Brand, so hard-sprung with rehearsals of what he would say if he got caught, when he got caught: 'This is my first time.' His excuse was so heavily embedded in the tip of his tongue, so closely impacted inside his readiness, that it had assumed the solidity of truth.

But, as measured by enumeration of times up those stairs and receipted financial transactions, it wasn't his first time, not his first time at all. Every stage of his approach, from the Hamlet-like passes by the doorway, the downstairs purchase, the resolution to leave and the celebration at that resolution, to the reversal, the joyous arrival, the final panic and the music of delusion and recrimination – all this was played out precisely as it always was.

The young white-suited man in the video section peered through the bead curtain all the way to the blandness of Dr John Brand's features. He saw what lurked behind those pacific blue irises sucked into a pair of Lifesavers by the traitorous pupils spread in ever-renewing shock. He could identify a man in shock: the impassive surface a scant mask for the turmoil stricken into him by this atomic-force riot of primary colours, candy pinks, ebullient reds and blacks, the cellophane whitelight shimmer which denoted the modern convenience, the ordered cleanliness and welcome. Frequency-modulated sound oozed from a sophisticated many-megahertz system, a virile beat filling the silence, as functional as urbane small-talk at a party.

John's eyes twitched towards the counter assistant: Chinese, young enough to be his granddaughter, though in here she looked oddly maternal. A woman. In all John's days of frequenting these shops, the only women were prostitutes with clients, counter assistants, and once in a blue moon a drunk couple, but ordinarily if you were in here you were among men who arrived alone and left more so.

'Can I help you?'

He jumped. Her pocket clip said JOY. Joy spoke slowly.

'Can, I, help, you, with, that, sir?'

John edged away, behind the salad-bar magazine rack. Joy followed him. Blushing, John shook his head and backed towards She-Males. Joy extended her palms, as if pressing him. JOY: name tag or slogan?

'Please, just stop, sir?'

All she wanted was his biography, to stash behind the counter.

'The rules,' she said patiently, as if to a deaf-mute. 'You get it back. When you leave.'

John let her take the Kouchner from under his arm. He flushed purple, content to be treated as a thief rather than a what-he-was.

He averted his eyes, inhaled the disinfected air, which smelt scrubbingly, falsely Dettoled and Jiffed like his surgery, to the degree that it was the disinfectant itself that turned the stomach rather than any smell it was masking. The excessive smell of cleanness only drew attention to the filth. He struggled to comprehend the material stacked around the walls, and the long literature bar down the centre. He'd seen worse on his computer, of course, but the proximity of other customers – beating hearts, oozing glands left and right – made the pictures themselves seem fleshly.

Soon he was able to focus. The wares were divided by category: soft from hard, A4 from pocket-sized, high from low production values, pretend glamour from proud disgust – he knew them, he knew them already – and further back the hardcore small-format publications, European-produced, no pretty women striking poses on the cover, oh no, oh no no no. He knew them all, and what he was looking for was not in that section.

He was here among men, scanning the shelves and seeking some hormonal command. John knew what he was looking for. He slid magazines out, scanned covers, the two or three acts from two or three angles portrayed with a stylised sameness, an enforced language like the standard postures of religious art. Everyone was looking for something.

John neared the speciality sections, but shied away, rounding the bar quickly. He felt he would be labelled – incriminated – by where he stood. Even if he positioned himself in front of the literature bar, he would be suspected of inspecting neighbouring Specialities sidelong, a deception within other concentric deceptions, oh why did it matter, but it did, it did.

The bleached surfer elbowed past, working a ring around his wedding finger, trying to get rid of the chafing by chafing it more. Shocking, John thought, how many young married men you saw.

From around the bar a middle-aged man, a new one, emerged at Brand's right.

'Scuse me I just get past you here? Thanks, ta. Bit tight in here donchathink?' He spoke softly, without insinuation, more dial tone than voice. Accidentally, John looked into his face or, more specifically, at a roseate jelly mole the size of a five-cent coin nestled into the wing of his right nostril. John's immediate reflex was to ask himself: Is it the jelly mole that makes him? Has he never been able to get over it? Or the nutbrown teeth peeled open by his cringing smile. The twiddled eyebrows like frayed fusewire. What is it that makes him and then what is it that makes me . . .

John's face pulsed a heavy wave of adolescent shame. Was there an absolute need for jellymoleman to be so verbosely polite, or so atonal, given that he had plenty of room to get by and need not have said a word at all? His politeness, probably an anti-tic, an overcompensation for being there, sent a shiver down John's back.

The centre bar had the magazines piled to waist level. He settled, brow knit. He flicked and flicked covers, plastic-static snapping in his fingers, until he fell upon what he had come for.

Her, on the cover of a two-year-old copy of *Cheri Movie Stars Special Edition*, Her spine a perfect S, rump pouting at the camera, lively smile cocked over the shoulder. Her hair was in its platinum phase; a tricoloured sheeny catsuit crackled on Her hindquarters.

At the sight of Her eyes, he felt the reaction he had been seeking: She remained faithful to their original contact.

He looked with his eyes and flipped with his fingers and smelt with his nose, but he listened with something else. Having decided on that magazine, he hid it behind another and left it on the stack. He didn't want to appear too eager, fearing that an extended look at the cover photograph would reveal his *thing* for Her. He found two more magazines with Her on the cover: a *Club International* and an *Adam Film World*. He secreted both behind the first one, his buried hoard. He cocked his ear to the little animal, wondering if She would rouse it with her siren call from some other shelf. He scanned female faces, faces with sockets, faces like ten-pin bowling balls. Organs. And hearts. Hearts abounded in there. On box covers, magazine lines, the packaging of totemic rubber and dolls with Insinkerator mouths, one word predominated:

LOVE

And one shape:

LOVE with the O as pink beating heart, a love-heart, bubblegum pink, throbbing, glistening with that little catch of light, a distended pink heart quivering with LOVE.

His own heart, meanwhile, worked overhard. The excitement jogged John's left ventricle. It belted against his ribcage like an ornery old boxer fighting out of habit but getting beaten up by younger, hungrier men. With each thump, his damaged aortic valve failed to close, allowing blood to rush back down into the heart, which in turn was forced to pump harder, causing a burp or belch of blood in the centre of his chest. Each beat hardened and enlarged the muscle of his hypertrophied heart, which hurt like any other tired muscle, a thigh or biceps, felt like it needed a rest, a brown-yellow streaky hunk of gristle, nothing at all like those vivacious pink candystore valentine hearts.

The further from his heart, the less blood. His hands, feet and head felt thinned by the low pressure. A healthy heart would have produced a certain tautness beneath his skin, but instead his extremities hummed on an economical but chancy supply, like an experimental car. Drained of blood, his bowels also weakened, the lower gut loosening. Between the shelves he walked strangely, clenching his buttock cheeks. Almost Pavlovian: erection, defecation.

He tottered towards his buried treasure, ready to pay and leave. Two men entered the store, setting off an electronic dingdong from the lintel and a flinch in John's neck. He could see them through the horizontal gap in the salad bar. One wore slack flannel shorts to the knees and a dirty horizontal-striped knit T-shirt that hung over the shorts to magnify the slop of overladen stomach propped up on his legs: hairy, fat, kneeless tubes. His mate was lean as a strip of jerky in a red Manchester United soccer shirt loose over black jeans, dandling a half-drunk bottle of Coca-Cola. They paused at the counter, the fat one foursquare in front of the jerky.

'Whewwa yo videos?' The voice an unmodulated honk. A wincing John thought: *Mentally deficient perhaps dangerously short-tempered definitely a virgin and goes without saying compulsive masturbator. With the weaselly skinny one, a Steinbeckian psychotic pairing.*

'Where'w your VIDeos?' the fat one repeated in mockingly clear English for Joy, who was in fact as Australian as he, but the fat one was losing whatever shallows of patience he had brought in, while behind him lankyboy shuffled foot to foot.

Joy pointed to the beaded curtain. The X-rated video section was not strictly legal, as John, frightened of a police bust, well knew. But X were still on sale in these shops and, as the lanky one took a step towards the curtain, 600 ml Coke Buddy swinging in his fingers, his fat mate held his ground.

'What do they wange fwom?'

Incomprehension – feigned? – from Joy.

'What do they WANGE FWOM?'

Joy shrugged and waved him dismissively towards the curtain.

'WHAT DO THEY WANGE FWOM?'

A big impatient bellow this time and lankyboy sidled back, muttered plaintively, 'Cool it, eh.' He shepherded his friend to the back room. They were in their early twenties, the prime of life. Joy must have pressed the button when the fat one raised his voice. A rumble of footsteps on the staircase preceded the arrival of the slab-faced man from downstairs. He went to the threshold of the video room.

'Help you, mate?'

'Ah, we just wanted to know the prices of the, um, videos,' the lean lad in the soccer shirt shuffled and stammered, while the fat one slouched against the door, his hanging arms pressed out by his rolling waist.

'Twenty to fifty, as marked.'

The security man stood by the beaded curtain to watch. He nodded gruffly and said 'G'day' to someone else who was already in there. In the main part of the shop, John Brand, feeling dizzy and cold, decided to buy his prized three magazines and leave quickly. He would hail a taxi and go back to the surgery, calm himself with his purchase, rest a while, then go home. He found Her smile and took his magazines to the counter.

As he passed the beaded curtain, he was bumped in the shoulder. He leapt. His heart accelerated again, as if out on the street sprinting from danger. The security man was escorting the two loud youngsters out of the video room. The bead curtain clicked. Up close the skinny one was viciously sebacious, red-nosed with pimples as if with a cold. John found himself face to face with the fat one, whose brown hair hung in a greasy veil over eyes buried in slits of cheek-and-brow, a face squeezed in on itself in whingey colicky pain.

The fat boy looked frankly at the respectable elderly man in the grey suit. John tasted the boy's sugary breath.

'No-one won't fucking help you get a decent fuck awound here, will they?'

John jumped out of his heart, mouth gaping like a landed fish, eyes boggling at this fat-faced vision from hell with sunken pellet eyes, addressing him as man to man, punter to punter, moaning about *a decent fuck*, this troglodyte, this rapist-in-situ, approaching John and making an honest complaint about the service as *one regular punter to another*.

John's knees and bowels turned to water. His withered aortic valve spat blood back into his overtaxed ventricle, which began to seize and belch. His pulse motored to three beats a second. One hundred and eighty! He reeled back against the rack and brought down three shelves of C---s With D---s and S---s With N---s, his last thought, as the boxes came tumbling over him, a childlike wonder at how there must be valves of language, like aortic valves, designed to close up over such words and stopper them from seeping back into the consciousness of good people like him. Yet, as he failed, so did the language-valves fail, flooding him with their putrescent euphemisms, their unspeakable rhymes. Chicks with Dicks, Sluts with Nuts. Chicks with Bricks and Clocks with Blocks. How gruesomely Dr Seuss it is, he thought, as infancy – but whose? his? his sons'? – infancy and old age came together and crushed the breath out of him.

'Hi,' the young man in the white linen suit stepped forward to rescue Dr Brand. The good Samaritan's hand reached across the beaded curtain to arrest the doctor's dead faint. Joy came from behind her counter to help. The customer and the security man helped the semiconscious John Brand out to the landing. Joy reached into a pigeonhole and brought out the biography wrapped in brown paper. She also gave the white-suited regular the three magazines John had bought.

The two disruptive customers took advantage of the confusion to sneak into the Suckatorium. As he was helped out of the shop, John came to. He'd only been unconscious for a few seconds. He saw faces – the jellymoleman, the young surfie, Joy, and the man from downstairs emerging to gather around The Guy Who Fainted In The Sex Shop – and a voice said:

'Yeah no, don't worry, I know him.'

Chris Brand fields at fourth slip for the opening bowler. Blond boy, nicknamed 'Simmo', not because Simpson is his name – it isn't – but in recognition of the desert between his ears. Simmo runs in. Chris goes into a crouch, settling in on his left knee first to ease the strain on the arthritic right, as if working his way down a rope. He watches the ball in the bowler's hand, then switches his focus to the bat, tapping, tapping, whirring into the set of triggers unique to every batsman, ending, this time, in a decision to let the ball fly through to the wicketkeeper. Someone who is not Chris lets out a mischievous howl of frustration, as if the ball had been a lot closer than it was, and someone else rips off a loud fart.

The ball is flicked past him on its circuit back to the bowler. He pushes himself upright, folds his arms. His hand feels the black tape around his left biceps. The tape pinches his sleeve. He fiddles with the loose end. He can't re-tape it: every camera in the stadium will be on him. Chris Brand taking off his armband? Don't think so.

Simmo runs in. Chris crouches. Another leave. Someone oohs again, but Tom Pritchard makes a mini-megaphone of his hands: 'Come on, make him play! These two balls! Come on, boys!' Geeing them up. Being a captain.

To Chris's right, Nathan Such says something to Chris. Chris ignores him.

The over finishes with an easy single to the batting team, and Chris and his teammates jog to the other end. He tries to vary his speed to be alone, but Nathan Such seems to be shadowing him, like a yacht covering tacks. Chris refuses to look at him.

He was lumped with Such this morning, before play. Pritchard decided, with his celebrated psychological astuteness, that it might be a good thing for the veteran to take the debutant under his wing. Chris walked Such out to the centre during warm-ups, the kid expecting him to say something. For an instant, Chris considered collaring the little prick and telling him the truth: *It never gets any better than this*. Telling him that your debut is a thrill you'll never know again. That your subsequent on-field achievements will be robbed by the bandits of videotape and newsprint. That even when you score fourteen centuries in ninety-three Test matches, you will feel only exhaustion and relief and the vague resentment of having to share. And the huge fucking resentment of having to do it again.

Did the kid really want the benefit of Chris's experience? Chris decided it was better, for both their sakes, to pretend Such wasn't there. He slouched over the pitch, hands shoved in his pockets. The longer he has played at this level, the more his favourite part of the game and therefore, arguably, the sweetest hour of his existence, is the hour before a Test match. The stands are mostly empty, save the keenest devotees and those most inclined to panic about traffic. The grass smells of dew, as green and turfy as it will ever be. The pitch is virginal. Its character is a mystery that will reveal itself over the course of its life. Five days from now, its history will be told in its imperfections: the abrasions, red cherry-skids, blockholes, middle-stump scratchings, cracks, slide marks, sunburnings, gouged bowlers' footmarks, bald spots and rogue eruptions, a cricket pitch's age-wrinkles and moles and scars. But for now its secrets are hidden beneath perfect skin.

He'd have liked to tell Nathan, *Slow down, take it all in, remember this moment, bottle it*; but instead he stood with hands rammed in pockets, breathing to the martial rhythms of balls cracking against the advertising hoardings as the other guys played throwdowns. Better to leave Nathan Such to find out for himself. Chris remembered each step up to a new level, from school to colts to grade, the thrill of rising from soft private-school cricket to mixing it with the sixteen-year-olds from the country who'd been competing with grown men, years ahead of Chris in sharps. Every promotion took him into a new sophisticated world with new things you had to learn, new mistakes to make. Then into State and Test cricket, and then the buzz of new countries, teams with strange ways of carrying themselves, practising, sledging, even stretching and exercising – every country has its own subtle ways. Fucking beautiful thing, the differences between people.

But it is a long time since Chris experienced anything new, and he lacked the words to bridge those years back to the awkward expectant twenty-two-year-old beside him. Chris led Such off the pitch. As they passed the South Africans on their way to the players' gate, Chris, sensing he ought at least to say something to the kid, squeezed out five words: 'Let's stuff these cunts then.'

Now they crouch for the second opening bowler, a young Aboriginal quick. Press love him, of course, though he's not really up to this standard. Chris watches his liquid run, then switches his eye to the bat. The ball kicks off an invisible ridge and hits the edge of the bat. At first it slews to Chris's right, but the pace and side-spin warp it back towards him. He has to do the hardest thing for a slips catcher: go forward to the ball. He reaches out with a cupped right hand, but something in his knee sticks, and as his arm goes out in front his bum pushes back. The ball bounces in front of his hand. He twitches away from it – you can lose your teeth going forward – but by pure fluke the ball sticks. His fingers close around it. A huge roar is choked off, heads are thrown back in anguish, and then the knowledgeable, or those who think they are knowledgeable, or at least the merciful, set off a round of generous applause for Chris Brand's excellent stop. A missed catch, a great stop – that's the difference when your old man's cooling in the morgue.

He tosses the ball to Nathan Such and folds his hand under his left arm. It throbs. The black tape is cool against his red-hot palm.

'Sweet stop, Chris,' Such ventures. Someone else gives him a pat on the bum. The Aboriginal bowler shoots him a quick glare – as Chris would hope and expect, the bowler thinks he's just missed out on a wicket – but after the initial disappointment the boys are congratulating Chris on a sharp piece of fielding.

They're all being kind to him. The last two days, in the nets, they've been patronising him with easy half-volleys.

'Hittin' 'em sweet,' they never miss a chance to say.

Everyone trying to talk him back into form. They need runs from him, sure, but there has been this sickly kindness around him since the news about Pa. He hates it: the *concessions*.

This morning, after their abortive walk to the centre, he and Such had played throwdowns near the fence. The ground was filling up. Chris remembered how he used to love the Sydney Test – his home Test – when the whole town was too hot to work, and everyone he knew, everyone he'd ever known, came out to watch him. Nowadays, in his twelfth year at the top, the Sydney Test fills him with anxiety. People he knows still come to watch him, but they're watching for him to fail. And does he know people anyway? When you're an international sportsman, it's hard to keep in touch with old friends. You just don't have the time, and when you have the time you find you don't have that much in common anymore. If you ever did. So the only people you really care about in the crowd are your family. Your wife and kids. Your Ma and Pa. Specially your Ma.

But Ma isn't here this morning, and this is a stadium full of strangers. Chris practised grimly. Children were calling out with their pens and programmes like baby vultures – cute, but vultures still. Did everything have to be a fucking spectacle?

As he was practising, Chris had locked eyes with a girl. Or not a *girl* as such – glasses, hair pulled severely back like a towel being twisted dry, could be any age between twenty and thirty-five, hard to tell, and wearing a T-shirt with an arrow pointing to the side and the words: 'STUPID'S WITH ME'. She propped a string bag full of books on the fence. Face dragged down by invisible weights. Something about her unnerved him. He tried a smile. The girl/woman looked away, picked up her bag and turned back up the ramp. In her hurry, she bumped a seat hard enough to bruise her thigh.

While Chris and Nathan Such played throwdowns, Tom Pritchard and the South African captain went out to the pitch to toss. Their smiles and creams and blazers got glutted in electronic cables and Ian Chappell and cameras. This, Chris thought, is majority rule: the sacrifice of the people at the ground to the millions doing their crosswords and ironing in front of their TV sets.

Chris wanted to bat first, but he tried to ignore the toss, play it cool. He wanted to get into it. Not sleep on this wretched fucking thing for one more night. Let's go. Am I good enough? Let's find out now. Get in there, put some runs on the board, shut those fuckers up. Then see fear rise in the enemy's face. Bat them out of the game. Drain their hope.

The youngest sprite in the ground knew Chris Brand's last six scores: 0, 0, 0, 0, 1, 1. Who has been in a pub, a schoolyard, or stood by a radio in the past fortnight and not been through the arguments? At thirty-four, can a bloke just lose it, even though he topped the averages on the spring tour of Pakistan? Is he washed up, or just having a run of bad luck? Should the selectors sack him despite, or because of, his father's death? Should he be 'rested', or given a tap on the shoulder to indicate he might 'retire on his own terms'? Opinions are like arseholes. Everyone's got one. That's Chris's opinion.

He had a good chat with Ma about it yesterday, on the phone. She'd been up at the hospital. Chris offered to leave the team camp to go view Pa, but Ma said it wouldn't make much difference.

'Not for Pa, but what about for you?' Chris said.

'You know how you can help me?' Ma said. 'Stay with the team, concentrate on yourself, and make some runs.'

She'd been amazing. She hadn't wanted to talk about Pa, instead making the usual small-talk about the game. Her effort not to seem worried about his form nearly broke his heart.

'Don't let them tell you you're out of form,' she quipped. 'You haven't been batting long enough to lose form! You've just been unlucky.'

Ma was the only person in the world who truly believed that. One thing matters and that is your numbers. 0, 0, 0, 0, 1 and 1 are six brutal spotlights. If you live by the numbers, you die by them. In the end, not even Chris believes there is such a thing as luck. Not in the long run. Christ – if luck had that much to do with it, any fucker could be here.

No, he thinks: it's a meritocracy, that's why we love it. No luck. Skill and application and nerve. Measured by numbers. Well, his skill and application have been tested for years, but the question of *nerve* is never quite settled. Nerve can desert a man. Nerve can be pilfered in the night. Everyone's time comes, everyone's nerve goes. And once a batsman passes a certain age – maybe thirty, thirty-one, thirty-two, let alone thirty-four – the nuance in the question shifts from 'When will he turn the corner?' to a more blunt 'Has he lost it?'

'Would you prefer to bat first or field first?' Ma had asked.

'Bat, I reckon. Get it out of the way.'

She was so stoical, with everything going on, Chris had almost choked up as they said goodbye.

'Don't let the bastards get you down,' Ma said.

'Ma . . . thanks.'

There was a silence on the phone.

'No need to thank me,' she said finally. 'I'm only your mother.'

'Well, still, thanks,' he swallowed. 'For being so . . . professional.'

It wasn't the right word. He didn't know why it had come out, compared with all the others he might have used.

'Sorry Ma, I didn't . . .'

'I take it as a compliment,' she said. 'But I'll tell you something, my love. I'm not going to become a professional widow. I know too many of them. So if you ever see me looking like a widow, tell me. I'm relying on you.'

Chris knew what she meant. He'd been to enough funerals with Ma.

'Ma,' he'd said. 'You've got me . . . all of us.'

Chris had been thinking about that conversation with Ma when a light groan rippled through the ground, seagulls scattered in disproportionate alarm, and the news was announced that South Africa won the toss. Nathan Such's face turned as white as his shirt. Chris saw that no matter how much he himself wanted to bat, get his torment over and done with one way or the other, the debutant wanted even more *not* to bat. Such wasn't ready. He needed a day in the field to get used to Test cricket, feel at home at altitude. Suddenly it made sense to Chris why he and Nathan Such had been thrown together. More of Tom Pritchard's pseudo-psychology: quarantine the two most anxious men from the rest of the team. Make sure their fear doesn't spread. Keep the two Potholes – everyone else wants to avoid them – together, away from the boys.

'Batting,' Such said in a Xanax voice.

Chris's gut tensed. He lashed a last ball at the fence. Right, let's go. He was striding up the astroturf race, purposefully telling Such, who tailed him like a valet, 'It's a 400 pitch if we get through the first hour.'

'No, Brandy, *they're* batting.' Such was blushing with his relieved smile.

Chris stopped, biting his lower lip. He uttered an embarrassment-hiding grunt. It was unlike Chris Brand to get something like this wrong. Nathan would report it to the others: another sign that the old boy is feeling the pinch.

But that's all gone now. We're fielding. He goes into the crouch again. Too much on his mind. *Fucking come on!* With his unhurt hand he slaps his thigh as if jockeying a wayward horse. Concentrate. The Aboriginal bowler fires in a short ball that clips the sweet shoulder of the South African's bat. Chris loses the ball for an instant against the dark Noble Stand. When he picks it up again, it is lobbing, with a nasty fizzing spin, towards him. It happens too fast and too slow. He has no idea what he is doing, but seconds later his teammates have converged on him in a wild hug, as if he has done something great, and even the young fast bowler is throwing himself onto the huddle as if this is Chris's wicket, not his.

Chris looks at their faces, these ten men collapsing onto him, and reads a joy and relief that they expect him to feel. *Okay, they're pleased I've taken the catch. But a ten-year-old could have pouched that. This is fucking excessive.* The crowd has gone up as if the game has been won. He clenches his eyes shut. *I've taken an easy catch. But now I have a whole country patronising me with their goodwill because I'm the poor bastard who's lost his form and his father in the same month.*

When he opens his eyes, Tom Pritchard is in his face.

'I told you! I told you! You've got it back!'

Chris shuts his eyes on Pritchard. He totters away, flicks the ball to the umpire and crouches down with his forehead balanced on his fingers. Behind him, his teammates still cavort. He can see the photo: oh so poignant, a team celebrating and the hero, overwhelmed, saying a quiet prayer, perhaps dedicating this catch to Father.

What a fucking circus.

He pulls at his armband, reties it to stop it pinching. He's the first back into position, clapping his teammates: 'Come on, let's get into 'em!' He's irritated beyond belief with the ceremony, the special consideration. The armbands bullshit – nobody told him about that until five minutes before play. Pritchard had lost the toss: Australia were fielding. Chris had stormed through the dressing room, tossing his bat unnecessarily hard on the floor, on into the bathroom, throwing the irrepressibly jubilant Such off his tail, and submerged his head under an icy shower. The water drenched his collar and shoulders. When he came out of the shower, a towel turbaned around his head and the fast bowlers stretching and running on the spot, the dressing room was unusually silent. Even the manager and coach and attendants, who customarily punched holes in the air with their talk, as a vent through which nerves could escape, were creeping around like night animals. Then he noticed. They were all wearing the black electrical tape.

'No,' he glared at Tom Pritchard, who was signing the team sheet. 'No.'

'Board's orders,' Pritchard said, without having the fucking bollocks to engage Chris's eye.

The silence clotted. Even the opening bowlers paused. History piled on itself like sediment: his own relationship with Tom Pritchard, the only other survivor from the 1980s, had been whittled back to a professional gristle ever since, three years ago, the captaincy succession was resolved in Pritchard's favour, due reportedly and fucking well definitely to Board doubts over Chris Brand's 'team spirit', his 'single-mindedness', which was an asset for his batting but a liability for captaincy. As if you had to be half a player to make a captain.

It all flowed from there. The captain advertises soft drinks, cars, photocopiers, air conditioners, photo film, a whole industry of sports gear tangentially connected to cricket. There are scales that quantify a sportsman's appeal factor, like a batting average, and Tom Pritchard inhabits the top rung. Chris Brand doesn't even rate Top Fifty. He has a contract with a hair dye company. There were meant to be TV ads, but he hasn't done any yet.

Maybe he should flog himself for an Audi endorsement deal. 'Audi', that's what those press cunts were calling him up to the last Test, after he'd scored four zeroes in a row: 0, 0, 0, 0. Then they had to change it, because in the last Test he scored 1 and 1. They changed it to 'Binary'.

'Well,' Chris had glared at Pritchard, picking up the length of black tape left diplomatically by his kit – his monogrammed *coffin*, though nobody calls them *coffins* this week – and said: 'S'pose if I need a score to save my place, I'd better not rock the boat.'

From there, the great white unblinking light, and a great cheer to wash the crap from the earth. National anthems, a nest of teardrop-seeking cameras in his face, the full fucking catastrophe.

He goes down into his crouch, cupping his hands loosely, resting his forearms on his thighs to take the pressure off his back. The batsman plays and misses. Fieldsmen and crowd ooh. Chris pushes himself up. How many times has he done this, gone into this crouch? It seems infinite, but the beauty of this game is that there would be records, if anyone sought them out, providing exactly this fact. How many balls has he fielded? Let's say, ninety overs a day, six balls an over, ninety-three Tests, same for 254 first-class games, then the 112 games he played for his club, the 201 one-day internationals, forty-seven State one-dayers, then games for Australia on overseas tours, and not to forget all the charity and exhibition games, and Christ, he thinks, Christ Almighty, maybe it is infinite.

The commentators have been saying he was riding into this Test on 'a wave of emotion', which was cute bullshit, because he is too experienced to allow himself to go into any Test match, let alone one as important as this – the series to be won, his position to be saved – on 'emotion'. Right at this moment, the commentators will be parroting the line that the Australian team are united in their 'emotional wave'. But Chris knows his team-mates. He knows cricketers. Who among them honestly has any capacity for an emotion beyond his own anxieties about his own performance? Not even – least of all – the great Pritchard. Any man who 'rides emotion' into this game won't be here long. For Chris it had simply been a choice, made long, long ago, an enforced habit, hardened into a character trait, tested and fired in the kiln of competition: *You develop the habit of not having emotions. You challenge emotions to make themselves felt. You defeat emotions.* Since yesterday's chat with Ma, Chris has been able to beat them. He hasn't given Pa much of a thought. Ma would be proud of him.

They gather for the first drinks break. Simmo has an ankle problem. He's sitting with the physio unlacing his boot. A sponsor's anthem pumps out in rumba time. Chris stands apart, sipping a red-flavoured sports drink. Now and then a hand passes by, smacking him reassuringly on the rump. He stares into space.

The crowd releases a deep unified sigh, followed by a pause, and rolling clapping. If you didn't know that sound, he thinks, you could mistake it for disappointment, or shock. But it is the sound they make when they see something they like on the big screen.

His teammates are watching a replay. Chris hates the big screen: thinks it has sucked the spontaneity from the game. He detests it when the guys, instead of geeing each other up, stand around like morons watching the big screen. Fucking hell. But this time, because it's a drinks break, he turns and looks at it himself. It's the second replay, the one where the camera shot is tighter, grabbing the very spin of the seam as it deviates off the shoulder of the bat and arcs at the hundred-and-twenty-odd degree angle towards fourth slip. A player he recognises as himself catches it.

It shocks him. This isn't how he recalls it. Instead of lolli-popping, the ball rockets. No wonder he'd lost sight of it. On replay, Chris Brand nonchalantly raises his hands at the last instant to cut off the ball's flight as it is about to crash into his Adam's apple. It looks like a feat of daring. One of the guys gives a soft admiring whistle.

'Like shelling peas,' Nathan Such says, taking Chris's drink bottle out of his hand.

The crowd sighs and applauds again.

Chris claps his hands, as if warming them. His right hand isn't sore anymore.

'Come on, get up,' he mutters to Simmo. 'Three more of these cunts by lunch.'

At eight o'clock in the evening, Davis arrives at the apartment hotel in the hollow of Circular Quay where the Australian team chooses to stay. A security guard asks him to show identification before keying the lift up to the cricketers' floor. It is bizarre and annoying that he should need *credentials* to see his younger brother. In a brief moment of challenge, Davis wonders if he could get away, on looks alone, with an outraged Do-You-Know-Who-I-Am? routine. It's the type of thing Chris would encourage him to do and scorn him for not doing.

Davis presents his driver's licence, which the security guard nods through. The elevator smells of recent male sweat. Davis composes himself for meeting his brother. They have spoken once since the news about Pa. Yesterday Chris rang Davis and said: 'You all right?'

Davis: 'Yeah, you?'

Chris: 'Yeah. Just checking. Gotta go.'

It was the day before a Test, after all.

The lift rises to the top floor. Davis checks himself in the mirror. He smoothes his hair into the careful trilobite-shape. He pinches his lower lip, runs his tongue across the little white scab. He stands back, offering the mirror a more global perspective. Could he even get away with it, looks-wise? He and Chris look more like cousins than brothers. Each resembles their mother and their father, but the genetic mix-n-match cards have fallen with regular randomness, giving Davis his father's fleshy lips and his mother's fine-boned build, and Chris his father's brick-red complexion and his mother's quick eyes.

The elevator mirror offers Davis no fresh insight. He looks like what he is. A doctor who sleeps too little. A son. A mildly familiar relative of the famous Chris Brand. A crop of pimples is lurking in the cleft of his chin. Ma's cleft. Pa's chin. Davis's pimples.

The lift door opens. He steps into the corridor and another security guard, seated at a desk, asks for his ID.

'You right, mate?' the guard says as he copies down Davis's particulars.

Davis swipes his brow with a handkerchief.

'Yeah, fine, mate,' he says, his voice sounding like someone else's. But that's the problem with his voice today: it's always sounding like someone else's. It sounded like someone else's when he finally reached Lucy on her mobile, on his way from the surgery to the hotel. She recounted her meetings – she likes to hear herself – before, taking a breather, saying:

'So how's your day been . . . Oh God, sorry sweetheart . . . I'm so sorry. How *has* your day been?'

He wanted to tell her about the unusual way he'd found Pa's death certificate. He wanted to tell her about how Ma had not spoken to him. He wanted to tell her about the phone call, and his discovery of the trousers with the imprint of a kiss, which he had taken outside and dumped in a garbage bin on the street.

Instead he said: 'Yeah, fine. You're breaking up.'

'Okay, not a problem,' Lucy said to someone else. 'Sweetheart, I'm *so, so* sorry. How's your mum?'

'She's good. But you're breaking up. I might come over later.'

There was a pause on the other end.

'Sweetheart, darling, I'm going to be really late tonight. Really late. Can you wait till tomorrow?'

'You're breaking up,' he lied. She was clear as a bell.

He raps a bright tattoo on Chris's door, which is held open by the little gold bar.

Davis anticipates the tired little dance. Chris will say: *What've you been up to?* Davis: *Nothing much.* He won't need to ask Chris what he's been doing, because fame leaves his younger brother with a certain unaccountability. *What do you think I've been up to? Don't you watch TV?*

Yet there are things Davis needs to know, which Chris cannot dodge.

'Enter.'

'Hi, Chris.'

'Davo.'

Chris grunts from the floor, legs splayed in front of him, back against the bed, clad in white bicycle shorts and a singlet, remote control dangling in his fingers like a cigarette. His hair is grey in the television glow. His cricket whites lie spread out in human shape on the bed, ankles hanging off the edges, a limp ghost of exhaustion. In the battle for possession of the room's air, the funky aroma of Chris's body has taken the upper hand over the nylony scent of five-star.

'Good to see some things don't change.' Davis nods at Chris's possessions – bats, pads, newspapers, clothes, merchandise, packaged odds and ends, occupying every square inch of space. Chris has always been the grub, the Oscar to Davis's Felix. No matter how salubrious the setting – and this hotel room, with its Bridge view and inch-thick glass, is literally twenty storeys higher than the type of places Chris started out in – the essential Chris Brand reveals himself in the Balkanisation of his gear.

'So they've got security for your hotels now,' Davis says.

Chris massages his temples. The undersides of his biceps are shockingly white.

'Gotta stop the groupies!' Davis gives a stringy laugh.

'*Groupies.*' Chris blinks at him, stretching his back.

'You don't call them that anymore?' Davis hazards a smile.

Chris shakes his head, more to himself than to Davis, and watches the television. Davis goes to the window, stepping over Chris's legs. A cruise ship is docked by the passenger terminal. The girders of the Harbour Bridge glow an industrial-era green.

'It always surprises me how tired you get from a day fielding,' says Davis. 'I'd expect you to look like this if you'd been batting all day . . .'

Davis tails off. Chris's eyes reflect the glassy screen. Davis stabs at a new conversational topic like a blind man lunging at a sound: 'They put in a nightwatchman. Pritchard didn't think you'd last?'

Chris seems catatonic in front of the television, but waves the remote with his thumb on the red button. He pushes himself arthritically to his feet. Davis perches in a chair, one of a cluster by the window, hands falling into his lap as if at an interview. He tries to loop an arm casually over the chair back, but it slides off. Chris flops on the bed.

'Don't try,' Chris's voice says from the crunchy pile of plastic-wrapped batting gloves.

'Try what?'

'You think meteorologists like chit-chatting about the fucking weather?'

'Probably do,' Davis says. 'Hey. A joke. What's the difference between an introverted meteorologist and an extroverted meteorologist? The extrovert looks at *your* shoes while he's talking to you.'

Davis cackles at his own joke to fill the silence. Chris pinches the flesh between his eyes – Pa's vertical lines, Ma's gesture and pliable large-pored skin. Davis wonders how it is that he always feels so awkward around Chris, as if Chris is the elder brother and Davis has to try to impress him. Chris seems worldlier, as if, through his fame and his sport, he has overtaken his elder brother. It contradicts all of Davis's ideas about life that he should feel this inferiority. There is no way a man who spends his days in hotel rooms like this, being chauffeured to cricket grounds, having his every whim catered for, who never has to put his hand in his pocket or organise a flight or a taxi or pay a bill, cushioned from all practicality to leave him prepared, monkishly, for the higher purpose of belting a ball around a park – no way such a man could have gained any experience of the real world, or at least, nowhere near the richness of experience gained by another man who spends his days tending to the full deck of ailments, physical and mental, in a public hospital. And what's more, Davis helps improve his world! He's seen the worst of the species, and the best. He stitches, soothes, medicates, treats. All Chris does is divert. Davis has done much more with his life than Chris. So why is it that Chris seems so much more grown-up?

'Yes,' Chris says, mechanically. 'He put in a nightwatchman. I'll bat tomorrow.' He changes channel, lost in his own world.

The bowlers had done well, getting the South Africans out for 227. But it left the Australians with a tricky last hour to bat, the light high-contrast, the fielders elongating into silhouettes. Two purple strips of sky-writing detritus wreathed the sun. Grandstand-sized shadow puppets clawed their way across the field until only an almond of golden turf remained. The crowd edged up the western stand to escape the encroaching sun-line, the top rows packing up as the ruler of shade swept upwards. In the late heat the wind built, thermals of rubbish and dust curling and clattering in surprise attacks under the stands.

As a player Chris knew this was when things happened, when every skin in the ground was stretched taut. In the history of the game, how much critical, match-turning drama happens in the last hour of a day? Everyone loves the last hour – except a batsman padded up in the pavilion.

Chris was lying face-down on the massage table, doing a cross-word and sipping a green-flavoured electrolyte drink while the physio gave his calves a rub-down. His toes soaked in a saucer of whiskey, a superstitious custom after a long day in the field and a cure for his chronic ingrown toenails, legacy of years crammed into cricket boots. His teammates avoided him.

Chris would bat at second-wicket-down. If one of the openers got out, he'd pad up. He lay on the massage table, aware that every drop of the dread, fear and hope percolating through him was shared, sucked away even, by Ma, in front of her TV set. The image of Ma watching him, fighting alongside him, was, as always, a granite lump of comfort in the pit of his stomach. She'd have turned both the radio and the TV commentary off now, because when she's most nervous she can't stand those has-beens and never-weres pontificating about her son.

He was almost through the crossword when the peculiar groan of a home disaster leached through the wall. Chris glanced at the monitor hanging from a motel-style bracket in the cornice at the rejoicing South Africans.

The Number Three went in. Tom Pritchard used to bat at Three – the position of Bradman and Richards and Chappell and Hammond – but a weakness of stomach has attacked Test captains in recent years, and now Three is the oven into which teams throw a young, promising batsman, to either destroy him or toughen him up. Three is now a weakness. Nathan Such, in his first Test, walked out to bat, his spikes snare-drumming on the concrete steps.

Chris jumped off the massage table, squirmed into his whites and started Velcroing himself together. In a sweaty flurry he fumbled with his straps. Acrid needles of Dencorub from his massage pierced his nostrils. He inserted his box and thighpad and for ten minutes sat perfectly still, emptying his mind, the usual routines, but difficult today, like shovelling sloppy snow. Going into bat now was a loser's game. Survive, and you have to start again tomorrow. Err, and you're gone.

But still he wanted to bat, and when the second opener got out Chris donned his gloves and picked up his bat.

His mouth opened and closed with confusion when he saw the wicketkeeper going out in his place.

He stormed back into the dressing room. He hurled his bat against a locker, dashed his gloves on the fibreglass casing of his coffin, cursing Tom Pritchard, who, when Chris looked up, was standing in the doorway.

'You're too valuable, Chris.'

Chris ripped off the Velcro of his pad straps.

'No ifs, no buts,' Pritchard continued. 'You're not batting tonight.'

There was a scene waiting to be played out between Chris and Pritchard that was overdue by three years – but neither would be careless enough to enact it here.

'You could've told me,' Chris said. Pritchard waited for more, but Chris was letting his Velcro do the talking.

'I know you think you don't need protection,' Pritchard went on with insulting tenderness, 'but I can't risk losing you tonight. No captain would do any different.'

And now, two hours later, all Davis can do is utter his offensive smart-arse comment about the nightwatchman, deliberately poking Chris's raw nerve. Fucking Davis.

Chris gives a tired flick of his hand. 'So how's Luce?'

Chris is the only person permitted – or who permits himself – to abbreviate Lucy. She likes it, from him if from no-one else. It's part of their snigger-at-Davo thing.

'She's great, great.' Davis nods hard and looks out the window appreciatively. He doesn't want Chris to see his face. Maybe, he thinks, he feels inferior to Chris purely because of how many women the guy must have had. Maybe there's an occult knowledge a man gleans from having had X-hundred, as opposed to, ooh, say, three. 'Yeah, *Lucy*'s great,' he nods, something clicking in the base of his neck.

'Can I have her?' Chris is doing some stretching exercises on his back, twisting on the bed with his hands crossed to opposite shoulders.

'Eh?'

'Wanna swap? You can have Suzie and her whingeing ngya-ngya-ngya all day. Here, see the holes?' Chris pauses to point to his cheek. 'Where the hen's been pecking.'

Davis pinches the scab on his lower lip.

'She's fucking driving me up the wall,' Chris says. 'Hey, matey, you're here. Can you call her up and tell her you caught me in bed, in the act, watching the news on telly? That'll really blow her mind.'

Davis rolls his tongue against the roof of his mouth. Chris has complained about Suzie's jealousy, and Suzie about Chris's womanising, since the day they met. Yet neither seems to tire of the routine, which, Davis has learnt, constitutes a complex ritual that inevitably ends in passionate reconciliation. There's no dividing Chris from Suzie. No war, no infidelity, no insult can bust the interconnected bunkers they've dug themselves into.

'She rang me after play today,' Chris says, 'and asked if she could come over. I said no, Davo's coming and I only have headspace for one visitor. So she starts accusing me of, you know, fobbing her off so I can go out on the tool. I mean, what do I say?'

Chris had taken the call from his wife in a cubicle of the dressing room toilet, a musty cigarette-stinking corner, known as the Domestic Shithole, where players can go and argue with their wives without being heard by teammates. It wasn't a fight, but it did belong to the fight family. She'd ended up accusing him and then, of course, crying. Crying always satisfied Suzie.

'You fucking cheating fucker,' she'd snivelled.

Chris couldn't be bothered fighting. What's the point, he thought. What is the point in anything? Should he have told her that he couldn't even be bothered to organise one of his regular Sydney girls? Should he have informed his wife of the crying jealousy fit one of these girls-in-every-port exploded into only last night when he said he didn't want her over? Or should he have told Suzie that in this state of mind he'd be tempted to get three or four working girls? Should he have told her that calling prostitutes, rather than picking up girls in bars or at the hotel, is increasingly popular among his younger teammates? Models, fuckbags, girls they didn't have to take to dinner, girls with bazooms that stood up while they lay down, and lots of them, four, five, six at once – should he have told her that? Should he have told her that the culture of this game had changed so much that whereas in the past it would have been shameful to pay for sex – especially a Test cricketer, who could find it anywhere – nowadays fame is a black paranoia, and therefore the safest as well as cleanest route is the root that costs nothing but dollars? Would it help Suzie to know this? Would it help him to tell her? Would it help their two daughters? Would it help their future, when he'd no longer be a Test cricketer, no longer living in hotels, no longer a famous face, just a sun-ravaged one – would this knowledge help her when she'd have him all to herself?

He had hung up on her. He was drained of desire for any woman. Too much to think about. But one of the enduring ironies of his marriage is that when he is out on the tool, he has fewer problems with Suzie. When her accusations have some foundation – when there is some girl he's off to meet – he and Suzie understand each other. She accuses, he lies, she knows he's lying, he knows she knows. Fine. On the other hand, if he tells her the truth, as he has tonight – that he's going to go back to his room and watch a pay movie and order room service and speak to no-one except Davis – she thinks he's lying. He can't win.

And the bastard of it all, he thinks, is that the only person in the whole world who calls Chris Brand a cheat is his wife. He's never thought of *marital infidelity*, if that's what it has to be called, as cheating. It's a fact of life, a perk of the job. It's no more cheating than having chambermaids to turn down your bed and leave a chocolate on the pillow. Yes, this life is not real: you are a celebrity, it's different. But it's not cheating. It's not deceitful. You're not breaking some contract. Chris abhors cheating! He's never saved his skin by refusing to walk, never sledged, never claimed a catch that didn't carry, never covered up or blurred the lines or been anything other than the straightest guy on the field. Chris Brand's reputation is spotless. A tough bastard, but rigidly within the rules. Chris Brand's name is a byword for honour on four continents. Every Test player in the world knows it: Chris Brand walks, doesn't cheat. He once famously overturned an umpire's decision on a catch he'd been awarded, and recalled the opposing batsman. The guy went on to score 200 and single-handedly win the match. Chris Brand became the first wearer of the baggy green cap to enhance his reputation through an action that lost his country a Test match.

He owes his reputation to his mother. That code of honour against cheating: he owes that to Ma. In his debut first-grade match sixteen years ago, fresh out of private school – soft, limp, cushy cricket that left him unprepared for the blinding daylight of the adult game, a step that usually defeats private school boys – two NSW State players had fielded close to the bat and spat across his pads. One had got him. But he knuckled down, taking the insults quietly, and scored 150. When Ma heard about the spitting she wanted to run out there herself and take up the fight. But Chris calmed her. The last thing he needed was a reputation for a feisty mother. He'd be finished.

So he stopped her, and Ma said: 'All right. I won't embarrass you if you promise me, promise me, Chris, that you never forget what is right and what is wrong.'

He remembered every insult and formulated his own code of revenge. His silence became, in the minds of opponents, an ominous quietude. He was a maniac for honour in a sport where being a maniac of any kind eventually played to your advantage. As long as you had the numbers. So he'd caught up, without being broken down by a system of cheating and sledging and proving your manhood by stooping lower than the next guy. And then he'd overtaken them all. For all his ambition and ruthless-ness, nobody has ever questioned his integrity. He's made his mother proud; and even if she truly knew him, she'd still be proud.

'So,' Davis swallows, 'have you been able to speak to Ma?'

'Yeah yeah,' Chris says with a dismissive frown.

'You have? Oh. Oh, yeah, I have too. I went and saw her this morning.'

'Good on you, buddy.'

'She tell you I'd been over?'

'Nah.'

'You got through to her?'

'Don't stick your lip out, Davo, it doesn't suit you.'

'Shit, I just . . . Well, this is one of the things I wanted to see you about. See, when I was up there, Bertrand was acting like the Minister for Information, and she was watching TV.'

'Watching me.'

'Bloody Bill Lawry was going on about you, and Pa, and . . .'

'Wanna swap places? You're jealous? You want the glory, the black armbands? Okay, you go and bat tomorrow. Make sure you get some runs for me. I need them, in case you haven't heard.'

'Stop asking me to swap.'

'So what else've you been up to?' Chris says without looking at him. He's stretching his neck, pushing it with his hand as if restraining his head from spinning off onto the floor. 'Teeing things up at the surgery?'

Davis clears his throat. His hand is against the window. When he lifts it, a humid imprint covers the Harbour Bridge, the whole arch in the palm of his clammy hand.

'Did Ma give you any idea why they said in the obituary that Pa was survived by *two* sons?'

'Ahhh.' Chris winds down from his back stretches. 'I think they mentioned Suzie and the kids, and Luce and you. See, you got your moment of glory.'

'I'm not talking about me. I'm talking about the "two" sons.'

Chris gets up and goes to the mini-bar. He pours himself a nip of what looks like Southern Comfort. Davis can't see in the gloom, and doesn't know for certain what it is, because Chris doesn't offer him one.

'I'm batting in the morning,' Chris says.

'Yeah, you're batting in the morning. The world stops while the great Chris Brand saves his career. Whoopee do.'

'Come on, Davo, I've got to go to sleep.'

'*Two* sons.'

'Matey, you should only be thinking of one thing now. Hey. Serious now, right? Think about Ma, and making things as okay as possible for her. I dunno what you're getting at, but you should leave her in peace. And the old man, too.'

'You're a fucking hard bastard.' Davis's lip trembles on the swear word. Chris, who peppers his speech with so many fucks that he doesn't notice them anymore, gives a contemptuous snort.

'That's what *all* the girls tell me,' he replies without humour.

Chris goes into the bathroom and pisses with the door open. He fires hard into the pool. Davis tends to aim at the bowl, for silence, and to shut the door. He puts the seat down if there are women around. Chris leaves it up. He doesn't even wash his hands.

'I mean,' Chris comes in, wiping his hands on the hair on his chest, 'Ian ran the obit by me. I told him to make it two sons. It was me, okay, and I'm fucking proud of it.'

'Come on, Chris.'

'No, *you* come on, mate.' Chris is poking towards Davis with a padded glove he has grabbed off the bed. '*You* come on. What's got into you?'

Davis shakes his head.

'Why wasn't Jim Cobcroft at your New Year's Eve bash here?'

As Davis speaks, Chris's feet align themselves in his batting stance as if the bowler's hand is the peephole on the back of his room door. His hands hold the invisible bat. He sees the line of the ball as it bursts out of the peephole, and then its length – it will pitch between the corner of the bed and the luggage rack.

He goes forward to meet it. It swings in, and he rocks back onto his right leg and tucks the ball off his hip, the flat of his left hand forming the face of the bat, between those crouching close-in fielders, Bed and Armchair. He sees the shapes, like ghosts of a set field, the boyhood daydream of cricket. At school he used to roll up his exercise book into a bat handle under the desk, seeing balls coming at him. Ma understood this otherworldliness. She likened Chris's daydreams to a poet seeing the shapes of words and memories – it was, in her eyes, as dignified as poetry or sculpture. More! Pa – uncoordinated, light-hearted – had tried to tease Chris about his little obsession. Even to the end, even with all that the game had brought them, Pa had never quite conceded that cricket could be a serious or worthwhile way for a grown man to spend his life. But Pa had been wrong – the balance of power had changed, and the joke was not that Chris dreamt he could play for Australia, but that Pa and Davis were grown men who couldn't catch a ball.

'How would I know?' Chris says. 'He was probably up in Noosa.'

'Do you think he could have been up in Noosa on New Year's Eve?'

'Do I look like Mrs Jim Cobcroft? Why should I be keeping tabs on where he is?'

'I just want to know. Was he in Sydney or Noosa that night?'

'What's it matter?'

'It matters because his signature is on Pa's death certificate.'

Chris stops practising his batting for a second. He seems barely able to restrain his anger.

'Well,' he says through thin white lips, 'I guess he must have been in Sydney then.'

Davis takes a breath. 'Where were you when it happened?'

'Jesus, Davo, you know where I was. I was here, trying to get rid of the guests so I could get some sleep. Trying to stop *you* drinking the mini-bar dry. You don't remember? Course not.

You were pissed as a monkey. Ma, Ian and Suzie all went home about half past midnight, I finally turfed you out around one am. You were the last to leave. I was still pretty wound up after the party, so I called up for a massage and watched a movie. Ian called me about two am. Okay?'

'You don't care to know how or where your own Pa died. Or,' Davis scratches the side of his nose, then, examining the tip of his finger, says, 'or who he was with.'

'Jesus, I can't believe you're coming to me, tonight of all nights, when you know I've got . . . Christ!'

Chris kicks the side of his bed. It rolls a foot off the wall towards the bathroom. He falls to the bed, holding his foot. Davis wonders how Chris would explain it if he injured himself, broke his toe, kicking the bed. Tomorrow on the TV, they'd be saying he hurt himself 'in a training accident'.

The air in the room has turned tropical. Chris's whites stink sweetly. He sits up on the bed and rubs his foot. He flexes his toes. Davis wonders if Chris didn't, just a little, play up how much it hurt.

'So,' Davis attempts a conciliatory tone, 'what do *you* want?'

'Runs tomorrow.'

'Serious. Big picture.'

'Runs and a win.'

'Come on. You're the one who's so big on being upfront, on letting people know where you stand. What does Chris Brand want? What's Chris Brand going to do for the second half of his life, eh? When he's not the big hero anymore? Go into politics like Ma tells him? Be a stuffed turkey in Canberra?'

'Fuck off.' Chris winces as he gives his foot a squeeze.

'You're so worldly wise and in charge of yourself and tough, and you don't even know where she's leading you. You huff and puff, but you're just letting yourself be led off to the yard like a good little lamb.'

'Be careful, matey, or I'll fucking snot you.'

'Well, stop bullshitting me.'

'What do you think I fucking well want? Same as you. A good life. A good family. A life like Ma and Pa have. Had. *Same as what you want.*'

'I'm not sure.'

'Not sure?'

'Not sure that's what they had.'

'You fucking moron. You're a goose, Davo. A deadset goose. But,' Chris lays his callused hand on the meat of Davis's shoulder. Davis looks up at him. In the choreography of family life, Chris is always standing higher than him. 'But I'm glad you came and brought it up with me. You've fucked up my concentration, and I'll probably get a duck tomorrow and then we can all find out what Chris Brand's gunna do in retirement, and thanks very much for that, but at this moment in time I'm just glad you've brought it up in front of me, not Ma. 'Cause she's the one who needs our help and protection. All right?'

Davis swallows. He realises now that he is not going to raise the other subject he came for. He is not going to tell Chris about the phone call he received, or the trousers he threw away.

'I don't commit myself strongly to an idea of other people,' Davis says.

'What the fuck's that mean?'

'You never know what's in people's hearts. It's all a mystery. I like to keep my mind open. So I'm never surprised.' He swallows again, drily. 'We don't really know what was in Pa's heart.'

Chris gives his brother a look of horrified disappointment. Davis has seen that look on television, when Chris has taken a clear catch and the umpire has turned down his appeal.

'You are kidding, aren't you?' Chris says. 'So, you mean, if I told you I was beating up Suzie, or I bit the heads off fruit bats – you're saying you wouldn't be surprised, because you never knew what was in my heart in the first place? Is that what you're saying?'

'It's what happens when you've seen people's bodies. In hospitals. You realise how much of their lives is a secret to everyone around them.'

'Then you,' Chris holds up his bat and points it at Davis, 'you must be one lonely fucker.'

Davis gets up to leave. He's not going to say anything yet, about the call. He's made an opening move. He tries not to hear the other whisper: *I am a gutless prick. I couldn't say it. I couldn't say it.*

Chris resumes practising his forward defensive stroke, grooving it.

'I just think we should do something about it,' Davis says shakily. 'We . . . we have a right to know what happened to Pa at the end. We have a right to . . .'

Chris comes at him in an onrush, a sudden attack like the charges down the wicket he's prone to after he's been off-strike for too long – one of his known weaknesses, this lust for confrontation, this impatience for assertion.

'So what's fucking wrong with wanting a life like our parents had?'

'Forget it. I'll leave you in peace.' Davis pulls open the door. It has a five-star heft.

'No, come on, don't walk away like the spineless goose again. What's wrong with wanting that?'

'Nothing at all.' Davis looks at Chris. 'Nothing wrong with that at all.'

'Come on, why don't *you* say what you think? Superior fucking bastard.'

Davis stands on the threshold, wanting to position himself for the last word. He looks Chris in the eye.

'I'm not saying there's anything wrong with it. I'm just asking if you really know what it is you're wanting.'

But Chris is more schooled in the combative arts than his pale, balding doctor brother. There are certain skills – footwork, anticipation, reflexes – for which healing the sick cannot prepare you.

'Well, bro, I should tell you something,' Chris says. 'Good luck with the surgery, but if I were you I'd give up on the locum.'

Davis stops in the hall.

'You're a fucking goose,' Chris says. 'Just be a help to Ma for once, will you?'

'What?' Davis's eyes are full.

'You've been following that locum around like a puppy for months. Jeez, don't look at me like that. Pa's the one who told me. Said it was an open secret around the surgery. Fucken Davo, smitten with a locum. Pa said he hadn't believed it, I mean, not the golden-haired boy. But he must've, in the end. He told me all about it a few weeks ago.'

'He'd never . . .' Davis stammers. 'He'd never tell you that.'

'Fucken disappointed in you, he was.'

'He'd never tell you that!'

Chris gives him a smug, superior sneer. 'Wouldn't he? Okay, if it makes you feel better, you go on believing that. Pa never told me a thing. He'd never share a secret with old Chris, would he?'

'I haven't done anything!'

'You're a deadset goose, Davo. But that's not telling you anything you don't know.'

November 18

At 6.02 pm on the third Friday of November, Dr John Brand was watering the back yard far enough from the house to maintain a credible pretence of not hearing his family arrive. Concealing himself behind a stand of gums, he pointed the hose seventy degrees above the back flowerbed and let the parabola of spray peak and collapse like fuzzy winter rain on the pink, white, indigo-and-yellow, and crimson flowers. The soil darkened.

The mid-November weather was still cool, though he took no pleasure in the fact. Stifling days were on their way, like relatives at Christmas, and their inevitability was enough to rob him of any enjoyment of this prolonged – Indian? – winter. Due to the soft sunlight and low temperatures, the garden did not need watering, but John watered nevertheless. He paid most attention to the garden when he wished to avoid the house, a habit unchanged since childhood. He had always fled visitors, even his own; at this late stage he still needed to be coaxed from shy solitude. This afternoon he'd prepared a roll of lamb with rosemary so hastily that he'd knotted the string with unstable double-bows, shoving it crookedly into the oven before making a run for the garden so he could be outside, far from harm, by the time the family came.

They didn't have to call out to signal their entrance. His ear was tuned to the pause of Davis's sports car, the race-and-cough of Chris's four-wheel-drive, as they breached the driveway. Above the static of the hose he detected distant delight – slamming doors, feminine laughter, parents shouting after children – and the sudden overfilling of the house's emptiness.

'Where is he?' he thought he heard surface from the babble. But they knew where he was. An eye out the back window would have made out the green-skinned hose snaking past the swimming pool. He was always deputing Margaret as the reception committee, not deliberately creating a cloud of mystery about himself but, at least in the case of the grandchildren, quite probably giving them a lifelong memory of a remote, controlled Grandpa.

In the heart of his family, a stranger.

Chris and Suzie and their two girls, Emily and Brooke, and Davis and Lucy: John could picture them in the kitchen, talking over the top of each other, Margaret at the centre admiring her boys and her girls and all of it.

Bad blood leaked down into his right ventricle. He wondered how long now. Fainting in that shop the other week – well, these episodes were getting closer together, tighter and harder, like a piece of paper you can fold only so many times. You never knew if the next would be the last. He sniffed up the green soily dampness. *Rather go down here than in that other place, in front of him. Quite respectable, really – I could start digging my plot here by the purple fireworks, the – what does Margaret call them? – the agapanthus . . . aggro panthers.*

He screwed shut the nozzle and spent more time than necessary coiling up the hose over a hook by the tap. He tidied with the procrastinator's rigour. Leaning forward, as if relying on gravity when his inclinations failed him, he passed the Totem Tennis pole and went to the back door. He stamped soil off his soles.

Friday dinner, he mouthed, grasping for the routine. Chris chatting with Margaret. Davis reading his mail and humouring his nieces by feigning interest in the insect-shaped wheeled vehicle they pulled by a string. Suzie and Lucy locked in young-women conference. He, John, patriarch, looking in from the far side of a flyscreen.

He rushed through the group to the laundry, apologetically flashing the black sickles of his garden fingernails.

Under the chill hard laundry water, his hands shook. Pink blotches betrayed failing circulation. Or did they? Couldn't they just be cold? As a doctor, he had always presented his family with the illusion of omniscience. For himself, he had only puzzles and best guesses.

Even in the kitchen listening to Suzie and Lucy, somehow snagged into their conversation, he felt on the far side of a window. What a mystery they were. He had never spoken to a woman until he was twenty, and had lagged ever since. Private schooling in the post-war era had a lot to answer for. His life was somehow the reverse of learning a language; the older he grew, the greater the unconquered vocabulary and the thicker his foreign accent. His whole experience disabled him from deciphering a generation of women like Suzie and Lucy: at ease, fluid, adaptable, Suzie to Chris's life, Lucy to her special arrangement with Davis. They were discussing the girls. Emily was six now, Brooke, he guessed with anxious uncertainty, around four? Not knowing what to say, but feeling he had to lunge out of his trembling muteness, he asked how the girls were going at school.

'Terrific.' Suzie addressed her response to Lucy. 'Em's a bit of a teacher's pet, and for the little one there are three boys waiting at the gate to take her under their wing and play every morning when I drop her off. God, they're gorgeous! Sometimes I'm so overcome I can't even put the car into gear.'

'In her mother's footsteps,' Lucy cracked in her low flat voice. Suzie giggled, her eyes seeking out Emily.

'But how's their reading?' John asked, with a roughness that coincided maladroitly with a throat-clearing. 'They keeping up?'

'Oh, at their age, learning to make friends is the main thing.'

Suzie appeared to have said this with reflex sharpness, a rebuke not to him but to a longstanding disagreement with Margaret and quite probably with Chris, too. John Brand wanted to ask forgiveness. He hadn't known why he'd asked the question. Just to fill in space. Of Margaret, Chris and himself, he was the least involved in this ideological conflict. It was Margaret, certainly, acting in Chris's name, and Chris holding a silence biased towards his mother, who pressured Suzie over things like the girls' 'progress'. Yet here *he* was.

He chewed the insides of his cheeks. Suzie and Lucy resumed their conversation as if he had left. Gloriously, intimidatingly beautiful women. How had his sons achieved such matches? How proud and excited he'd been. How sorry that they didn't feel comfortable with him, or he with them. His needs only ever surfaced as false self-assurance.

He hovered until he felt creepy, a dirty old man.

'Anything to drink?' he blurted for something to say.

'Oh. Um. White for me, I s'pose. White?' Suzie looked at Lucy.

'White if it's a nice one,' Lucy winked at him. 'Unless it's just a bottle for the relatives?'

John laughed too loudly, shaking his head, and moved off.

The bar fridge was next to where Davis knelt on all fours with the girls and a bumblebee on wheels. John Brand kicked the bee towards Davis. The girls chased it.

'How's the ward?'

'Okay.'

'Much happening?'

'Not much.'

'Any problems?'

'Not this week.'

He poured Davis a beer, taking extra time to manage the froth, glad for the task. He paused as Brooke jumped on Davis's neck, then he handed his son the beer. Unlike Margaret, John didn't chafe for Davis to become a father. Evidence of Davis playing with the girls didn't mean he'd be a good father, or that he'd want to be a father at all. John knew that Margaret would, in the course of the evening, have something to say about it. But it wasn't that Margaret wanted to influence Davis, force him and Lucy to do something they didn't want. She simply couldn't help herself. She didn't mean to place pressure on them; she just asked for the same reason John asked about the little girls' progress, to lay planks over the ever-threatening abyss of silence. John saw no change in Davis's attitude to children: great joy in playing with them, equal relief in handing them back at the end of the day.

Davis. *His* boy. Never had a cross word for him, except once when they'd caught him smoking marijuana with a friend. Davis had been twenty-two, an adult. John had exploded, then pleaded with Davis: 'Don't throw it all away.'

There had been no need to define 'it all'. John hadn't needed to point out how much Davis, how much they all, had to lose.

John knelt and said to Emily: 'What's this, then, a bumblebee?'

The older girl responded in her usual way to formal inquiries from her grandpa. She ran off to hide behind her mother's legs. The bold little one, Brooke, rolled the wooden toy towards him and announced: 'Dungle bee.'

'Bumblebee,' he corrected. His knees were aching. He had to get up quickly before he couldn't at all. But he didn't want to abandon the girl when they were making such progress.

'Are you, ah, having fun with, ah, your Uncle Davis?'

'Uncle got a willy like Daddy!' Brooke beamed.

Davis laughed. 'I'm sure there are regiments of women who'd like to know that.'

John Brand pushed himself upright, dusting nothing off his palms.

'Where do you think up things like that, eh?' he said to Brooke, who grinned back.

'Uncle got a willy!'

John Brand looked awkwardly at Davis, who said: 'Looks like she's moved into the anatomy phase. I was hardly out of the car just now when she bounded up and asked if I had a willy.'

'Oh, for goodness' sake,' John Brand muttered into the bar fridge. 'This chardonnay isn't cold enough. I'd better get a colder one from the laundry.'

Somewhere, he thought – maybe as early as Chris's birth – he'd lost the knack. He'd only had one serving of fatherhood to give out. A failure with Chris, a failure with the third, a failure with Chris's girls. Women a mystery, children a superior force.

In the kitchen, Chris and his mother had already fixed themselves vodka-tonics. John wondered if he should ask them to empty the dishwasher – his mental calculations estimated a dead heat between the amount of cutlery clean in the drawers versus the amount they'd need to feed themselves. But Chris was using his hands to describe the exotica of Pakistan, where he had just toured triumphantly. The muscularity and ease of his movements bewitched his mother. Margaret adored him, struck by pride, the words of love dancing on her lips.

But John could also see the cogs turning behind Margaret's gaze. She was picturing how Chris's manly authority would translate from the cricket pitch to the floor of Parliament. Margaret was plotting his run. He'd retire from cricket in two years and sail straight into preselection.

Since Chris had turned thirty, Margaret's anxiety had gathered incrementally, like lint. What would happen to him after cricket? Where would he slot in? How could she keep him going, stave off the musty irrelevance that overcame all those others whose careers had ended when they were still boys? John consented tacitly, less interested in Chris's parliamentary future than in the convenience: it kept Margaret's hopes occupied.

'Get that email?' Chris murmured to his father as he came back with the cold wine from the laundry fridge.

John shuffled noncommittally and looked around as if he were being watched. He'd noticed, over the decade or so of Chris's *fame*, that the boy's success gave the whole family a kind of rarefied perception of themselves. Certainly Margaret, and even Davis, acted in Chris's presence as if the outside world were imagined witnesses, as if the Brand family's doings were of wide importance. Some of their public performance – the overbright faces they put on when they chatted with Chris in the Members' Stand at the SCG – had seeped into their private lives.

'You did or not?' Chris said through the side of his mouth. 'I sent it on Tuesday.'

He had sent his father, as he commonly did, a wallpaper-of-the-week that had originated with teammates who liked to obtain particularly degrading Internet material. This week's was a photograph of a donkey mounting a beagle. The donkey stared ahead; the beagle, on a high gurney, at the camera.

'No, no, not yet,' John Brand lied. He wished Chris would stop sending them. Chris seemed to find them funny, poking his father for a response. John had no other way to show his disapproval than to pretend he hadn't seen them.

'Liar.'

'No, no . . .' John was looking at a large buff envelope on the kitchen bench. 'What's this?'

'Change the subject, why don't you,' Chris said. 'It was in the letterbox.'

'You brought it in?' John picked it up, trying to look casual. He didn't need to read his name closely or examine the stamp. He knew what it was.

'Yeah, it was in the letterbox.' Chris was looking back at his mother. 'Hey, and in Peshawar, they *all* carry guns. AK-47s. We had our photos taken with them before the one-dayer. Big fans, these guys. Crazy.'

John delivered the wine to Lucy and Suzie, who had procured glasses of mineral water in his absence, as if they'd only asked for wine in order to give him something else to do. When Ian

Bertrand arrived, John took advantage of the momentary atmospheric shift to disappear upstairs into his study.

He threw the envelope onto his desk and fell into his ergonomic chair, legs spread at the angle of a peace sign. His hands cupped the plastic armrests. *It has come to this*, he thought. *It has come to this*.

He slid a paper knife under the envelope flap and drew the magazine halfway out, then pushed it back. He didn't need to see it: the *Adam Film World* with Her on the cover.

This was the third and, he hoped, the last to be posted to him. There was never a note or any other communication. The deliveries *were* the communication.

He had revived John when he'd fainted in that place, put him in a taxi home, and mailed him the magazines. One by one. In the most dangerous and threatening ways: the first John had found in the letterbox when he was with Margaret. He'd been opening it right beside her, sitting in the car! He rammed it back in the envelope before she could see. She'd asked what it was. 'Pharmaceutical advertising bumf,' he'd said with a cough.

These mailings were a direct incursion, a terrorist attack on his homeland. With the first, the *Club International*, John had bundled it among newspapers and ordinary garbage, taken it not to the Brands' own wheelie-bin, but to those belonging to the townhouses beyond the back fence, under guise of a normal household chore. Later he had lain awake in bed imagining some janitor finding it and cleaning it up and taking it home for himself and making an educated guess as to whose house it might have come from. One must never underestimate a rubbish collector's detection skills.

Then the second one arrived, the *Cheri Movie Stars Special Edition*. Margaret herself had brought the envelope in with the rest of the mail. John had virtually torn it from her hands. She hadn't noticed.

John had ripped it up – turning Her image away so he couldn't see the injury he was committing – and incinerated it in the back yard. He'd do the same with this third one, when he had the time, but for now, with all the family here, he'd secrete it among his taxation papers at the back of the filing cabinet.

He sat back and breathed. The young one had been laying traps for him. Blackmail, almost. There were the magazines in the post, a business card John found in his suit jacket, evidently planted there when he'd been put in the taxi home, and then there were the computer messages.

John's laptop was open beside him. He looked out the window: blue skies were breaking through the cottony grey, an ominous foreboding of summer. Downstairs Ian Bertrand laughed. John tapped in to connect, listening to the frying-eggs-and-bacon sound. He picked up the Bernard Kouchner biography. Inside the cover he'd slipped the business card, having taken it out of the suit where Margaret could so easily have found it. He turned it over in his fingers. Strange kind of card: the front displayed the name, the word 'Founder', and a logo of a bone, a cartoon bone. The company had no name, but on the reverse side was an advert-isement for a phone service: 1-900-CORNHOLE. Seducing the camera, spreadeagled in lingerie, was a very pretty girl whose face looked familiar. John reversed the card again. Below the bone was an address in the south-western suburbs.

He told himself he'd deal with that later. For ten days now, since he'd collapsed at that place, he'd been telling himself: later.

A draught blew his study door shut. He got up and pinned it open, kicking into place an iron doorstop shaped as a magpie. He didn't want to be surprised. Downstairs, Chris was shrieking his strangely high-pitched laughter, perhaps a joke at John's expense. John knew how he looked to his second son. A timid man. And just as some boys reacted cruelly to sloth or mendacity or vagueness, Chris loathed timidity. When Chris detected a lily-liver on the cricket field, he would savage the man like a fox diving in on a wounded horse. A weak spot. Chris must have sensed it from the very first with his father, this man, John Brand. *My fear of him*, John thought. *A grown man afraid of a baby*. John had never been able to disguise it. He couldn't get rid of babies quickly enough. The rank smell of his terror spread. Davis found it endearing, but Chris had shown contempt: his father was not fully a man. John hadn't wanted to hold his infant grandchildren, for fear of squeezing them to death or letting them slip to the floor.

John Brand pulled up his most private email account, the one Margaret would never find even if she had the skills to turn on the machine and open windows.

His hand reached halfway to his knee. His ears picked up the slightest changes in the family noises downstairs. The exposed floorboards from the kitchen upstairs to the study would amplify any approach.

He needed to do it. He calculated the odds.

He set himself, with the laptop over his knees, facing the door, so that even if someone should sneak up on him nothing could quite be seen. He rehearsed, mentally, the quick concealments he'd have to make. He could do this with a bare minimum of unzipping and movement and mess.

Margaret and Chris cackled in the kitchen. John saw the beagle wallpaper file, and deleted it. He opened something more to his taste.

Unlike the magazines in the mail, seemingly aimed at en-dangering John's marriage, the emails had been arriving like a coded aid package.

The three magazines had left the clue to what John liked.

His eyes darting towards the doorway, he clicked. He had been sent, this time, eighty-two jpeg images.

Photographs of Her, fully dressed: in street clothing, officewear, cocktail dresses, swimsuits, studded leatherwear, a fireman's uniform, a police uniform, a wench get-up, pirate's gear, khakis, a baseball uniform, skintight latex, French maid, Indian squaw, Tahitian grass skirts, and a grease monkey's overalls complete with engine part manufacturers' patches. He loved the potential energy She stored in her clothing. He preferred photographs of Her fully clad to the somewhat predictable organisations of nakedness. And in Her films, he liked seeing Her acting, as in *talking*; but regrettably, the standard format was to get Her nude and punctured as quickly as possible.

His special interest was not the worst, nor even especially monstrous. Compared with what was available. But who, if they caught him, would be comparing it to what was available? Would Margaret say: *Oh, at least it wasn't . . .*

In addition to pictures, he had been sent written material: reviews of Her films, descriptions of scenes, interviews, shot lists, profiles, press clippings, and of course directions to Her own website, which among other things contained a facility wherein the consumer could engage in 'cybersex' with Her. John had tried this a couple of times, but Her 'responses' were patently pre-programmed to reveal parts and arrangements of Her body that held no allure for him. His requests were more unusual, and beyond the capabilities of an automated-response system.

John eliminated most of the photographs in an agile businesslike fashion. Deleted: images of poor quality owing to bad lighting or cheap reproduction. Dead eyes, ravaged bodies, anonymous roughness. He deleted the photographs of Her posing in the four or five standard ways, routinely unerotic, devoid of motion or, in his inner language, *connection*. Every user is a fetishist, and this was John Brand's: he wanted eye contact.

John Brand picked through the emailed photographs, imagining himself a Red Cross officer on a battlefield, sorting living from dead eyes.

The living from the dead.

This left him, out of his original eighty-two pictures, with just eleven. Time was too short to indulge in extrapolations. His body was tensed to the sounds coming from the kitchen, the pregnant dangerous silence of the stairs – the jarrah alarm system.

The eleven photographs highlighted Her eyes – or, specifically, moments when Her eyes were making a connection with the camera. One showed Her gazing up through half-moon pupils; in one jolly good one, Her eyes rolled back in Her head.

He unzipped, holding the laptop as a protective screen.

What a revelation, this technology. Until the age of sixty-two, the only pornographic images John Brand had seen were *Playboy* spreads of the 1970s and the covers of raunchier magazines glimpsed at the newsagent while he bought a *Herald* or a *Bulletin*. He had been vaguely aware of tapes in the Adult section of the local video library, but assumed these depicted simulations, not the real thing. In the mid-1990s, when he and James Cobcroft had installed computers in the surgery, John had become connected to the Internet for professional purposes. It had taken him a year before he was game to do more than turn the thing on and go straight to his useful medical sources, like a man who has moved into a forty-room mansion but sets up camp in the front foyer. Then, day by day, he had taken his first timid steps to the inner rooms. He had typed 'sex' into his search engine – just as an experiment, mind, just because he had heard that 'sex' was the most common word on the whole Web. This first domino had toppled others, and soon he beheld the first image of a man and a woman making love – Was that the term he would use? No, but nor could he employ the nomenclature adopted on the screen – *making love* by a swimming pool. Everything about them was improbably swollen. John's old man's eyes had widened, and he had reeled away in stunned shock. There was no doubt about the actuality. The woman's blissful expression might have been fake, but the act was real. Could there be people who did this, who stood in front of a camera and did this? He had quickly shut his machine down and paced circles in his surgery. This had obviously been happening all along, and he had been unaware – totally unaware. His unworldliness shamed him. He lay in bed each night with that image in front of his eyes. The woman was dark, Hispanic, the man polished and well-muscled. John wondered who they were, this man and woman, and who else there might be. How long had this been going on?

It was a month before he dared look again; he spent a day trying to retrieve that first image. He could not, but on his search he came across many more, profoundly diverse, riotous, revolting and arousing in equal measure. As his exposure increased, the question of satisfaction arose. None was fully satisfying. There was something about every single image that held out the promise of something more, something totally fulfilling, just out of reach. He studied them at angles, like a child trying to see around the corner of a scene in a painting. He stepped up his pursuit. His shock gave way to a consuming curiosity. He started to recognise familiar faces and bodies. He developed favourites. He would go off on a random search, finding what he found, but would inevitably end up going back in pursuit of his favourite models, who, he discovered, had names and histories, even if those histories were merely lists of their film appearances. He discovered the confluence of the *celebrity* and *hardcore* sub-genres in the cult of personality, the *Superstar* fetish. Familiarity and revelation, best of both worlds. He knew them, and they, he fantasised in his silken moments, knew him. They shared a secret that recalled his teenage years when, at birthdays, he had to make a secret wish as he cut his cake. *Please God*, young John used to whisper, *let every woman be in the nude, and let me be the only person who can see them*. He could look into Her eyes and think: *You and I, my sweet one, we know each other*. The fantasy of knowing, and being known, and cherished, conquered him. Soon he was ordering moving pictures piped through the Internet. They took him around that blind corner, gave Her three dimensions. He discovered magazines – 'fanzines' – showing that She was a real person, with a hometown, a 'touring schedule', ambitions, ex-husbands, parents and, conceivably, needs. Before long, beneath his desk, in his surgery; a five-hour-a-day habit.

And here he was, six years on, taking time out from a family gathering.

He found one he liked. Some element of accident in the photograph caused an expansion of the tingling, a pressure against the soft fabric. The little space had cleared, that delectable breath, that awakening music. Blocked from lift, expression in elongation, each eddying expansion traceable to a particular photographic stimulus.

And here. The best till last. Two fine shots of Her.

Well, there was worse. Doctors self-medicate, like any other addicts, for all sorts of troubles, and he tended to see this as a form of palliative and preventative care. He had succumbed to a reversion, an affliction of the middle-aged. There was nothing to do but manage it. John Brand's reasonable case management had its scruples and boundaries: he had never given any patient an impression of any kind. He was not a molester. He hermeticised the final stages of the act. It was not that he would not be embarrassed. He would be mortified. But it was far from the worst. He had convinced himself that this strengthened his loyalty to Margaret, the time-efficiency of this process, the emotional simplicity, the ablutionary cleanliness. At least, that was how he got started. And then a new series of reactions, pathology rather than choice, had begun to take effect.

The email, blessed messenger, had delivered Her onto his lap. Her honey blonde hair washed over Her shoulders. A male hand gripped Her neck between ear and collarbone. Her eyes, wild, glazed, impish, snarled up. Her mouth gaped, tongue extended and grooved like a pink runnel. This was Her and She was real.

Her eyes were the truest expression, windows to her intimate interior. She was looking at *him*. Those eyes: a darker shade of jungly green over her slightly hooding lids had made them recede, like magic; a little yellow concealer covered the light-blue bruises beneath. She was squarely on him, on John. He choked down, feeling Her hand, gazing into Her eyes. With his free hand, he took two tissues and laid them across his lap. He moved the free hand to his mousepad and manipulated the frame of the image. He narrowed it. He cut out the man's hand, Her shoulders, Her chin, now even Her mouth. He narrowed and narrowed until all he was left with was Her eyes. Hazel, outlined, orbs of adoration. Flecks of bronze. They engaged with John Brand's blue eyes. Her eyelashes were long black curled branches; Christmas lights could hang from them.

It was Friday dinner. The floorboards were silent. His wedding ring cooled him.

The most perfect creature.

Ian Bertrand's voice said: 'So did you get up to the Kashmir border? I've heard it can get hairy up there.'

With minimal movement, John Brand had achieved. Everything concealed behind the keyboard, in case of interruption. With a tuck and a zip, done. He closed his emails. He sat for a second or two and inhaled.

Bertrand was making party chat with Chris.

'Do the wickets turn much?'

John Brand closed his eyes. He arranged everything back into place. The air smelt of lamb.

At 7.15, John merged into the kitchen traffic. He felt warm in his face, but nobody looked at him. Davis and Margaret were huddled around the two little girls. Chris and Bertrand were on their way out to the back patio to join Lucy, who was pointing at something in the pool. Suzie was fixing portions of salmon salad for Emily and Brooke. None of his family seemed to have realised John Brand had been out of the room.

He checked the lamb, which was an inscrutable yellow in the oven-light. He looked to Margaret, but she was occupied with the children. The lamb smelt right. The double-bows in the string had held fast. If he cut the lamb the right way, there'd be enough left over for a nice three-night curry. He heaved open the stiff door and, a tea towel wrapped around one hand and an oven mitt on the other, lifted the Corningware dish. Somebody made appreciative sniffing sounds.

A post-catastrophic happiness filled his home. He remembered when the family had been complete. The laughter had had a different quality then, white like an unbroken bone.

But they'd healed up, hadn't they? Didn't bones heal stronger?

Ian Bertrand came back in, sipping his beer. He said there was a funnel-web in the pool. Chris was fishing it out with the scoop.

No, John thought. *It's just been so long since we were a family that we've forgotten how to tell the difference. We've forgotten what we've lost.*

Bertrand's hands semaphored some point to Margaret. They never seemed to run out of things to say to each other. Soul mates. Nearly every day, John regretted that Margaret's soul hadn't found its mate in her husband.

'Refill, anyone?' John said.

Nobody needed a refill. John let the lamb rest. He wished he could rest. He pretended to fix himself another drink and pretended not to watch Bertrand and Margaret. A thought interrupted him: better empty that dishwasher. He swung open the door, causing Bertrand to step aside, which he did without looking around, so comfortable was he in this kitchen. Margaret shot John a look asking him to relax, just relax.

'Oh, Lord, what have you done now?'

Margaret was staring at John's fly.

'What? Nothing.'

'You've been poking into the fridge, haven't you?'

Margaret pressed his nose like a lift button. He backed away, but she had him against the kitchen bar. She went to the sink and rinsed a Chux. John Brand looked down. A teardrop of whiteness had fallen onto his casual trousers, just to the left of his fly.

He raised a hand as if warding off attack. Margaret dipped to kneel in front of him and in front of Ian Bertrand. John looked to Ian for help, but the man's pointy face grinned genially and he raised his glass and his eyebrows.

Margaret dabbed harshly at his white spot. John swallowed, clamping his eyes shut. He wondered about odour. He clenched his fists, realised that not only had something spilt onto his trousers, his wedding ring was sticky too.

Margaret made motherly public noises, dabbing him at arm's length.

'Stand still, you grotty man,' she muttered, cranky-loving.

His eyes watered. How she would have been unable to say such a thing had she known its truth.

Davis, who had resumed reading his mail, said: 'Careful of the crown jewels!'

'I don't know, I can't leave you alone for five minutes.' Margaret pressed the Chux with unambiguously defiant strokes. A cloth she might use for cutlery and benchtops. Naughty little boy, spilling something on his pants like that. 'You've had your nose in the humus, haven't you?'

Lebanese food having arrived in the Brand household only in the late 1990s, Margaret pronounced the chickpea dip homophonically with the decomposed stuff in soil. John stood at rumpled attention, overwhelmed by the number of places he would rather be.

The next few seconds occurred as a breach, a seam in the quality of time. John Brand was the first to see the little girl, Brooke, over Margaret's shoulder. She had raced in, flushed with the excitement of her father slaying the funnel-web outside. Had anyone else seen her, they might have held her back. Emily, her sister, once bitten and shy for life, was doing the right thing, playing somewhere her grandpa wasn't.

It was the tot, bold Brooke, venturing into the whirlwind of her grandfather's disorder. Margaret's knees cracked as she pushed herself upright, bunching the Chux in her fist. When she turned to the sink to rinse it out, little Brooke charged in with all her love.

'Grampa got dungle-willy!'

The girl had her arms around his hips, bracketing his confusion. Her face went joyously to his groin. The chills in his back were sharpened by the tiny hot circle her mouth was condensing at the wet patch by his fly.

When he opened his eyes, he saw Chris's red face belching laughter across the kitchen bar.

The Brands were the type of family who would have pretended, if they could, that Brooke had just tripped over. But the girl was catapulted across the linoleum, skidding once on the repeating patternwork before her spine broke her flight against the four handles of the utensil drawers.

Brooke howled. Margaret, whose back had been turned, rushed to the little girl. Suzie's high heels slipped on the lino. Davis went white. Ian Bertrand swallowed. From Chris's sunburnt cricketer's face, the laughter was still receding, like a television screen that takes a few seconds to lose its glow after being turned off.

John Brand's finger trembled as it rose towards Chris.

'You filthy disgusting creature, you think you can bring up your children, my grandchildren . . .'

Fishlike, John Brand's mouth gasped for words.

'Steady on, Pa.' Davis took half a step forward. In the flat fluorescent kitchen light, everyone looked brightly two-dimensional.

'Your own children, you bring them up like depraved savages, you filthy . . . And you send me those pictures, when there are children in the –'

'Hey, baby, no probs.'

Chris was moving towards Brooke with a reassuring grin, following the accords of life as it had existed prior to the last ten seconds. Brooke's face was collapsing upon her thumb. She was all right – just a bruise – apart from the shock, from which there were no adults fit to spare her.

'You disgust me!' John's trembling finger made amoebic shapes in the air at Chris. 'You . . . !'

'Steady on,' Davis repeated. Lucy, out of focus but strongly lit, appeared behind him.

None of them would come near John Brand. His wet groin turned cold in the kitchen air.

'All of you, get . . . get . . .'

They waited for him to say it. He didn't.

'I'm going for a walk.' He looked at Margaret, who was crouched over Brooke, hushing her gently. 'The lamb's ready to carve.'

He nearly tripped over Emily as he made for the front door. She saw him coming, though, and jumped clear. Nobody was crying, not even the winged Brooke.

Soon after stumps, the curry smell that has been massing all day coagulates into the solid matter Ian places before her in a deep ceramic bowl.

She stares at it in her lap, cradled in her hands, while Ian switches the news to mute and returns to the kitchen for forks. She hears him clattering about in the wrong drawer – after all these years. She reaches for the remote and turns the sound back up.

Ian settles down beside her and watches the television agreeably. Margaret forks pieces of lamb into her mouth. It tastes more like a real Indian curry than its smell promised – more Indian than John's curries. Nonetheless she wishes Ian hadn't chosen this, hadn't tried to cook a John meal. She doesn't want a man wearing a John mask. She'd prefer Ian cook something he does well, an Ian meal. There are so many delicious Ian meals! That ocean trout with chamahli (or was it chermoula – something Moorish and more-ish), or the five-spice crispy beef he does. A dab hand with the Chinese is Ian – those noodles with deep-fried tofu – who'd have guessed, tofu! He's never been anywhere much, but Ian's travelled the world in his kitchen. He's a gifted, adventurous cook. Such a shame, then.

She chews obediently, letting the TV do the talking. Why are they eating in the armchairs, when the table's only two steps away? It was obviously Ian's choice, for her sake – to avoid the pressure of sitting at the table having to think up things to say.

The cricket highlights come on: the armbands, the minute's silence, the catch. As if the game were a setting for the Brand family drama.

'Have you ever seen a better catch?' Ian points with his fork. 'It should have been worth two wickets!'

He sits strangely, his back hunched forward like a question-mark over the dot of his bowl. She realises after a moment that he's sitting like this to avoid spilling food on the rug. Margaret feels faintly hostile against him. If he's going to put his back out, why sit in here? Why not do what civilised people have always done and eat at the table?

Ian bangs on about the catch, the choice to send in a night-watchman, the state of play. He is giving her what he thinks she wants. Duplicating her world – a habit of Ian's which has always brought such blessed relief from John's obtuseness. Yet now, without John here, Ian's agreeability feels intolerably bland. As if Ian's presence only made sense as a counterpoint to John.

Poor sweet Ian, she mustn't blame him for being what he is. But he really ought to go home before she loses patience and says something.

After they've eaten, he goes to the sink and washes up with more noise than necessary. He hums to himself. She's never heard that before, has she? But – Lord bless him – once he's done putting away, he comes and plants a dry kiss on her forehead.

'See you in the morning.'

The beauty of Ian is that she doesn't need to see him out, doesn't even need to glance him a goodbye. She sits in her chair, pinching the skin between her eyes.

There's nothing on the television, and she's exhausted after the day, so she decides to go to bed. In the bathroom, she restrains herself from making any noises, acutely self-conscious. She never troubled especially to hide noises from John, but she doesn't want to hear herself now.

Wrapping herself in a dressing gown against the unseasonable chill that seems to have invaded the bedroom, she lies in bed and switches off the light. Her eyes were drooping before dinner, so she didn't think she'd have any problem sleeping, but once she's here that optimism appears to have been misplaced. Her fatigue was a false advertisement. Her eyelids are sprung open. When she blinks, they make a clicking sound.

Now she's the one wearing a John mask: insomnia was his affliction, not hers. She's always been a good sleeper, though she tends to fret if she doesn't get her eight hours. John was the one who'd get up and rustle around all night, make the darkness his own. Sleeplessness strikes Margaret rarely, but with a vengeance. Unexposed to the germ, she's never built up an immunity. She is switched to full power, her mind racing. She tries staying awake to let it overcome her, tries counting but loses concentration. Her mind drifts too fast from one thought to the next. Watching television all day has left a heavy band of fatigue across her forehead, but otherwise her body is not ready to sleep.

The luminous bedside clock reads half past nine when she sits up and tightens the dressing-gown cord. It shouldn't be so cold in here. It was such a warm, airless day, yet she needs to hug herself. She goes to the window above the trousseau chest and tries to slide it shut, but the pane sticks. She'll have to get Ian onto it tomorrow.

She goes downstairs, her steps guided by the glow of electronic lights from the kitchen: the green oven clock, the red television eye, the white video clock, the lemony microwave clock. An indoor constellation of cruel unblinking stars.

Their verdict is unanimous. Even downstairs, it's not yet ten o'clock.

Fresh air, she thinks. She steps out onto the back patio. Frogs croak in the rockery above the swimming pool. Cars whish by distantly. Semi-trailers. On what roads? From what direction? She's aghast not to know where, exactly, these night sounds originate.

Where is the main road along which these trucks travel? How can she know her surrounds so scarcely?

Clouds cover the moon and stars, bringing down the canopy of sky like a mosquito net, robbing the garden of depth and distinction. The blue clouds seem as near as the bushes, a claustrophobic closeness that disturbs her senses: sounds are visible, shapes are smellable, scents whisper. A dog barks somewhere over the back fence, and she sees a forsythia bush vibrate. Someone is doing something indistinct in the row of townhouses on the other side of the right-of-way – hosing? But why would anybody be hosing at this time of night? She senses the sound as a smell of rubbery water. Perhaps it's not hosing, but something else.

It's all a bit much. She focuses on items in the yard, tightens her eyes against the low sky. The Totem Tennis pole: must throw that away. The trampoline: likewise. They've been keeping these things for Brooke and Emily, but surely when they're old enough to scoff and laugh at their dad's old games, they will. Ian will have to throw it all out, though it will give Margaret a pinch in the heart to give up the Totem Tennis pole. There is Des to leave resting in peace, and also the memory of stealing the pole from their neighbours on one of those awful caravan park holidays back when the boys were young. These people pitched their tent too close and rose too early in the morning. The thwack-thwack of their Totem Tennis drove Margaret insane. So one night she and John conspired to nick the thing. Without anywhere appropriate to dispose of it in the caravan park, they'd stuffed it into their car. It had come with them to the next park, and the next, and the boys so loved playing with it that it came home. A family secret! But now that John is no longer here to share the memory of the pole's provenance, there seems no point keeping it.

She knows the name of every plant in the yard. As a stratagem against insomnia, she enumerates them one by one: zinnia, forsythia, camellia, azalea, prunus, agapanthus, rhododendron, hydrangea, jacaranda (that silly Des!), pansies, crepe myrtle, Christmas bush, lisianthus, the roses, irises, oleander, coral tree, black bean, tree fern, staghorn. She should be able to close her eyes and name them, plant them in their precise position from memory. Perhaps that would put her to sleep on her feet.

John was the gardener, really, though he hardly knew the name of anything. He smirked at her for knowing so many names, implied in his innocent, wordless, deceptively meek way that the names were nothing – what really mattered was something behind the names, the private names he had for them all. The things in themselves. He condemned her, not to her face, but by keeping the peace. For all she knew, he might have given these bushes human names. What's a good name for a plant? Violet? Flora? Lily? Did they always have to be women? Maybe he had boys' names for them: Russell, Leif, George Bush. His secret mates. Now, in the dark, their indistinct shapes appear to mock her with their barking, their hissing and their hosing, and prove John right.

A feeling comes across her that someone is in the house. Oddly enough, she has no fear. To the contrary, the action of grabbing a saucepan and clocking a burglar over the head would be a great relief. But it feels more as if someone is waiting for her to go in and finish a chore: the washing, the dusting. She goes back inside. She's moving through the ground floor room by room, like a prowler herself, when it strikes her, not for the first time, that a normal woman would probably be missing her husband more than she is. The thought brings her to a standstill. If there were a sound in the darkness, or a suspicion of movement, a normal woman, a widow, would cry out for her husband and tearfully break down in renewed realisation of how much she misses him.

It troubles her, this not-missing John – but it's only been lapping up in wavelets, as if at the tranquil shore of a lake, rather than breakers crashing onto a beach. As a matter of fact, it troubles her most when people are around her, expecting her to do certain things and not others. Suggesting she ought to be missing John more. Davis, for instance. He seemed to expect something of her today. She shouldn't have shunned him, but she didn't want to talk to him – he can keep his possessiveness of John, his complex ideas of family ententes and balances of power. Davis has something ulterior about him that she cannot address at present.

She must be practical about this. She hates the manufacture of emotions, and is not about to start wailing and rending her clothes like the Middle Eastern women she sees on television. It's not inappropriate – it's just not her.

She wonders if she has prepared herself for this moment a little too well. She has seen too many friends fall to pieces when they lose their husbands. For years now, she has been making ready: missing John in advance. He encouraged her in this. He'd say: 'You mustn't rely on me. When I'm gone, I don't want you to give me a moment's thought.' She'd treated it as a typically morbid joke but, in practice, she had always been prepared for life without John. Why, forty years ago, the story had been writ in their very first evening out together. John had invited her to a musical. Margaret waited at home for him to pick her up, growing steadily more anxious, then angry, when he failed to arrive. The start time for the musical passed. She hid from her parents' pity. Then, very late, there had been a ring at the doorbell and here was John, formally dressed, his shirtfront absolutely drenched in blood. Margaret didn't care – she was so livid with him! But then he produced, like a rabbit from his hat, a young boy, his face caked with dry black blood. John said he had been walking from the railway station to Margaret's house when he witnessed an awful car accident. He'd wanted to pretend he hadn't seen it, and rush on to Margaret, but he couldn't. He'd dragged injured people from their cars and helped them into ambulances. This little boy's parents had both been badly hurt. John looked, full of trust, into Margaret's eyes and asked: 'Can you clean him up and look after him? I have to go back to the hospital, they need me.' And Margaret had taken the boy inside, washed him and settled him down. There is a purpose to all this, she had thought as she put him into her own bed and read him a story. True, she had missed out on *Hello Dolly*, but she had fallen in love with this man who trusted her, implicitly, to manage without him.

Yet now – *now* – she wonders if her years of independence, of preparedness to be alone, have not succeeded too well. Yes, the blow of John's death has been softened. She is not falling apart. She is managing her grief capably. But just now, it feels like a hollow victory. Life seems, perversely, too easy. A string of such victories. She is managing – but she is not sure if she wants to be managing quite so well.

Suddenly there is a noise – a real noise – from outside. Holding her gown closed across her chest, Margaret goes to the back screen door. It sounded like a wall collapsing, a deep rumble followed by a crescendo of a dumping wave, and now the reverberations of rubble. She hears a shriek of teenage laughter, receding. Mouth ajar, she stands still and listens. There's nothing more. She doesn't know of any building sites, though that was what it sounded like: a retaining wall falling over.

To her wakefulness is added curiosity. That dog barks, but no human sounds punctuate or corroborate the collapse-noise. It came from the townhouses on the other side of the right-of-way beyond the back fence. She and John kicked up an almighty stink, back in the late 1980s, to stop that development. The council's zoning policies had fallen into the hands of a corrupt few – scandalously, members of her own father's party – but she had been unable to exert any influence, and the lovely Federation-style mansion across the right-of-way was flattened and replaced with six chalky Gold Coast townhouses, a whitewashed rank that put her in mind of war graves. As she predicted, they have been filled not with respectable or houseproud types, but with renters. The only satisfaction of the endless troubles over the years has been to be able to say that she was right all along. If they have to be there, they may as well prove Margaret correct.

She crosses the lawn, goes out the side gate and turns to the top of the right-of-way. It runs downhill at a moderate slope. In the middle of the paving is a shape. She treads towards it, confidently, as if calling its bluff. When she gets to the prone object, she gives a snort. It is a wheelie-bin belonging to the townhouses. Someone's teenagers have come along and pushed it down the hill. That was the roaring collapsing sound. It has spewed out its plastic recyclable innards: bottles, yoghurt pots, tins, moulds, wrapping, disposable plates. Their drumming fall was the rubbly noise she heard. Satisfied that she has traced the mystery to its source, happy to have seen another example of the townhouses' inappropriateness and to know that the silly renters will have to clean it all up, she wipes her hands and returns to her house. She bolts the door behind her and goes upstairs.

PART TWO

Davis Brand discovers himself lying on his stomach at 6.29 am. His legs straddle the clothes of his kingsize bed, the left lightly goosepimpled in the open air, the right twisted with his penis like a creeper through the chainlink of cotton sheet and polyacetylene doona filling. The small of his back is sheened by an oval of sweat. His right hand snakes out from under the pillow and hovers above the clock radio. The 6.30 am strike triggers a single sonic howl transformed, by the fall of Davis's open palm, into newsreaderspeak.

He rolls out of bed, feet falling into the Moroccan babouj slippers left meticulously in a toes-outward position. He sits on the bed, focusing on the view through his window: the toylike sailing boats bobbing on their harbour moorings; the waterfront unit blocks on the far shore; a ferry roiling in from the east, crossing bows with an oceanbound tanker; light patches of sandbank revealed by a low tide against the harbour blue.

Automatically he articulates his intimate surroundings for Claire – how would she like it here? Would he ruffle things up, to disguise how anal he is? But then with an inner groan Davis remembers last night. The consequences hit him like doldrums hitting a yacht; Davis's emotional spinnaker drops limply.

He steps to the bathroom. The nap of woollen carpet gives him the vague sensation of walking on air. His hands turn the shower taps to points marked with black texta: the exact optimal mix for a hottish morning shower (other points, in red, mark the settings for a hotter evening one).

Davis's mouth opens and fills with shower water, which he lets flood over his chin and down his chest. He soaks his stubble, thicker on the jowls, tougher on the chin, before taking to it with a twin-bladed razor in the same pattern he follows each day: long upward strokes on the cheeks, angling towards the nose on the left side so as to cut perpendicularly against the grain; cross-strokes right to left under his chin, taking care across an old scar; masque contortions while undertaking the more studied sweeps around his mouth and nose. He runs the razor around the nape of his neck beneath the line of his hair, picking up the fluffy growths which produce that untidy slipped halo, premonition of middle age, at his collar. His cheek reddens under the blade.

It returns, like a hangover: Pa knew about him and Claire. What did Chris say? An 'open secret' at the surgery. Dear God. An open secret. Has it been that obvious? It must be – it would *have* to be obvious to penetrate Pa's general cluelessness and his loyal habit of taking Davis's side in a fight.

Yet Davis is beginning to wonder just how much Pa was, in fact, on his side. It is more than a year since Pa last saw Davis for a prescription or referral and, Davis has to admit, the undeclared end of their doctor-patient relationship did entail less time spent alone together. He can't remember his last informal lunch, or evening stroll after work, with Pa. Surely it didn't end because of Claire? Scrolling the garbled pages of his memory, Davis recalls – or reconstructs – a chill between himself and his father that seems to have coincided with Claire's arrival at the surgery. Davis would drop around, and Pa would make excuses – he was taking his walk with Jim Cobcroft; he and Jim had to go off for a meeting with their accountant or solicitor. It seemed Pa had switched allegiance, in a subtle way, invisible at the time, but now devastatingly clear, from Davis to his trusty old partner. But why?

Was it Cobcroft who discovered Davis's thing for Claire? It's possible. Ever since Davis decided to study medicine, Jim Cobcroft had braced himself against Davis like a territorial old bull. In medical discussions Cobcroft liked to deride Davis's inexperience, humiliate him even, in front of Pa. It was as if Cobcroft were a jealous first wife, furiously undermining the young rival, desperate to retain Pa's affections. Yes, it must have been Cobcroft who'd detected how Davis was acting around Claire, then poisoned Pa's mind. 'Your married son is mooning around after the locum.' God, it's even Cobcroft's kind of phrasing: 'mooning around'. Pa, being Pa, would have laughed it off, but all the same he'd stopped using Davis as his doctor. And finally, he'd taken Davis's secret to Chris. To Chris! And Chris had lifted Pa's gloom, turned it into a joke, helped Pa mock Davis, 'the goose'.

If the image of Chris and Pa laughing together at him is intolerable, and if that hardens Davis's determination to reassert himself as Pa's son and *find out what happened* in the end, to uncover the truth that nobody else, least of all Chris, cares to discover, then there is an even darker realisation lying in wait for Davis. Worse than Pa knowing, worse than Cobcroft's success in turning Pa against him, worse even than Pa confiding in Chris.

Claire must know.

He rinses his face, soaps and rinses his armpits and groin, turns off the taps. He stares for a moment into the Danish plate mirror. His hair dries easily and in place: tiny droplets trickle pleasantly to his scalp like dewdrops down blades of fresh-cut grass.

She knows. What a pathetic prick you are.

He pinches his noble lower lip to raise the incipient lesion, the mother-of-pearl scablet that has remained for several months, unhealing. He flicks it with a gentle index finger, almost casually, to see if it will come off under mild trauma. Like a silly patient.

At the embrasure of the curved harbour window, he performs his breathing exercises: inhaling the kinks out of his lung lining, filling his redcurrant alveoli.

Claire, he thinks, *would love it here. Pity she's never going to see it now.*

After leaving Chris's hotel last night, Davis didn't go home. Instead, he parked near the reserve between Claire's apartment and the waterfront. He'd discovered her address, not far from his own, while nosing through her employment registration file. He sat on a bench and pretended to speak into his mobile phone, in case she saw him and found it odd that he was sitting there.

He was not untouched by the idea that what he was doing might, technically, be classified as stalking. But he posed no danger to Claire Mullally. Far from it.

Completing his calisthenics in his eyrie, he suffers a stab of some feeling he can't quite identify. He's unsure whether he feels more regret at losing the opportunity to impress a young woman with his handsome lifestyle, or at the fact that this very lifestyle has been created for him, fitted onto him, by his wife.

He's married, he remembers, a fact that would seem inconsistent with sitting in parks at night outside young women's apartments. He's fucking married!

Last night, he had dialled Lucy. He sat there, on the incriminating park bench, and gazed across the harbour. Were it not for the ridge of Kurraba Point, he and Lucy would have been able to signal across the water.

It was after ten, so he'd called her at home. Her phone rang six times and diverted to her voicemail – breezy, cute, insouciant.

'Hi sweetheart, it's me,' he mimicked her breeze. 'I know you're there . . .' His forced smile curved his words into her machine, and he imagined them curving out into the large spaces of the flat across the water. 'I'll give you five seconds. Pick up the phone. Five . . . four . . . three . . . two . . . we have ignition. Oh well, just . . . just confirming dinner tomorrow night. Call if there's a change.'

Tuesday is Davis and Lucy's midweek special: the night they see a cheap movie, grab a cheap meal, and slip back to Davis's place to play at being a couple. It is lovely, they've always held, to be married and yet not give themselves a chance to tire of each other. Their other weekly night together, spent at Lucy's after dinner at Davis's parents, is Friday.

But last night there had been a change: Lucy called straight back, from what sounded like a very crowded room, and remarked on how late it was for him to be calling.

'You're not at home,' Davis said, seeing her mobile number on his caller ID.

'No, we went out after we finished up.' She reeled off a string of eight names. A large group, Davis. A large group. 'I've had my home voicemail send me an alert whenever there's a message. Did you know you can do that?'

She was intensely coherent. Davis knew that she never sounded sharper and more precise than when she was drinking.

'I can't make dinner,' she said. 'I have to work tomorrow night.' She outlined, with a liar's comprehensiveness of truthful detail, the meetings she would have to attend on their designated Tuesday night.

'How about a coffee tomorrow morning?' Davis said, trying not to let his frustration show.

'Oh, I'd love to!' Lucy said with a brightness that made him want to be sick. 'Love to!'

Carrying Pa's old leather briefcase, battered pale at the corners, Davis walks, preoccupied, up the hill into Kings Cross. The morning is clear, sunshine illuminating the leaves and airbrushing the facades of the old apartment buildings. A caretaker vacuums the porch of one of the grandest deco blocks. A well-known fashion designer, to whom Davis has occasionally prescribed emergency tranquillisers, emerges from the wrought-iron doors with her cocaine-dealing boyfriend, the pair showing telltale baggy skittish eyes from the previous night. Davis slows to avoid having to say hello. One can live too close together. While locuming for Pa, Davis has paid house visits to patients in most of the blocks around here. He is aware that the division of post-codes, between the stigmatised Cross and his own well-padded suburb, is unrecognised by the human body. A blossom-faced jogger hurtles down the hill from the Cross, patched with sweat, as if fleeing dark forces. Illness and medication know no post-codes. On both sides of the invisible border are the mechanists who think their body is a machine unrelated to their mind and blame it for their sickness; the counterbalancers who take differ-ent cocktails of medications to erase each other's effects; the disease groupies who self-diagnose and linger lovingly over their ailments' names; the deniers who call him in only after their sickness has progressed to an advanced stage; the hypochondriacs who come in before they're sick; the embarrassed, who apolo-gise for being sick; the know-alls; the know-nothings; the faithful, who believe his arrival will cure all evil. A doctor is a fisherman: all he has to do is dip a net into this place, and he will find more democracy than human hopes could imagine.

Too many people, each a need. He has learnt to resist, the way Pa never could learn. Pa gave himself to these people. But Davis keeps something in reserve. The world has changed. A man needs a life. You can't live on good deeds. And yet – what is there left but to play your part to the best of your ability? He wonders if he will arrive at the end of his life feeling he has lived too sensibly, stopped too short, left too much in the tank – wasted his father's legacy. And yet, after seeing those lipsticked trousers and the death certificate that raised more questions than it answered, Davis asks himself if this shadow, this monument of a paternal legacy, might not be quite what it seemed; yet even if it is not, he asks himself further, does he really want to be party to tearing it down?

Lucy is sitting outside the café on Victoria Street. She doesn't see him approach. She has already ordered, is stirring a milky latte, her legs crossed elegantly, immaculate in a sand-coloured pants suit. Pearls in her ears.

'Hey, darling.' She gets up and air-kisses both cheeks. 'I'm so, so sorry about tonight.'

'I'm still sorry about last night.'

She shapes to say something, then smiles. 'Do you realise we haven't even seen each other since your dad died?'

Lucy can't help it, but she makes it sound as if they haven't seen each other since an exciting social event.

'Yep, well, that's how it is.'

She checks her watch. 'I really wish I could be there for you, but it's been a hell of a week, it's the Americans, you know, they just refuse to recognise our summer holidays!'

'Ah, the Americans.'

Lucy gives him a look that is so friendly that he wonders if she even recognises him. 'You're not mad at me, are you?' she says in her Cute voice.

Mad at her? She has given him the perfect life: the balance of liberty and love, the maturity of friendship-in-marriage that they, alone among all the people they know, possess. What right has he to be mad?

'Of course not.'

'Well good, because I'm really sorry and I feel *so* awful about it. Okay?'

He lets her hang a while longer, unable to deny himself the pleasure of her need to hear his blessing, her need to get to work.

'I've just – something a bit odd's going on.' Davis pauses while a waiter comes and takes his coffee order. Lucy doesn't ask for another. She rechecks her watch. Her skin has the stretched look of glazed clay. She is probably, he thinks, hungover.

'I've been checking Pa's death certificate,' Davis says, his right index finger tracing a diminishing spiral of spilt sugar on the table, 'and a few things don't add up. First of all, it's been signed by Jim Cobcroft – who I don't think was Pa's GP.'

'Does that make any difference?' Lucy smiles at someone across the road.

'A death certificate is meant to be signed by a doctor who's seen you regularly, or recently, who's familiar with your history. Especially when he puts down heart failure as the cause of death.'

'Your poor mother.'

'But see, the thing is, "heart failure" is always the cause of death. It's just something doctors write when we have to write something. The person's heart stops. It's like the default setting. I've written a hundred heart failure death certificates. It's what you do when you don't really know what's gone on, but there's no real problem and you just want to save the family the hassle of a coronial inquest.'

'I never knew your father had heart trouble.'

'That's what I'm saying! He didn't! Or not that I knew. And what's more . . .' Davis pushes forward on his seat. His coffee arrives. He sips it and burns his lip, the lower lip with the white sore. 'What's more, the death certificate mentions aortic stenosis. Pa never had any aortic stenosis. It's a chronic problem, a narrowing of the aorta. He'd have told me if he had stenosis. I'd have known.'

Lucy's eyes film over at the medical terms.

'Well, why don't you just ask Dr Cobcroft?' she says, glancing again at her watch. 'Listen, sweetheart, I'm really sorry but I have to . . .'

'That's the other thing. Jim's up in Noosa. And I'm not sure when he went up there. He must have signed Pa's death certificate and then jumped on the next plane. It's weird, don't you think? Hey, that reminds me – on New Year's Eve, at Chris's hotel, did you hear anything about why Jim wasn't there? I'm having a few . . .'

'Look. Sweetheart.' Lucy has her wallet open. She takes out a twenty-dollar note and anchors it under the sugar canister. 'I don't know how to say this, and I know you're a doctor and it's good for you to be concerned about dotting the i's and crossing the t's. But I'm just not sure if this stuff matters enough for you to be worrying yourself about it. It's just details.'

She pats his hand and gives him a smiling eye contact she can hold, he notices, for barely an instant.

'You're right,' he says.

'Good.' Lucy stands and brushes down the front of her slacks. She checks her phone, which twitters with new messages. 'God, I knew I shouldn't have turned it off.'

Davis studies her and thinks: She has a dickface. Like the ones they used to draw in the bus. Round eyes, blunt nose, symmetry. It's not that she isn't attractive. Princess Diana had a dickface. Nothing wrong with dickfaces. But there it is: my wife has a dickface. Funny I never noticed it before.

She bends down and air-kisses him again. 'I'm meant to be at the office half an hour ago. I'll call, maybe let's reschedule dinner. Sorry, darling. Ciao!'

'You're right,' he says again, softly. Lucy doesn't hear him. He watches her sweep away, onto the street. She snips her fingers at a taxi. Davis says, answering Lucy's cheerful wave: 'You didn't know how to say it.'

And realises he never got around to what is uppermost in his mind.

He couldn't be worse-prepared if he tried. This is what he thinks as he blinks into the sun. The white light floods his eyes, already sticky from sleeplessness. He coughs up some of the phlegm that has built up since the early hours when he lay counting the grey folds in the hotel curtain to bore himself to sleep. He spits through the grille of his helmet.

In his padding, he feels embattled. His thighs knock against each other. He waddles, hips swinging, to the centre. He hasn't been able to rest since Davis came last night. At least, he thinks, I'll know who to blame.

Holding his bat upright on the crease, he asks the umpire for a line to centre stump, and finds that when he has to move the bat a few millimetres he has no feeling in the ends of his arms or legs. The umpire asks if he wants to take centre again, but Chris shakes his head. He looks around the field placings, supposedly memorising the gaps, but sees nothing. He blinks hard, contorts his face, stretches his mouth as wide as he can to try to induce some pain, some rush of endorphins that might wake him up. He'd scream if he could. He can't.

He tamps down rough spots on the pitch with the end of his bat. The umpire extends his arm like a fence rail as he waits for Chris. The bowler scuffs the ball once against his hip to remove the palmsweat and lacquer grease. The umpire winks. 'Right there, Chris? Okay – play.'

At the top of his run, the bowler windmills his arms and fixes the ball between his fingers, seam upright. His enormous boots stutter into the first steps. His boots flash silver spikes, divots spitting from his footmarks. His shoulderblades work into shape beneath his white shirt as he prepares his arms for the whirligig delivery motion.

Chris blinks hard, trying to lubricate the fatigue out of his eyes. He fights for concentration like a man overboard. When the bowler goes into his delivery leap, Chris surrenders: his body will either remember how to play, or it won't. There's nothing he can do. He gives up. *FuckenDavisFuckenSuzie.*

Every batsman has a complex set of triggers to activate the reflexes needed to play the shot. Chris's back foot takes a step in rhythm with the bowler's leap to the crease. His front toe steps forward, pivoting and pointing to the ball. If the ball loops fully, Chris's foot will commit further forward; if the ball cannons shorter into the turf his foot will press him backwards. That is, if his body obeys; if it doesn't just freeze.

The scarlet ball travels fast and straight for fifteen metres. Its mirror-smooth hemispheres part the air, which flows around the ball and gathers a frantic turbulence in its wake. As the ball slows, the turbulence catches and grips it. The moisture in the air combines with minute adjustments in the arc of the bowler's arm and body at release to curve its flight into Chris's pads.

He reads the curve: a hooping in-swinger. Yet when the stitches land they snatch the grey-brown turf crust. The stitching bites, and the ball deviates the other way – *away* from Chris's legs – so that it has now changed direction twice in the last quarter of its millisecond journey.

Chris adjusts desperately, but has no control over where the ball will go – if he hits it.

It misses. It misses his pads, misses his bat, misses the off stump which he has left exposed.

The ball travels another twenty paces to the wicketkeeper, whose head snaps back, lips an anguished O. The fieldsmen gasp and sigh, clutch their heads. The bowler pinches his goatee and places a hand on his hip. He wants to catch Chris's eye, wishing to impress on him how lucky he is not to be undertaking the return to darkness.

Chris ignores him. We all know what's happened, he thinks. He turns, jogs on the spot, tilts his face up to the sun, blinks hard, mutters to himself, springs into a series of knee flexes.

Puff, it's gone. Fucking forget it.

Sensing a quick kill, the South African fieldsmen yammer in their violent guttural Afrikaans. Fuck them, Chris thinks. Why can't they speak English? You don't know if they're sledging you or not. Like the Pakis – urdu urdu urdu – or the Windies – uggabuggadugga. Okay, here's the ball. Shut the fuck up.

This one is fuller, tempting him to play the big shot to ease his nerves and get off the mark with a cracking boundary. It bleats large in the air: Hit Me Hit Me Hit Me! Nothing would be better, Chris thinks, than to slam it to the fence. In one shot he could register his highest innings of the series.

But that's what they want him to do. Just as he's ready to launch himself, he notes a late swing in the ball's flight, and, with a jerk that hinks his wrist, he pulls out of the shot.

He leaves the next two balls. He still hasn't found that nice, confidence-filling sensation of bat on ball, and he's been beaten pointless, but something strikes Chris: he's *seeing* it. There's no other way of describing this feeling. Even the first ball, he saw it all the way. It beat him because it was a damn good ball. But he saw it. He tells himself not to worry. Eventually – here's the plan – he'll make them bowl it where he wants it, rather than him going off chasing where they want it.

Sure enough, the next one is angled into his pads. Chris twitches it away and runs 2, which might as well be 100 for the cheering.

'That's the over,' says the umpire, and only now does Chris realise fully that his batting partner is Nathan Such, the kid. He was so distracted by his annoyances, the crowds of thoughts and plans and arguments raging in his head, he hadn't even noticed that it was the nightwatchman who got out. Australia three wickets for 38 runs. Deep trouble.

'Nice one,' Such says to Chris, who gives him a withering look. The boy mumbles: 'It's doing a bit in the air, bit off the deck.'

Chris gives him another look. Such taps the pitch, hiding behind his helmet. To the outside world, they must look as if they're in earnest discussion.

Chris says: 'Let these cunts get you out and I'll make sure you never play for your country again.'

He returns to the non-striking end, where he crouches and runs on the spot and tries everything to revive his energy. It's hopeless. He hawks against his lungs again, raps the face of his bat against his legpad. A South African fielder walks past him and mutters something in Afrikaans. Chris played against these pricks when they first came back from apartheid. It was unnerving then, the Afrikaans. But always a buzz. This was the great thing about the game – the different cultures, the ways people have of speaking, of doing things. The first time against any nation is always special, even if it does put ideas in your head. Like the Sri Lankans and Indians: always in your face, like flies. And so dirty and fucking numerous. You wave them away, more fly in. He can't stand Indians. The Kiwis he doesn't mind, they're inoffensive, cut-price Aussies really, except they're unbearably cocky when they get on top, like they can't quite believe it. The Poms are similar – bad gloating winners, good blokes when they lose. We Aussies, he thinks, are the other way round – gracious winners, terrible losers. The world's a happier place for everyone when Australia beat England. Then there's the West Indians. They're all swagger, all confidence. At home, and when they're on top, they'll tread all over you. It's a macho thing. But when they're down, they start bickering, they drop their heads and give up. The opposite of Aussies, who need adversity to bring out their toughness but suffer from hubris when they're leading. Australians like a scrap.

Nathan Such misses the next ball. He's not up to it, Chris thinks, but he's still here.

The Afrikaners gibber away. They love to irritate you. Just last night, two Yaapies got in the hotel lift with Chris. He knew they usually spoke English together, but one of them started speaking Afrikaans. Just to give him the shits. Luckily the other kept on speaking English. Just some crap about what they were doing later that night. Arseholes.

Is he racist? He often wonders. You meet different races on the field, and you form opinions, and whether you want these opinions or not they're grafted onto you, cooked in this furnace, and then they're part of you, and the rest of the world may think you're racist or bigoted or whatever, but it's not that simple, it's not that simple. You have to be a player to understand.

It's the end of the over. The Yaapies jump around. Busy, punky, athletic. They think they're like us, Chris muses, but they're not, fucking not at all. Something in their history makes them tough but insecure, hard on the surface but soft-centred. They fight and fight and never give up, but when you've beaten them, there's something in them that accepts it. As if deep down they're too guilty to take the last step.

Chris faces up. He's happy to have seen through that over. He's been in for five minutes now. His concentration is still shot, but his hands are starting to decompress. He can feel his fingers. A line of sweat streaks down between his arse cheeks. He goes into his stance and the bowler comes in. From the sleepless night his eyes still itch, and he's distracted, as the bowler comes in, by trying to get in one good soothing blink. He's thinking more about his eyes than the ball, which kicks off a length and spears at the outside edge of his bat.

He doesn't need to look around to see where the ball's going. He feels as if he's on a moving footway: walking along at normal pace but the world is flying by. A premonition of departure hits him.

Maybe this is what Pa felt. In death. Death as dismissal. Thank you, you're out. Give someone else a bat. Off to the pavilion where you can have a good long look at yourself.

He's walking. He's off, twirling his bat underneath his arm, ripping his gloves off. He's been dismissed in Tests 141 times before. It's not as if he doesn't know how to walk off. So he's not watching when the South African third slip fieldsman, coincidentally the same one who provoked Chris last night by speaking Afrikaans in the lift, closes his fingers on the ball too early. The ball prongs into the middle finger of his right hand and pops up in front of him. He has ample time to regather his senses and catch the ball, but juggles often set off an electrocutive panic in fieldsmen. His head whiplashes, his hands scrabble, the ball goes down.

The crowd groans, sighs, cheers. Chris doesn't hear this, doesn't hear anything except, having taken three steps towards the pavilion, the shout of his young batting partner.

'Wait! Wait!'

It's a running call, but it might as well be a cry to save Chris Brand's career.

When Chris looks around, the South Africans are standing with their hands on their heads. It looks comical for a second. Simon says, Hands on Heads. Simon says, Ball's on the Ground.

'Wait! No!' Nathan Such holds his gloved palm in the air. Chris lowers his head and steps back to the batting crease.

He lets the next four balls go, and the last of the over he nicks over the top of the leaping wicketkeeper for a boundary.

At the change of overs, the kid looks as if he doesn't want to come down the pitch unless Chris beckons him. Chris comes halfway and stands, resting on his bat, one hand on his hip, until Such understands that this is an invitation.

Such taps a divot in the pitch, afraid or unable to say a word.

'Eh,' Chris says. 'Never forget this. Your first Test. Soak it all in, mate. Never gets any better than this.'

'Thanks.'

'Don't thank me till tonight, matey. Now let's stuff these Yaapie cunts. They feel too sorry for me to get me out. Let's make 'em pay.'

But the weird thing is, the weird thing is – he takes a deep breath and settles over his bat – it has come back. It's like something's protecting him.

He is watching the ball and letting thirty-odd years of repetition, burnt into instinct, play the shots for him.

Something changed in Chris when Ian Bertrand told him about Pa. Relief? Not quite.

Clarity.

In recent weeks, since his 'slump' began, his mind has been fizzing with solutions and suggestions, ways of attacking the problem – play more shots, play fewer shots, move the feet earlier, move them later, run harder between wickets, get forward, get back, eliminate the hook and the cut, play straighter, all the interior conference-calls of lost belief – but now Chris's mind is drained. There is no longer a need for solutions. There is only a ball, and his bat. The first principle: *Hit the ball. Use the bat.* His bat and the ball start arriving in the same place at the same time. The scratchiness, the hesitation, the undecided shotmaking of recent weeks seem to have fallen away like a snake's skin, a decayed product of his last form cycle.

At lunch – Chris 23 not out, Such 29 not out, the ship steadying – nobody in the dressing room says anything about Chris's form. Superstition forbids utterance. He has to save his position with his bat. He wonders if they've discussed it among themselves: creepy that Chris's form returned the moment his father died.

And to him it's ironic, given Pa's attitude to cricket. It wasn't that Pa didn't care – he just didn't think it amounted to very much. He hadn't been in awe of the whole apparatus of fame and international success and Chris being a public figure.

They hadn't really been estranged. Estrangement, to Chris, suggested some concrete problem, and unless you thought a lifelong mutual awkwardness was a problem, there was none. He and Pa never fought. It was just that they had nothing to talk about. Chris was Ma's son, belonged to Ma's camp just as Davis belonged to Pa's, but they weren't warring camps, at least as far as Chris was concerned, no, they were just natural pairings. Chris and Ma had sport to talk about, and Davis and Pa had medicine. So between Chris and his father, there was just a big hunk of silence which Chris might have described as comfortable.

That is, until Pa's blow-out at that family dinner just after Chris got back from Pakistan. Lost it completely. Went *beresk*, as the boys in the team would say. Blew his stack. Did his nana. Everything Ma had always said about bottling things up, still waters running deep until there's no deeper and they explode, proved correct. Whole aquifers of rage blew out through Pa's top, in front of children, children-in-law, grandchildren, Bertrand, the full deck. It was that bad.

But it was so bad, it was good. Pa's explosion had released quantities of toxic waste that dissolved barriers around him, at least from what Chris could see. (And frankly, all Chris *could* see were those sturdy mute fences between Pa and himself.) The eruption seemed to liberate the old man. Out of the blue, during the first Test in late November, Pa phoned Chris at his hotel in Brisbane. Chris didn't know what to say. Pa mumbled apologies, then started asking Chris about his Test preparation in a blindly groping way. Chris had been unready. He'd cut Pa off, and gone to practice.

Next day, Chris got out for his first Test duck in five years, an umpiring decision of historical ineptitude. That night, Pa called again.

This time, they'd talked – or Pa talked, in a self-unburdening gush. He spoke of turning over a new leaf, being a new man, he and Chris carving out a new relationship. In a rare gesture of confidence, Pa told him about Davis mooning around the locum. Pa thought it was funny that the one person who seemed most upset about it was Jim Cobcroft, who for some reason wanted to cut Davis's nuts off. 'He's running to me, telling tales like a hurt schoolboy,' Pa said of Cobcroft. 'If there's one goose who's a bigger goose than Davo,' Chris said, 'it's that goose Cobcroft.' He and Pa had a good laugh.

Although bemused at this sudden change, and residually pissed off about getting out for a duck, Chris was all for reconciliation. He arranged for Pa to come visit him and Suzie, alone, without Ma, when Chris came back to Sydney after the second Test. Pa had seemed really happy about that. Pa said, again, that he didn't want his behaviour at Warramunga Avenue to drive a wedge between them, particularly between himself and his granddaughters, and Chris said that the very act of phoning him up would help to mend things. Pa said sorry again. Chris contributed a sympathetic observation about the Personality his father had always seemed under pressure to present, even in his own home. It reminded Chris of the Personalities his fellow cricketers crafted for consumption in the team community and for the wider public. It was Chris's opinion that the further that Personality strayed from the individual's true nature, the tighter the stretch. He'd seen cricketers get lost between their Personality and the guy they really were, as if falling into a crack in the earth. Chris himself had never yielded to this temptation – for him, the great beauty of sport is that you are your numbers, you are free to be yourself, as tetchy or affable as you want, because your stats dictate how people see you. In the cricket community, it doesn't really matter whether you're a nice guy or a total prick. You'll be a nice guy who couldn't do the job, or a prick who earned respect out in the middle. Take Bradman.

Pa liked that story. In the SCG Members' pavilion there are washed-out prints of the Queen in more splendid times and Bradman in times more splendid still. The first time Chris brought his father into the dressing room, Pa looked at the portrait and said: 'No oil painting, Bradman, was he.'

Chris and Pa looked forward to hooking up again. But in December, Chris was always too busy to have that special meeting with Pa. And suddenly Pa was busy too, God knows why. So they put it off to the end of the season, but even as they were putting it off he sensed that Pa's enthusiasm was waning, his concentration drifting. Pa's outburst at that family dinner had opened a window of opportunity for them to make something new together, but the window had only stayed open for a short time.

And now he's gone, and Chris's form is back. He's thinking about Pa, yet his bat keeps hitting the ball. It's like there were things he wasn't allowed to do, ways he wasn't allowed to feel, when his father was still alive.

Weird how things work out.

Davis sits at his father's desk with palms down, sucking calm from the white laminate. He rings his mother's number, wishing to reassure her that he's not mooning after the locum, wouldn't dream of it. He's a good faithful husband, a good son, good, good, maybe it's time to sound out Lucy about children. Yes. But Ian Bertrand picks up and says Ma is busy and how could Davis call at a moment like this, when Chris is batting?

'Of course,' Davis says. 'How insensitive of me. How's he going?'

'He's into his eighties. You mean you're not listening to it?'

'I'd forgotten.'

Ian chuckles, as if getting a joke, and says he has to go back to the television.

Davis writes, and junks, a long email to Claire Mullally. He saw her outside the surgery this morning, when he arrived. He was sure that she saw him and ducked away to avoid him. He rushed up the surgery stairs and into Pa's room to stew over his abortive conversation with Lucy. Soon afterwards, he heard Claire arrive, telling patients she'd be with them shortly. Her door closed. Davis pressed his ear against the dividing wall. Sounds of a readying nature: a handbag being hung, a computer being booted up. Her voice called for the first patient. Davis's mind's eye saw how her face folded up on itself when she smiled.

He types another draft of the email, telling her she cannot automatically expect a continuation of her locum work when Dr Cobcroft comes back from holidays, and while her service is appreciated, et cetera et cetera, she might be doing herself a favour by seeking to further her career elsewhere.

Mooning after her. Sure.

Davis thanks his good luck that he never slipped up and revealed anything to her. It would've been a disaster. For a start, she's a smoker. Through the exercise of his profession, he has never been able to overcome the nagging belief that cigarette smokers are less trustworthy than non-smokers. If they can lie to themselves – as they must – then smokers can lie to anybody. And on top of that, her gawkiness, her Olive Oyl figure. She's not willowy. She's scrawny, with a cartoonishly backward-leaning walk, toes flung out in front of her as if she's overcompensating for a fear of falling on her nose. He has noticed, also, how her white skin goes unattractively goosepimply and blotchy with high emotion. Today she is wearing high black leather boots, which accentuate the poultry-like whiteness of her knees and thighs. In all, he thinks, with her black turtlenecks and tartan skirts she has a dress sense that connotes a kind of desperation, a young graduate on the make, a lonely quest for medicine's tawdry dreams. Yes: a disaster.

The phone rings, causing Davis to almost hit the ceiling with fright.

'Davo.'

'Ah – hi.'

'Did you talk to him?'

'Chris?'

'Mm-hm.'

'I went to see him last night.'

'Did you ask him? Show him the pants and stuff?'

'It's just – it seems too early. Chris is fighting to save his career, and –'

'Yeah no, it's all about Chris.'

'Well, if I don't have Chris onside, I can't see how we can get through to Ma. And . . . she's in shock. She's sitting in front of the TV like a zombie. Understand – nothing's going to happen for a while. It hasn't really hit her yet. She can't take much in.'

'That's why we have to pull her out of it.'

'We have to be gentle, take our time. I'm just thinking, if you can be patient, we'll work on her gradually. Once this Test is over, Chris will come around, I know he will, and then we'll get to work on her together, and . . .'

'We have to do it now, know what I'm saying? For the funeral.'

'But see, why – why can't you wait? Why do you have to do this so – publicly?'

'Because the truth must be shared before we say goodbye.'

Davis tries to brush off the strangled, alien intensity coming through the phone.

'Well, I'm trying to think of what Chris, and Ma, would say to that, and –'

'Don't need your –'

'– and listen. Just listen. I think they'd say, well, we'd all say, that truth isn't the most important thing right now. It will be eventually, but not right now. For now, we have to organise the, um, funeral or whatever we're going to have, and just be compassionate, be dutiful, do what she wants.'

'Compassion. When was that ever shown to me?'

'Come on, be reasonable.'

'Piss-weak, man. Too piss-weak to ask her yourself. Yeah no, you're going to Chris because you want to put it all onto him, and then come back to me and say you've tried your hardest,' the voice rants, wearily despotic.

'Look, I'm just saying in the short term . . .'

'Truth at all costs. That's what Pa and I discovered together.'

Davis flinches at the thought of some shared secret knowledge.

'The pants,' he says. 'Are you going to tell me about the pants?'

'In my own sweet time. Why don't you look up his email folder? Too fucken gutless, that's why.'

'Hey,' Davis says. 'Don't say I'm not interested in the truth. I've been doing some digging, and I'm thinking there's something not quite right about the death certificate. It's been signed by Jim Cobcroft, and it says heart failure, and aortic –'

The rasping laugh on the phone sounds like something tumbling downhill.

'What? What's so funny?'

'I'm thinking there's something not quite right,' the voice mimics Davis.

'Well, there isn't.'

'Fucken gimp.'

'What? I'm only searching for, trying to make sense – oh, shit.' Davis feels the blush spread across his face to his ears. 'You know, don't you. You know what happened.'

'The sound of pennies dropping.'

Davis thinks of the trousers. A woman. 'You were there, weren't you?'

'Why don't you do the right thing for once, Davo, and go tell them what I want?'

'You were with him.'

'Yeah no, you'll all find out the truth, once you stop being such a bunch of fucking control freaks.'

'What happened? What happened?'

The line is dead. Davis stares into space, placing the phone sleepily, almost tenderly, on Pa's desk. Some minutes later, he finds himself staring at the email he has written Claire Mullally. Rather than send it, he saves it. He can send it tomorrow.

He opens up a new window and follows the directions into Pa's personal email folders. The password has been saved. He pulls the monitor square and wipes dust from the screen.

Margaret Brand wears her thick spun-tungsten hair pinned up from both sides, its healthy density giving the impression of padding, something soft encasing something hard. Her hands are on the armrests, fingernails clicking on the leather as if playing a piano accompaniment to Chris's innings.

His great innings.

Chris has saved his position, got himself onto the overseas tour, saved his career from an ignominious ending, put Australia in a good position for this game, brought a twinkle to his mother's eye.

'All right?' Ian brings her a cup of tea.

Her eyes blink affirmatively. She pinches the flesh above her nose between thumb and forefinger. Ian goes out to clean up the kitchen.

Bolder friends of her sons used to see Mrs Brand as the type of mother they could share a joke with. But Margaret's twinkling eye denoted mischief rather than laughter, ambition and a touch of cruelty rather than humour. Boys would try to share a joke with Mrs Brand, but their sarcasm fell flat. She was too literal, defusing their exaggerations with a quick contradiction. Ian admired her for that. He told her she had a sense of ambition you rarely found when you lived and worked in a school. A Big Wheel by temperament if not situation, Mrs Brand moulded her world to fit. She created a 'scene' around Chris's teams, her initiatives to supply the boys with transport and food earning her the nickname 'Auntie Marg'. She would scout opposition games and come to midweek training with dossiers about strengths and weaknesses. It was 'only professional', she said, causing a certain number of jaws to drop. None of the other mothers could guess where she got the energy or motivation, and threw off at her behind her back. She tended to watch Chris's games on her own, fiercely. That was another thing that drew Ian to her: she was strong enough to stay out on her limb. She came in full voice, cooking cakes for teatime, supplying the newfangled waterbottles with the squeeze tops – for all the boys, not just for Chris – and marking the scorecard. She even offered to umpire, but was banned after her one performance when an opponent questioned Chris's eligibility for an under-seventeen game considering he'd driven up to the gates in a Volvo. Auntie Marg snapped from the square-leg umpiring position: 'He's been shaving since he was fourteen, so mind yourself or else I'll give you out.' All in the sweetest voice, her snub nose and delicate make-up and pinned-bolster hair concealing the killer inside. A soft glove, all the better to swing with.

'That's it!' Bill Lawry cries. 'Chris Brand, one hundred runs, huge crowd, on their feet, Sydney Cricket Ground.'

Chris looms from the screen, helmet in one hand, bat in the other, blond hair sweat-pasted. Lawry calls it 'a tremendous battle against the odds'. Chris performs one revolution, acknowledging all corners of the crowd equally. He doesn't give an extra flourish to the dressing room, or a vindicated sneer to the press box. His eyes are buttons, expressing nothing but blank fatigue.

Margaret's fingers loosen on her armrests.

'That,' says Richie Benaud, 'is one of the finest innings you'll ever see.'

Ian looks expectantly at Margaret. Her eyes seem to mirror Chris's – dim with exhaustion, flat with relief.

'He's done it,' Ian says.

Margaret doesn't reply. There is a movement in her chin, as if she is chewing the inside of her lip.

'That will silence the critics,' Ian feels himself ploughing on. 'Tea?'

Margaret shakes her head without looking at Ian, her eyes fixed on Chris as he replaces his helmet, tucking his chinstrap firmly.

'He's only just started,' she says.

'You're right. Looks like a BCC.'

Davis is close enough to note the colour of Claire's eyes. Hazel: golden sunbeams angling into green sea. It's not often that green and gold, together, can look beautiful. He likes her voice, too. She makes a basal cell carcinoma sound like a freckle.

He would never have come so close to her if he hadn't had his brilliant idea.

Hi, he pretexted her, got time for an extra patient?

Claire releases his lower lip from the pinch of her fingers. She goes over to the sink and washes her hands. He speculates if his two hands, thumb to thumb and pinkie to pinkie, could encircle her waist.

'It's different when doctors examine each other.' She wipes her hands on a paper towel. 'It's not like a patient's asking me a question and I give the answer. With this, you've already diagnosed yourself and you're asking if I concur.'

'More pressure,' Davis says.

'On both of us.' She gives him a noncommittal smile and sits on her side of the desk.

'And we're one-all,' he says. Claire has listened to his heart, measured his blood pressure, and found that he's suffering from nothing more than stress. His fears of heart trouble are imaginary.

But the lesion on his lip will require a trip to a specialist: Professor Birch at the Bourke St skin cancer clinic.

As Claire writes out a referral, Davis tries to think of something to say, a plea for time, for the grace of her presence.

'How have you been going with Jim's patients?' he asks.

'Oh.' Claire scrunches her nose. She finishes the referral with, he notices, a flamboyant signature. Without looking up, she says: 'Sometimes I think I'm losing them.'

'Call it population control.'

'No.' She leans back in her chair. It rocks. 'They keep living, and they keep turning up. Where I'm losing them is in the bedside manner. A girl came in this morning convinced she had giardia and depression. Street worker. She has a bit of gastro, a few other odds and sods, but not giardia. Even less depression. Could I convince her of that? Not a chance. She just went on about how her boyfriend had had it, how her mother had it, and then we were into the long version of her relationship with her mother, and I was sitting here thinking about something entirely different.'

'Ah, that kind of losing them.'

'They only hear what they want to hear. I'm just a dispensary.'

'We're like dole officers. A disagreeable checkpoint before they can get the goods.'

'You remind me of your father. He said we're passport-stampers. If patients are polite with us it's only because they feel that's the quickest way to get what they want.' She wipes her nose. 'But he'd say, "If we weren't here, who would they have?" God, I miss him. I can only imagine what it's like for you.'

Davis brushes it away, like a compliment he's heard too often.

'Days like this,' Claire says, 'I loved to go into his room, or take a walk with him, and just have a good old whinge. He'd let me complain about the patients, and was so non-judgmental. He'd just chuckle and tell me a story. You know, I got firsts in medicine and surgery, yet it was your father who taught me how to be a doctor. I can't believe I'm not going to go on, and learn more, with him around. I'd schemed him into my future. He was a permanent fixture. I just feel, I don't know, cheated.'

'Yes, well.' Davis has never been gladder that he deleted the email message he was going to send Claire, telling her she was no longer needed. Love and hate, he thinks. Love and hate.

'I'm sorry. You don't want to hear any of this.' She gets up, takes a sheet of paper towel from the dispenser, and blows her nose. 'There's your referral on the desk. Sorry.'

Davis doesn't get up. He taps the edge of the envelope on the laminate. Claire glances at her watch.

'I suppose you've heard about Chris,' he says.

'Oh?' Claire says, eyes glittery. 'I don't really follow sport.'

'He got a century.'

'I assume that's a good thing,' she smiles.

Davis's laugh breaks the tension.

'Depends.'

'I don't envy you. All the public scrutiny.'

'We've made things worse for ourselves. Chris authorised the obituary which said our father only had two sons. You know there's a third, Hammett. Our youngest brother.'

'Um. Jim Cobcroft told me once.'

From Claire's silence, Davis assumes she knows at least the bare bones.

'And other things have been getting up my nose,' Davis says. 'Hey. Do you know if Jim was my father's personal GP?'

'No, I don't.'

'I guess we could look up his files.'

Claire gives Davis a searching look.

'Probably better to wait for Jim to come back,' she says.

'Yeah.' Davis exhales, staring at the wall. 'Probably. But see, a few things don't add up. On Pa's death certificate, it says aortic stenosis. He no more had aortic stenosis than I do. Which, we now know, I don't.'

143

'Maybe he did,' Claire says cautiously, 'but he didn't tell you.'

'Nah. Sorry, I don't mean to be dismissive, but he would have told me. Pa and I – you know how some fathers and sons talk football? That was how Pa and I were with medical matters. We told each other everything. He wouldn't have hidden that from me.'

'Have you spoken to Jim?'

'That's the other thing. He's up in Noosa, but he signed the death certificate. So he must have been down here on New Year's Eve. Yet he wasn't at our do, at Chris's hotel. Which is kind of odd. That he wasn't there, but he was around a couple of hours later to declare Pa, you know . . .'

Claire shrugs and shifts in her chair.

'It's good for your mother that Chris has done well.'

'A couple of other things,' Davis continues. 'I found the death certificate, and it was on Pa's own pad. Not that that means anything, but why wouldn't Jim have done it on his pad? Why did he have Pa's? And then there's the cremation certificate. A cremation's been organised. That would have needed Jim to have his cremation certificates with him on the night, sign one off, and then go to Noosa. I mean, it's not as if we carry them around with us.'

'Oh, well, he must have been prepared.'

'Very well prepared. Very well prepared.'

'I can't go through his files. You know that.'

'Sure! Sure!' Davis gives a weird little shriek, folding his arms and leaning back to examine the ceiling. 'I'd never dream of compromising you!'

Claire clears her throat.

'You ought to be asking Jim about this, not me.'

'You know what? I ought to. You know what else? I ought to be talking about it with my mother, and my brother – Chris. But nobody wants to talk about it with me. And that's what's driving me up the wall.'

'Maybe when all this cricket blows over . . .'

'Yes, in another two years. He's saved his career now. He'll go on until he drops. And that'll give him and our mother all the excuses they need to dodge the reality, the things we need to face up to.'

'Davis, I'm really sorry.'

He has been talking with his eyes on the ceiling. He has noticed Claire's fidgeting, her evident unwillingness to discuss this.

'I've got patients waiting,' she says, gently.

'Oh. Sure.' He jumps up, with a sunny smile. 'I didn't mean to take up so much of your time.'

'Don't be silly.'

She comes across the room and stands almost close enough to touch him. Davis taps the referral against his palm.

'We all miss him,' Claire says.

'You know who I miss?' Davis says.

'You must miss your mother.'

'My mother.' He gives a dry laugh. 'No, I miss my youngest brother.'

'Hammett.'

'It's funny,' Davis says. 'You don't ask any questions about him. Nobody asks any questions about him.'

'Well . . .'

'I'm off.'

Abruptly, almost rudely, Davis leaves the room. Claire takes half a step after him, but the next patient comes past Davis, without any ceremony, and plonks himself in the chair. Davis gets his mobile out of his father's room and slams the door on his way out. A message on his phone says Dr Cobcroft has been calling for him. Davis mutters something under his breath and takes the stairs, two at a time, down to the street.

December 12

His outburst had tugged like a rip beneath every minute. How many times had he relived the moment when he stood in the kitchen, stiff as a mummy, while Margaret tamped him clean? The family watching her wipe away his, his. What did he feel, later? Heartbreak? Terror? Humiliation? Anxiety? No, none of these. He felt nothing but a mild regret for pushing his granddaughter a bit too hard. When he unmoored himself from the house and struck his toes through the long grass in the field around the investment townhouses, he reflected on how unjust was family orthodoxy. Family orthodoxy held that Chris had inherited none of his 'mental discipline' from John. Orthodoxy held that Chris's 'cool' and 'toughness' came from Margaret. But orthodoxy, John found, was premature. This ability to retire from feeling in a crisis – this animal numbness, this lighter-than-air detachment, this death in life – must, somehow, be a gift from John to his famous son. It saddened him that the unspeakable source of his discovery prevented him from claiming credit.

It was from this sense of renewed kinship, rather than to apologise for his embarrassing outburst, that John essayed contact with Chris. In the first week of December, Chris was playing in an inter-State game in Sydney. It was meant to be the 'breather' between Test matches, at a more relaxed and unpopulated level of the game, for Chris to regain form after a duck in Brisbane. Instead it had rained walls of water for four days. John and Chris contrived conversation, awkward yet pleasantly novel, in the Members' Bar. They planned to 'hang out' – Chris's tentatively casual formulation – just the two of them.

Yet Chris was busy that week, and in any case the promise sufficed. John was busy too. Since his outburst, the business card with the picture of the young woman had been burning a hole, as it were, in John's desk drawer.

He abandoned the surgery to James Cobcroft and took long walks through the city, his mind frantically debating plans of action. After the rain, summer had arrived. A high-pressure system was passing over the south-east coast sizzling a fried egg of isobars on the synoptic chart.

At 3.33 pm on the second Monday in December, John left the surgery and picked his way through Kings Cross as if walking along a beach taking care not to tread on bluebottles. The air filled with the lower, distinctive hum of Falcon and Commodore engines, taxis' shrill brakes. Car alarms sent off their impotent symphony of alternating sirens. Wheelie-bins stood out for collection. Building sites, building sites: Sydney was like a geriatric patient, constantly being patched up, never quite right. If it wasn't one thing, it was another. Near the surgery, a community centre had been bulldozed for a block of units: Style Has A New Name. Contact So and So For Details. Selling Fast. Labourers crowded the pavement, faces grey with cement dust like those of Japanese actors. One of them shovelled scree out of a gutter, making a noise to wake living and dead; another crouched like a footballer in the tray of a utility and hauled dense bags of metal brackets over the footpath to land against the chain fence. John paused, wondering whether to cross the bags' flight, but the labourer stopped throwing and irritably waved the old man through.

The old man's head was full of Hammett, whose bombard-ment of material, through the post and by email, might have constituted harassment if John were not so cravenly consuming it. He had ceased throwing it away. The damage to his nerves caused by the flood of magazines, articles, videotapes, DVDs and CD-ROMs arriving for him at home and at the surgery was, monstrously, being soothed and cured by the consolations he was finding in that very same material.

He urged himself to do something. He had Hammett's address on the card – a mute invitation. Surely what Hammett was doing was pummelling him for attention, crying for his time.

He had met Hammett in the shop. As he fainted. On the second Tuesday of November. Hammett had picked him up, dusted him down, put him in a taxi. John could acknowledge the sequence of events now. More than that, he was beginning to see in the coincidental meeting an omen. Or perhaps he, John, had been unconsciously wishing for, even orchestrating, the encounter? He could not rule it out. It was arguable that everything in the past five years had been leading to this.

John wandered down the leafy end of Kings Cross, and turned back up the hill. He tried to distract himself from his thoughts by reading the text of his neighbourhood. Black T-shirts and renovated apartments gave way to souvenirs, leather, Sasuki, Minami, Shogun, For Lease: Huge Exposure Retail Space. Victoria Bitter. Angela's Jewellers. Kings Cross parking station: twenty-four hours seven days. Stock sellout. Pizza, Seven Day Food, bookshop, Indian Home Diner, souvenirs, continental deli, real estate, natural therapy centre, travellers cheques money exchange cambio wechsel, free appraisals rental and sale . . .

John avoided the naval officers coming down the hill in their white outfits, the army in their khaki, the fat drivers standing outside their minibuses herding their Japanese charges or querying anxiously into phones. In the gardens, the dandelion fountain sprayed. A man lay corpselike under a blanket; other winos gathered seriously, as if for a convention; two Aboriginal women bickered in country voices under the shade of a palm tree while a pair of beat policemen ambled by. McDonald's cups and scrunched brown bags performed a tango in a gust, a chocolate-smeared sundae container landing on, and sliding off, the blanketed man. Pigeons hustled beside a pair of young addicts, both of whom John knew as patients, who were trying to wheedle a fresh clean syringe out of Marie, another sometime patient, who was too bombed out to know what they were asking. Marie wore a dirty Santa Claus cap. John considered pausing to help – he could give them a syringe and spare Marie – but dozily, she palmed them one out of her string bag and they took off with a skip up to the purple Funk House backpackers hostel.

Women approached, and John Brand's eyes triangulated in their repetitive pattern. Left breast, right breast, face. Left breast, right breast, face. Even if his mind was engaged elsewhere, his eye tracked this set pattern: left breast, right breast, face. His eye tracing the same triangle in the same way, right-eyed, as if crossing the right leg over the left by lifelong habit.

Something had worn out in him since he had turned sixty. It must have been wearing out for decades, but only in the last few years had he become aware of it. Edges, once sharp, were blurred; fatigue took the form of a mental looseness, an inability, soon an unwillingness, to examine things too closely or hold onto them for too long. He stared into space for increasing periods. He idled. He ceased to listen to Margaret; attention seemed to require Everestian effort. He had stopped wanting to be good! Could it be something that straightforward? Perhaps it was. Perhaps it was.

As a young man, John used to think constantly about death. The death he witnessed, almost daily, convinced him that the noblest aim in life was to die well. As a young man, at around the time he met Margaret, dying well had been a consuming goal for John. He read religious and philosophical works which, combined with his first-hand observations, coalesced into a working idea of death. For John, a clean conscience gave you a painless journey, at the moment of death, through the pivotal moral moments of your life. If you had been good, you would rejoice in what you had done, and the revision of your days could give you the illusion of those days relived in lingering detail, like a highlights tape you can view as often as you please – a life after, or at least in, death! Planning for this moment had seemed incontestably worthwhile as a man's life's work.

On their wedding night, in a South Coast motel, he had felt emboldened to explain it all to Margaret, and she had listened to him. But he knew, as he told her, that this was a discovery one made for oneself. One couldn't sell it, or be sold it. Margaret had listened, patiently, and said something like, 'Isn't it a bit early to be thinking so much about dying?' She had laughed, John had laughed along, and he had never mentioned it to a soul since.

In his thirties and forties, he kept at his project, but the lessons of one's early adulthood fade, and John's guiding philosophy grew brittle. Learnt in the pitiless light of forty-eight-hour emergency ward shifts, John's philosophy staled as he grew more comfortable and the brutality of his early years in medicine leaked away into the past. It cost him increasing effort to submit his every act to the spectre of a final reckoning. Which was so far off. So far off. Margaret had been right. Life is for living. John had grown tired of being good all the time. Paradoxically, as death came closer, dying well mattered less. He knew scoundrels, like his father-in-law, who died in perfect peace, the ghost of a smile on their lips. He knew good people, the best, whose reward was a lingering death in cancerous agony. The nearer he got, the less point there seemed in pursuing what he now felt was a youth's callow idealism. Strangely, as the other doctors he knew grew older, they became more and more interested in reading philosophy, or speculating on all the deep thinking they would undertake in their retirement. For John, deep thinking was an embarrassing memory.

Weary with being good, or simply weary, he had eventually sought out the sensation of being bad. He tried various agents – the pictures, the videotapes, the computerised images – and found that they were more potent, sharper in outline, than what ordinary life had to offer. He medicated himself with these doses of richness. He developed a fixation with Her. In the street he followed women who resembled Her, a palimpsest over his longing. The adventures of watching yet not being seen, the art and technique of spying in window reflections, through car windows, gave him something akin to a shot of heart-starting adrenalin. He chanced going to those shops rather than purchasing the products over the Internet. He courted risk.

And yet, it seemed now, he might only have been leading himself towards the boy. Hadn't his troubles, his degeneration – his *degeneracy* – started when he lost Hammett? Was all this perversity – he freely recognised himself as a *pervert* – merely an avenue back to the boy?

Blessedly, he had found him. Could he not, now, make the most of his luck?

Turning back towards the surgery, John tried to subdue himself, *take the edge off*, as his patients said, with the music of signs: Kodak Photo, tax free, mixed business, Croissant d'Or patisserie, For Lease, Hong Kong 7,571 km, Bangkok 7,537 km, Cape Town 11,017 km, Amsterdam 16,645 km, Rome 16,330 km, Moan, moan, moan – that's all we ever hear from our customers. Old Sydney Bourbon Bar. Old wares, fine wines. Hair skin body. One hour Internet free with every drink downstairs. Girl power, dare to be different, Kingsview, Fountain Tobacconist, gay lesbian Australian made, make your own, unlimited design, raunchy. Singles, twins, doubles, dorm. Juice stop. Alcohol-free zone. The Globe Backpackers. Black-market. Sleevemasters Tattoo. Stripperama. Nick's Tobacco. Freedom. Taste of Freedom. Where did I come from? The year is here. Studley says no rest for the wicked. Graphite deodorant. It's your Sydney: eat it, watch it, work it, wear it, love it.

It was no good.

This is not my world.

This is not my world.

He slid the card from his wallet. On the reverse side was the phone-sex advertisement, the sprawled brunette with come-hither eyes.

For the first time in he did not know how long, he felt proud of what he was about to do.

December 12

Five weeks after he fainted in the shop, three weeks after his outburst at the family dinner, six days after his stunted reconciliation with Chris, John Brand responded to the invitation on the business card.

At 4.32 pm on the second Monday in December, he left James Cobcroft with the last patients of the day and told him he was going home. Instead, he drove to the shire of Liverpool. He headed south-west, and ninety minutes later was still in Sydney.

Absurd that at sixty-seven he should sneak away with the thrill of truancy.

But there it was: rebelling, hitting the road, venturing on a secret mission.

He didn't trust his Morris on the freeway – or rather, he didn't trust the combination of Morris, freeway and himself – so he drove the slow way, down Old Canterbury Road through suburbs of plywood, grille and graffiti, radio off, fingers tapping a non-tune on the wheel. The variegated road surface altered the quality of the car's sound as he drove over graded greytop, slabbed concrete, blue-metal conglomerate, sun-softened bitumen, unredeemed potholes. The wheels sent rhythmic two-beat vibrations through the car as they passed over the seams in the road, tar between the slabs as waxy as scar tissue. The beats sounded like a nail gun linking piece by piece his road back to his boy. He stopped at a pedestrian crossing for a United Nations of school-children. Girls in Muslim headdress crossed furtively. He hadn't been in these suburbs since Greeks were exotic. It was a foreign country in his own city, a blind spot behind the freeway noise barriers.

He had had to come out here once, years ago, for an emergency call, to a flat above a vacant shop in Campsie, or Belmore. A man had died in the kitchen. But it wasn't just that he'd died. He'd been dead for six weeks. He had no friends, no visitors, and it was only when the stench filtered out to the street that someone called the police. It had seemed to John that this kind of thing could only happen out here, in this kind of place, never on the North Shore. But perhaps, he thought now, that was just another illusion, another callow judgment, and people died under our noses every day, everywhere, ghosting among us until the odour grew too strong, leaving us to calculate how long they'd been dead.

The metropolitan centrifuge spun him out to the south-western fringe where the malls were gutted by boredom's fires. Scratched holly and snowflakes were stencilled onto shop windows. Mullet haircuts and hooded tracksuit tops peopled the bus interchange outside a train station, and the suburbs had Anglo-Saxon names of spiteful blandness, like the impassive faces of hardened criminals: Miller, Cartwright, Busby. Here, three-bedroom houses brought the same price as a bedsitter near his surgery.

His eyes strained. He felt he was discovering Sydney the way he had discovered foreign cities: late in life. Since this *thing* had come to life inside him he had travelled widely, accepting any and every invitation to medical conferences. Margaret never came. On his own, in faraway places, his first act when he checked into a hotel room was to order room service, in order to conceal on his bill his next move, which was to decipher from the in-house movie menu what was on offer in The Best of Non-Violent Erotica.

Next he would scan the local yellow pages for the city's adult bookshops, X-rated cinemas and gentlemen's nightclubs, then go out and orientate himself by these sights. This was how he came to know the difference between American and European cities: not by their art or architecture, their theatres or operas or museums or parks, but by their red-light districts. American cities shot their smut to the peripheries, to warehouses in industrial zones, alongside panel beaters and freight forwarders and light manufacturers, to isolated roadside turnouts hidden behind billboards. European cities hugged their red-light districts close to their bosom, painting their prostitutes and their XXX against the romantic backdrop of once-grand shuttered doorways, geranium-filled windowboxes and frosted-glass hostelries.

He liked both. The world, he'd found, was an interesting place. He travelled to be free, to indulge in orgies of self-abuse, nights when he didn't know who he was anymore, a last frenzy of replenished youth.

His favourite? Paris, city of light. Paris – he'd gone for a conference on migraine run by a pharmaceutical company one March. As Chris was touring the West Indies, Margaret opted out of Paris, preferring to sit up late watching cable television at home.

John had been to Paris once before, as a medical student. He had spent his days in the Louvre and the Invalides, the Orangerie and the Place des Vosges. He'd stood up at café-bars, unwilling to pay the sit-down price, and dreamt of what he would do when he'd return with money. Now, in his late middle-age, he was booked into the 2,800-franc-per-night Hôtel Lutétia on Boulevard Raspail just west of the Luxembourg Gardens. The conference would detain him for three hours of the middle morning and two of the afternoon. Otherwise, he had Paris to himself. Paris! To himself! A cultured, world-loving, mildly Francophile man, wealthy and free, he arrived at Roissy and took a train to the Gare du Nord. When he emerged from the confusion onto the outside steps, he cast his eye over the bank of taxis towards the Rue de Compiègne. The first word that snagged him was: SEX. A yellow vertical sign, one word, the letters oozing.

As if called by a pitch of sound only audible to himself, he moved towards it. SEX. With every step, the Paris of his mind – boulevards, plane trees, restaurants *prix fixe*, gardens, the Seine, the *bateaux-mouches* – dissolved behind him. All that remained was SEX. *Ooh*, he thought, *la-la*. He wasn't even going to make it as far as his hotel.

His feet took him to a doorway, down each side of which ran diagonal fluorescent words: *Nouveautés*, *Vidéos*, *Magazines*, *DVD*, *Cabines*. The international language of filth. And Poppers. He didn't know this one. Poppers, what were they? Books by Karl Popper? Something homosexual, he suspected. Perhaps this was a fairies' lair. He'd go inside, and his destiny would be taken from his hands. No, no, no. *Non, merci*.

He reeled away down Compiègne. The tussle between the Paris of his memory and *this*, if indeed there was any fight in John, was detectable in the sweat on his forehead, the butterflies in his stomach. He pressed on down the rue, past a shop called '*Littérature et Articles Erotiques*'. Then one called '*Erotisme et Sexologie*'. Then '*Aphrodisiaques et Lingerie de Séduction*'. Trust the French, he thought, to make it all sound so intellectual. The next shopfront was a reassuringly blunt '*Projection X*'.

He kept going with his carry-on luggage, telling himself he was on his way to Hôtel Lutétia but by foot. He needed some fresh air, some streetlife: he would go to the Seine, or to a cafe. But his legs tricked him into taking a turn towards Clichy, where he swam in an ocean of *nouveautés*, *cabines*, *livres*, 'Poppers', faded photographs of strippers papering the entranceways, the temptation of *la burlesque*, chunky aromatic men plucking at his elbow and beckoning him in their poor English. When he ignored them they switched to hopeful German, then Dutch, wildly speculative Russian, Swedish, finally a forlorn query in Italian.

To escape, he turned into a normal-enough-looking place with *vidéos*. Inside, the force of it hit him – I am in Paris, and Paris is the same as everywhere, a galaxy of skin and familiar American faces, and here is Her face twinkling from the shelf, or is it Her, no it is not, her sister maybe, how diabolical the trickery! He ran outside with his small suitcase, which contained toiletries, a biography, two spare shirts and ties, and three changes of underwear. He'd flown in his suit. He liked to fly formally, not in the tracksuits favoured by some, which brought to mind going out in public in one's pyjamas. His big heart thumped staunchly, his armpits gushed, his back a great Africa of clinging stain. And wasn't Boulevard Clichy a lovely street when you stood back and looked at it, with its reserve down the centre and its art nouveau *Métro* portals?

Then he was back again, inside another place, making inquiries at a counter about the use of the *cabines*. His French had deteriorated since his youth, when his school learning had still been fresh enough to get him by. Now, through handsignals and broken Franglais, he understood that if he went into the *cabines* he could only see the videotapes already playing, six films in, John imagined, an eternal sisyphean loop. The man assured him they were all *'ardcore*, all *très bien*. A black man came out of a *cabine* requesting more change. John asked the man at the counter, who sported a drooping moustache, if he could bring a videotape from another shop and play it here, *dans une cabine*. He wasn't interested in the six tapes on offer. He only wanted a specific tape with a specific actress. Could he buy it somewhere else and bring it here?

'*Je reste dans un hôtel*,' he apologised. '*Je ne peux pas regarder mon vidéo là*.'

The sex shop man shrugged. '*Point d'animaux, point d'enfants, tu comprends?*'

John nodded eagerly. He waved his hands expressing disgust at the idea of animals and/or children. He was not that kind of man. Then he wondered if, perhaps, he might find a tape of Her on the sale racks, here. Haltingly, he asked the *mec* if this shop had its videotapes catalogued alphabetically, '*ou peut-être par l'actrice?*'

The man's reply was rapid, but John caught the word 'complexes' and understood the man to be saying that they didn't catalogue their tapes by starlet, as it was unhealthy for shoppers to develop a complex about a particular actress, because, what do you want, they are all *égales*.

John left the shop, humiliated. The man hadn't meant it personally, but he had relegated John beneath the lovers of megaboobs, he-shes, Asians, teens, bondage, leather, gay, black, shit, piss, everything – he was the weirdest of all, the man who had developed a *complexe* about an actress, the man who had mistaken fantasy for reality, the man who did not know that in porn, in SEX, *égalité* ruled.

Night had fallen on Clichy. The tips of the Moulin Rouge's wings bobbed above tour buses. A team of end-of-season shinty players in kilts sang their way down the boulevard. John Brand darted back into the first shop, where he thought he'd seen Her on the box cover. He'd lost the position. He went through the shelves quickly, his finger running along the ridged spines. He found it: Herself indeed, coupled with another beauty. Without bothering to check the price or calculate the exchange rate, he bought it and took it back to the other shop where the moustached man seemed to be waiting for him, palms flat on the counter. This dirty foreigner *avec ses complexes*. John Brand ripped the brown paper off the box. He thrust it across the counter with a challenging look, as if daring the *mec* to refuse to play it.

The man's moustache undulated like a grub as he regarded the tape with a suspiciously expressionless expression. He matched the name on the tape with the name on the box cover, as if it mattered – or perhaps he was checking it did not contain *enfants* or *animaux* – and informed John Brand that he was going to have to charge him double.

'*Pourquoi?*' John asked.

The man sighed and looked beyond John's shoulder. *Pourquoi pas?*

'Okay, *d'accord*, okay,' John said in a rush, slapping down a 200-franc note.

'Do you want to see ze whole story?' the man said softly, in English, as if having to treat John carefully. Like a mental patient. As if to watch the whole story, dialogue and all, would be the ultimate perversion.

'*Oui*,' said John, thrusting out his jaw.

A hint, from the man, of a consensual shrug. He saw all types.

'*Cabine numéro deux.*' The man made a peace sign.

John set himself up in his *cabine*. There was a vinyl bench and a Kleenex box and a plastic fliptop bin. It smelt of Dettol and faded urine. The tape quality and the age of the machinery degraded the experience. Nonetheless, there was an introductory scene in which She remained fully clothed in tight houndstooth officewear, 'interviewing' a 'job applicant', and for one precious shot her eyes locked in on the camera. John stored the moment. The scenes without Her being insufferably tedious, he sorted through his hotel voucher and conference documents in the dark while he waited. She re-appeared and did a lesbian scene, then a scene with a not-very-nice-looking man who performed with the sweaty resignation of a convict breaking rocks. Ingrate! Checking his watch, John went out to the moustache at the counter and asked if he could rewind the tape and just play the first five minutes. He returned to his booth.

When it was over, he left the videotape with the moustache, letting him know that he might come back later tonight or tomorrow, and he would pay 200 francs to see that first portion of the movie.

'I do not need the whole story again,' he said.

If he didn't return, he added, the shop could keep the tape as a donation. The man nodded passively. He'd seen it all now.

When John emerged onto filthy, yob-choked Boulevard Clichy, it was nearly midnight. He had been in Paris five hours. He had not eaten. He didn't eat. He checked into the Hôtel Lutétia and slept poorly. Next morning, he spent an hour at the conference before ducking out and catching a taxi. A different man was at the counter of the shop, but evidently he'd been informed about the weird old *étranger* and his special tape. It was even cued up to the scene where Her eyes engaged with the viewer and she kept her clothes on. John watched it twice, then returned to the conference. Superstitiously, he couldn't help pondering the significance of the conference's location: XX arrondissement. That evening he declined an invitation to the Opéra and dinner on the Ile St-Louis, deciding instead to go out for a walk, some fresh air, a relaxing stroll up to Clichy.

On his way back to the hotel later that night, he bought a souvenir for Margaret: an expensive colour catalogue from a Musée d'Orsay exhibition of Rodin sculptures. He could think of nothing better, and it would be appreciated more than a bottle of duty-free perfume from the airport. It might also suggest he had been to the exhibition himself. He planned to memorise some facts from the catalogue on his flight home. John also took a magazine back to his hotel room for his last night of freedom. The magazine, *Adult Video News*, contained an interview with Her in which she talked about Her childhood on the road with Her circus family. The next morning, he slept through his wake-up call and had to leave in a rush, inadvertently leaving both the magazine and the catalogue in his room. At the airport, he felt stung by the loss of the 150-dollar art book, and considered calling the hotel and asking them to send it on. But if the hotel staff had found the book, they had also found the magazine. He knew that this particular hotel would never be hearing from him again. He went to the duty-free shop and bought Margaret a bottle of Chanel.

Since Paris, he had been to conferences in Los Angeles, Seattle, Dallas, San Diego, Brussels, London, Madrid, Bologna and

Lisbon. He saw little of what is conventionally seen in those great cities. He had intimate knowledge, however, of what he wanted to see and how to see it. Manners and methods varied all around the world. Cultures differed everywhere. But within the differences he found a pleasing sameness.

Between 4.37 pm and 6.03 pm on the second Monday in December, John Brand drove from Kings Cross to the outskirts of Sydney. Without coastal breezes to flush it out of the hollows, smog settled like a tired traveller in the new suburban tracts. When he arrived at his destination, John drove past the house several times. It was what John had heard described as a McMansion: atrium in front capped by a fanlight window, brick gables with circular ventilation holes, and at the side a glass-topped cupola, a conservatory crammed up against the next property. A tall fence painted 'heritage green' surrounded the house, which was built into a hill overlooking all the other identical two-storey mansions. There was a turning circle in the front, a ragged garden, immature shrubs stunted like a gypsy family around the tumescent brick edifice. He'd never seen an uglier house in his life.

He sat in the car, unable to get out. Like an arrow fixed in a bow, his thoughts needed to travel backwards in order to go forwards. Memory bore down on John. This guilt was his to bear alone. Margaret could never know John's fears that this *thing* of Hammett's was inherited, somehow passed on by John. Could Hammett's problem be inherited? As a medical man, John would have found it absurd, Lamarckian claptrap, as silly as the one-armed man who conceived a one-armed son, or the women who claimed that the image of a past lover in their mind at the moment of conception would cause their offspring to resemble that lover. But John knew also that nothing was cut and dried. When the mistake of Hammett's conception had occurred, what was in John's head? Was he thinking, *I forgot to do it today, why didn't I do it today, damn I wish I'd done it, oh no oh no oh no oh yes*, and thus had passed some of that fever on? Was his *propensity* somehow imprinted on the whirling confusion of Hammett's DNA?

When John was forty-two, he had so loved the nuclearity of his four-square family that the idea of another child, nine years behind Chris, loomed as a threat to throw the unit off-balance, as if adding a long fifth leg to a stable chair. Margaret wanted another. John posed normal and often contradictory practicalities as roadblocks: they should wait until his practice had settled into its stride; wait until he could afford to take time off. Their life had a hard-won lightness, now Davis and Chris were growing up, that John did not wish to surrender. Perhaps they should travel? Perhaps cast off their moorings rather than throw out another anchor? John feared making a move – any move – that would cause him, at some later deathbed date, to regret this moment as the peak after which all things declined.

Margaret persisted and, in time, they began *trying*. John was not exactly wholehearted in his efforts. Oh, there was no question of raising suspicion by refusing to *try*. Nor would he have wanted to cease the act that constituted the very heart in their happiness. Instead, John resumed that habit which had waxed and waned and waxed again, rather than simply died away in his teenage years, and *flushed himself out* between times. That was the way he thought of it: flushing himself out, performing a contraceptive ablution, expending his vital fluids rigorously, privately, so that when it came to trying with Margaret his ejaculations would be sensually convincing but germinally dry. To be sure, he flushed himself out three or four times a day.

He knew of course that this was a far from dependable contraceptive method. But it was comforting to tell himself that masturbation was merely a cover for the important matter of contraception. He was still young enough to kid himself. Never would he have admitted that contraception had become the cover, masturbation the need.

This pattern of behaviour had been going on for some time, during which, for the sake of eliminating boredom, John had managed to expand the vision of his mind's eye during his flushings-out from a purely ablutionary darkness into the florid reveries that had served him in his youth. His inner cinema screened these and newer fantasies, starring certain actresses, wives of friends, friends of his wife, women of his generation.

It was an ineffective vigilance, however, and somewhere along the line he was taken off guard by something particularly alluring in Margie's way, some perfume, some softness in her face first thing in the morning, and, as a consequence, they had – as Margie observed later with uncharacteristic bawdy glee – *put a bun in the oven.*

The moment Hammett slid into the world, John realised how fervently he had not wanted this child. He and Margaret named him after her family, as they had named Davis after John's mother's line, but a name could not paper over the unanticipated, unspeakable, unspoken problem. Without being able to confess, they had in the previous nine years developed parallel lines of love with Davis and Chris. It might have been called ownership. John had *his* son, Davis – placid, reflective, sensitive to the feelings of others, gentle, like John himself. A boy equipped with what might in a more agreeable language be praised as a strong feminine side. Margaret had never been a speaker of that language, and, to her, Davis's thoughtfulness was code for concealment, plotting, deviousness. The way Margaret saw Davis, you neither saw what you got nor got what you saw.

It had come as a tremendous relief to her when the second son, Chris, turned out altogether more in her image. Chris's passion, forthrightness and simple force were more to her taste than the oblique angles at which Davis deflected her gaze. Chris's physical vigour seemed to relieve stresses that had built up inside her own body. From the start, she – not John – threw the balls for Chris to whack into the privet hedge. She let him play inside the house when it rained, keeping a hollow plastic golf ball 'alive' by hitting it, over and over, against the cushions of the leather lounge they used to have in the family room. She taxied him to matches, took him to the SCG, bought him books of cricket history. She coached and umpired. She *watched* him.

So Chris was her son, and Davis his. Even in the youngest days when they went on trips together, in walks across a field or a pedestrian crossing, John instinctively took Davis's hand while Margaret took Chris's.

What then of Hammett? Whose was he? To whom did he belong? The equilibrium had already been settled, the spoils divided. John had his, Margaret hers. What to do with the unbalancing fifth? In truth – though there was no truth spoken, ever – and in the absence of so appalling an admission – that they each owned a son – they let Hammett go to the default. That is, he belonged to no-one but himself. Hammett might have had his mother's name, but he was his own boy, his own man, too soon, granted an independence that he seemed to grasp all too instinctively. He was on his own. As a child his outstanding talent was for disappearance. Very early he understood the political alignments within his family and withdrew into his own world of secrets, familiars, intimate conversations with his own projects.

Had John cursed his son? Had his selfishness transmitted itself into the genetic material? Absurd, yes, but there was no doubting the other traits he had passed on. Hammett had taken on his father's tall sharp-angled frame, his scintillant blue eyes, his tendency to roll his right shoulder in a nervous clockwise gesture when faced with uncomfortable situations, his habit of scratching his nose with his left forefinger as he shook a new acquaintaince's hand, his need to hear bad news repeated twice before his ears were convinced to pass the message to his brain, and sundry other predispositions: melanoma, snot-nose, a tendency to sweat heavily but for that sweat's scent to be not sour but sweet, slightly fermented like a part-rotten pear, tinea between the toes, warts on the knees and a blistery eczema that appeared on the palms of the hands and soles of the feet at moments of stress or unseasonal heat.

Other traits Hammett got from Margaret: the tendency to store tension in his lips and between his eyes, the predisposition to constipation, the lightning temper, the singleness of purpose, the habit of pinching the skin between the eyebrows when overcome with frustration, the obstinate inability to drop a job until it was finished.

But this other tendency – for years John had carried the private burden of wondering if he had passed that on to Hammett, too.

They had thrown their youngest son overboard, five years ago, as if jettisoning an unpleasant burden. But, like a careless sailor, leg tangled in the anchor rope, John had gone over too. As Hammett sank, so had John. Yet not together – had they been together, perhaps they could have helped each other.

Where was their vigilance, the guardianship that it grieved John to realise now, too late, should have been the first duty of parenthood? Had they simply looked the other way? Had they known, but blotted it out?

There had been early tics, habits that had not appeared in the two elder boys: Hammett's early love of nudity, his traumatic misunderstanding when other toddlers would not be permitted full nudity for play. He would tear his clothes off at kindy, try to tear off others'. There were reports of him 'bothering' other boys and girls. What had he done, specifically? In those days, embarrassed parents didn't ask and embarrassed teachers didn't explain.

Hammett loved to disappear. When the family went to New Zealand, to the steam pits of Rotorua, six-year-old Hammett vanished into thick white air, triggering a half-hour's panic in his parents, panic which in turn branched out, like a dye in the family blood, producing high anxiety (John), hardfaced anger (Margaret), derision and contempt (Chris), and fearful visions (Davis). When they found him, nude, scampering in the steam,

Margaret took charge, smacking him for what she saw as more attention-grabbing behaviour. Had they been more clear-sighted, John felt now, they'd have taken Hammett's disappearances at face value. He wasn't crying for attention. The boy liked to be alone and away. He liked secrets and cubbies. He made friends his family never knew about. As a seven-year-old he had been caught with a little girl neither of his parents knew in the back laundry of a caravan park shower block. His brothers would in the same circumstances have shown remorse. The girl was without underpants. Hammett was naked, seven years old, lying back on a pile of dirty laundry like a pasha inspecting a new addition to the harem.

There had been something foreign, something abominably fast-maturing, in him. At eight, he was tongue-kissing girls both older and younger. And this was only what John knew, through the outraged parents of the girls. There must have been more. One day, Margaret ran onto the front lawn to catch Hammett talking to a stranger in a car. The man was leering from his open-top black convertible, golden bouffant and gold chains gleaming. As the man screeched off at her approach, Margaret saw that he was wearing nothing below the waist. He had beckoned Hammett from the garden and asked for directions.

What was it about the boy? There were other incidents, on their holidays – or was it only on holidays that John was around to notice? Older girls, and boys, and Hammett. Strange men and Hammett. Nothing like this had ever happened to Chris and Davis. What was it about Hammett? Was there some scent that these men detected? By the age of ten he was exploring teenage girls' bodies. When he was eleven they'd found Danish and German magazines among his things – women with bottles, vegetables, slackjawed addicts spreading for the lens. Then, when the boy was not even a teenager, there had been the dalmatian. Margaret and Chris had walked in to see Hammett and the dog, Des: Des licking jam off Hammett, the boy's eyes clenched tight with what his mother and

166

brother assumed must be pleasure. Thank heavens, at least, he was not hurting the poor animal. For years it had been a secret between Margaret and Chris, a silent agreement never to talk about it to John, who'd been at work, or to Davis, who had left home to attend university. Margaret and Chris had sewn their bond tighter with this terrible knowledge. It was not until years later, when Hammett had *gone away* and *come back*, that Margaret told John about Des. John asked Chris if he had known. Chris turned it into a joke: 'Hey, Pa, didn't you ever wonder why Des hanged himself in the tree?'

Something musty clung to the boy, an early adolescent smell, a lifetime's sexual worldliness somehow born within him.

When the final act came, Margaret responded with cool-handed resolve while John reeled about in shock. Hammett, at the age of seventeen, already suspended from most of his classes at school, a non-sportsman, a non-achiever, a stranger in their midst, was caught by police. A peeping tom. He loitered outside houses and watched women. Sometimes he took photographs. It wasn't always indecency – often the woman wasn't undressed, but going about her ordinary chores – and Hammett was not caught exposing himself or masturbating. But he had a long, long record of unofficial cautions which, somehow, he'd managed to conceal from his parents. When he was arrested by the police he was charged, convicted and given a suspended sentence. The sentence was enacted when, three weeks later, he was caught again. The police informed John and Margaret that, yes, unfortunately they already knew Hammett. The odd incident. Him and 'his bits and pieces'. They needed to put him away, for his own good. Protecting the community from him, and him from the community. He served two months, came out, and within a week was caught again. He grew violent on capture, and was hit with eighteen months for indecency, wilful exposure, assaulting a policeman in the course of his duty and resisting arrest.

Only his broken-hearted father visited him. Never his mother.

Neither of his brothers. And then, five years ago, when he came home and disgraced himself at Warramunga Avenue, Margaret's word stamped finality: Hammett would not be readmitted. John struggled against it, but blindly. He was outmanoeuvred by his own confusion, his new speechless sorrow. Whenever he neared Margaret with a new tactic to persuade her, she would produce some new recollection of an abominable thing Hammett had done, to counter and silence John. That was when she told him about the dalmatian, Des. She was sad too, but her sadness was older, harder, ossified, a firmer foundation for action. And she was supported by Chris, whose outrage took on a physical dimension that frightened John. Chris said he would kill Hammett if he turned up at home. There was so much at stake: the profile-writers at the doorstep, fickle selectors and national administrators. For Chris's sake, they had to cut this off at the pass. This family had become public property. They were people of interest. As a politician's daughter, Margaret had grown up with this kind of thing. Never allow badness to spread. They could not let Hammett jeopardise Chris's future.

John and his little boy had been routed. The father defeated, the son banished.

Yes, a rout.

He sat in his car. Harsh lights blazed in every window of the appalling house. John was on his own. He pressed back in the seat, feet slotting into the resistant floor between the pedals, trousers riding up his thighs.

It came almost as a relief when his heart started to misbehave. If he was dying, it meant he was still alive. The tachycardia set in. He paused and shut his eyes to listen to the three-beats-per-second music of his aortic regurgitation. Dead blood flowed backwards through his ravaged aortic valve cusps into his left ventricle, which by now was the size of a bodybuilder's biceps. He didn't know what caused it. Possibly rheumatic heart disease when he was young, or infective endocarditis, myxomatous degeneration, ventricular septal defect with aortic valve prolapse.

Or maybe a bicuspid aortic valve, or ankylosing spondylitis, Reiter's syndrome, psoriatic arthritis, the arthritis associated with ulcerative colitis, luetic aortitis, osteogenesis imperfecta, dissecting aneurysm of the aorta, supravalvular aortic stenosis, aortic arch syndrome (Takayasu's disease), rupture of a sinus of Valsalva, giant cell arteritis, Ehlers-Danlos syndrome, myxomatous transformation in patients with Marfan syndrome.

He knew too much, too little.

His left ventricle weighed more than a limb now, more than his liver. He sweated, his pulse slapping like a water hammer. He slumped back in his seat, laid a finger on his femoral artery and heard the double Duroziez murmur. The large carotid pulsations in his neck were called Corrigan's sign. The head nodding resulting from the ballistic force of the large stroke volume was de Musset's sign. The pulsatile blanching and reddening of the fingernails when slight pressure was applied as he gripped the steering wheel was called Quincke's sign.

His body bore diagnosticians' names the way young bodies bore tattoos. My death, he thought, will be called Brand's sign.

He blinked away tears. His pulse steadied: he wasn't going to die here in his suit.

John breathed. Not yet, but not long now.

The business card had turned moist in his hand.

He got out of the car and buzzed the intercom, saw a curtain part. The gate moaned open. John made it to the top of the driveway, his right fist closed around the card. A front light flickered on over the turning circle. His heart flipped over and over, like a fish in a bucket. He steadied himself against a fluted pillar, clammy hand slipping on the gloss white paint, his toe bunting the welcome mat, his nostrils flaring for breath. The front door swung open, and John closed his eyes, thinking how helpless he must seem, collapsing like this for a second time in front of Hammett.

Six-thirty on a January evening. The day has just become toler-
able, even beautiful, with a bushfire haze burnishing the sun. The
grandstands empty into the carparks and the pubs. Around
the country, a long summer evening begins: bare feet rest on cool
chairs, men light their barbecues and mosquito coils and sigh,
How 'bout old Brand?

While the boys play a frisbee game on the twilit SCG, Chris
warms down by banging balls against the fence. Nathan Such
throws for him. The ball cracks off Chris's bat against the hoardings and comes to rest near the pile of ten or twelve abraded red
pills by Nathan's feet.

'So why weren't you hitting them like this all series? Just trying
to give us heart attacks?'

Chris shrugs and, to let the kid know not to press the subject,
drives one back at his chest. Such hops out of the way. The ball
clatters into the seating on the Brewongle concourse, where an
optimistic autograph-seeker, the last in the ground, clambers to
seek it and throw it back.

On the ground, Simmo and the other fast bowler wrestle
over the frisbee. Chris adjusts his gloves on his fingers, rotates
his right wrist, a mannerism seen perhaps a thousand times
on the field today between 11.20 am and 6.10 pm. He flexes

his knees, bone scouring bone.

The autograph-hunter lobs the ball from the seats back to Nathan. Neither he nor Chris pays her any attention.

'Yep, well.' Such tosses a ball. Chris creams it against the fence. 'It's not how, it's how many.' Nathan Such, who only left Chris's side when the shadows of the Members' Stand minarets crept onto the pitch, talks to Chris with the warmth of a new friend. They scored 201 runs together in five hours. Such made 96.

'Wipe that fucken smile off your face,' Chris says. 'You've got no reason to be happy with yourself. Another half-hour, you could've started again in the morning. And got a ton. Dumb fucken prick.'

Nathan Such tries to put on a stern face, nodding as he throws the next. Chris smashes it over the fence. The autograph-seeker goes after it. But Nathan can't help smiling into his hand. He's over the fucking moon. Sure, he's meant to be disappointed. But fuck Chris, crusty old cunt. Fuck him, scraping out his hundred like the burnt bits off the bottom of a frypan: 113 not out, 350 minutes, 279 balls faced, eight fours, no sixes. It is what it is.

Behind Chris, the boys cringe as the frisbee curls out of control in his direction. No-one has the guts to call out a warning. The orange disk shaves past Chris's sunburnt ear and lands near Nathan. Chris continues tapping his bat on the ground, unawares, still locked in his own world.

It's not the first time he's played an innings like this, but he wouldn't have expected it today. He's still mad at Davis over last night, at Suzie over the messages on his voicemail, at Tom fucking Pritchard for the nightwatchman, at himself for opening the door on this Hammett business – and even if he'd closed it again, he'd opened it enough, hadn't he? He's angry about the full list of grievances against his two brothers – got a day to spare? Usually a century leaves you walking on air, yet he's rarely felt so out of joint, so scratchy, so bloody tired. But – here's the weird thing – after that early chance, when the Yaapie goose dropped him at slip, Chris never felt for one instant that he was going to get out. Never hit a ball in the air, never missed one near his stumps. He was hit on the pads and body plenty – his torso is a galaxy of grey nebulas, purple-yellow contrails, blue zodiacs – but he can't remember one serious appeal against him. The future won't remember how, only the how-many.

Chris goes down on his haunches and peels the velcro off his pads. An unreasonable number of people are pissed off at him, given the circumstances. The coach, Jimmy Dent, will report him to the Cricket Board after he refused to appear for a press conference. Despite – or because of – his being the so-called 'biggest story in the country' (Dent's words), Chris said he wouldn't talk to the press until after his innings finishes tomorrow. 'I'm not going to answer all their shit about am I gunna dedicate this innings to the old man,' he said. Dent threatened to do 'the contract thing' on him, one of these inventions, like new technology sprung onto a manual worker, requiring players to make themselves available for 'reasonable requests' for interviews.

'Yeah, yeah,' Chris said vaguely, his mind still out on the field. 'So what do you fine me, ten grand?'

'Five is standard,' Dent said.

'Well, I'm getting off light.'

'It's worth five grand not to spend twenty minutes in a presser?'

'Worth every brass razoo,' Chris said, pointing to Nathan Such. 'Anyway, why don't you send him in? He's a bigger story than me.'

In the hour since that exchange, word of Chris's fine has spread through the team. To be honest, Chris thinks as he tucks up his batting gear like an archer's quiver, I'd give anything to be happy with what I've done. But I'm not. I can't help it. I'd give anything.

He's passing through the gate when the autograph-seeker who was collecting balls on the concourse looms through the fence. She can't get into the Members' area. Chris considers giving her the brush, but what the hell, he's in no hurry to get back into the dressing room. He bears heavy contempt for cricketers who ignore their fans. Most of the world can get fucked as far as Chris Brand is concerned, but you've got to respect the serious fan.

She hands him a greasy, stained scorebook of today's play, and a Bic pen with a chewed tip. She points mutely to where she wants him to sign. He does. Then she unrolls a commemorative panoramic photograph, one of those Channel Nine merchandising scams – 'Limited Edition of 50,000' and all that – of Chris scoring a double-century in Calcutta a couple of years ago.

'Genuine collector's item,' he mumbles. 'They weren't exactly a big seller.'

The girl's hand is trembling as she points to where she wants him to sign. He does. She rolls the poster back up. He's about to make his way to the dressing room when the girl pulls out a bubblegum card to sign. It still has the gum powder and synthetic pink smell. He's smiling in the photograph.

'That's another rare one.' He signs beneath his smile.

Again he's about to leave when the girl produces a poster of the Australian team. It has no other autographs on it. Silently she motions towards the inset photograph of Chris. Uh-oh, he thinks, we know what we've got here – a genuine hardcase.

She's still a girl, he supposes, though she could be almost the same age as him. Her elfin looks and drawn-back hair blur her age and sex. In the compressed world of cricket, Woman is blonde, trussed, pinned, cut from a stencil, and the men of cricket usually only recognise Woman in her conformity to that model. Irregularities cause confusion.

A gust presses her loose T-shirt against a hint of rumpled bra. With her flat chest, twin-barred gold glasses, pimpled chin and light stature she looks like a science graduate, small but not petite.

'You want me to put a name on it?' Chris says.

'Yes! Chris Brand!' she blurts, then blushes again. 'Oh, I mean . . .'

Her apologies sound defensive. Eyelids heavy as manhole covers. Mouth goes rabbity when she talks. Honest, candid, human, straight. What makes her prickle is when people say she's prickly. Chris knows the type.

'Nah,' he smiles at her distress. '*Your* name.'

'Eve,' she squeaks. 'Eve Garforth.'

He sees the way she's examining him, reassessing the famous face up close. He knows he's better looking on television than in person. The faux youth of his centre-parted yellow-blond hair clashes with his burnt red face. His mouth is greasy from sunscreen. His eyes never blink, like those of a lidless fish.

'To Eve, all the best,' he reads as he writes, then hands back the poster. "That it then?"

'I've got some more . . .' Her bag leaps up at her face, swallowing it as she searches for something.

'They might have closed the gates, you know.' He looks around. Two teammates watch from the players' balcony. A high yee-haa rings out.

'Here, here . . .' She pulls out a couple of old scorebooks. They record centuries Chris has made on the SCG before. One goes back eight years.

'Impressive.' He signs them both.

'You weren't.'

'What?'

'Impressive. Today.'

He wonders if her face will ever fully recover from the blush that covers it.

'No,' he chuckles, 'I wasn't very, was I.'

'But you stuck with it.'

'Guess I did.'

She scratches her armpit violently.

'Do you think . . .' She loses her voice in a dry swallow. 'Do you think that sometimes batting is easier when it's harder?'

'Meaning?'

'I mean . . . No, I'm not a cricketer. Thanks for the autographs.'

He's still holding the last scorebook. He pulls it away from her reach.

'Uh-uh. Spit it out. I'm not giving it back till you do.'

He's shocked, inside, to hear his voice. He's *flirting*. With *this*.

'Um, um, well, I just wonder if it can be easier to bat when you're not expecting a lot of yourself. I mean, you weren't in any form at all today, you were shocking – sorry – but I wonder if, in your head, when you think you just have to fight to survive, it kind of focuses you on each ball and you don't get, um, you know, carried away, so you don't take risks or think . . . Um, I'm sorry. Can I please have that back now?'

He hands the scorebook across the chain fence.

'You've never played.'

She shakes her head with the same blushing violence, the visible nervousness.

'Um, sorry, I have no right . . .'

'Well, you've obviously been watching a lot,' Chris says, 'because you've pretty much hit the nail on the head. I felt like shit – scuse the French – my timing was off all day. But sometimes, like you say, when you're not expecting yourself to dominate, you do play within your limits. You're feeling too shithouse to do anything stupid.'

'Gotta go. Bye.'

She tears off, half-tripping on the seats. He watches her drop, then regather, one of her scorebooks. Bits of paper and cardboard poke out of her string bag like the head of a pineapple piercing a shopping sack. Chris shakes his head and makes his way up the race.

Later, alone in his hotel room, he tries to watch a movie but can't concentrate. He's exhausted by all the thoughts the world wants to know. The cricket tragics, like that girl, the autograph-seeker. Inhabitants of the interior land of Cricket where the stumps are never drawn. They know more history than the players and journalists; they love the game more; their stake is unattached to their own glory. Ma's a tragic. She goes to inter-State games where there are less people paying than paid. She sits out rain delays when even the players would leave the ground. With her rugs and cushions, wireless, and boiled eggs in foil, she really stands out when she's one of the only ones there.

Fuck he wishes she could've been there today.

Maybe, he thinks, he'd have been better off going to the presser, just spewed it all out like some of his more 'extroverted' (read 'commercially opportunistic') teammates. Yeah, he could make a headline. And he probably should have taken the heat for Nathan Such, who, because he went to the presser, will get the major coverage, which is nothing but bad news for a young kid.

But fuck it, he thinks as he turns on the shower and strips off. Fuck them all. Fuck Davis in particular, that gullible prick, that bleeding heart, that sad excuse for an elder brother. Out of some misguided sympathy for Hammett, Davis is risking sending Ma into a place she may not be able to come back from. Chris is angry, but anger feels better than the emptiness following his innings. He needs an enemy.

A little while later, Chris sets the gold bar across his door so it won't close, and wanders out into the corridor. He's had his shower and his room service and his massage and his annoying phone call from Suzie, all the rituals of an evening in the home season, and suddenly he feels like company. Next door, the wicket-keeper sits in his room. Back in the days when cricketers had to share, Chris and the 'keeper were regular roomies. Funny guy, the wickie. He was such a light sleeper, he used to stick a bandaid over the infra-red eye on the television panel. Came across in black moods when you least expected it. Chris pushes open the wickie's door.

'Outski!'

Chris backs out, palms in the air. The wicketkeeper is online, crouched over his laptop. As Chris moves down the corridor, he hears the wickie slam his door.

In the next room, Simmo and the other fast bowler are also huddled at a computer. With the glassy attention of teenagers at play, they beckon Chris over. He stands behind them. They're in a chat room, posing as twin sisters, blonde and big-chested, laughing themselves silly at the replies they're getting out of the hapless john at the other end who could, for all Chris knows, be the wicketkeeper in the next room.

He finds himself knocking on the door of last resort. Tom Pritchard opens up.

'Come in, mate.'

Pritchard lies on his bed watching a pay movie. Thankfully, Chris thinks, not a porno.

'Interrupting you?' Chris says, standing with his hands in his pockets.

'Nah, heap of crap,' Pritchard hits the remote, zapping the TV silent with a quick motion that has something, however slight, of the way his hands move on the bat handle or take a catch. A supremely coordinated guy.

'Can't get a word out of anyone else.' Chris slumps on the edge of bed. They both seem content to let their years of acquaintance paper over the recent coolness. Chris picks a practice ball off the floor and tosses it, with a leg-spin over-the-wrist flip, from hand to hand.

'Playing with their mouse?' Pritchard says.

'The old days, we'd have been on the tool. Now it's phone sex, Internet sex, and five hookers at the end of a Test match. All too professional if you ask me.'

'Yeah, but in the old days we weren't half the players these guys are.'

'We have to save our positions.'

177

Pritchard lets this slide. When it's all turned out well in the end, everyone's a mate and every man a genius. Unknown to Chris, Pritchard has just given a television interview only half-jokingly claiming credit for Chris's return to form. 'He might have needed a nudge from his skipper,' Pritchard joked with the camera. Tomorrow morning, Australia's senior pair, Pritchard and Brand, will go out together to build the lead. The nation can sleep easily tonight.

'But it's not just about playing better, is it?' Chris tosses the ball hand to hand. 'When I go out to pasture, my fondest memories will be of the friendships.'

Pritchard widens his eyes and puffs his cheeks.

Chris frowns. 'All the friendships I've made in this game are the ones I made in my first two or three years in the Test team. What are these young guys now doing for mateship? What are they gunna look back on? Great nights with their laptop?'

Pritchard shakes his head.

'Maybe they are building their friendships,' he says, 'only you're not part of it. Maybe it's all going on same as ever, but . . .'

'So it's not them, it's me.'

'No need to get stroppy, Brandy.'

'You're saying I'm not contributing?'

'I'm saying that when you were new in the team, the senior guys were the ones that built all the good stuff you're talking about. Which some senior players still are.'

'But only some. Others are Potholes, right?'

'Well . . .' Pritchard gives a shrug that strikes Chris as punchably arrogant.

Chris isn't so blind as to miss the hypocrisy of his views. He has been a prototype for the machine professional. He knows it. He just doesn't like it. Teams only have room for one Chris Brand. But he's not going to admit that to this cunt Pritchard.

'We've all fucken changed, Skip.' Chris gets up. He pings the ball on the floor. It rebounds up and hits the ceiling, leaving an angry red cherry. 'Some of us used to be mates, and now we're boffing the Board chairman's daughter.'

'I'm not "boffing" the chairman's daughter, Chris.' Pritchard is famous for his patience, his unflappability. He's not even showing a shade of anger. He stands up and reaches with his thumb to rub out the mark on the ceiling. 'Jane and I have been married for six years.'

'Six years? In that case, skip, I take it back. You wouldn't be boffing her at all.'

'And you seem to forget certain things about the good old days,' Pritchard goes on, ignoring him. 'How many guys' careers were cut short because they couldn't hold a bat they were so hungover? How many guys never got over hamstring strains because they were out on the tool all night? And those great days? We were busted, remember? We had to clean up our act. People got hurt. That's why things aren't the way they were. These guys can't go out anymore the way we used to, because some prick's going to catch them with a camera. And why's that? Because we screwed it up. Our generation got bitten, and the young guys are shy.'

'So it's our fault?'

'It's the world that's changed, mate. It's not you, it's not me, it's not the young guys. It's the world that we've created. And now we have to keep up with it, or drop off the pack.'

'So does that mean the world's allowed to stick its nose into my family affairs?' Suddenly Chris gets, or thinks he gets, why Pritchard is needling him – it's all about his refusal to come to the press conference.

'You have a duty to the game,' Pritchard says. We're just custodians.'

'Yeah, my role as a "custodian" is to spill some sob story about my family, because, yeah, we've all got to keep up with a *changing world*.'

'Ah.'

'What "ah"?'

'Chris.'

'What?' Chris is at the door.

'We're gunna kick their backsides tomorrow.'

'Yeah right. As long as I don't run you out in the first over. Prick.'

'Sleep well, mate. Glad you dropped by.'

And the fucked-up thing about Pritchard is, he means it.

When Chris returns to his room, the phone is ringing.

'Chris, it's Jim Cobcroft here.'

'Doctor Cobcroft. I thought you were in Noosa.'

'I am. But I'm cutting the holiday short and coming down tomorrow, first thing. Has she set a day for the funeral?'

'We're thinking the day after the Test finishes. But nothing's set in st –'

'How is she?'

'Fine.' It feels strange to Chris, talking to James Cobcroft with this muted intimacy. He has only known Cobcroft through Pa; socially, they have been two points in a triangle, with Pa the ever-present apex.

'And you?'

'Good. Had a lucky day.'

'Lucky?' Cobcroft sounds perplexed, momentarily appalled, before there is a gasp down the line and he says: 'Ah, goodness, I forgot. You were batting today? Sorry, we're a no-television, no-radio, no-outside-world house up here. You did well?'

'Three figures, still going.'

'No doubt about you. That'll give your mother a real lift. Terribly sorry for forgetting . . .'

'No worries.' Chris feels lightened, in a funny way, that there is someone who doesn't give a flying fuck about what he did today.

'Listen, Chris, I'm trying to get hold of Davis. Any idea where he is?'

'You've tried his pager?'

'He's switched it off. The hospital's put him on compassionate leave.'

'He was at the surgery putting a few things in order before he moves in. I saw him last night.'

There is a silence in Noosa.

'Yes, I've been told he's been there.'

'Anything wrong?'

'Not as such.' There is another long pause.

'What is it?' As he says it, Chris feels he has to qualify his sudden sharp curiosity. 'If you can say.'

'Ah, just tell your mother to stay well, and I'll give Davis a call.'

'Are you worried about the death certificate?'

'Why do you ask?'

'Um, Davis seemed a bit stirred-up about it.'

'What did you tell him?'

'The truth. That Pa died at home, in his sleep, some time after midnight on New Year's Eve. But Davo wants to start bothering Ma about it, and I'm buggered if I'll let him.'

'Good, good, thanks for that.'

'Don't thank me, I'm only –'

'He died peacefully in his sleep.'

James Cobcroft says it in the monotone of a prepared statement.

'So is that why you want Davis?'

'Ah, that as well.'

'As well as?'

'Chris, ah, I'd prefer you kept this to yourself for the time being.'

'Goes without saying.'

'Ah. There seems to have been some sort of misunderstanding. About the surgery. Davis has been in there. Fortunately he hasn't seen any patients.'

'You don't want him to?'

'It would be illegal. Strictly speaking.'

'Illegal?'

'Davis . . . Davis seems to be labouring under a slight misunderstanding that he will automatically take over John's share of the practice.'

'You mean he doesn't? He's not the only one who's misunderstood, then, because Ma . . .'

'This will all come out in the wash, but . . . well, the arrangement between John and myself was that in case of misadventure or death, if anything happened to either of us that might, ah, threaten the good name of the surgery, then his share would fall to the other. John's solicitor will clear this up with you all eventually, but I'm trying to get in touch with Davis so that he doesn't see any of John's patients.'

'But there wasn't any misadventure, so why should –'

'Quite right, quite right. But Davis isn't acting in his own best interests if he raises questions about the circumstances, you know, of John's . . . Damn fool just went in his sleep, didn't he, made things easier for us.'

Chris emits a lukewarm laugh at Cobcroft's attempted humour. Chris knows Cobcroft would love to elbow Davis out. Cobcroft's low opinion of Davis has always been obvious to everyone except Ma and Pa. As far as Chris is concerned, Cobcroft and Davis can both get stuffed. They're as bad as each other.

Cobcroft goes on: 'I've got the name of the practice to think of. We want to make sure there's no . . . no stigma attached. We have to protect our name, and if there's anything to do with John's death that . . . Damn shame I'm away.'

'I'll tell Ma you sent your best wishes.'

'Don't tell her anything, I don't want her worrying.' Running off and telling Ma is the last thing Chris was going to do. Like Ma needs two spare arseholes right now.

'Okay, okay. Thanks, Doctor Cobcroft.'

'Jim.'

'Oh. Er, thanks. Jim.'

The draught refrigerates the bedroom. Earlier today she would have blessed the cooling night breeze, but tonight, wrenching vainly at the stuck panel of the window, Margaret lets out a malediction.

'Damn you! You be damned!'

She gets off the stool she positioned to reach the sliding pane, stomping her foot on the floor like the boys used to do in their temper tantrums. She feels like breaking something, but only destroying the window itself would give her the requisite satisfaction.

'Blast!'

She throws on a skiing jumper, a third layer of insulation over the pink batt of her dressing gown and the flimsier protection of her nightie. She lies in bed and shivers. She pinches the skin between her eyes, as if to localise, and trivialise, the pain and the chill. Why should the night be so cold when the day was so hot?

She turns away from John's half of the bed, whorls herself into the shape of an ear.

She sent Ian away after he cooked dinner, more brusquely than she needed. Poor Ian. But he does irritate her at the moment. 'And a more absorbing hundred you'll never see,' he said at stumps, giving her shoulder a condescending pat. Margaret still bristles at the words. Poor silly Ian can only pretend, unconvincingly, to understand how Chris plays this game. 'Absorbing' is a received idea, a code Ian has learnt to utter when he is bored. But even she saw, when Chris reached his century, raising his bat and removing his helmet, the deflation in his eyes. She shared – shares – it. She is angry that he had to do this, angry at John, angry at everyone who has turned this game of bat and ball into a family drama. She feels no joy at Chris's triumph. Instead, fatigue, annoyance and a strange emptiness.

Ian went quietly. A look from her was worth all the arguments in the world. Perhaps he didn't want to stay, anyway. For all she knows, he might have tapped his heels together with glee the moment he shut her door.

A mystery, even now! She recalls the time, donkey's years ago, when Ian suddenly disappeared from their lives. Fifteen years ago. They'd had a weekend house party, and Ian had been his usual convivial self. Yet he called her on the Monday to apologise for 'being so grumpy all weekend'. Margaret said she hadn't even noticed. But he seemed irreconcilable, apologetic out of all proportion. Then he didn't call for weeks. Nor did he return Margaret's calls. It was unfathomable. Perhaps he was the one who felt insulted? Margaret raked her memory for some offence she may have caused him, but there was none.

This nonsense had gone on for three whole months until, just as she was reconciling herself to the puzzling possibility that Ian may never speak to her again, he called to invite her and John to dinner at the boarding house. John, who had paid little attention to Ian's absence, made nothing of the invitation and prepared for a routine evening. Margaret was trembling. She dreaded some confrontation. Ian was going to corner them in his gloomy quarters at the school and reveal, or demand, some terrible truth. Tormented, she fell sick with flu the day of the dinner. But John told her it was just a cold, and dosed her up for the evening.

As if mocking her anxieties, the dinner passed off as though those three months hadn't happened. Ian made absolutely no mention of it. He chatted gaily and played some pieces on his cello. He showed them some paintings he'd been working on, and some by his students. He was a model of normalcy.

After that night, relations between Margaret and Ian resumed as if the breach had never occurred. Like a stone dropped into a pond: the surface closed over it.

Relief overriding puzzlement, she never gave it much thought. Now she wonders what was most strange: Ian's disappearance, his failure to acknowledge it, or her failure to ask him.

You never know, do you. She looks at the clock radio. It's just after ten. Little wonder she's not sleeping: she sits in her chair all day and expends no energy save what she needs to hold up her mask of concentration on the cricket. It's something she's promised herself: to preserve her dignity and *not look like a widow*. She has enough friends who are widowed to be familiar with that telltale trait – something ajar, something just slightly unkempt, a single unclipped whisker, a smear of mascara, a lump of dried yellow matter poised on the end of a nostril – that betrays a woman who does not live with her groom. For years she has been absolutely determined, if anything should happen to John, not to let herself develop that widow-look.

But it is so hard. Merely to keep going, from one hour to the next, is such an effort all of a sudden. It seems to Margaret that she has not changed since the other day, since New Year's Eve when she was making everyone comfortable in Chris's suite, when life was still rollicking onwards; but rather, the earth itself has shifted angle. The 'privilege' of her life can be measured in a slightly downhill tilt of the earth, along which she has pushed her men, her plans. Now, in the last two days, privilege has been withdrawn, and the earth's gradient is uphill. She finds herself barely capable of taking a single step. Everything seems to cost so much effort. Was this how John felt? Did his . . . problems . . . have the effect of tilting his path uphill? The simplest tasks seemed to cost him so much strain.

The pillow chills her cheek. She turns, lets a leg creep across to John's half. As her weight shifts, the bed whimpers like a small mammal. She's still not missing him as much as she ought. But this is odd, this bed business. There's no reason for her to be cold, she thinks. The wall thermometer still reads twenty-three degrees, yet she is freezing. She is not getting a flu. Nor can it be that she misses the warmth of his body. Since the very first night, way back in the Menzies era, when they had shared a bed, John and Margaret had appreciated each other's willingness to yield a free zone down the centre. They hated the thought of another body clinging, creating heat, moisture, adhesion, through the night. Sleeping without touching was one of the first grateful discoveries of their marriage. So she cannot be missing his touch.

She lies hoping for sleep, but her thoughts are failing to unravel into the absurdities that prefigure dreams. It's no good. She hoists herself out of bed and goes downstairs in her slippers. She pulls the screen door aside, disentangling some Christmas tinsel, and stands on the patio. Frogs croak in the damp rocks around the swimming pool. The rotten ball bumps the Totem Tennis pole in the light breeze. Dramatic clouds beard the moon. Even with the Totem Tennis, she pushed the boys. They forged their strength here in this yard, this muddy Culloden.

One night, only a few weeks ago, John surprised her with a comment about the boys. They'd been at a party function, where she'd presented Chris to more preselectors, and he had distinguished himself by giving a light-hearted speech to dissipate the tension caused by an unfortunate incident involving an engagement ring. She could see the branch committee's astonishment that a *mere cricketer* could speak as diplomatically as Chris. Afterwards John was unusually warm and, even more unusually, came to bed at the same time as her. They chatted away – she remembers saying how smooth Chris's run would be from cricket into the preselection – and then John said: 'Have you ever thought about Davis?'

He'd come out with some twaddle about doctors being well regarded by the electorate. She had pooh-poohed this, but he insisted: 'I do mean it, sweetie. Are you sure Chris is cut out for politics? You haven't really asked him, have you?'

After a long period of shallow wakeful breathing, she said, 'John, where has this come from?'

She tilted herself up on her elbow. He was blinking at the ceiling with a strange, tense excitement. Typical John: waiting until the very, very last moment before saying, almost as an aside, what was on his mind.

'Why,' he pressed, 'are you only ambitious for one of our sons? What happened to the other two?'

He was opening a door for her, but she wouldn't enter.

'John,' she said, 'what are you doing?'

'I don't know. What am I doing?'

She slumped back onto her side, curling away from him.

'I think we should discuss this in the morning,' she said.

But there never was a next morning. John went to work, and the matter was dropped, like every other obstacle. They were a family who circumvented. Even that Friday-night *fit* of his in front of the family (she'd selected the appropriate word, after testing out a few others, for her inner glossary) still went un-discussed.

It still prickles her, however, his sneering at her ambition. Without her, where would Chris and Davis have ended up?

Margaret remembers the day about thirty years ago when she enrolled them both in the local rugby club. She volunteered to coach. She'd have made a wonderful coach, football and cricket, but would those fathers let a woman coach their boys? Not a chance. It had been utterly frustrating. But Chris made up for her disappointment, showing extraordinary coordination from a very early age. He was well ahead of Davis, who was rather timid.

187

Because Chris was so strong and skilful, and Davis so shy, they were put in the same team. In that first game, a boy from the opposition went down injured on halfway. The game continued. Davis, who was supposed to be playing fullback – the last line of defence – was crouching down with the hurt boy, asking if he was all right. And the opposition broke through and ran straight past him! John thought it was delightful. But Margaret was incandescent with rage. She and Chris teased Davis for being 'a girl'. They were different times, weren't they? She felt calling Davis names would toughen him up, encourage him to try harder. But here was John, boasting that they had another doctor in the family. Margaret said: 'This is not a good thing, John. This is a bad thing.' She was furious! She didn't like it that Davis had been nice to the other boy, and appeared happy to forget about the game. That showed precisely what was lacking in Davis. He was not fulfilling his potential.

But John never cared for any of that.

So it wasn't her fault and John had no right to renegotiate the future as Davis's advocate. She, not John, was their generation's norm. People she knew were like her – competitive and ambitious for their children. If your children didn't achieve, they – and you – would slip away and be lost. There were the rails, and there was going off the rails, and nothing in between. She wasn't unusual, far from it, in holding those beliefs. She certainly had the boys' welfare at heart. And one day they'd thank her for it.

Yet now, as she stands in the breeze, on her own, in their garden, overlooking the pool, with the moonlight shining down on her like a lonely trumpet, she knows what that conversation in bed was really about. It wasn't about Chris, and it wasn't about Davis.

She tilts her face up and looks at the stars, pinpricks of a brighter light behind the perforations of a threadbare universe.

She crosses the patio and sniffs the jasmine, little bursts of sweetness, and touches the long cigar branches of the frangipani.

It's really a lovely garden. John planted it so that something would bloom every month of the year. This was where he came when he was sleepless or quietly desperate, and she can see how much it has to recommend it. She spends so little of her life alone – she's not a person who's ever felt she could achieve much on her own, stewing over things – but tonight, and last night too, she feels solitude as a relief from the oppression of the people around her. Poor Ian. It would devastate him to know. But it's not just him: they're all getting on her wick. She wonders if this was how John felt most days, if this was why he made the darkness his own. He used to sneak down here, into the very back of the garden, when he thought no-one else knew. Whenever the family came around, for instance, off he'd dart. Chris or Davis would arrive, and wink: 'Where's Pa?' They all knew where he was, and he thought he was so subtle about it. Eventually he'd show up on the back step, wiping his hands, and give them a look of surprise as if he'd forgotten they were coming. Priceless, that look.

How sharply her eyes have adjusted to the night. She can make out all of John's beloved nameless trees, right down to the access lane. I have come here, she thinks, for a reason.

Funnily enough, it was Margaret, not John, who'd come down here to hide on that day when they last saw him. Hammett. Five years ago, when the boy was nineteen, a week after he had finished his year and a half in the low-security institution. It had taken a full week for Margaret to consent to Hammett's entering their property. Their meeting was gruesome, a disaster.

Margaret had been gardening – right here, watering the privet hedge. John met Hammett at the door, and brought him through the house and out by the swimming pool to see his mother. Margaret pretended to be very busy, and Hammett had responded by dragging an outdoor chair – this banana chair – to the corner she was watering. He was gibbering hyperactively, telling stories about his time inside that awful place. Evidently he found it very humorous, laughing at his own stories, filling the all-too-obvious silence.

Margaret watered the privet.

The boy was strange, as if the places he had been were more strongly burnt into him than the family from which he had sprung. He grew red and breathless, though he affected a light-hearted air, as if coming home from a holiday, and as if these events he was relating could possibly interest or amuse his mother. He was telling them about a 'friend' of his, 'inside'.

'Yeah no, he was on a patriot kick. Wanted the boys to tatt "God and Country" across his shoulderblades. Instead we pinned: "God and C—t".' (Margaret cannot say the word to herself, though she remembers the distressingly easy way it tripped off Hammett's tongue.) 'Got around, and guys'd ask him to take his shirt off, they wanted to see it. No point fighting it, and in the end he liked it. It was his Thing. He was the God-and-C—t guy, and he'd even introduce himself to newbies as "G-and-C" and ask them if they wanted a squiz.'

Margaret continued watering, presenting Hammett with her square back. She had rehearsed a speech to welcome her son. She had been prepared, after making her point, to give ground. But Hammett swamped her with his nervous details, this sense of humour which, more than anything he might have done or seen or anything she might have imagined, was the most alien, repulsive, poisonous thing. He told his stories as if expecting her to laugh along.

Without the benefit of a reaction – not counting Margaret's stoic non-reaction – Hammett pressed on. She'd left him nowhere to go but up.

He began talking about a night when he was ten or eleven years old. Margaret paused, a tremor in her watering hose, as if willing to listen. Hammett said that in the middle of the night he had been unable to sleep. He'd walked by his parents' room. Hammett said the bed had squeaked rapidly, then stopped. Then he'd heard a happy sigh – his father's – and 'a big smacking kiss, a familiar goodbye-I'm-off-to-work kiss'. Then the deep sigh again, and through the sigh his father's voice: 'Thanks, darl.'

It was a cruel enough story. It may have been true. That was hardly the point. Margaret continued watering with a furious kind of stillness. The worst was not that he'd chosen to tell this story – the worst was that he told it as if fondly recalling happy family times.

Until that conversation, Margaret had forced herself not to think of her family as a random collection of coincident beings – the cruel, adolescently 'logical' view advanced by Hammett. Hammett did not know how bitterly she had battled to hold onto this idea, against all the persuasions of her society and the wrenching of her grief. But as Hammett prattled on in this garden, about his friends, his tattoos, and then about what he thought he might have heard while eavesdropping on her and John, it dawned on Margaret that by the end of this meeting her fight would be over, and they would be too far from each other to ever be anything but strangers.

'Well,' Hammett interrupted himself. 'Fuck youse, then. I'm off.'

John had tried to prevent Hammett leaving but, giggling manically, the boy spoke of an urgent appointment. Margaret had moved on to the camellias. When John returned to the garden, having seen Hammett out, Margaret said simply: 'Never again.'

Her interdiction wouldn't have mattered. Hammett never tried again. Hadn't called, or let them know where he was. That was the end of it.

Afterwards, John had fretted over Margaret's reaction. Was it the 'fuck' that had angered her, or the 'youse'? John kept picking at it like a boy at a scab. As if it mattered! Why, she wonders, are the *details* so important to these men? Hammett couldn't let it rest, couldn't take it for granted that she knew enough already. Davis, these last couple of days, pressing, pressing, to know every minute detail of John's death. What does it matter? And then there was John and his carryings-on these last couple of years. Whatever else she is, Margaret knows she is not stupid or unobservant. Did John think she didn't have a fair idea of what he did when he got holed up with his computer all night? Did he think she was so naive about men and their bits and pieces? Could *he* be so naive, after all the terrible Hammett business, as to think Margaret was blind to what was going on in her own house?

He could have just come out and said it: a simple word. She would have stopped it at his lips. She would have said: 'John, I know all I need to know. I don't need the details.' But it was the details that burdened him, made him so wretched and lonely: always with men, the details of things that they convince themselves they cannot share.

She shuts her eyes and listens to the frogs. She is rubbing the warmth back into her toes when that crashing sound comes again, making her jump out of her skin. Her blood freezes, then moves again. This time she can break the sound down into its component parts. The deep rumble is not the earth shaking but the wheelie-bin rolling down the hill. The crash is not a wall collapsing, but the bin falling over. The subsequent cascading is not rubble falling down a slope, but bottles spilling on the paved right-of-way.

She's not irritated so much by the adolescents who do this sort of thing as by the adults who live in the townhouses and let it be done. Children will be children; the adults have no excuses. She works herself into such a lather of annoyance at the renters that she marches through the gate at the bottom of the garden and up to the top of the right-of-way. She stands in her dressing gown and skiing jumper, aghast. To her horror, she beholds not one but *two* wheelie-bins lying on top of each other, promiscuously, their combined rubbish mixing on the paving. These people have not even bothered to pick up the bin from last night! They will just leave it for someone else – that's what these renters are like – or wait until they have to drive down this road in their cars. Even then, they'll just crush the filth with their tyres. Disgusting, disgraceful people. Her hands are shaking as she goes back through her garden. She drives them into her pockets. Why can't people be reasonable? How long would it take them to clean up the mess – five minutes at most? Why must they always leave it for someone else?

She will ring council to complain – not about the vandals who create the mess, but about the tenants who refuse to clean it up. She shuts the back door behind her and climbs the stairs to the bedroom. Twice in two nights! Where will it end? These people are animals. It's just too awful.

She pours herself a glass of water in the bathroom. The sounds of her swallowing seem to echo. She pours another; her throat is as dry as if she's been conducting all these thoughts in an open forum. She's hoarse. Still vibrant with anger over the wheelie-bins, she clears out the bathroom cabinet and gives shelves, mirrors, taps and basin a good clean. She might as well make something clean, leave some tiny patch of this earth in a better state. Bonnie and Clyde are coming on Thursday, and she has to make the place presentable for them. Which reminds her of the comment Davis made when he visited, about Margaret supposedly wanting to get rid of the cleaners. Where on earth did Davis get that idea? It was always John, not Margaret, who wanted to sever Bonnie and Clyde, while Margaret argued for their retention – out of obligation, rather than any notion of the efficacy of their work, which both John and Margaret agreed was non-existent. Margaret's compassion had won the argument – so why was it that John got the credit? That's the thing with your children: they fix an idea about you, and you can never shake it loose.

Just as she puts the cleaning things away below the sink and presses herself to her feet, she catches a sight in the mirror: haggard, wisps of hair flying out as if electrified, a ridiculous Austrian alpine jumper over a quilted pink dressing gown.

A widow, she thinks with a wry smile. The thing is, you never know you're doing it. That must be how it tricks you – you never know when you are doing it.

PART THREE

PART THREE

January 4

Wednesday has dawned sultrily, a milky mist softening the view from Davis's apartment. He tilts the venetians just wide enough to catch the mother-of-pearl light. The heat rakes a flat pain, like poured concrete, from his eyeballs over his scalp.

He goes through his empty kitchen in a state of mild irritation, a hard ball of frustration in his stomach. He's left nothing in the fridge. He checks the messages on his phone.

Lucy's voice says she wants to meet him 'urgently' tonight. He calls her back, and her message voice answers. The sheer hard work of courtesy exhausts Davis. So, to Lucy's unacceptably cheerful voicemail, he finds himself saying: 'Yeah, it's me. I have to sort out some things tonight. The funeral and everything. Couldn't be helped. See you.'

He sits by the harbour window, pondering his next move. But he's too depressed and hungry to think.

Last night he sat under the moonlight outside Claire Mullally's apartment, dreaming she might float out like an angel into the park and answer his silent prayers.

He calls his mother. Surprisingly, the phone rings. Unsurprisingly, Ian Bertrand answers.

'Davis, Davis, how are you?' he says with unwarranted vigour.

'You're there already.'

'Just doing what I can. At this moment, eggs on toast.'

He pictures Ian in one of Ma's aprons, fussing around the kitchen. No wonder Pa never saw the wolf for the sheep's clothing. Davis is more certain than ever that Ian Bertrand and Ma are lovers. Have been for years. It makes total sense, but was just too obvious for everyone to acknowledge. If Chris can say, 'Everyone knows you've been mooning after the locum', then Davis can say to his mother, 'Everyone knows you've been having an affair with Mr Bertrand.' So there.

'Can I talk to my mother?'

'Is it all right if you give her a break just now? Chris is . . .'

'Ah, yeah, let's all wait for Chris to bat and then we can talk.'

Ian lets the silence sit, as if daring Davis to push it. Davis remembers an urban myth from school: Mr Bertrand's Spinning Wheel. Bertrand had this big leather swivel chair in his office. He'd gather his advanced English students there, six or seven of them, every lunch. The story went, Bertrand would get the advanced English boys to surround him in a circle with their mouths open, like laughing clowns. Then he'd whip out his knob and spin himself in his swivel chair, his knob going bdbdbdbdbdbdbd around the circle like the *Wheel of Fortune* wheel. Wherever he stopped, that kid had to slob the knob.

Parents, Davis thinks, have no idea of the world their sons concoct. And vice versa – he thinks of the trousers, the material on Pa's computer. Cluelessness cuts both ways.

The conversational pause becomes uncomfortable. Davis pictures Bertrand as a fish, hovering over a baited hook.

'I can hear your mother calling. I'd better go.' And swimming away.

'You do that,' Davis says.

The air feels like a full sponge, waiting to be squeezed out in rain. Davis clamps a cold washer to his forehead and lies on the chaise longue. The lesion on his lip throbs in time with his headache. And now the phone rings.

He screens the call. The caller ID says: Lucy Office.

Damn her. He can't be bothered talking to her though, nor, it seems, can she be bothered leaving a message.

It is midmorning when he calls the surgery. The receptionist must be off, because an automated voice asks Davis to press this, then that, followed by the hash key. Sometimes he thinks he is spending his entire life being followed by the hash key.

While on hold he fixes himself a cup of coffee, hoping the caffeine will speed the headache through, and out of, his system.

'Davis, how are you? Holding up?'

'Yes, fine. Thanks. Ah, you're back from Noosa.'

'I've been wanting to talk to you.'

'Mmm, Ian Bertrand told me.'

'What did he tell you?'

'Nothing. Just that you wanted to speak to me. But that's, ah, fine, because I wanted to speak to you.'

He waits for Dr Cobcroft to speak. Dr Cobcroft must also be waiting for Davis to speak.

'I have a few questions about my father's death certificate. First of all, it mentions aortic stenosis, and this is the first I've heard of it, which is a bit strange.' Davis's voice is trembling. He inhales, exhales. 'Secondly, the certificate is signed by someone who was not my father's regular physician. Thirdly . . .'

'Davis –'

'Thirdly, the certificate is taken off Pa's pad. His own pad! Forgive me, but I don't quite understand how this came about. And fourthly, fourthly –'

'Davis, calm down.'

'Fourthly, I can't see how the person who signed this death certificate did it. He must have been up on the North Shore after midnight on New Year's Eve to see my father, then gone into the surgery on the other side of the harbour, got Pa's pad, also got a cremation form, then raced back up to the North Shore, completed the documentation, then disappeared to Noosa, all in a few hours. I don't know about you, but to me that sounds like –'

'Davis, your father is gone.'

'Ah, but not forgotten! See? Not forgotten, Doctor Cobcroft, and I want my questions answered!'

'He died of heart failure. You've read the certificate.'

'Which is typed. Not handwritten. Typed. This Superman of the medical profession must also have had time to find a typewriter at that time in the morning, and then, and then . . .'

'Nonetheless, he died of heart failure.'

'What do you mean, heart failure? That's how everyone dies. Their heart stops. And how can you certify his death? You weren't his doctor.'

'You don't know that.'

'So you're telling me you were?'

'Davis, do you want your father to go to the state coroner? Do you want to challenge this and put your mother through an inquest? I can understand your questions, boy, but you should think very carefully before you take that step. Very carefully indeed.'

'So were you his doctor or not?'

'Come on, boy, you know what he was up to.'

'I know, do I?' Davis's voice breaks into half-laughter, half-tears. 'What the hell do I know?'

'You know what he did when he stopped seeing you. He just, he went to anyone, got referrals and scripts when he, when he needed them. Bulk-billers, medical centres. Any old place. He wanted to go out alone. As he'd always said he would.'

'You weren't his doctor, and you broke the law. You certified a death when you don't know how he died. You made up this garbage about aortic stenosis to avoid an inquest.'

There is a long silence, which, this time, Davis steels himself not to break.

Finally, Cobcroft sighs: 'Show me a doctor who wouldn't save a family the trauma.'

'It's my own father, and nobody's being straight with me.'

'Davis.' Cobcroft's voice has a fissure running through it, as if he is so tired he might fall over. 'You want to consider your own interests.'

'What's that supposed to mean?'

'Your whole future is at stake, Davis. You want to open this can of worms? Do so at your own peril. You won't be able to control the consequences.'

'What do you mean, my own future?'

With a gentle solicitude that annoys Davis more than any harsh rebuke, his father's partner informs him of the legal arrangement affecting the ownership of the practice.

'So I won't be getting Pa's share,' Davis says. 'Well, congratulations, Jim. You've got what you wanted.'

'We've got a lot of things to work through, and there are a few, well, circumstances surrounding your father's –'

'Yeah, yeah, whatever.' Davis needs, with an urgency that almost sucks his face off, to end this phone call.

'I'm sorry, Davis, but we'll let the dust settle and then –'

'I've got to go. Thanks for telling me where I stand.'

Davis hangs up the phone with a killer's gentleness, then rips the jack from the wall.

It takes him five minutes to find the drawer in which he has buried his season pass.

There is one activity that can transport him, allow him to surrender to time's passage and be as lazy and wanton as he wishes. There's one non-psychoactive, non-pharmaceutical activity that you can do for a whole day, surrender your soul to, yet not have to worry about the hours you are wasting.

It is only when he arrives at the SCG that Davis remembers why he so seldom comes to the cricket: the traffic, the humidity, the sleazy promoters who emerge from Sydney's undergrowth. The terrible pitch, the tussocky football-abraded outfield, the effrontery of the architecture, the unreliable facilities, the shopworn tackiness. His heavy old binoculars twisted by the strap, dividing his fingers into red meat and white tips, he joins the flow outside the Members' entrance. Midday mugs hot penitence out of a Christmas-tired city. He keeps his eyes down on the path's porous skin, its chewing-gum moles, its skateboard-wheel scars.

He'd expected to be inside the ground in five minutes, but as Ma has always told him – as she always told Pa – the Brand men carry five-minutes estimations like coins in their pocket. 'Everything's five minutes,' she used to complain when Pa was late. 'You think the Bridge toll is twenty cents and everything takes five minutes. When you think something's going to take five minutes,' she said, 'why don't you take inflation into account?'

As in airports, people at the cricket bring their own dress codes. Loose singlets jostle buttoned blouses, thongs tread on leather boots, careful make-up mingles with suncream. Physical adjacency throws differences into high relief. Yet the romantics, the dreamers, bless the cricket ground as the great mixing bowl of the classless society. It's bullshit, Davis thinks as the queues curdle and the classless society funnels apart. Towards the Members' Stand go the long trousers, crepe-soled shoes redolent of top-dressed lawns and air-conditioned cars, smart walkers with grey leather and perforated vents. Davis has always loathed the Members. Their pinstriped shirts, moleskins, club ties, navy blazers, Foster's farts hissing from glistening puffed lips. Their wrinkled underdone-egg eyes floating on bloodspecked whites. Their shoulder-slapping laughter spilling indecently. A gaggle of Young Nationals swings in, their path a drunken sine wave. Their cackling cracks off the prison-brick walls. One amuses the others with an impression of a barking dog and a joke. 'What's better than licking a mandarin? Eh? Licking Amanda out!' Among them is a guy Chris told Davis about, an ex-player who won dressing room bets with dick tricks. He'd stack dollar coins on the end of his penis and stretch his foreskin over them. He could twist his penis around itself, like a corkscrew, ten times. Davis can't help his eyes sliding to the man's moneymaker, imagining it ragged and weary, an organ-grinder's superannuated chimp.

The barking-laughing men turn their eyes on Davis, laughing at him, or just turning towards him as they're laughing, but suddenly he's something to laugh at too. Led by the dick-tricks player, they jump the queue and waltz in the VIP gate.

Meanwhile the General Admission people slop to the public entrance, their hairy thonged feet and droopy-hemmed sundresses and eskies rimed with the dirt of bus-stop waits. The Members discuss where they'll watch the match. The unwashed have no choice: they'll spill to their controlled seats in the rain-drenched sun-warped concourses and Hill.

Inside the gate, Davis climbs the steps to the Members' Stand. The first-deck bar reeks of kegged beer and cologne, blue blazers and club ties. The early starters – more florid young men than old, denims and collared shirts and deck shoes, refugees from agoraphobic open air – use it as a halfway house: out, but not outside.

The morning dawned too hot not to rain, and sure enough the game has been delayed. Layers of hessian and blue tarpaulin cover the pitch. Ground staff in myrtle-green raincoats huddle like sea birds. The colours of the crowd have smoothed to the slickness of raincoats and umbrellas.

Davis moves into an undercover seat in the Members' area. He inhales the SCG cocktail: tomato sauce, cigarette ash, beer, bitumen, pie meat, boiling fat, hot chips, fresh-cut grass. An elegant woman in front fidgets irritably, sighing and tooth-sucking to get the message to a fellow in the row behind her, a bald man with binoculars annoying the strangers around him with droning prognostications on the state of the game – this game and The Game. A man in a panama wheels around: 'Save your forecasts for the weather.' People chafe against each other, as on long-distance flights. Something about these strangers will stay with them. One day they will see one of them in a shop or a train station – can't quite place them, but you know them and know you dislike them. Seven hours is a long time to be thrown together.

When the rain eases the umpires come out with their hats off, looking naked. A relieved cheer greets the announcement that play will soon begin, and half an hour later Chris and Tom Pritchard come out, rolling their arms and twisting their torsos, stopping to flex their thighs by pulling each ankle up behind a buttock, blinking up at a sun that has broken through like a boil.

The game restarts. The morning rain has freshened the players like plants. The grass glows green as England. Wild-eyed and dangerous, rainforesty, both teams throw themselves into the struggle. The air's coolness grips the ball and curves its flight. Beneath its rain-laden covers the pitch has sweated, so when the ball hits the seam it ducks and bounces and cuts. Sprightly, wide-eyed in the post-rain cool, the South African bowlers are rejuvenated. Their fielding cordon claps and shouts as if it's party hour. The crowd, also renewed, rouses itself and cheers with pent-up force. The bowlers threaten a rout under the low clouds. Tom Pritchard takes a wild swing: Out! The next man, bewildered, follows. A perfect ball takes the next: three wickets in ten minutes. But although the ball is zigging in the air and zagging off the pitch, it is finding the heart of Chris's bat. Fours fly through cover and over square leg, fielders dive to make dazzling saves, coating their trousers with grass stains like gumbo. Mobile phones trill as friends call eyewitnesses.

Chris has come to work thinking monuments: a grand tower of an innings to crown it all. The finest batsmen are remembered for the one edifice: Taylor's 334 at Peshawar, Border's pair of 150s at Karachi, Waugh's 200 at Kingston, Lara's 375, Gooch's 333, Laxman's 281, Hayden's 380. Just one big one would satisfy him.

When he's rid of that cunt Pritchard in the first over, Chris feels blissfully alone. The steady fall of wickets at the other end, the inability of his batting partners to cope with the conditions, entrenches the feeling that he is living in a parallel world where he sees the ball larger, slower, fatter, where the gaps in the field are hardwired into the strength of his muscles and the tilt of his wrists, where he knows what's going to happen just before it does.

Noise and pressure wash off him like water. In front of all these people, he is alone.

A monument. It's not beyond him.

From where Davis sits, the field is a heartbeat. As the bowler gallops in, fieldsmen converge on both sides like a contracting muscle. As the ball is released the muscle tightens to maximum tension and then dilates, fieldsmen easing upright, pausing for a clap and a shout, then sliding back out to their starting points. One beat. From down here – where it's hard to see the ball – you must deduce its whereabouts from these movements and body language. From down here it is a game for the educated. Deprived of the ball, you must be able to read the codes.

Now Chris is facing. The South African bowler rolls in. His run-up has viscosity, as if he's wading through water. His action is a violent whir of chest and arms, discharging the ball at great pace. The arena fills with a rising roar, crescendos with the delivery, and bursts like a gum bubble as he lets go.

His first two balls pass through to the wicketkeeper. The third is straighter; Chris must play. He constructs his body and equipment into a watertight defensive stroke. The ball kicks, hits his bat handle, runs up his thigh, strikes his stomach, drops to the ground, exercises its residual spin and bobbles back to his wicket. His head darts around in every direction except where the ball has gone. It barely grazes the bottom of the stump, unsettling one of the bails, which falls in a tinkle known to batsmen as the death rattle. The fielders leap. The crowd, after a confused pause, responds to the players' celebrations with a groan. But Chris is staying, not walking. He's adjusting his glove. Eyes go to the umpire, whose arm is extended to signify a no-ball. As the realisation spreads that Chris Brand is not out, saved by a technicality, the SCG revises itself into a giant locus of joy. Even the elegant woman jumps like a girl, and the panama-hat man dances a hornpipe.

The over ends in pure carnival. Chris, swashing but not buckling, lashes the next three balls to the boundary. Davis is amazed: his brother never bats like this. He's still wearing the black armband, so there's an unseemliness to this bacchanalian riot. He steps away from his wicket, in contravention of technique, and hoicks the ball for another boundary to end the over.

The tea break arrives, and Chris comes off with more than 200 runs, more than the entire South African team. Children cram below the players' balcony, crying out for Chris, the hero. Helmet under his arm, he pauses and signs autographs. Davis is repelled by them, as if by a naive younger self. Yes, he used to collect autographs, but he threw out his collection when Chris's rise familiarised him with the swaggering immaturity, pettiness and crass stupidity of cricketers. *I grew out of cricket.* Davis would like to block these children from coming near a man such as his brother. A hero, a hero.

He's past 200 now. The only thing that can stop him is a declaration from Pritchard. But if there's one weakness in Pritchard for which Chris is grateful, it's his hunger for popularity. Tom would be crucified. It'd be like telling Michelangelo that half of the Sistine Chapel is good enough, mate, give someone else a go now. They'd lynch him.

Brick by brick Chris builds his monument. Now and then he casts a glance to the press box. All those pricks who said he should have been dropped. Audi, Binary – he'll order them a serving of crow followed by a dessert of humble pie. They can get fucked. Maybe they'll have to acknowledge him as a 'genius'. But they never would, would they: Chris Brand is, at best, a 'master craftsman'. The man you'd want batting for your life. For 'genius', there has to be some kind of sex appeal, some aesthetic satisfaction of which they, those limpdicks in the box, are the sole arbiters. It's to compensate for their own impotence, their sad inability to step over the white line; they try to impose some other kind of judgment on players that is not made by pure runs. Well, if that's the way they want to be, Chris will give them genius. He'll play like Viv and Bradman. Give them no choice.

Will it ever stop? Maybe he can build one giant wall that will block out all criticism, all challenge. But will it stop? Even now, every moment he's out here – crack, another four – he's correcting Suzie. Will she ever stop? Will his brothers ever stop?

After he came back from Pritchard's room and stripped off for bed last night, he called Suzie. Too weary to argue, they had a nice chat. She knew what he wanted – his calling from bed was code for a specific request – and she'd given it to him, nicely, with a tremor of forgiveness. 'Tidy,' he said. Then, relaxed by their little interlude, he opened up about how he'd been feeling when he was batting. He told her about Davis, and Ma, and how it all played on his mind while he'd been batting, but somehow he'd been able to fight through it.

'I can't seem to push this stuff into the back of my mind,' he told her.

'Of course you can't,' Suzie said. 'You're trying to stuff down all the things you're going to come back to later – at the end of the Test, at the end of your career – but there's no space back there. The back of your mind is full, Chris, it's full, there's nowhere left for you to stuff your feelings away.'

He hadn't known what to say. What she was talking about was her, her and him, their marriage.

But – crack, four – Suzie's just another critic, in the end. She knows that. He always bats well when she pisses him off, when they're fighting, when he's pushing against a strong wind, when he has an enemy. 'Baby,' she'd said, 'would a little harmony kill you?'

Yes. That's just it. Yes.

After tea the grandstands drain out. Rather than watch Chris roll on eternally, mums and dads prefer to get to their cars and beat the traffic. The Hill remains crowded, obeying the timetable of the liquid afternoon. Beer-gutted men step over seats with over-laden cardboard trays, oblivious to the on-field action. They punch an oversize beach ball overhead, or chant to a fieldsman: 'Hey X Give Us A Wave', followed by cheers or boos depending on X's response. They stage Mexican waves, really a pretext to boo the Members for not joining in. In the corporate boxes, guests pick over the remains of their chicken and Greek salad and finish off the chardonnay, glancing at the cricket now and then, an afternoon of big talk with the former players who cling to the game like a faded beauty grasping at her youth, trading reminiscences, living only to be asked about a long-past match, or an innings, the vividness of which has died in everyone's memory but their own. In the Brewongle Stand, children fold up their '6' cards into paper aeroplanes and set them into flight off the top deck. They crane over the balcony to watch their craft circle, spiral and dive into the unwary masses below, then squeal delightedly, pulling back from the rail to avoid being seen.

In the Ladies' Stand, the wives and number-one girlfriends perch like budgies in the front row. Cookie-cutter blondes: Jodie, Shauna, Maree, Tracy, Lisa, Donna, Tash. They lean across each other with glossy-taloned emphasis. Silhouetted, their hairstyles all of the moment – or a few moments ago – they resemble Barbies remaindered from last Christmas's stock. As they proudly occupy their stall, their husbands have been arranging for notes to be passed to eyecatching girls in the crowd, the rising hopefuls vibrating on the fringe of the Members' Stand, clutching their Day Passes, waiting serenely for the prearranged signal – Room 426, 10 pm – which will be folded like treasure into their purses.

With a grim smile, Davis fixes his binoculars to his eyes and examines the roofs and support stanchions of the grandstands, wondering where he'd start if he were to pull it all to the ground.

Too many people.

All this life out here – he thinks of that girl/woman, the cricket tragic who came up to him last night and showed she knew more about his inner state than anybody in the team or in the press box – there must be thousands like her, who are tuned into him, Chris Brand, into his very essence, because they can see it in his shots. Every eye is trained on him. He is naked; the game reveals him. It's shocking beyond belief that they might know what he's going through. They have the experience, or the empathy, to know him better than he knows himself.

In the tenth hour his innings begins to overwhelm him, like a building too heavy for its own superstructure. It's not just this innings. It's the last twelve years, and the twelve competitive years before that: he never realised, in the deep way that he is realising it now, how many people have watched him. Stupid, he thinks, of course there are people watching – that's why you're under pressure, that's why you're good enough for this, purely because all those eyes make it so tough for you. But until now he's never sensed it, in his gut – the multitudes, the size of the crowd, and all of them with feelings and souls like his own. Multitudes within multitudes. That girl.

Far from building his sense of vindication, the size of the crowd begins to mock his ambitions. He's constructing a monument? What bullshit. What will it mean? That he's put on a good show for a few days, won a single Test match among the thousands?

It's all so fucking petty. He's weary, unable to hit the ball off the square. Why the fuck am I doing this? Do I know anybody, outside cricket, who needs to prove himself in this way? None of his friends needs this. That's why they've all deserted him, left him to his fame. Suzie doesn't need it. She'd be happiest raising the kids on a North Coast farm. Davis doesn't need it, Pa didn't need it. Fucksake, Ma doesn't even need it.

But they all need *him* to be doing it.

He doesn't score a run for thirty-five minutes. A Bronx cheer when he squeezes one away to move to 251. Christ. He's fucked. He can't go up and face her. They're in the same goddamn city, and he's pretending every night that he cannot go up and face his own mother until the end of the match.

But he can't, alone.

Why is he the only one who has to do this? Why does he have to be the martyr?

Chris stops the game. The substitute runs him a fresh pair of gloves and a bottle of water.

'Anything wrong?' the sub smiles. He's talking to the finest batsman of his generation – a man who has taken this game apart, with all this pressure on him – standing atop his monumental innings. Chris looks the kid in the eye.

'You'd never guess.' His voice sounds like an old man's.

'Tschk!' the kid winks, making a winker's noise through his clenched teeth. 'I only hope I can, one day.'

Chris takes a deep swig of the water and hands the sub the empty bottle and his sodden gloves.

'Get the fuck off my field.'

The sub laughs as he runs off. Chris takes a breath and thinks: I'm not going to let my own body get me out.

December 12

At 6.11 pm on the second Monday of December, Hammett caught
John collapsing on his porch. He helped the old man inside. John
hadn't lost consciousness, but now lay weakly on a white leather
couch in front of the largest television he had ever seen. It was
penned in the room like a domesticated big game animal. On the
screen a woman in a police uniform perched on the corner of a
desk. Behind the desk a pale man sweated in a suit. The sound
was turned down, but the woman was punctuating her speech
with wafts of her nightstick. John slumped back into the seat and
closed his eyes.

'Nikki Dial.' Hammett came into the room with mugs of tea.

John took the mug Hammett handed him. It read: 'Sexpo '99'.
He sipped tentatively, not quite trusting Hammett's cleanliness.
White and sweet: Hammett had remembered how his Pa liked
his tea. John wondered if the boy also remembered Margaret's
habitual joke: 'Would you like some tea with your sugared milk,
dear?'

John looked around. The gigantic TV, the grossly ostentatious
house, the boy's white suit, the hair hanging wetly behind his ears,
the earring like a suspended droplet of water – it was as if John
had entered the home of some Gold Coast spiv. And yet this
was half, or less than half, of the story. The white leather couch

was a larger version of one he and Margaret threw out only a few years ago. To John's right, towards the back of the house, was a glass sliding door leading out to a desolate yard. An absurd, stately trousseau chest sat against the door – a shinier replica of their chest at Warramunga Avenue. On the mantel were family photos – John and Margaret together, the three boys in a caravan park with a dam wall in the background. For a boy who had seemed permanently vigilant against the threat of becoming like his parents, it was moving to see how he had tried to set up an outpost of the old North Shore.

'Nikki Dial, eh?' Hammett said again with a chuckle. He was inspecting the business card he'd purloined from John's hand. He turned it over to the photo of the girl, the advertisement.

'You know Nikki Dial?' He flashed the girl at his father, whose head was shaking from side to side. 'Yeah no, lot of the phone-sex ads use her. Nice girl. Big American superstar of the nineties. Natural, understand? Gorgeous *as*. Never works now. Nope, her day has passed, this fruit has ripened and withered and dropped off and rotted and probably been chewed up by fucken vermin. But in a phone-sex ad, she's, like, forever young.'

John had heard the name Nikki Dial before. He had been standing in a shop one day, trying to find a videotape with *Her*, and two men had come in beside him. One had picked out a tape and said: 'Nikki Dial, love your style.' They had laughed, the two men.

Hammett shot him the amused look again.

'Uh-huh, I know what you're thinking. You're thinking, yeah no, how can *I* advertise a phone-sex line with an *American "actrine"* on it? Uh-huh? Like any chump would phone up a local chat line and be talking to . . .' He held up the photo. 'She was a gorgeous girl but.'

John cleared his throat and looked away. He wanted to die. His heart settled, but his fainting episode had left a dizzying sense of movement, a pitch and roll, in his stomach. His mouth was dry.

His temperature felt wrong, both hot and cold, as if he were getting the flu. It cost him all his strength to remain alert and upright on the couch.

'Oh, uh-huh, sure, *you* don't *use* chat lines,' Hammett winked. 'So.' He perched on a box on the far side of the room, blinking at his father expectantly. 'So.'

Something in the boy's look – the way his mouth fell, fleshily relaxed, ready to smile – spoke more of his origins than his present circumstances. His was a look that could be described as a *mien*. It was not easily described, this cast of his neck, this fall of his mouth, yet it was as unmistakable as an accent of speech or a label of dress. It was a face seen at rugby internationals, private-school councils, ski resorts. Hammett could try as much as he liked to deracinate himself, but John was looking at one of the Brand boys.

John sipped his tea. His aching eyes wandered around the room. Against the non-couch wall was a chaos of removalists' cartons, polystyrene electronics mouldings and packing material, bubble wrap and polystyrene pellets like petrified toothpaste-squeezings, unruly stacks of videotapes, DVDs, computer disks, magazines and folders. The floor was tiled in white diamonds, like a foyer or a bathroom. Sliding windows looked onto the back yards of neighbouring mansions and the fences that restrained them all from eating each other.

The white walls of the room were bare but for a set of framed posters leaning against one corner, waiting for hooks. The topmost depicted a snarling woman in red latex, her breasts aiming out of the poster like twin cannon. In dripping red script: 'Ashlyn Gere is on her back, and this time its personel'.

'Yeah no,' Hammett nodded at the poster, following John's eyes, 'if there's one thing everyone in the adult industry has in common, it's that they spell like kids.'

John sipped his tea and offered a tight smile. He noted that the boy still clung to the minor speech impediment he had developed as a child and was too proud to dispose of as a teenager. It wasn't a lisp so much as a hint of squelchiness in the side of his mouth. Margaret had sent him to a speech therapist, but Hammett wagged lessons. It was typical of Hammett's peculiarly proud self-consciousness that he preferred the security of the squelchiness to the possible embarrassment of being observed to care enough to work on it.

'Yeah no, you want to know what's going on.' Hammett sprang to his feet. He walked over to John and knelt in front of him. 'Well, Pa. You reckon you've got the sand for it?'

'The what?'

Hammett winked. He had become a winking type of man.

'You got the sand for what I'm about to show you?'

Laughing, Hammett clapped John on the shoulder. With a jerk of his neck he flicked his greasy hair off his forehead.

'C'mon upstairs.'

John floated, zombie-like, in his son's wake. His nausea and hot flushes came and went in waves, and at moments he wondered if this was it, if this was to be, as he'd once heard it described, 'the significant moment'. Frightened and submissive, he followed the boy. In John's state, somehow Hammett represented a source of strength, a stable handhold to clutch.

He observed Hammett from his point of meek dependence. Of course the boy would be strange: after everything, after five years, a stranger. But a strange type of stranger. It would have been hard for Hammett to surprise his parents. Their pictures of his hell had been vivid – but limited by the scope and era of their imaginations. John could never have guessed this, could never have anticipated the strutting young buck taking him on a 'guided tour' of his 'enterprise'.

Hammett lived amid disposable goods. The rooms had a synthetic, new-computer-goods smell, an air of temporariness.

Even though computer terminals were set up with office furniture in each of the bedrooms, even though Hammett boasted about 'turnover' and 'margins' and 'supply chains', interjecting upon himself with motivational gobbledegook, the place still resembled an operation that could be packed up and moved on, or deserted, at a moment's notice.

Hammett told him, in the needily proud tone of the business-man, about his thirty-strong payroll *customising packages for clients' special tastes*. Hammett's business was a catalogue of *product*, chopping it up into scenes and photo layouts, compiling taxonomies and cross-indexes and summaries and reviews, before re-selling it over the Internet. So if a customer wanted a particular type of actress, particular images of particular actresses, then Hambone.com would furnish it. *Filling a gap in the marketplace*.

'E.g, the choice material I've been sending you,' Hammett winked. John's eyes fell upon something very interesting on the toe of his shoe.

How had it started? How had little Hammett come to this? Hammett was only too glad to explain, to answer his own questions. While *on detention* (phrased as if no different from being on detention at school), he discovered that not only was pornography read more keenly than newspapers, books and magazines combined, but there existed 'a level of knowledge and taste that could only be called connoisseurship, uh-huh?' Inmates had their favourite models and actresses, whom they knew by name and about whom they gossiped the way others gossip about Holly-wood stars. 'A lid for every saucepan,' Hammett said. 'It's all about niches. We've just created a means to fill every niche, know what I'm saying?

'There's a huge gap in the industry,' he went on, his hands measuring the gap like a politician or inspirational speaker, 'between the consumer, who has very specific individual tastes and desires, and the producer, who just pumps out standardised rubbish, uh-huh. But if someone steps into that gap, sorts through the rubbish and marries it with consumers' tastes, we're doing everyone a great service. It's the next stage. And man, you wouldn't *believe* the margins.'

When he left detention, Hammett, armed with a client list of current and former inmates, expanded with the help of the Internet. Within two years, he said, 'I was running a three mill a year subscription business, identifying and fulfilling consumer behaviour. We make things easy for the end-user, who's usually too gutless to assert his consumer rights.'

Then, he said, he was bought out by an American company that threatened him with a copyright infringement suit. He was flown to Sherman Oaks, 'where I got taken round the sets, met all the stars, everyone, I was a pig in fucken poop – and it was either join this gang or they bury me. So that's where it stands now – not as fun as working for yours truly, but I'd rather be part of the scene than six feet under, uh-huh, you bet. Market's expanding, and we're growing. I pull down about three-hunjie a year, keeps me off the streets. In this house we've got the biggest library of videos and magazines anywhere outside the USA,' he said, as confidently as a millionaire showing off his accomplishments – but wasn't that what he was? A millionaire? A businessman? 'Yeah no, fucken monstrous, fascinating. Another year and I'll have to move somewhere bigger, like a fucken *industrial area*, imagine that, live in a fucken *industrial area*, yeah, uh-huh. Twenty-one thousand, three hundred and six videotapes, 2,412 different magazines, 671 paperbacks, and lost count of the other bits and pieces, pieces and bits. Pretty fucken impressive, don't you think? Yeah? Uh-huh?'

Hammett perched on the arm of the lounge. They were back downstairs, and John had still not spoken. His fingers were numb, his racing heart acidic with pain.

'Cat got your tongue?' Hammett punched him lightly, then pointed a remote control at the television set, on which the policewoman, stripped of all her standard-issue uniform but for cap and boots, was being handcuffed to a banister by another woman.

'Yeah no, I'd never have placed you as one for the idol stroke, Pa.'

John looked at his mug of cold, half-drunk tea. A cradle-cap of skin floated on the surface.

'Idol stroke. I-D-O-L.' Hammett pointed the remote control at the television, as if it were illustrating his point, then turned it off. 'Yeah no, there's lots of strokes, Pa – I've seen them all, believe me, there ain't no stroke I don't know. There's nasty strokes, and there's Asian strokes, and he-she strokes, and fetish strokes, and kiddie strokes. There's all kinds of strokes, uh-huh. Yours is the idol stroke. It's not uncommon. That's what the studios play on when they create this superstar thing. Some men get obsessed by particular actresses. But you, my own Pa, wow, I'd never have guessed, uh-huh.'

John shook his head and swallowed. He couldn't meet Hammett's eye. Hammett went to the window, where he gazed out at the neighbouring fence as if it were a view of Sydney Harbour.

'Pa – don't shit me, right? Of all the ways you were going to get *caught*, this was the right way. By me. Eh? Yeah? Right? You must have had powerful fantasies about getting caught. Did you see yourself paraded before the public? Your friends, your colleagues? Or was it Ma that scared you most? Yeah? I wonder, uh-huh. Or did you worry about dying, never being able to explain yourself? Yeah. But you'd never have fantasised about *this*, though, would you. Being here? With me? This would never have entered your mind. You fucking tell me I'm wrong. Tell me!'

Deep ruts of sleeplessness were scored across the boy's tanned forehead. There was a look in his eyes that John knew, medically – a look that often led to a misdiagnosis of stimulant abuse. Hammett, on the other hand . . .

Hammett was the ugliest man John had ever seen. This was somebody's son.

Hammett lunged at him. John flinched, as if the boy were going to attack him. But at the last moment Hammett veered at John's hand and snatched away the tea mug.

'Getting cold,' he said, strolling out of the room. Washing-up noises came from the kitchen.

Hammett squeezed his forehead between his left thumb and index finger playing with the fleshy nub between his eyebrows. John wondered what Hammett would say if he knew how this very gesture, this precise fingers-to-the-brow reconsideration, had been inherited perfectly, unalloyed, from Margaret.

Hammett went to one of the boxes on the floor and fished out a foolscap envelope which he spun sharply, but not violently, into John's lap.

'Get a load of some real porn,' he said, and left the room. John heard him stomp upstairs.

Feeling he must cooperate or risk something terrible, John took a stack of prints from the envelope and laid them across his lap. The first photographs, trembling in his unsteady hand, showed two pink-faced women and a shirtless man with tennis rackets, on a clay court. In what looked like a hotel room, a beefy man and a blonde woman toasted champagne flutes. A red-haired young woman sat at a desk signing something. A blonde in a kitchen tried to push the camera away while she was cooking what appeared to be scrambled eggs. An Asian woman and a black man slouched on a sofa watching television. The man's thumb was raised cheerfully to the camera. A tall dark-haired woman in a loose tracksuit was getting out of a car. A woman carried a baby down a set of wooden stairs. A group mingled around a barbecue.

There were more. Women in tight-fitting evening dresses stood queuing for a toilet. One gave the camera the finger. Men and women sat around a table on a balcony overlooking the sea. They played cards. An untidy woman looked up while hunting through a pile of washing. Two female faces peered out through the window of a sports car. A woman in a baseball cap posed for the camera with a dark pig. Another posed with an Alsatian.

'She loves her pets,' Hammett said as he came back in.

John snapped the photographs together and fumbled them back into the envelope.

'Recognise anyone?' Hammett said significantly.

John winced, lips tight, feeling as if he were going to throw up.

Hammett's smile fell, changed, almost without a muscle moving, into an impatient sneer.

'Here . . .'

John flinched again as this young man came at him and scattered photographs across the floor before pushing a selection at his father's face.

'Here . . . and here . . . and here . . . Uh-huh?'

They came too fast for John to focus. He turned his face away from the rustling and scattering and cursing.

'It's fucking Double-K, Kelli Kittering, okay? I *know* her, Pa. I *know* Special K. This one here . . . with the dog. Here! Why won't you look at it?'

John felt the sheet brush his ear. Hammett's loafers clicked to the other side of the room. There was a wheeze as he threw himself onto the second couch.

John looked at Hammett. He didn't pick up the photograph.

'Oh, come on, Pa, don't pretend you're not *curious*. I know what you are. Uh-huh? You have no secrets here. Why don't you just enjoy yourself? Jesus, you still reckon you can get away with this? You're just a punter with a bad idol stroke for the biggest fucking name in the business. Yeah no, I mean, you could have at least been original. But – fuck you, you're dying to look at my secret porno pix – she's only, like, the woman who rewrote the history of human masturbation.'

John's mouth opened to object to the word. Nothing came out.

'Pa. She'll do anything for a camera. Even sit and pose with her pet dog. Come on, the least you can do is be impressed with me. This is the heart of my collection: my happy snaps. Everyone you've just seen is either a porn star or a porn producer. These are my friends. These are my colleagues. And Kelli – boy, I could tell you a few stories about K-squared.' Hammett shook his head, chuckling. 'Oh boy, a few stories.' He sprang forward onto his haunches and glared at his father. 'And don't tell me you don't fucking want to know.'

One of John's shoulders came up in a circular motion, a tic all his sons had either got or got over. He didn't know what to say. His great new skill, discovered so late in life, was to travel elsewhere while seeming to remain in the familiar circuits of home, family and work. But now that he was in the other place, the elsewhere, where was there for him to go?

He tried an appreciative nodding grin, but it emerged as a grimace.

'Fuck ya!' Hammett's face was between his knees. 'Sanctimonious fucken prick!'

John could hear the slight squelch.

Hammett sat up, his face crimson.

'Come on. You want answers? You want to know how we managed to run into each other in the stick shop? You want to know how I know Kelli Kittering, woman of your dreams? You want to know *who I am*?'

John Brand couldn't look at his son. The dregs of his circulation shook in his fingers. He could not speak. He emitted words through a cough: 'You . . . ? I . . .' He shook his head over and over, as if to shake something out of it. He wished he hadn't come. He tried to look at Hammett, but it was like trying to look at the sun. He could believe what he was hearing – he could believe anything – but he struggled with relating this speaker to himself. Was this his son? Well, it was Hammett. Hammett had always been different. He could accept that Hammett had done these things. But . . . that Hammett should be so manifestly *pleased* with himself.

'Oh come on. Come on. Pa? Where did we meet the other week? Where were we? Where were you? You might think it was a coincidence, but it wasn't, was it? I spend a lot of time in stick shops. I have to keep up, see what's selling. And so – you had your own reasons for being there. But please – let's not pretend. You're only ashamed, that's all.'

It had to come to this. They weren't talking about Hammett. They were talking about their common blood, this thing they shared. Why John was here.

'I'm not belittling your shame, man. You don't think I was ashamed? Shame was the first thing I knew, and for a long time the only thing I knew. Yeah no, I saw how you all looked at me. You were ashamed of me, all of you. I was ashamed of myself before I knew what I'd done wrong. I was even ashamed of my shame. Yeah! *Ashamed of my shame!* But that was the first step out of the dark place. My shame became a thing outside of me, that I could examine and do things with. And that was the first step to enlightenment.'

'I . . . I . . .' John swallowed drily. The business-speak, the self-improvement drivel – was there a language both he and Hammett could speak?

'Yeah, Pa? Guess I should let you say something.' Hammett leaned back and made a tepee of his fingers.

'I didn't come here to . . .'

John looked up at his son, who was grinning as if expecting an accolade.

'Yeah? Uh-huh? Caught you by surprise, haven't I? Rags to fucking riches!'

John exhaled. He realised what it was about Hammett – apart from the clothes, the hair, the house, the boastfulness, the tinge of Americanism. It was that he was a *businessman*. Generations of Brands had plied their trade as doctors, pharmacists, dentists, even solicitors and public servants. There had never been a businessman, an entrepreneur. There had never been a risk-taker.

'I came here . . .' His voice still shook. He forced himself to speak through it. 'I came here to ask you to – to stop bothering me. Stop sending me this . . . rubbish. It's . . . leave me alone. Please. Your mother almost saw . . .'

As he looked up at Hammett, John had the feeling that he had been riding a roller-coaster. The prating of Hammett's voice, his boastful smugness, was the rattle of the carriage climbing the highest peak. Rattle, rattle. Up to the top, to where you can see for miles around. And now it stalls at the top. It stalls, and you are untethered from the earth, floating free, dizzy, relieved for an instant from the sense of what will happen next. And now, down you go.

The boy had always been strong. Had he played sport, he'd have made a fine rugby breakaway, fast and fit and muscular and constructed of pitiless energy. He never played sport. He'd preferred his own company.

Hammett had him up against the wall, hand pinned to his throat, John's larynx the only buffer between Hammett's claw and the gyprock. John sucked for air. He felt his throat bruising, the muscle dissolving to blood in Hammett's fingers. The heel of the boy's hand narrowed John's windpipe. The knot of John's tie was also in there, like a barb, playing some supplementary gouging role. Salt tears clouded his vision. He shut his eyes with the effort of keeping his airway open.

Hammett let John pour himself into the floor.

'You could at least thank me.' Hammett was back behind his desk, arranging pieces of paper and videotapes.

John drank in air off the floor.

'You could at least thank me. You could at least do a lot of fucking things. You could thank me for saving you the trouble of having to go out and get your stick material yourself. Thank

222

me for saving you the agony I saw you go through when you were sucking up the guts to go into that shop. Thank me for not phoning up my mother right now,' he picked up a white cordless phone and waved it in John's face, 'and telling her where we met. Uh-huh? But no. No thanks. No praise. I'm the most successful fucking son you've got, and what do I get in return? I get you coming here, to my home, all the way here, oh you poor old man, bet you needed the fucken *Gregory's*, oh my what a pain in the neck for you, the first time in five years you have to dirty your sweet white fingers by seeing your own son, and here's poor me thinking my old Pa's come to make peace, to thank me, and maybe I can show him a few things about myself, show him how far I've come, show him how fucking *proud* he should be, and instead he asks me to stop *bothering* him.'

'But – Hammett . . .' John was on his feet. He stayed near the door. He loosened his tie and leaned against the frame. 'When you think of all the things you could have done . . .'

'To me, Pa, it's your life that sucks, uh-huh. Look at what you do. Why shouldn't *I* be asking *you* the question? But no. Yeah no, you're a fucken arsehole, okay? You're a fucking arsehole. You come here and . . .' He did the hand-on-forehead gesture again, the one that reminded John so much of Margaret. He felt Margaret was here all the time; he heard Margaret's voice, her cranky imprecations to do something about it. Oh, but Hammett had done something about it.

'We can sit down and talk, son. You, Ma, myself. But you have to stop sending me this . . .'

Hammett straightened from the screen, regarding his father with amusement.

'It's you and Ma who have to talk.'

'Ach . . .'

'*Ach* yourself. Now piss off before I get angry.'

Hammett hustled John to the foyer and then, without a word, took the stairs two at a time and slammed a door behind him. John let himself out. He sat in the car and massaged his neck. It was the shock that hurt, the quick turn to violence and then the equally unpredictable flicker to politeness. A minute after Hammett had had him by the neck, it was as if nothing had happened. John waited in front of Hammett's house until his strength returned. As he drove back, it struck John that Hammett had acted like a suitor who, his suit rejected, proceeded to pretend that he was the one doing the rejecting. Such a pitiful, childlike response. John should have known. He cursed himself for not standing more squarely on his feet, for not taking charge, as a father would have.

He went back, the next day. At 12.58 pm on the second Tuesday in December, a young man who looked like an engineering under-graduate let John in, then walked away to a computer terminal. When John found Hammett in one of the upstairs offices, sitting at a desk, Hammett barely looked up.

'You're not,' John essayed a smile, 'you're not surprised I came back?'

Hammett's eyes did not leave the screen.

'I'm all you have left,' he said.

'What is it you want?'

'What makes you think I want anything?'

'You, that material you sent me. To compromise me. What is it you want?'

'You're asking the wrong bloke, old man. It's what do *you* want.'

'I think,' John said. 'I think that you and I want the same thing.'

'Know what shits me?' Hammett jiggled a teabag, squeezed it between his fingers, placed it carefully on the white-tiled floor beside his moccasin-shod feet. 'Yeah no, it's that the four of you really did think you were special. Other people were more ordinary than the Brands. What shits me is that I *really believed* it.'

'Your mother believes it even now.'

'Yeah no, but that's just because of fucken Chris. We are special people because of what he's done.'

'You have to understand – it's why she clings to his career for dear life. Even more after you . . . She needs Chris. It's why attacks on him are taken as attacks on her. Why his victories are her victories.'

'Fuck him,' Hammett snaps. 'Fuck him fuck him fuck him. It wasn't me that fucked it all – it was this.' He flung a hand at the television screen. 'Television. Cricket. Television. Same thing. Don't you remember the family dinners we used to have? Yeah no, we played games, talked to each other, played cards, Monopoly – I remember that right up to the time I was seven or eight. Yeah no, I loved dinnertime. The friends you brought home, the way you talked to Davo and Chris like they were adults. It was a gas. We were one of those families that *talked*. And then, I remember the exact night. I was just at that age when a kid gets the first thrill of being able to talk, properly, to grown-ups. Something clicks. You can look adults in the eye. I was turning some kind of corner. But then – it was summer, see? And the Test was on in Perth. And Ma and Chris decided they had to have it on. And instead of talking and playing games among ourselves, we let our guard down. We were watching it. Then the day-night matches, and we started to eat dinner in our laps. The whole lot of us – just forgot who we were. And the cricket season ended, but we didn't move back to the table. We were bogged in the TV room. Then Davo and Chris moved out. I figured it had all been engineered to stop me being part of the family. I was ready to grow up, join in, but you lot stopped the conversation. All that was left was me, you, Ma, and acres of fucken television.'

'Yeah no, I never knew who you were,' Hammett said softly. 'That's the thing. You were never really there. You worked every day, weekends, sometimes nights. And when you were at home, your head was somewhere else. Fuck, man, your own wife doesn't even know you.'

John thought: It's hard to listen when the truth comes from such a source. To Hammett, he offered a nothing-shrug.

'Not even your wife knows you,' Hammett went on. 'You know what? I used to invent characters for you. At school, I said you were the real James Bond. I said you were a pirate. The Prime Minister. The other kids hated me – I was such a bullshitter. But see, I had no fucking idea who my dad was. Do you remember that night when the homeless man came to our place?'

'What, years ago when the police came?'

'Yeah. You and Ma had gone out to the opera or something. Davo, me and Chris were at home. They must have been sixteen or seventeen, and I was about six. We were all in bed, and then I heard something in the living room. I thought it was Ma and you getting home. I went down to see. But in the kitchen, there was this guy I'd never seen before. He had grey, wispy hair, like he'd just got out of bed. I was frozen solid watching him. He went round the kitchen fixing snacks out of the fridge. He wore pants that stank of wee, and a holey jumper. Fucken filthy. His skin was, like, green. Then he noticed me watching. He looked scareder than I was. But I didn't move or cry out or anything, and after a minute he just ignored me and went about his business. Then he sat down to eat, and beckoned me over. I asked who he was, and he said: "I'm your father." I said, "Bullshit, he's at the opera with my Ma." But even when I said it, it hit me that maybe he was right. Maybe this was my Pa. And the guy I knew as Pa was some impostor. I stood there and listened while this guy spun out a long yarn of how he'd raised his family in this house but had been turfed out for no reason at all, left to fend for himself on the streets, while his wife married a new man and his children went on existing here. I said, "I have a real Pa!" He just laughed and said: "I sit outside and watch you with your pretend father, and it brings me to tears." And then he started crying. I was crying too. He called me over to give him a hug, and we cried together. We cried and cried.'

'He was a child molester, Hammett.'

'That's what you all said. The noise of us crying had woken Davo and Chris, and they came down with cricket bats and rounded up the poor bloke into the laundry.'

'He was interfering with you.'

'He was hugging me. I was hugging him. We were crying.'

'No, you were crying because he was hurting you.'

'They called the cops. Then you got home, and he was taken away. And I screamed out: "You can't take him, he's my father!" But they took him away. And no-one listened to me.'

'He was a known criminal, Hammett – an insane man, a lunatic.'

'So you say. But how could you be so sure? Who was that guy who came home every night, calling himself my Pa? I was the only one prepared to keep an open fucking mind on the subject.'

At 11.44 am on the second Wednesday in December, John Brand was sitting at his desk in his surgery. Bruises had come up on his throat, the bleeding no doubt aggravated by the state of his heart – he told Margaret a patient had attacked him, and she cursed him for working in 'that godawful place'.

Hammett called, stumbling over his words in excitement.

'Got a treat for you, Pa, uh-huh, got a treat, pulled a few strings and made your dreams come true, yeah no, big special treat.'

John said nothing.

'I'm telling you, Pa, your dream's come true! You're gunna meet the – she who rewrote the history of human –'

227

'Please, Hammett.'

'Your fucking idol stroke, Pa – here! – in the flesh! And you're going to meet her.'

'Sorry,' John sighed. 'I don't –'

'Yeah right! It's her! It's Special K . . .'

'I'm not,' John swallowed, 'a teenager, er . . . posters of . . . popstars.'

'Chill, hey, what's weird about an obsession with strangers? We live in an age when every man, woman and child is obsessed with perfect strangers. If you wank to –'

'Oh.' John gagged.

'Yeah right. You don't wank, and you're not unfaithful to Ma. Yeah no, you and your fucking technicalities.'

'Please. I want to tell you . . .' A hiccup entered John's voice, the pop of something coming loose. 'No.'

As he listened to the word, John felt as if he were somehow mouthing it hollowly, for some public record, as if he were being taped, as if preparing for some future court room, when he would be judged for this, and he could say: 'I didn't want to be part of this.'

'Uh-huh, right, I get it! You don't believe me, do you?' Hammett went on, misreading John's silence. 'Yeah no, you reckon I'm bullshitting. But Pa, see, I am Hammett, I get things done.'

'Your . . . language . . .'

'Pa. Just fucken listen to me for a moment. Just one moment. All this stuff you don't want to admit? You think it's just your lust coming out. A little bit you can squeeze out, and it's just fucking . . . fucking excess fluid. But you know, that's wrong, wrong wrong wrong, and I'm your fucking son and I've done you a big fucking favour here, so the least you can do is thank me and pay me the respect, the basic human respect you'd pay anyone who did you a favour, and come and see what happens, because you know you want it and if you say you don't you're fucking lying. Uh-huh? It's not your lust coming out, Pa. It's your self. You have a right to enjoy who you are. Okay? She's coming. She's gunna be here. Here, Pa! You fucking have to!'

'No.'

But why would he be preparing his excuses, laying down his alibi, if he would not have some use for it? That was what struck him as he spoke. He was protecting himself, giving himself deniability, only because he was going to fall. It had an irresistible power, the future. Horrified as he was, he was also exhilarated. He was talking to his son. His son was talking to him. Hammett's offences were inessential: his hair, his house, his voice. What remained was truth, and Hammett was dragging the truth out of him. It was so tempting to let himself fall into this bed of nails his son was laying out for him, because, well, as the boy said, he wanted it.

Come on, John thought. Fall.

A golden sheet of sun levels through the towers of the old stands. Chris Brand blocks the final ball with his pad, tucks his bat under his arm and walks away from the other players, making a solitary exit amid the cheering.

From the Members' Stand, Davis observes through a flutter of nerves. His brother's innings has impressed Davis in its way, but it'll only make Chris harder to sway. His mind will remain out on the field. It'll be as it always was: Chris Brand, a simulacrum of a human being, a hologram of presence while his heart is still fighting battles on the pitch.

Davis sits in a dark corner of the Members' concourse while the stadium empties. The odd spectator gives him a second look, estimating, perhaps, that he might be Chris's cousin. The stands fill with silence, and players go out onto the field to warm down. The ground staff cover the pitch and watch the cricketers playing with a frisbee.

In the concrete and plastic stands, desolate as Russian steppes, teams of contract sweepers and cleaners emerge like nocturnal insects. The sweepers scatter through the tiered seating. Their brooms chafe the paving. A roar of blowers, high-tech brooms whooshing the rubbish against walls and fences, rises from the lower deck and bounces off the ceiling girders. The cleaners, the dust devils, slouch in shapeless blue prison-like uniforms. They bicker like brothers and sisters, which perhaps they are. They're not here for the cricket. This ground, for all its magic and history, its echoes of pleasure, is for them a place of business, a contract.

It's a place of business for Chris, too, Davis thinks as he sees his brother re-emerge, hobbling with fatigue, from the dressing room onto the field. Chris goes through some routine stretches with the coach, a guy called Dent whom Davis has never liked. There is little emotion on Chris's face.

Davis notices a female sitting in the front row of the concourse near his brother. She holds a string bag overstuffed with paperwork. Chris and Dent ignore her, though it's clear she wants an autograph. Bastard, Davis thinks as he goes to relieve himself in the still-crowded Members' toilet.

Down on the field, Chris notices the girl. He finishes his stretching, gets up with his hand in the small of his back, and finds himself smiling at her. Her response is a twitch of cheek and lip muscles that may also, in sum, constitute a smile.

'How're you doing, Eve?' he says. Jimmy Dent rolls his eyes and goes off to join the team.

'Good.'

'Just good?'

'Been a good day,' the girl says.

Neither seems to know what to say next. Chris is stumped by tiredness and perplexity, Eve, apparently, by sheer terror. She thrusts out a pen and programme.

Bemused, Chris opens the programme to its cover page. It's from the early 1990s, the one-day series when he emerged onto the international scene against Sri Lanka.

'You've kept this all this time?'

She shrugs defensively. 'Maybe you can sign your pen pic.'

She helps him find it. When his young face and blond mullet

beam out from the page, a laugh explodes through her nose. She swallows, licks the insides of her lips.

'It was great,' she says finally. 'Today.'

'You think so?' he frowns.

'Three hundred and thirty-one not out,' she says. 'I was sure you were going to get past Bradman's score today. And Taylor's. And Hayden's even. But we'll bat on tomorrow, I guess.'

'Doubt it.' He shakes his head. 'It's a team game. We've got enough runs. I'm going to suggest to the skipper that he declare overnight.'

'The press will crucify him.'

Chris shrugs, with an impish smile that reveals for this girl, like some privileged insider, the depth of antipathy between him and Pritchard.

'It wouldn't be the first time he thought he was Jesus Christ,' Eve says.

Chris gives a laugh that brings up a blush on Eve's forehead.

'It was great,' she croaks. 'Just great.'

'Any other comments?' He's looking over her shoulder. 'Got to go feed the chooks,' he says. 'Press conference.'

'You know what they'll say,' she blurts, honks, her voice coming out with unintended panic. She ploughs on: 'They'll say you had a lucky spirit looking down on you. How you were dropped before you scored? How you were bowled by a no-ball? How you hit anything you swung at? How you survived that last hour even though you were so cramped you couldn't run? You know what they'll write? That you had your father's spirit looking down on you. They'll rob you of what you've done – they'll say it wasn't really you – and it pisses me off.'

His lips tighten as if biting off a thread.

'You know way too much,' Chris says. 'Why don't you come to the hotel for a drink? We can, you know, talk cricket. It's not often we get to meet fans who really know what they're talking about. Hey, where are you going?'

The girl has stuffed her programme into her string reticule and bolted like a frightened filly up the concourse, cutting Chris off mid-sentence. She barks her knee on a seat, lets out a painful yelp and disappears. Chris wonders if he has ever come across another quite like this one.

He's on his way up the race when a familiar face comes at him out of the darkness.

'You can pick up better than her. Or are you running out of choices?'

'Davo. Fancy seeing you here.'

'Congratulations.'

Davis and Chris shake hands. Chris looks at the space the girl, Eve, has vacated.

'We've got to talk,' Davis says.

'I'm about to talk to the world, Davo. Why don't you come down and hear the unedited version?'

Davis is jumpy, guilty-looking, as if being followed, his skin a blotchy map. He chews the insides of his cheeks.

'You were brilliant,' he stammers. 'I never thought of you as so . . . flamboyant.'

'I'm always better in the flesh.'

The museum, where press conferences take place, has the odour of shut-in men. Davis slips into the circular room behind Chris and, to keep in countenance, inspects memorabilia: Clive Lloyd's three-pound bat with its five grips, coloured shirts from the 1992 World Cup, the ball with which Shane Warne took his 300th Test wicket. Cameras, lighting and recording equipment are set up in a hive around the improbably modest desk and cardboard-thin sponsor's backdrop that will come up, on television, as a stately formal setting for Chris's golden words.

The media people talk confidentially among themselves. It's easy for Davis to distinguish the press – sweaty polo shirts, ruffled hair, thick spectacles, unfashionable posture – from the television people, who wear crisp uniforms and concreted coiffures. This has all changed so much since Davis last came, early in Chris's career. Back then there were a couple of cameras, no Internet channels setting up their digicams. Chris used to tell him that the men and women of the press were an extension of the team, 'part of the effort'. Nowadays, he looks on them as a more combative adversary than his opponents on the field.

Chris's appearance sets off a flurry of clicking and equipment-setting, like a boxer arriving at a fight.

'Gentlemen.' Chris sits down with a parchment smile.

The forty or fifty professionals in the room cram Davis into the back. Under the lights, Chris's face turns coppery against his blond hair. The cameras occupy the centre of his view, while the press reporters rush to place their mini tape-recorders on the desk in front of him and move to the sides. Two print guys share a joke and laugh loudly. Television sound recordists, their furry micro-phones poised in the air like koalas clinging to branches, turn and hush them.

'So,' a fruity voice says from the side, 'you would, I suppose, claim something of a psychological victory.'

Eyes turn to Chris.

'Not really.'

He pauses, looking into the air as if at some floating ball that contains his answer. He watches it drop at the feet of the questioner.

'Given the conditions,' the deep voice persists, 'and the extreme humidity, you must have been pleased to get this far ahead and give your bowlers time to bowl South Africa out.'

Chris is wearing a synthetic tracksuit that strobes in the lighting. His tongue runs along his bottom lip as if lubricating it for a speech. He blinks.

'Yep.'

There's a collective sigh. A tall moustached print journalist throws his hands up in the air.

'Your own performance has been criticised in recent weeks,'

another reporter wades in. 'Even your captain hinted that this might be the end of the road. Do you feel as if you'd answered the critics?'

Chris gives an internal smile, shaking his head a little as if to say he isn't fooled by the passive grammatical construction. Everybody knows it is these very people who criticised him and construed some of Pritchard's pre-match comments as a suggestion Chris would be dropped.

'No, not really.'

Another reporter drags on a Ventolin spray and has a try.

'Mate, watching you out there today, it seemed like you were, I dunno, trying to get a bit more, I mean, side-on in your shots, than, you know, well, you didn't really have time to lose form in Adelaide, I s'pose, and Perth you got run out, that kind of thing. Or did you? Sorry, well, it's like, there's been a bit said about your technique getting more, you know, front-on, and, I dunno, you know what I mean? I mean, I mean, maybe the South African bowlers get less of a, you know – or maybe you don't agree. I noticed today you were sort of, you know, closing down the movement, or maybe not, maybe that was more your plan yesterday. Um. Your thoughts?'

An amused flicker runs through Chris's eye. The corners of his mouth curl up.

'You said it. Mate.'

The questioner seems to reconsider.

'So . . . So, um, can we get a quote from you on that?'

'Not really.'

'Then you disagree?'

'I can't remember if there was a question in there.'

A heavy corporate rustle rises from the television nest. Davis notices that the press guys ask questions from the sides, so that Chris's face will be turned at right-angles, in profile to the television cameras, rendering his responses, for what they're worth, even less useful to the networks.

Davis understands why Chris is the way he is. Having spent the day composing their great words, the reporters are trying to put them in Chris's mouth.

Davis knows that Chris minds the television people less than the press. They're all blazer and haircut, but Chris recognises their faces: there's a certain brotherhood in fame.

'Chris,' says a television voice directly behind a camera, 'what do you think your old man would say if he was looking down on you now?'

Davis swallows. The old man? How dare they. Davis sees the cloud on Chris's face. But it's too late – the pens are already jotting, the still cameras clicking – his expression is being noted as 'the moment when all the emotion finally overcame the ice man'. Davis wonders how Chris can keep his cool. The pressure to respond quickly and decisively is as intense as anything on the pitch.

'I s'pose he'd say,' Chris looks directly at the cameras, 'what are you doing stuffing around with journos, you should be having a beer with your teammates.'

The tension escapes through a slash of sycophantic laughter. Even Davis smiles at his brother's cunning: his answer has effectively neutered the question. Hearing their laughter, Chris smiles too. He knows they won't use this quote – reporters can't bear to hear themselves mentioned; it would puncture the illusion of the fourth wall.

'Brandy,' says a television reporter. 'Any thoughts of going out on a high now?'

'Do I know you?' Chris says.

After a brief awkward silence, the television reporter laughs loudly and says: 'Good one, good one. Um, Chris, so – any thoughts of retirement?'

Chris looks at the ceiling and says: 'I'll keep going for as long as I'm enjoying the game.'

'Chris,' says another television voice, 'did you have a feeling in the last few days that an innings like this was around the corner?'

'Well,' Chris breathes, 'you often get that feeling but it doesn't count for anything, does it? I had that feeling before the last four Tests. I have it before every Test match. I always think I'm going to score runs.'

'Was there anything different in your preparation for this one?'

Everyone in the room looks at the questioner, who must have been on Mars for the last week. It's a petite blonde from a cable network. She frowns at Chris, apparently expecting an answer. But Davis knows, from what Chris has told him, that it's often the dumbest questions that get the best answers.

Chris inhales, exhales.

'You know, I was having a chat with my wife and daughters two nights ago, and my youngest girl said I was going to score a triple-century, and I said, well, if you say so, then I guess I will.'

It's pure bullshit, Davis knows, and Chris's laughter is of a different nature from that which fills the room.

The following questions nudge for details: Which child said it? How old? Where was Chris when he had this conversation? What time of night was it? Davis can see it all. Chris has just written their leads for them. 'It took a prophecy from his tiny daughter Brooke to trigger the finest innings of Chris Brand's career . . .' The fruits of experience, Davis thinks. How his brother loves yanking their chains. He can't help a surge of love for the guy.

The questions subside, and the television camera and sound guys begin packing up to leave. Chris is about to push himself to his feet when a high-pitched, nerve-choked question comes in from his extreme left.

'Chris, are all your family going to be at your father's service?'

Chris doesn't look at the questioner. The squeaky voice identifies him as the *Herald*'s guy, who has a rusty voice that sounds like it isn't used much. There is an amount of censorious 'tsk-tsk'ing in the museum. Having got what they wanted – a choice morsel about

Chris's family life – the journalists disapprove unanimously of this incursion onto sensitive territory. Not that their disapproval stops them from keeping the cameras and recorders running.

'Yes, Suzie and the girls will all be there,' Chris says. 'That all?'

He knows the curtness of his response will end the interview. He places his palms face-down on the sponsor-logoed paper table-cloth to push himself up.

'I mean your brothers,' the squeaky voice says. 'Will they both be there?'

Chris's neck muscles tighten as if pulled by a drawstring. He's just made mincemeat of four of the best bowlers in the world in front of forty thousand here and millions on television. Does this prick think his nerve is going to break in front of a couple of dozen drunks and misfits?

'My oldest brother's here. Why don't you ask him?'

Faces whirr around at Davis. But the squeaky voice drags them back to the front.

'Will your younger brother be there? Hammett? Ah, it is Hammett, isn't it?'

There is no time to gauge what the guy knows. For an instant Chris's eyes flicker in confusion and then search for Davis, but he is invisible behind the lights.

'Okay, thank you gentlemen.' Chris gets up. Some of the tele-vision journalists mob him and shake his hand. A sound tech-nician asks him to sign a programme. One of the print journalists congratulates him on his innings and murmurs confidentially that the press guys all reckon the *Herald* correspondent is a scumbag, so just ignore him.

Davis links up with Chris's retinue as they leave. At the stairs to the dressing room, Chris stops to sign a kid's miniature cricket bat. Davis stands with his hands in his pockets, whistling-but-not-whistling, affecting nonchalance.

'I'll assume you had nothing to do with that,' Chris says without looking at his elder brother.

'And I'll assume I don't need to dignify that with a reply.'

Chris gives Davis a terse nod. When it comes to the press, the Brand family is united. The 1991 tour of the West Indies was Chris's first, and when it was blighted by a journalist who posed as a friend of a player, insinuating himself into recreational team outings and then writing a book of scuttlebutt, Davis was the first to Chris's defence. Suzie was distraught, but Davis was the one who talked her into believing in Chris's innocence, even though Davis didn't quite believe in it himself.

'Fucking journo scum,' Chris says, guiding Davis by his elbow to a quiet corner beneath the Members' Stand. 'See what I have to put up with?'

'You're the one who brought family into it. You raise it, you're fair game.'

They've stopped in a windswept corridor, military green, ancient paint shiny against the night lights.

'So. What brings you out here, Davo?' Chris chucks his brother on the chin. 'Came out to see some quality batting?'

'Picked a good day, didn't I?'

'Well, you picked a bad day to get under my skin the other night.'

'You mean, if you'd failed, it would have been on my head.'

'That's character, I guess. Rising up against adversity. That's the way I've always been. Anyway – I accept your apology.'

'That's the way you've always been.'

'So you wanna come back to the hotel? Dinner or something?'

Davis, taken aback by the idea of dinner alone with his brother, shakes his head hard and stammers: 'No, no, no, I've got some work to do.'

'Right. Fair enough then.'

'Sorry.'

'Why be sorry? I'll be celebrating. Ain't nothing can knock me off my perch now.'

'Well . . .'

'Hey, Davo.' Chris punches his arm, hits the bone, sees Davis wince. 'Don't give me that look.'

Davis swallows. His arm rings with pain. A dead-arm.

'I've been speaking to Hammett.'

'Good for you! I should have put you up in the interview, you could have told them whether my fucked-up pervert little brother is coming to the funeral!'

Chris forces a laugh.

'He was with Pa. Hammett was. Pa and Hammett. The last few weeks. I think he was with him on New Year's Eve. That's what Hammett is trying to say. He's been phoning Ma, but Bertrand won't let him through. He wants to come to Pa's funeral. He wants to give a eulogy.'

Davis spurts it in short sentences like tomato sauce coming out of a bottle, stubborn at first, yielding in gobbets, but now pouring. He tells Chris everything he's discovered, through Hammett, about Pa and Pa's interests.

They stand in the breezeway outside the Australian dressing room. From inside come bursts of Tina Turner, Cold Chisel, John Williamson (he launched Pritchard's autobiography last season). Strumming truly, bluely, for patriotic boys. The cricketers' tastes fall into pedestrian step: polo shirts, Jim Carrey, left-lobe studs for nights out at Hard Rock Cafés. The boys' standards: standard boys. No matter how individually talented, no matter how great they all think they are, no matter how their stomachs churn as they lie awake at night, the glue that holds them together is the lowest common denominator. They're boys.

Chris looks around, checking nobody is listening. Conscious of the proximity of the dressing room, he walks Davis out to the nets area, where words can be carried off by the fresh evening breeze. Chris nods with a plotting kind of patience. Finally he surprises Davis by giving him a hug. It is a hard, cold hug, an unfamiliar feeling, as if Chris is doing it not to embrace Davis but to restrain himself from some act of violence. Davis clamps his mouth and eyes shut against the taste of Chris's tracksuit, the stench of homo athleticus.

'And?' Chris whispers in his ear.

'And what?' Davis steps back, wiping his mouth on the back of his hand.

'Exactly. And what?'

'What do you mean? I came here because – because I want Hammett to come to the funeral. And you should want him there too.'

'Davo, Davo, Davo,' Chris chuckles. Sometimes Davis hates this coolness, this poise under pressure, that Chris was born with and he without. Davis needs his anal-retentive routines, his formality, the bindings and trussings of his manners, to hold his basic rage together. For Chris, control comes more naturally. Infuriatingly naturally.

'You don't care what happened to Pa, do you?'

'So what, Davo? So old Pa looked at pictures. Let me tell you a secret. He's not the only man.'

'But . . .'

'Jeez, he'd only have needed to keep half the filth I've emailed him, and he could have been arrested.'

'What?'

'It's *funny*, Davo. Don't you get it? Filth is *funny*. It's no big deal, no dark secret. Grow up! What do you think happens in the big world out there? Bloody hell, stick mags, thigh pads, liniment – the boys buy stick mags in airport lounges, you know. We pass them round the plane. 'Cause it's *funny*. You know how the TV cameras come onto us while we're on the players' balcony watching the game? And some moron says, "Oh, there's Chris Brand, he's reading the *Form Guide*"? Well, Chris Brand might have the *Form Guide* wrapped around a copy of *Penthouse*!'

'This wasn't just *Penthouse*.'

'Hardcore? Big deal! Christ, Davo, I was introduced to hardcore porno in State under-sixteens. That's just the way it is.

God, come to the team hotel tonight and I can personally guarantee that at least half the squad will be watching a porno on the pay channel. And the other half will be marinating their meat with someone on the Internet. What's the big deal? Listen, when we go on tour to India or Pakistan, and you can't get any porno there, we take a team VCR. The manager keeps a stash of hardcore, and we watch it. As a team, or if someone wants to take it off on his own, then that's a healthy way of relieving tension. I don't see why you're so hung up on it. It's a good laugh – a social activity. Everyone does it.'

'But Pa, um, Hammett . . .'

'Listen, all Hammett ever needed was a clip over the ear. We should have been tougher with him. Given him a sense of humour. Because this stuff is *funny*. Remember Hank Johnson at school? Caught buffing the bishop in a dunny? That was *funny*, wasn't it?'

'Not for Hank.'

'Ar, yes it was. He was a nobody until then. Bet you can't even remember his real name. He became a character when he became Hank. No worries. Hey. Remember the '96 World Cup? It was in the subcontinent, right? Turns out every team has its own stash of pornos, its own travelling VCRs – everyone's into it. And the World Cup being a great cultural exchange, everyone gets together to share stuff. Turns out one of the Paki guys had this filthy farmyard shit, you know, donkeys and mules and whatnot. Amputees and twenty-inch wangs and dwarfs. It gets passed from the Pakis to the Yaapies to the Windies to the Aussies and finally we're in Madras for a quarter-final against the Kiwis. So after the game, we're all together, and someone shows the Kiwi boys this video. And I mean, it's hideous. Totally off. But there's this Kiwi, whose name shall remain undisclosed – hahaha! – who really wanted to make a copy of this tape. Wanted to show it to all his inbred mates on the South Island, right? But we're in India, aren't we, and the chance of finding a tape-to-tape recorder's as easy as finding a piece of fish that won't give you the runs for a week. So what he does is, he gets his Handycam and plays the tape, and stands in front of the TV recording it. Fine. So he's made this bootleg tape, which he starts showing around to some of the boys. But see, the problem is, when he was taping it, the light in the room sort of reflected him off the screen, and if you're watching this shocker of a bootleg of this fucking stick movie, when the screen goes a bit dark you can see the reflection of this Kiwi boy with one hand busy, know what I mean? And jeez, if that story didn't spread like wildfire. Now you know why everyone calls him SHV – "Single-Handed Viewing".'

'We're not talking about your cricket mates. We're talking about Pa.'

'But the Kiwi dude took it on the chin, right? It's *funny*. Fucksake, man, don't you and Luce do it?'

'Do what?'

'Watch pornos together?'

'What's that got to do with Pa?'

Davis's heart flip-flops. He wonders if Chris might be able to see it thumping in his shirt. It feels like a whale breaching, rising up and crashing down hard. He shuts his eyes to stop the cricket nets spinning.

'See, Davo, you won't "confirm or deny" it.'

An image comes into Davis's mind: Chris and Suzie going through their paces athletically, like porn actors: the correct cadence and volume of moaning, the correct technique, the pro-forma positions and locations – hot tub, kitchen, car, floor rug – and both of them coming in PC – Pornstar-Correct – paroxysms.

'And when we met,' Chris goes on, 'Suzie wouldn't even do it with the lights on! Now she's a tiger. Why do you think they call them marital aids? Lighten up!'

'I think,' Davis sighs, 'you might be missing the point.'

In the half-light thrown onto the practice nets, Chris's eyes are blank sequins.

A smile steps up onto Chris's face.

'Haven't you been watching, buddy? Chris Brand doesn't miss *anything*.'

Davis looks to the dressing room. An attendant comes out with a coffin, casts them a glance – pretending not to pry, busying himself with sitting the coffin upright – and scoots back up the stairs.

Davis persists: 'Whether you like it or not, you're part of a family. A family that can't manage to come together. At a time when we really need each other.'

'Thanks for the moral lecture, Mr Locum-Lover.'

Davis is about to bite, but finds traction against his skidding, sliding emotions. For him to retaliate is exactly what Chris wants.

'We don't even know what happened to him at the end,' Davis says. 'Hammett knows the truth. He can tell us. I'm sick of all these people trying to stop us finding out what really happened.'

'Are you going to challenge the death certificate?' Chris gives him a look of pure hatred. 'Because if you do, I will fucking knock your block off.'

'I shouldn't need to challenge it. Of course I don't want to. But I need to know what happened. He wasn't sick, he hadn't even been to a doctor, and suddenly, you know . . .'

'Don't be a fucking idiot. Leave it alone. Fuck off, leave me alone.'

'Someone's lying.'

'Boo-fucking-hoo. It's all a conspiracy. Hey, maybe I'm lying! Everyone's lying to poor little Davo.'

Davis senses someone coming from behind, then stopping by the nets. Probably a team flunkey, he thinks, come out to hold Chris's hand and lead him to the bus. Davis doesn't care. Chris is his little brother.

'You've confirmed everything I suspected about you,' Davis says.

Chris's smile passes, like a change of weather.

'What's that, matey?'

'How you endure the pressure. How you can function when so many people are watching you, and ready to criticise you. I've wondered for a long, long time, Chris. What it is that sets you apart.'

'It's called training and discipline, Davo. Something you've never . . .'

'But that's not all, is it?'

'No, mate, no, it's not all.' Davis knows he's got him angry now. It's the only way he can assert anything over Chris. Cook his blood. 'There's got to be something special,' Chris says. 'You've either got it or you don't.'

'And you've got it.'

'It's called composure, Davo. Staying calm.'

'Yes, that's the line I've swallowed until now.'

'Oh yeah? Why don't you tell me about myself, Doctor?'

'Really, what it is is, you're not fully alive.'

'Come and stand in the centre of the MCG in front of 90,000 before you tell me what it is to be alive or not alive. Doc.'

'Someone who's fully alive would throw up, shit their pants, run for cover. You're different. You're not really there. Something in you – the part that feels – is dead. Cauterised.'

'Wow, you're so smart.'

'And you have no compassion. You're dead, Chris. It makes me really sad to say it, but you're dead. If you weren't dead, you'd be more interested in getting our family back together.'

'Well, matey, since you know what it is to feel fear, why don't you talk to Jim Cobcroft? If you let that prick Hammett come into our Pa's funeral, and spew out all sorts of bullshit, then Jim's not going to let you have Pa's share in the surgery. Right? You're wrecking your own career. Ta-ta surgery. He's very sensitive to repu-tation, Jim is. Okay? Feeling a little *fear* now? Feeling *alive*, Davo?'

Davis can do exactly what Chris has not expected. He can see the warmth of his smile reflected in Chris's eyes, its heat melting Chris's physical superiority.

'I don't care,' Davis says. He feels ten feet tall. He lays a magnanimous hand on Chris's shoulder. 'I don't give a stuff. We have to do what's right. And it's more than just pictures. I found evidence that Pa was having an affair.'

Chris smacks Davis, with a firm open palm, in the chest. Davis stumbles and slips on the moist turf. Chris steps up and starts kicking him. His right foot pummels Davis like a power tool. In the ribs. In the legs. In the groin. Chris is chanting with each kick:

'Don't you fucking touch me! Don't you fucking touch me!'

By the time Davis can open his eyes, Chris has broken into a brisk jog-trot in the direction of the departing Australian team bus. He runs past the girl with the glasses and string bag, the autograph-hunter Davis saw with Chris earlier. She is getting a book out of her bag as Chris passes her. Arrested mid-gesture, she watches Chris climb into the bus. Her face turns back to where Chris came from, tracing his path back to the nets, where Davis is pulling himself up into a prone position. Tears make dewy spots as they hit the grass below his face.

January 4

As she watches Ian's headlights widen through the window, raking the room like searchlights before turning away, Margaret is, for the first time today, happy.

Not even Chris's innings, which had an unsettling frantic desperation to it, had the power to soothe her. She has sat up in her mourning mask, as if lying in state, and brooded. Ian has been unfailingly, oppressively kind.

She wanders around the house, arms folded, relaxing. Ian has fed her, tended her, but best of all he has left her. She breathes out her frustration. She'd never have expected that John's death would release her from all obligation – foremost from the obligation to speak.

Mischievously, she discovers she likes the nights. If she can survive the catatonic day, hiding in broad daylight, then her reward comes at night when she can breeze about the empty house, companionably alone. She fixes herself a dessert of ice-cream and chocolate sauce, and lets them melt into each other before stirring them with a spoon. A *thickshake*, the boys called it – and it is delicious. Scandalous that she never let herself discover such a treat before. She cleans the kitchen joyously, readying it for Bonnie and Clyde. Then, unable to read a book or magazine, she goes out into the garden and sits under the stars in the banana chair.

She is too gleeful to sleep – that's the appalling realisation – she is alive with glee, at having tricked Ian, tricked everyone. How scarcely they would guess! She feels as if she is inhabiting John's body in all those times he hid behind his taciturnity and came out to this very chair to feel, probably, this same solitary delight.

When she met him, the glow that emanated from John had this same self-sufficiency, this absolute satisfaction with his own company. Most boys she knew were chatterboxes, children who needed to fill silence. Muteness was a sign of awkwardness. But John was happily quiet, absorbed in the mere pleasure of being, a man with whom she could take a two-hour walk and never say a word and yet feel, at the end, the satisfaction of time contentedly shared. Once she asked him if he ever felt awkward. He said: 'Constantly.'

They'd had their moments, but those early years were sweet indeed. She and John were still young when they had Davis and Chris, and the four of them grew up together. Children evolved so quickly, and as a young parent you felt you were keeping pace with them. But later, by the time Hammett was born, Margaret had the feeling that she was already a fixed quantity. John had seemed to want the third child. Margaret too. But she found, late in her pregnancy, that she had reached that age when one realises how long one is going to be old. One reaches a point, and stagnates – ossifies. How violently she changed her mind, halfway through her pregnancy! It was the worst thing she had ever done: to regret a child, to dread its arrival. She could not, of course, tell a soul.

Hammett grew and changed as quickly as any other child, but relative to her own fixity his growth seemed an insult, a challenge, a racing-past. And he developed so very quickly.

They were helpless in front of this raw natural force. She'd never thought of herself and John as fair-weather people. Far from it. But Hammett had come, and they were somehow too solid. Inflexible. Probably, she reflected, too satisfied with the way they already were.

Hammett had run wild. That day in Rotorua when he'd disappeared, John was apoplectic with worry. Margaret sat in the car watching the clock, stewing over how late they'd be arriving at Mount Egmont. When Hammett was found, running around naked, his own mother hadn't been able to look at him.

'Don't worry,' she had said to the ranger who asked if she wanted Hammett's clothes found. 'If he wants to run around like a naked savage, he can sit in the car like a naked savage.'

As they had driven off to Mount Egmont, Hammett had delighted in his nakedness and begun to make obscene gestures at his parents. Chris hit him. A fifteen-year-old punched a six-year-old with full swings. Even being bludgeoned, Hammett continued to waggle his thing at the front seat. Davis tried to reason with both him and Chris. They screamed abuse at Davis.

'Oh, for God's sake!' John pulled over to the side of the road. Snow-capped Egmont, emerald fields. John got out of the car, and Margaret thought he was going to the boot, to the luggage, to find some clothes for Hammett. She had been about to suggest he pull over so she could dress the boy. Enough was enough. This was the thing with Hammett: whatever battleground you chose, he would beat you.

But John did not go to the boot. He walked away from them, down the straight road towards Stratford.

The boys fell silent.

'Where's he going?' Davis said.

'See?' Chris snarled at Hammett. 'Pa's left us forever because of you!'

Margaret sat in the front seat, watching her husband walk away. She had no idea where he was going or what he was thinking. They were in New Zealand; he had nothing but the clothes on his back. Yet for a moment it seemed totally conceivable that he was going to leave them there, to disappear into the mist and become another man with another life. Another family? No, this new man would have no family.

Then she did a wicked thing. She turned around and said, gently but impersonally, like a hostage negotiator addressing a terrorist:

'Hammett, do you want clothes or no clothes?'

'No clothes!'

'Is there anything else you want?'

'Ride in front!'

'All right then, you can come into my seat and ride beside me.' She got out of the car and went to the driver's seat. Smirking at his brothers, Hammett leapt into the passenger seat. He made lewd gestures towards Chris. Margaret ignored him. With her eyes she begged Chris to do the same. 'All right, boys,' Margaret said, clipping in her seatbelt and adjusting the rear-vision mirror so she could see Chris and Davis. 'Let's go and see if we can pick up any hitchhikers.'

She drove on. Without a word, John got into the back seat. Margaret drove them to the motel. Things were as she wanted them: her three boys in the back, safely uncontaminated by Hammett. All she had to do was last the distance, get him out before he could do them too much harm.

She'd given him up. Yes, too late to deny it: she'd given him up. She knew, intuitively, that she and John did not love the boy as they had loved Davis and Chris. A shocking thought – that they could not be true parents to this alien presence. So shocking that they had never broken their silence on the matter.

They became the opposite of what they were. They became bad parents: not by reputation, for their friends would always forgive one bad apple. But she knew within herself that she was a mother-gone-bad. Wordlessly, but with sweeping unanimity, she and John had cut a bargain not to allow each other, or Davis or Chris, to be hurt by Hammett. They ceased arguing with him or contesting his will. In every decision pertaining to Hammett, they followed the line of least resistance. She sent him to speech therapy classes, she enrolled him in sport, she had him moved from school to school. Ah, the public pretence of action! But the truth was, the moment Hammett resisted – wagged classes, missed training, got himself expelled for some new horror – Margaret let him have his way. As if the fear of pain were as much as they could cope with, she and John closed ranks pre-emptively, before the boy could make that fear actual. They closed ranks against a helpless child, let him have everything his own way. What people they were!

She could face the truth, now: she had cut him loose a long time before he repaid her with his own flight. He had swept through his childhood, loveless, repaying them in havoc. Making it impossible for her to change her heart and begin loving him.

She'd been guilty, of course, but her guilt came out as resignation, not apology. When she discovered terrible things about him, she felt like making amends, but where on earth did one start? As he got older and his behaviour went from wayward to unspeakable, she just wanted nothing to do with him. Left him to his own devices. Her plan was to hold out, survive, until he was an adult and off her hands. She almost made it.

She would like to talk to him now, but while it does not seem too late for regrets – which keep their own timetable – it is too late to find a way, practicably, to find and speak to him. To whom could she admit it? Ian? Davis? Chris? Pointless. Pointless. She has made her great mistake.

She could have admitted it to John. It would have meant something.

These thoughts have ruined her good mood, and she is getting up to go back into the house and try to sleep when that blasted noise of another vandalised wheelie-bin roars through from the right-of-way. Fierce with anger, she runs to the side gate, hoping to catch them before they run off. She scampers to the top of the hill, but her slippers are not the best running apparel and the whooping teenagers are already echoing behind the townhouses by the time she reaches the corner, from where she can see the third bin mounting the first two, their combined rubbish spilling off the sides of the paving and into the high grass.

Margaret cannot remember being so livid, so *incandescent*. Heat prickles her cheeks as she strides down the hill. If anyone stepped into her path, she doesn't know what she'd do. She is a woman, late in middle-age but sturdy, and she is capable of murder.

But instead, with no-one to murder she sets the three bins upright and goes about picking up the rubbish.

The bins have different-coloured lids: red for glass, yellow for plastic, blue for paper. At home, she's never bothered with recycling. The earth is still large enough to let Margaret Hammett Brand reach the end of her days without sorting her garbage like a bag lady. But here, with the bins so clearly marked, it offends her sense of order not to direct the right refuse to the right container. Her back hurts as she bends to loop as many orange-juice bottle handles around her fingers as possible. Soon her face is flushed not with anger but exertion. She finds a certain comfort in the rigour of dividing the rubbish and filling the bins back up.

The glass-only bin has the lowest tide, and she is forced to throw, rather than place, bottles inside. They crash shrilly against each other. Alerted by the noise, a face appears at the window of one of the townhouses above Margaret. She catches the silhouetted head staring down at her. She picks up three beer bottles in one hand, her other hand going to the small of her back, and drops them provocatively into the bin.

'Sshh!' the unfortunate person says.

Margaret looks at him for a moment. He's a man, around her age. Possibly a divorcé – these townhouses seem to attract single men who have come out on the wrong side of a marriage split. Hopeless types, men who have given up.

'Don't you care?' she says.

He stares back mutely. With his bathroom light behind him, she cannot make out his expression.

'Don't you?' She waves her arm to indicate the rubbish.

Another two faces appear at another window. A light goes on.

'You let this kind of thing happen,' she says, 'and you don't do a thing!'

One of the lights goes out again. She hears a muttered curse, then laughter.

'You just wait for someone else to do it,' she addresses the first man. 'You don't care at all.'

He goes on staring. She picks up some more glass bottles and dumps them, forcefully percussive, into the bin. They smash.

'I don't even live here!' she cries at the man. And now, she realises, she is crying. There are tears on her cheeks. Her voice breaks. These people – they are animals, animals.

'I don't even live here! And not a single one of you cares!'

The sobbing overcomes her. She heaves, but the tears are a natural force, like her poor little boy, a natural disaster, far greater than anything she could staunch. And why should she? Why the hell should she conceal anything from people like these? What do appearances count in the zoo? The man is still examining her, as if only a freak could do what she is doing – he's accusing her of being the one who pushed the bins down the hill, and the only explanation for cleaning them up could be that she is guilty.

'It wasn't me!' she weeps, her voice hardly carrying beyond herself. 'And I don't even live here!'

The man at the window looks at her until she has cleaned it all up. Wiping her runny nose on the sleeve of her jumper, leaving a snail's trail down her arm, she finishes the job. All the rubbish is in its right place. She lines the bins up together. If someone wants to put them back at the top of the right-of-way, they can bloody well do it themselves.

Back in the house, she cleans herself up. In the bathroom mirror, her nose is blotched and her eyes swollen. She scrubs her hands over and over, adding disinfectant to the soap, soaking them in hot water, changing the water and rinsing them again until they feel like the hands of a baby in a bath, wilted like pink petals.

The bedroom is desolation. She hasn't made the bed today, and it resembles a bird's nest of sheets, blankets and eiderdowns, everything she could hold against herself to keep out the cold. She doesn't have the heart to go in there.

Instead, she finds herself in his study. Whether she knew it or not, she has been steering clear of this room. Not once in her nocturnal roamings has she been in here. She sits in his office chair, uncoiling her hands, letting the rawness run out through the tips of her fingerprints into the grey, hot-plastic-smelling air.

This was where John came when he couldn't sleep. More than the garden, more than the kitchen, this was where he hid out. During the day, too, he hid in this office while she took care of the world. But what is there left to take care of? Now that he's gone, where is the world?

She sits looking at the grey shapes, the boxes into which Ian packed all of John's things with unseemly haste. The objects in the dark room are unfamiliar, stylised totem shapes, all angle and shadow like a cubist painting. The soft edges are sharp, the sharp blurred. The space does not feel like their house. She feels as if inspecting real estate – this room is potential, cold, diminished. How could they have fitted so many years in here? It's only a warren of little boxes, brick, mortar, plywood, tile, beams and batts. A wave of pain rises in her back, and as she rests against the desk she gives a start – she must have disturbed something, and the computer comes to life with a light static fizz. There is a screen the colour of Mediterranean water, and two columns of small pictures with coded names. She wouldn't know the first thing about this machine or what lurks inside it and, to be frank, she doesn't want to know.

She turns around and looks at the boxes, which have inherited the screen's green glow. Everything seems to have slipped into place only just now, as she turned around to look, as if the boxes themselves have been doing other things behind her back.

This house is her domain, a finite place where she knows all. Nothing escapes her.

The quality of the light on the boxes changes. She turns back to the computer screen, which has gone black but for a six-coloured shape that bounces off the perimeters. It is a cube – red, dark blue, green, light blue, purple, yellow – but now it is a spiked weapon, like the head of a mace. As it bounces up off the bottom of the screen it becomes a ball, a beach ball, but the sections of the ball distend into slightly rude bulges, male-looking things. It flirts with the spiky mace shape but reverts to the beach ball again, then the cube, and now the cube's walls are sucked in as if by vacuum force. Now it bounces off the side and it's the beach ball again, and now the rude shape.

She knows what they call it – a screen saver. It's meant to save energy. But how can it save anything when it is so frantic, so energetic, so nervous? What is it *saving*?

And they say computers are logical!

She's not going to delve into the machine. She knows they all want her to – but she won't. Ian also suggested she 'go through' the 'floppy disks', in such a slyly casual way that she wanted to send him out of the house there and then. How dare he? As if it were merely a matter of sorting out share certificates or annuity statements.

She works open the lid of a plastic box and shakes the disks. Ian suggested that if she didn't look through them (as he well knew she wouldn't – couldn't!) then she should let him. She shook her head. Like a lawyer in court, she didn't want to ask a question to which she didn't know the answer. That's what these disks are – John's final testimony – but without John to answer for them, it's unfair to raise the case.

She knows these are malign. Alien things. She pulls one out. Why are they called floppy disks? They're square and stiff. More computer logic! It has no label: it is just a stiff square blue thing. She turns it over in her hand. It has a science fiction feel to it.

So John's secrets are on these silly misnamed science fiction squares? She blows a half-raspberry.

John's secrets? If only they knew the difference between truth and detail. These disks may contain the latter, but not the former. The truth is filed away somewhere else. This machinery would only contain irrelevancies, distractions. Margaret doesn't much care for details. She knows John. He was right, after all, about the trees in the garden. The names, the labels and details, mean nothing. It's the essence of the trees, the private names we give them, that carry truth. She knows the living soul inside her husband. She doesn't need the details. That's what Hammett was always on about – the details, the details, as if it were important for them to know exactly what he'd been doing. But she didn't want to, and she doesn't want to. It's about – sex, yes, sex. That's all she needs to know. John had his hang-ups. All right. But the details would not clarify John, they would obscure him. She thinks of how she saw him in death: how calm he seemed in the hospital. What a great price his self-control had cost him, a price visible only now that the mask had fallen off.

She has been flicking the metal guard on the edge of the floppy disk. It makes a pleasant spring and snap. She notices something inside – glistening, smooth, slightly organic in appearance. She bends back the aluminium: feels the thrill of breaking this science fiction thing, reducing it to weak metal and flimsy plastic. She works her fingernail into the seam of the plastic. Snap! Her nail breaks. But who cares? Does she? Not tonight. She has done her caring for the evening.

Finally she works the two halves apart. The circular thing inside comes out, slick like a strange thing living on an ocean floor – more like a plasticky organism than plastic itself. It flops rudely in her fingers. This is it: the floppy disk out of its shell, defenceless, disgusting. She giggles, waves it about in her fingers. Silly, silly thing – how can they condemn John's soul into something like this?

She breaks open another. It reminds her so much of an oyster, or a mussel, that she gives the parts corresponding names: the blue halves of the shell, the aluminium case of the valve, and the slippery innards, the flesh. She separates them into three piles: shells, valves, flesh.

Oh, she's grown to like being alone. She looks around the room. Her eyes have adjusted. This was what he came here for, at this time of night: the peace of being the only one awake.

She gets to work on the rest of the disks.

Late that night, Claire Mullally turns out the lights in her flat and draws the curtains so that, unseen, she can keep an eye on him from her window. For several nights he's been hugging the shadows of the park between her balcony and the harbour shore. He's careful, veering away from the pools of light cast by the park lanterns. Sometimes he sits on a bench, or else he leans against one of the palm trees or paperbarks lining the path. He pretends he's not watching her flat, sitting with his back to her, his hands laced behind his head, going over to chat with the guys who dangle a fishing line off the sea wall. Lovers come to cuddle, enjoy the prospect of the water, or share a joint. Homeless regulars nest down against the sandstone retaining wall behind the toilets. But he's always there, always alone, pretending with an almost endearing ineptitude that he's not watching her.

He's been leaving messages on her voicemail. Sometimes he wheedles, sometimes he bullies, sometimes he insults, sometimes he appeals to the past: pushing every button. And now – she's sure – he's stalking her.

She has tried to go to sleep, but gave up. She can only relax by keeping an eye on him. The last few nights, he's gone home soon after twelve. Frustratingly, she never gets a good fix on him. The moonlight has shone off the water, and all she can make out is his silhouette against the dappled harbour and the orange lights of the North Shore.

It's almost midnight when he sidles towards the marina, his usual escape route. Claire resolves to put an end to this now. She bustles into her bedroom and throws on a pair of tracksuit pants and a jumper, wraps herself in a shawl. Through the curtains, she takes another look. He's darted off to the side, but she can intercept him if she's quick. She pockets her cigarettes and keys and presses the lift button. No clunk of ancient gears: someone must be using it on another floor. She runs down the fire escape. She's got no reason to fear him. He'll see sense. *No hard feelings, but I've drawn the line – it's over.*

She still wonders if she should have seen it coming. He was onto her from day one: discussing cases for longer than was necessary, offering help she didn't need, thrusting his boxy gym-built chest – his vanity did erase the age difference. He'd started by inviting her to the café where he lunched, and she'd been flattered enough to accept. He pressed a little, and she resisted. He'd retreated behind his marriage, then slyly emerged again. This quiet conquest, under the guise of mentorship, had lasted for months, and then he'd found the weapon of leverage he'd been seeking. He held the promise out to her, and she'd been weak enough once – once! – to enter the trading ring. After that regrettable incident, he pressed for new terms. He was going to make good on his offer, but he also expected her side to continue, as if she wasn't a stupid girl who'd surrendered to one moment of venality but a mistress, a young woman to adore him. It is not a price she is able to pay. *It's over*, she repeats.

Lips moving over her words, she heaves open the bevelled-glass front door. The globe in the porch lamp has gone, darkening the steps. She walks past the barred-up ground-floor windows towards the park. At the fire hydrant booster, she pauses and listens. Fruit bats squawk in the Moreton Bay figs. Waves lap against the sea wall and drum against hollow hulls. Cables clang flatly against masts, like dead bells. As she steps out into the darkness of the park, the croaking of frogs envelops her.

He's gone, the coward. A voice makes her jump, but it's only the guy who lives in a kombi parked permanently on the park's edge. Dope smoke billows out with music. The guy takes a pee against a rubbish bin, as if that's more couth than going against a tree.

She returns to her building, cursing whoever jammed up the lift. Undelayed, she might have caught him. She's fiddling with the keys, about to step up onto her porch, when she bumps into, of all people, Davis Brand.

'Oh! Hello, there.'

'Evening.' He's wearing a polo shirt, loafers, and shorts ironed to an edge that could draw blood.

He tamps down his sparse blond hair, which is beginning to show the characteristics of an incipient comb-over.

'I suppose I shouldn't be surprised,' Claire says.

'Oh?' Davis's Adam's apple jumps.

'We're more or less neighbours. It's probably more remarkable that we haven't bumped into each other.'

'Yes, ha!' He releases a choked laugh, as if dislodging a piece of food.

She smiles at him. He swallows loudly.

'What brings you down here, Claire?'

She wonders, for a moment, whether to tell him. But his expression so reminds her of a beagle's – you can kick me, you can pat me, it's all the same, I'll still like you – that she lights a cigarette and says: 'Come upstairs for a cuppa?'

'I don't think I should,' he says, with a grimace that makes her think she might have committed a faux pas.

'Oh. Okay, whatever.'

'Thank you for the offer,' he goes on with a stammer. 'But no, no thanks. I mean, it'd be under false pretences.'

She laughs, too quickly. 'I won't even go there!' she finds herself giggling.

'But if you'd like to go for a coffee, that'd be nice.'

'Um,' she laughs again, 'I don't know where you're thinking of going, but it's nearly midnight and I'm not really dressed for it.'

He utters an apologetic surprised grunt, as if the lateness of the hour has only just struck him.

'But – a walk?' she says. 'You were out getting some fresh air? I'll take a turn around the park with you?'

'That'd be . . .' He gives her a hopeless look. She hooks her arm through his and guides him towards the park, wishing, at the back of her head, that James might still be lurking and see her with another man. That would stuff it right up him, the dick.

They walk in silence. He doesn't seem to mind her closeness. Putting her arm in his seemed the natural thing in the awkwardness of the moment, and now she's glad, as it seems to relieve them of the need to speak. They walk like an insomniac couple under the fancy cornices of the waterfront buildings, along a path spattered like a Jackson Pollock with ancient white bird droppings. Davis, she fancies, is walking oddly, as if trying to conceal some physical pain. But it might just be the strangeness of the situation. They pass the wrought-iron canopy over the bubbler. Davis half-trips on the roots of a Moreton Bay fig, but doesn't relinquish his grip on her. There's a strong smell of stagnant mains water and gas leaks.

'Don't you think that smells of B.O.?' she says.

'B.O.? Um, I did have a shower . . .'

'Not you, silly. That smell. Stop, sniff it. See? It's these old buildings, they get this smell about them. On a good day I quite like it, but on humid summer nights like this, it smells like B.O. Do you think it's possible for a whole street to smell like B.O.?'

'Around here, it'd be very high-quality B.O.'

She rewards his attempt with a laugh. All of a sudden she's feeling effervescent, buoyed by a late-night second wind.

'Sometimes I think it's overrated, living by the harbour. If it's not the B.O., it's the rotten stink off the water.'

'Mouldy.'

'Exactly! Kind of crotchy. Or the wind. It can be vicious, like a bad dream, the way it whistles through the windows. And then there's the view. Look at this – all I can see is the Garden Island cranes, the ugliest buildings in Sydney, and the backside of the marina. It's not exactly the harbour of the brochures.'

'Keep your voice down. Seditious talk around here, you'll be done for treason.'

They fall silent again. Moonlight glitters off the flat water. Channel markers flash green and red. Davis clears his throat but says nothing. He seems to be limping slightly, wincing as he walks.

'I came down here,' Claire says, 'because a man I was involved with has been sitting here every night watching me.'

She sneaks a look at Davis out of the corner of her eye. He is staring straight ahead. 'It's a long story,' she goes on. 'Short version is,' she clears her throat and tightens her arm through Davis's, 'James.'

Davis's eyes emit an audible click as they blink. 'Jim Cobcroft.'

'I know, it's embarrassing. He flattered me. I guess I didn't know any better.'

'I had no idea.'

'Oh, it was all a state secret. James has too much to lose, too many cars, too many houses, too many children.'

'And you dumped him.'

'What makes you say that?'

'Whatever else Jim is, he's not insane.'

Claire laughs. 'It's not that we've ever been, you know . . . I don't know. It just seemed important to James to assure himself that I haven't fallen out of love with him. It was meant to be no-strings-attached – except that I go on loving him for the rest of my life.'

'You said . . . he'd been down in this park, um, watching you?'

'I can't be sure it's him, because he sticks to the shadows. But it's James-like behaviour. He's been, um, harassing me lately. And I've said no. At long last, I've said no.'

'You sound proud.'

'Well, it's not just James. All my friends and family say I have this thing for charismatic older men, that I get starstruck. It's the big family joke. Claire's crushes. My parents have always worried about me and the Unavailable Successful Man. It bugs me. But hey, with James I guess I proved them right.'

'So it's a relief to finish it and prove them wrong.'

'Right! I just wish I could have come out here and pushed his face in.'

She looks at Davis again, but he seems to be sustaining a great exertion not to look at her.

He's always been a bit this way with her. She remembers last year's surgery Christmas Party. Davis avoided her. Whenever she moved into his orbit or he, inadvertently, into hers, he veered clear. But whoever was nominally engaging his concentration became a prop by which Davis could station himself and watch her. When she'd catch him staring, her smile would fold up on itself, exaggerated, like a nervous actor, too many muscles in motion. He left early.

'So,' Claire says to stop the conversation going completely slack. 'Your brother's going well? That must make you all proud.'

'Hm.' Davis grunts.

'You okay?' she says.

'Yeah, yeah. Fine.'

'Well. I don't follow cricket, but since meeting your father I've taken a distant interest in Chris. It makes me feel as if I'm part of the human race – you know, for once in my life I have something to say about sport.'

Davis's silence is a vacuum, sucking words from her.

'A journalist came to see me yesterday, as a patient. At least – you know, it hasn't struck me until now, but maybe that was a ruse. He was asking a lot of questions about the funeral. Maybe he came to investigate.'

'Like what?' Davis looks grimly curious, as if this was just the kind of bad news he'd been expecting.

'He seemed most interested in knowing if your youngest brother would be going.'

'Hammett,' Davis says, in a tone unfamiliar with the name, talking about a family he only knows vaguely.

'I didn't tell him anything.' She pats his arm. 'I was quite the guard dog.'

He asks her the journalist's name; it's the same one who harassed Chris at the press conference.

With a sigh, as if being coerced, Davis tells her about Hammett wanting to come to the funeral to make a speech about their father. Once he's started, Davis warms up. He tells Claire he'd like Hammett to come, but that Ma and Chris oppose it, and if it's going to be so much trouble, then perhaps it'd be best to keep Hammett away. Claire listens patiently as Davis builds up steam. Soon he's pouring out such torrents of distaste for Chris, and someone called Mr Bertrand, that she starts to feel uncomfortable. After some time, noticing her silence, Davis exhales.

'I don't suppose you'd like to say something at the funeral?'

Claire laughs, but Davis gives her the stony look.

'I hardly knew your father. I mean, I'd be honoured, I'm flattered, but – you're just kidding, aren't you?'

'Sometimes I think it'd be better if someone who hardly knew him does the speaking.'

A flush travels up Claire's spine, first confused, then annoyed.

'It's your father! It's – Doctor Brand!'

Davis is shaking his head.

'You don't understand. It's not a matter of not having nice, appropriate things to say about Pa. I could fill a book, you know? But . . . it's the occasion of . . . it's getting up in front of people. We're not really a family who says these things aloud.'

'What about Chris?'

'You obviously don't know him. Put him in front of a crowd, and he clams up.'

'In front of a crowd?'

'Take away his bat, and Chris is the most shy person I know. When we were kids he refused to have birthday parties, or if he did he'd run from the room when the cake came in and the singing started. He loathes being the centre of attention.'

'Funny career choice then.'

'That's the paradox of my brother – for a guy who's so driven by the desire to be on his own, alone, he's chosen to be a person who can't walk to the newsagent without being asked for an auto-graph. Anyway. Chris and I aren't on the best terms right now.' He winces, rubbing his side.

'But what about you? Surely you're the logical choice.'

'I can't.'

'How come?'

Davis chews the insides of his cheeks, as if considering whether to reveal something. His hand continues to massage his ribs.

'I . . . I've learnt things about Pa . . .' He takes a deep breath and sighs. 'I have an understanding with Hammett that if he isn't allowed to talk, then I won't either.'

'Oh!' Claire puts a hand to her mouth. They round the end of the park. Bats fly in from the Botanic Gardens, senses trained on fruit. There's a beachy stench at this end. A fish jumps, slaps down on the water. Claire tightens her arm through Davis's.

'Perhaps they'll have to give Hammett a go,' she says. 'He won't say anything horrible, will he?'

Davis shakes his head. 'If I can convince my mother to trust him, I reckon he'll come good. But if they don't trust him, that's where he'll be dangerous.'

Despite the sombreness of their discussion, Claire feels inexplicably light.

'You don't mind if I smoke?'

Davis looks as if he is about to say something more, but shakes his head. She takes her cigarettes out of her tracksuit pants. Bugger it, she thinks. If Davis objected to her smoking, she'd be disappointed. James banned her from smoking. Men always want to put bans on you, change the way they find you. She blows a shaft of smoke up to the stars.

'Did your father ever tell you about his episode with the dwarf?'

'Dwarf?'

'At the surgery, not long after I started, there was a little girl with leukaemia who broke everybody's heart. A gorgeous six-year-old who fought like a tiger. She came for check-ups between chemo sessions at Vinnie's. Your father used to try to cheer her up by pretending to be an animal – an ape, a chimp, a horse, an elephant – and jumping out of corners to scare her. She'd scream with delight – she'd wet herself! He was her special doctor. One day, he decided to be a crab. He put his glasses up on his head so they'd look like crab's eyes on stalks. He scuttled along sideways up and down the stairs. He was hilarious, all bandy-legged and with bent elbows and turning his hands into claws. He scrunched up his face as ugly as possible. When the girl saw him, she laughed like crazy. Then at one point she had to go to the bathroom. Your dad . . .' Claire pauses to wipe her snub nose dry with her non-cigarette hand, '. . . your dad waited outside the bathroom door. He hears the toilet flush, and goes into his crab pose – he's all squinched-up and nasty-looking, and crouched down, with his eyes on stalks – but what he doesn't know is that in the surgery that day, there's a dwarf, you know, a small person. A patient of James's. And the dwarf has gone into the bathroom before the little girl. But your dad doesn't know that.'

'Oh no.'

'Oh yes. The bathroom door opens, and your dad is scuttling up and down, on his haunches, making this terrible face and making terrible noises . . .'

'And the dwarf comes out.'

'For a second they just freeze, the dwarf and your dad as a crab, and stare at each other. Then Doctor Brand straightens up, rubbing his back, mumbles an apology, and darts off to his room.'

'Oh, jeepers.'

Claire's laugh is unrestrained, coughing. She butts out her cigarette into the bin that smells of fresh urine.

'If I had to speak at his funeral,' she says, 'that's the story I'd tell.'

They arrive at Claire's door. Davis's hands are plunged into his pockets, his eyes intent on his shoes.

'You really do remind me so much of him,' she says.

'Is that a good thing?'

'It is.'

'Um, it's after midnight.'

'I'm glad we bumped into each other.'

'See you tomorrow then.'

'Davis?'

As if cutting short anything she might say, he reaches out a hand. She looks at it as if he's held out a slab of steak. It appears he is offering a handshake. She looks at his face, but he's grimacing painfully at his hand. She shakes it, thinking: This is surreal.

'Are you sure you're all right?' she says.

He shakes his head violently, with a scowl.

'Davis, funerals are for family. I don't know if it's my place to say this, but however uncomfortable you feel about it, I think the consequences of avoiding it will be a lot worse and last a lot longer. And, well, I think I owe you an explanation as well.'

Davis looks at the ground. Claire sniffs, then blows out, like an athlete standing on her mark.

'Jim's offered you my share in the surgery,' he says.

'You knew?'

'It all makes sense now. What with you and him, and . . .'

'I'm not taking it.'

'Oh?' He looks at her through the tops of his eyes.

'I can't go against your father's wishes. It's not very nice, James's conniving. I don't like the way it's being handled. He's trying to exploit some kind of loophole, which he can only do by, well, if something happens to your father's reputation. And he's using me as a lever. Well, I loved your father, Davis – sorry – I loved your father as if he was my own father – you understand? He was a wonderful doctor, and a great mentor – and I'm not going to be used. So you can rest assured. I don't want your share. I'm thinking of moving on, working somewhere else.'

Davis gives her a real smile, his father's smile. She realises she was wrong about him not liking her.

'You want to know a secret?' he says. 'I don't want it either.'

'You don't?'

'Let's leave Jim to sort out the mess on his own.'

'Are you serious?'

'He's been working to freeze me out for years. And frankly – what you've told me tonight, it sickens me. I don't even want to look at him, let alone go into partnership with him.'

'Well, it looks like he's lost two of us for the price of one.'

Later, Claire sits up until dawn. Something hums inside her, stopping her sleeping; but it's a happy insomnia. Davis's peculiar vulnerability moves her – he tries to hide it, but it escapes as confusion and courtliness and the strain for propriety, while deep down he knows he's vulnerable and is content for her to see it. What she's discovered, in her scanty experience, is that all men are needy, and the differences between them are the different measures they take to hide it.

There's a certain beauty in good manners, she thinks, in his declining her invitation to come upstairs, in offering the handshake.

As she settles down with a mug of tea and a cigarette, tucks her legs under herself and watches the harbour turn from black and silver to grey, she reflects on what a nice change it is for a man not to make her feel like a fragile or amusing child. And as the park turns green, she remembers why she likes living here. It's Sydney Harbour. By the time the bats have gone off shift and the birds come on to replace them, Claire has fallen into a dreamless sleep.

December 24

By Christmas Eve, Pa had failed to respond to Hammett's invitation to come and see Kelli Kittering on tour in Sydney, so Hammett decided to apply some pressure.

Christmas Eve, pig of a day. Night was falling as Hammett sat in the back of a taxi, shirt sticking to his shoulderblades, a parcel of tapes and magazines cradled on his knees. The driver wore a Santa hat at a tilt, white pompom bumping against the plastic security divider. On the North Shore they passed a hairdresser's that resembled a restaurant, a hospital that resembled a school, a school that resembled a jail. A domed skyscraper in North Sydney had a giant Santa hat over it, tethered with ropes, limp in the clotted air.

The North Shore, Hammett thought: a choking shroud of uniformity fell on you, like a kidnapper's blanket, the moment you left the expressway at Willoughby.

Christmas fucking Eve.

Hammett knew it was time to force the issue when Pa didn't call him back. Pa just wasn't going to move without a prod. No initiative, Pa. Crisis was the motivating force, and Hammett held the crisis on his knees. He drummed his fingers on the package.

The taxi turned into Warramunga Avenue. No greater violence, here, than the digging up of bitumen for television cables.

Hammett asked the driver to stop two hills before the house.

He paid the guy and cautioned him to count to ten before doing his three-point turn on the crest. Package under his arm, he walked towards the Cape Cod house.

Before the house he turned down the right-of-way. A loud laugh, which he identified as Chris's, bounced off the side wall. There used to be a group of sheds down the right-of-way. They were the common property of the scouts and the local council, usually abandoned to boys with BB guns who'd shoot bottles against the wall, graduate to currawongs, and perhaps move up to blowing the windows out of the school bus. The sheds were now buried beneath the yards of six townhouses. Hammett crunched through the bracken, pausing to switch the heavy parcel to the other arm and wipe his brow. Night had fallen and the Brands' windows shone brilliantly, a golden grid through the trees.

Hammett had spent much of his childhood in and around those green corrugated-iron sheds. He'd wander into the bushes searching for treasure. Found scraps of centrefolds, magical waxy paper, piled around dead campfires or stacked in rubbish bins in the picnic grounds of the national park, and hoarded them in the shed which local men, not his father but others, used to store tools. Hammett stashed his treasure in an empty metal chest he found among the electric grinders and lathes and power drills, the rusty antiques and house junk. Sunlight would claw in through the high barred window. It was a nice dark place, smelling of earth and oil. Other suburban boys were learning how to bowl a leg-spinner or ride a bike or chat up their sisters' friends. Hammett lurked in the shed and wandered the bush.

Down by the river had a particular charge. As he fossicked for pictures he became aware of other activities. Wherever there were school and scout excursions, there were solitary men too. Hammett wasn't interested in the cub groups or girl guides or other young adventurers; it was the men he liked to spy on. There was something intoxicating about watching the watchers. They would sit absolutely motionless, like the most patient forest animals. Just. Perfectly. Still. Not doing anything, but their stillness tempted contemplation of the frenzy inside their minds and their hearts and their guts. Then, after agonising hours, they would make their move. Darting to a point where they could intercept the target's progress, these men knew the bush like marsupials. They had their unique style at the kill.

Once Hammett saw a man jacking off atop a rock near the scout hall. Five cubs screamed and ran away, and the man jerked away merrily to the sound of their escape.

The man was zipping himself up when he caught Hammett watching him like a fly on a tree.

'Hello, boy.'

'Hello, man.'

'Nice day for it.'

'I can make a solar still.'

'Solar still, eh? Like to come and show me? I've never seen a solar still.'

Hammett walked over to the man, who had reversed his motion of zipping up his fly and was now wheedling his brown tube of gristle into the open bush air again. The man took it in his hand and worked with it, reminding Hammett of the way Ma rolled her stockings down her leg.

'So, boy. Tell me about the solar still.'

'First,' Hammett said, watching the man's expanding thing, 'you need to dig a hole. You put leaves and stuff in, then some plastic over the top, and then you need a stone to weigh it down in the middle.'

'A stone, eh?' The man was getting short of breath. 'There's some stones here, near my foot, here. Why don't you bend down there and show me what type of stone you like.'

'Okay!' Hammett said. The man's eyes were glazing. Hammett walked over cheerfully, not too close to the man, not where he'd been pointing, and picked up a pie-sized chunk of sandstone. 'Like this!'

'Isn't that a bit . . . big?' the man said, clenching his teeth at the last word.

'No, it's just the right size.' Hammett weighed it in his hand. 'For this, ya perv!'

He flung the sandstone as hard as he could at the man's ugly brown donger. He didn't stay long enough to see if he'd done any damage, but the guy let out a massive howl. Hammett ran up to the next ridge. The man was below, on his haunches.

'Get stuffed ya fucken perv!' Hammett screamed again, letting out an Apache holler before jogging back to the sheds.

The parcel under his arm, Hammett now eased open the side fence and entered the garden, Christmas bush flopping in an almost effete manner onto the ragged grass. He crossed the lawn to the pool rockery, laid his parcel on the ground, undid his fly and pissed onto the rocks. He rotated his neck, vertebrae clicking. The joy of pissing outdoors! He pissed heavily, like the first man must have pissed, the way man has pissed for thousands of years, bodily pissing, natural, territorial like a dog pissing, pissing on the world, their world, the only world, as far as he could piss and as far as he could see.

He shook himself off, picked up the parcel and stepped up the side path. Through the window, he saw them at the table: Pa and Ma at the ends, Chris, Suzie, Lucy, Davis, Mr Bertrand and the two little girls spread equidistantly between. Ma carved the turkey. Bertrand passed around a plate of sliced ham. Suzie and Lucy laughed at something Chris said. Davis, wearing a paper hat, pulled crackers with the younger girl. Pa nodded along, slightly out of it, the lights strung around the Christmas tree behind him.

A Christmas card in itself. The tip, Hammett thought, and the iceberg. I am the iceberg. The tip floats along, buoying itself with jokes and cheery sarcasm and pretence. All tip and no iceberg.

In all the years since his last Christmas here, Hammett had never thought he'd missed much. What did you miss without your family? Turkey? Discovering your relatives are actually quite weird?

Why am I bad and my brothers good? I am true. So why am I here and they there?

When he was fourteen, he ran away before Christmas lunch was served. He'd gone to the neighbours' houses and peered through their windows, to see if their Christmas was different. And they were – in the other homes, the children were all the same age. Nobody was like him, a pesky adjunct to the adult world. When he ran away, as he did increasingly, Christmas or no Christmas, he fell into this habit of looking at other people's lives. He saw how they ate dinner. He followed them from their dining rooms into their bedrooms. He watched husbands and wives arguing, boys and girls setting up whispered assignations, girls and girls and boys and boys plotting against each other, mothers complaining about their children, mothers boasting about their children, fathers evading talking about anything. Neglected in his own house, Hammett explored the houses of others, the domesticities, the warp and weft. And just as one can pick up a grotesque education from television, so did he from peeping through windows: a gesture-rich, fervid life, movement stripped of sounds, eternities contained in blank looks and minute flinches. He never involved himself. His desires were quenched by looking on.

Hammett knew he was fucked up as hell. But his fucking father lived the same way! As he stood at the Christmas table and worked the cork off the champagne bottle, Pa stood in his own little space from which he peered out, through his fearful little slit, at the others. It was that little space that gave him his distinction. Chris had it too. On the sporting field it was called composure. It bred heroism. They acted their roles, Pa and Chris, and were rewarded. *So how the fuck did I get to be the family loser?*

The back door was open. A wave of coolness almost knocked him over. He pulled the door softly behind him and sniffed the damp indoor air, scented faintly with burnt matches and turkey flesh. In the dining room, he heard a cracker pop and a loud, ironic hurrah, the sound of an adult humouring either a child or an old person.

He poked into the storerooms at the back of the kitchen. The family's old fads still resided in here, gathering cobwebs – the underwater camera (see the awful out-of-focus framed pictures on the wall, everything the colour of green olives?), the windsurfer, the surf ski, the Atari computer, the chemistry and electronics sets.

This house – he re-entered through the moist dark passage linking the storerooms with the laundry – throbbed with charge. He tiptoed up the stairs to his parents' bedroom. The drawers – folded trousers, matching argyle jumpers and socks, Pa's Y-fronts, his leather gloves, his pressed shirts slipped back into their plastic-cardboard packaging each day – now, in perpetuity, those drawers an archive, a museum to a family.

He went back downstairs, pausing on the landing to check that there were no footsteps on the floorboards between dining room and kitchen.

He'd always thought they were very rich, even more so since his banishment. But in the kitchen he saw the linoleum was worn in a rut between the pantry door and the sink; the wooden window casements were bowed with moisture; the striped wallpaper was peeling, gracefully, near the door jambs; the cold water tap dripped onto a brown rust stain; the oven dial was stuck on the alarm symbol; the open griller tray was caked with archaic blackened cheese; the dishwasher stank vaguely of something old and dead, a smell dispersed over the years, the thing in there so old and so dead that it was mummified.

The parcel still under his arm, he went down the side hall into the library, its papery scent bringing back those days when he fucked the cushions, fucked the ottoman, fucked the chaise longue, brought in schoolmates during his fleeting summer of popularity when they circle-jerked around the waxy-papered relics he'd gathered in the bush, before that, like everything else, ended when the others grew out of it, grew embarrassed in front of each other, and finally embarrassed themselves of Hammett.

How much had his parents known about him? Probably, he thought now, as little as he knew about them. Who can be as foreign, ultimately, as family? There can be points of observation and collection – call it evidence – but their evidence of him no more resembled what he was than an acorn resembles an oak. They had had years to twist, whisk, pummel and chew their idea of Hammett. Then years more to speculate, ward off, ignore, suspect, re-form, toy with, deny thrice, suggest and regurgitate that already highly refined and processed secondary product, that sausage of what they allowed themselves to *think* they knew. How much did they really know? Ma's sight was less blurred by hope and absence: it was sharpened by having raised him herself and focused by her instinct. She knew more than John. But even she knew no more than the shadow. How could she know anything? It was only a matter of reconciling themselves to the vastness of what they did not know. But they wouldn't reconcile. They had to extrapolate. They were parents.

They'd never have known his dreadful power, the curse that started with Old Faithful.

His crime against Old Faithful had begun one day when, in year seven, he wagged school. His science teacher had sent him to the Headmaster's office as punishment for collecting chemicals in a single test tube, then smashing the tube away from what had congealed into a nasty glutinous substance, which he had then hurled at the ceiling. The tubular knob-head had hung like a stalactite. Hammett had already told the Headmaster that this science teacher wasn't fit to teach him, and there was little to be gained from going over that ground again so, rather than see the Headmaster, Hammett went to the train station intending to go home. On the way, he decided that rather than explain to Ma the tiresome saga of the blobby thing, the science teacher, the Head-master and his early homecoming, he'd go to Kings Cross.

At twelve, he had already accumulated a store of first-hand anatomical knowledge of females to which, no matter how much longer he lived, he would – could – only add increments, addenda and errata, gap-fillers and obscure footnotes. He'd covered all that without having to leave the North Shore. The next conquest would be geographic. He'd heard of Kings Cross, seen it on tele-vision. He came out of the train station, past the heroin addicts and drunks and sluts and dealers and pimps, his head turning from side to side in wonderment at the people and the smells of kebab fat, grease, puke, cigarettes, dope, stale beer and cheap perfume. He *knew* this place. He fitted in here. Immediately. He roamed the main street and the back streets in his school uniform, his mind empty, his senses pure receptors of all this: the bong shops, sex shops, strip joints, souvenir shops, nameless bars, the runaways, the tourists, the sailors, the homos, the tittering old men who acted too coy and besotted to invite him to the places they took girls like Hammett. He was twelve years old and blessed. He'd made six or seven passes of Kellett Street and Darlinghurst Road, marvelling at the subtle changes each time as day kerbcrawled into night. As darkness fell he went to The Wall, which he'd heard about, and checked out the pale boys not much older than himself. He got lost down an alley between Tewkesbury Avenue and William Street, a mini-canyon, and found himself amid a roaring meat district of transvestites and children and inching traffic. He was offered drives by men in cars, but he knew these men, he'd been fending them off for years.

He wandered back up to Darlinghurst Road, where he felt comforted by the overflowing old ladies slouching in the door-ways smoking cigarettes and chatting among themselves about getting their cars fixed and where they'd had their hair cut. They called Hammett Sweetie and Sugar and Pumpernickel. One of them, occupying most of a doorway between a pinball parlour and a fruit shop, was a large-breasted black lady, a Maori or a Samoan. Hammett had never been so close to a black lady – or even a black person, with the exception of Raymond Bandeau at school, who was not black as such but a Pacific Prince from the birdshit island of Nauru. This lady had frizzy hair, on which she balanced an old-fashioned pillbox hat, like the ones the Queen Mother wore. A meshy veil hung over her face. She had pink lips the colour of meat in a butcher's window and clear-rimmed glasses that magnified her smiling eyes to look like specimens from the science lab. She was the one who called him Pumpernickel. She flashed her lovely smile. Her teeth were big piano keys. She wore a black skirt and a black blazer in some sort of shiny not-plastic-but-not-leather-and-not-quite-snakeskin material that managed to both retain and amplify her figure. Beneath the coat, only a tight fishnet thing intervened between her night skin and the night air. The blazer was parted just wide enough to show the sides of her breasts, long folds of flesh veeing like bow-waves from her chestbone.

Hammett, hormones gushing, realised he was wearing shorts. Khaki school shorts. The black lady noticed too, and tapped the side of her nose. Hammett blushed and walked, half-bent, away down Darlinghurst Road.

The next few times he passed her doorway she was not there. She must have finished her shift, or been picked up. Hammett knew the score. He headed towards the train station. He was in one of the lanes between Macleay and Victoria Streets, a little lost, when he glanced up at a second-floor apartment window and saw the black lady. She'd taken her coat off. She wore her tight fishnet top. She smiled and waved her cigarette hand at him. Her breasts were obscured by the windowsill, but he could see how they drooped low, sweaty, flat and round, could be any shape you wanted. She called out some words but the only one he could make out was 'Pumpernickel'.

In what he intended, in his twelve-year-old mind, as a friendly gesture to a new acquaintance, Hammett bobbled his eyebrows at the lady. She paused, her cigarette hand suspended near her mouth, and regarded him with a narrowness that halted him. Then she disappeared from the window. His erection tented his khaki shorts. He shifted on the kerb.

Her hand closed like warm meat around his. He never had to raise the matter of money. She would accept nothing but his school badge, as a souvenir. He was with her for two hours. Her skin was rough, papery, her hair unpleasant, like steel wool rubbed thin. She stank of sweat. She was all around him at once. She made him strip for her, slowly, like a white slave. She proceeded, with an old camera, to take photos of him. He came four separate times in the two hours. At the end, when he confessed that he was meant to have gone home, and his mother was probably freaking out, the black lady scolded him and put him into a taxi home, for which she paid.

It had been a misunderstanding. All he'd meant was to nod hello from the street.

When he stood outside windows and took photographs, and made the ladies strip for him, he was innocently rekindling Old Faithful.

But they'd found him guilty.

He'd gone on detention, and Old Faithful remained by his side. When the bad things happened he travelled back in his mind to Old Faithful, who wrapped him in her blanket of flesh. She was always there. That first spring evening in year seven continued to burn slowly and evenly like a good true coal, feeding his fantasies for years. Whenever he doubted himself, or who he was, or had trouble, or his mind wandered, he could always come back to Old Faithful.

But then something bad happened. It was while on detention that Hammett first noticed a pattern of events surrounding the women who peopled his most powerful fantasies. There was a mother of a friend of his, Mrs Charles, over whom he'd done himself silly. Mrs Charles was killed in a level-crossing accident. Then there was a teacher, Miss Humphrey – a precursor to Old Faithful in her fantasy-reliability – she'd got cancer. When he was inside, and becoming familiar with porn stars, he realised that the pattern was more than just coincidence. His favourite, since before he knew who she was, had been Savannah. Savannah committed suicide. He dug Tricia Devereaux, who got AIDS. To test this power – see if it could travel forwards in time – he thought a lot about Trinity Loren, a nice actress with fat natural breasts. He borrowed her videos and put a poster of her on his wall. Then Trinity Loren died of an overdose. There were more uncanny victims, and more.

As his eighteen months drew to an end, Hammett grew scared. When he was released, the first thing he did was catch a train to the Cross, not for the customary prison-to-Cross purpose but on a quest of his own. He'd gone up and down Darlinghurst Road, searching for her. She was nowhere to be seen. He asked other prostitutes if they knew where the black lady was – 'with the thick glasses, and the veil'. Nobody knew. She'd been there for years, then one day she'd left. He waited for hours outside her flat, but she never came back and the light never came on. He went back up Darlinghurst Road and, by chance, ran into one of the old prostitutes. He described Old Faithful. It had been a long time, but his memories were vivid. The old prostitute nodded, tucking her bottom lip below her teeth. She interrupted Hammett with a shake of her head.

'She's gone. Dunno where. Just up and left. While ago.'

Hammett didn't need to hear more. *I've killed her*. If anyone was going to come to harm, it had to be a person who had given him such joy. There was a universal balance – women who visited Hammett in his fantasies paid the price. It was a macabre, devastating power. Still shaking his head with grief over Old Faithful, he went and visited his parents. It was a debacle. His mother threw him out, or as good as. He booked himself into a four-bed dorm room in a backpackers' hostel and, that very night, tried to fix her in his mind – his own mother – and *do something to her*. But no, nothing. He tried, but it refused to happen. He must have shorted out something in his own circuitry that day, because ever since then the gears would not engage. Within a few months, he gave up trying. He became busy, with business, and it didn't matter anymore. Those days were behind him. He just serviced the needs of others, and for his good work was relieved of the burden of guilt. Or maybe he'd sacrificed his ability to feel pleasure so that others may feel.

He lived on: priestly, celibate, penitent.

Just another thing they didn't know.

He returned to the kitchen and picked some slices of ham out of the refrigerator, eating them cold. It was here that the worst humiliation had occurred. His progress from one category to the next was always the same. It went something like discovery – fulfilment – tang of boredom – curiosity about more – daring to go the next step – desire for something more authentic – the leap. *Farmyard Friends* and *Animal Crackers* led to Des, right here, on this linoleum floor, roused to an overwhelming sense of disgust with himself, as if waking from a sleepwalking nightmare to discover himself about to cross a busy highway, when Ma and Chris appeared at the door.

Of all the hideous moments of which his life, at that time, seemed composed, this was the worst. He could see what they saw. But he could also see what they did not see: his revulsion, his decision to stop himself from this appalling act. The mortification of being caught was nothing to the inexplicability of being innocent.

Ma would not talk to him. Chris said he'd kick him until his teeth came out through his arse. Hammett ran away.

But not far. He'd done as he was doing now: lurking around the home, spying on them, trying to make sense of them. He saw

Ma and Chris in fraught conversation in one room while Pa and Davis watched television, oblivious, in the next. He saw Ma crying in Chris's arms. When they'd re-convene as a family, they'd paper it all over with their wry normalcy, a joke at Davis's expense, a laugh at some idiocy on the television.

He wanted, more than anything, to explain. But where would he start? And where would they insist he finish? His mortification ran so deep that there were no ledges on which he could catch his descent. There was no language for apologies. Why was there no forgiving in this family? Why no apology? There had been no way he could look his mother in the face and ask her to forgive him. He doubted she even wanted him to. She was through with him, finished. Rid of him.

But, now he knows a little more about his Pa, he knows there is another dimension to it. If she started admitting weakness into this house, where would she start and where could she stop?

The running-away, and the looking-in, had become as much his talent as cricket was Chris's. Hammett got himself expelled from school classes intentionally, to free up his time for more important projects. Since the episode with Des, Ma had as little to do with him as possible without raising Pa's suspicions, and hence the need to explain it to him. For some reason she'd do anything to protect Pa from this knowledge. She became Hammett's mother only in name and the compulsory mechanics of feeding and clothing him.

By the time he was caught by the police, people knew from one glance what he was. He was caught, and caught again. He found out where he belonged: the green-clad brotherhood of wankers, pervs, freaks, stalkers. They answered advertisements for Inflate-a-Mates and penis pumps, Spanish Fly and one hundred videos for ninety-nine cents. They bought videotapes regardless of the quality of script, lighting and whatever – the quality had come down to meet them in the marketplace. They went to Friends of X-Rated Entertainment conventions, and tried to start up conversations with X-rated performers, and sometimes were thrown out by burly men in black shirts with earplugs. They jerked off while writing fan letters. His people. His place. The lonely, the scared, the unparented.

He let himself out the back door, locked it and returned the key in its gladwrap to the soil of the pot plant. He went back around the side and watched them through the window. They were still the team they'd always been: Ma, Pa, Chris, Davis. Pa was talking with some animation now, spittle flying, hands waving. The little girls watched him warily, the adults politely, Ma with excessive delight. Plenty of tip, plenty of iceberg. Who was Hammett to deny Pa his fleeting happiness? It wasn't all Pa's fault. Humiliating the old man wasn't what he wanted. He wanted to show them that he was fit to join them, to be admitted as an adult. And he could, now, because he was as good as them. Chris was a fading star, Davis drifting into aimless middle-age, Pa caught in his own oblivion.

It's for the strong to forgive. As he watched them through the window, Hammett realised that he was the strong one. To leave this parcel for Pa, to get Pa caught out, would be a pointless punishment, reheating the miseries of the past. What Hammett wanted was something new. He was a man now. He wanted them to see a man, not a gutless boy who'd sneak in, leave an incriminating parcel and sneak out again.

He walked out the side gate to the top of the right-of-way, jammed the parcel into the overfull red-lidded recycling bin belonging to one of the townhouses. He couldn't get the lid shut. As he pressed, the bin's wheels went out from under it. Losing control, Hammett gave it an exasperated push. As he turned and walked off down Warramunga Avenue, he heard the bin roll down the right-of-way and collapse in a clatter. Maybe the gift would burst its packaging and lie in the open, waiting to be found. He thought: Some lucky kid.

PART FOUR

PART FOUR

Ropy with lack of sleep, Davis is sitting in his father's surgery waiting for his appointment with the skin cancer specialist. For seemingly the thousandth time, he revisits his conversation with Claire last night. It's falling into place now. The silver lining, if there is one, is that Claire is unaware of Davis's feelings for her. She was never in on the joke. But everywhere else, Davis sees the clouds of Cobcroft's duplicity. Cobcroft, eh? Dirty dog. He'd had more than one motive to turn Pa against Davis, hadn't he? Well, Jim Cobcroft is going to get his.

Davis is musing about this when Suzie Brand calls his mobile. Chris's Suzie. Her voice quivery with fury or tears, she complains to Davis about a reporter who called with questions about Hammett coming to the funeral.

'You deserve that,' Davis says finally.

Silence, then, freezer-cold: 'I'm sorry?'

Davis and Suzie rarely speak. Generally, Suzie calls when she and Chris are fighting and she wants to pump Davis for clues and sympathy. Mainly clues.

'Chris was the one who made his family the subject of public knowledge,' Davis says. 'It's a two-way street.'

'Why are you being like this?'

'Maybe it's time to tell the truth.'

'Maybe it's time to show a little support.'

'Truth can be support.'

'What are you talking about, Davis?'

Davis tells Suzie that Hammett wants to come to the funeral. He doesn't tell her that Hammett seems to have been with Pa on New Year's Eve. He doesn't tell her about the things he has discovered about Pa. He doesn't tell her that Chris kicked the shit out of him last night.

'I want my family back,' Davis says. 'I want to give Hammett a go, and . . . you're talking about supporting each other? How about we, for once, support Hammett?'

'Have you spoken to Chris about this?'

'Obviously he hasn't spoken to you about it.'

'Obviously.'

'Then I think that's where you should start, Suzie.'

'What does Lucy think?'

'Lucy doesn't know about it.'

'Oh, right! So before you start accusing me of –'

'Lucy doesn't give a stuff. She's too busy. All right? So I don't think you should say another word. Try getting your husband to start telling you things.'

After the phone call, Davis breathes pure air. Truth is good, a helium lightness. He wonders what stopped him, what has always stopped him.

Probably the same thing that stopped Pa. Davis looks around the spare, functional room. Boredom? Loneliness? Sitting here, in his father's chair, Davis tries to put himself inside Pa's skin. The Internet must have come as a cataclysmic shock to the old man. Davis knows of men – through rumours, second-hand tailings – whose marriages have collapsed in their late middle-age when suddenly they came into contact with images from which they have been protected all their lives. Obscenity laws are meant to protect the vulnerable. Everybody assumes that means children, but men like Pa – who grew up in an era when pornography was cheesecake, when hardcore meant a flash of 'pink' in someone else's wild seventies – these men were utterly unready for the things they would find on the Internet. They're the ones whose lives have been up-ended by the shock. On whose soft, pliable inner eye the images are stamped. Who lie awake at night wondering what is wrong with themselves. Grey-haired men. The worst thing about Internet porn may not be what it does to children; it may be that it is breaking up forty-year marriages. Ending families. Jesus, Davis thinks. Going by what's on his disks and emails, Pa had a ten-hour-a-day habit. No wonder he stopped talking. It wasn't just Davis, and Cobcroft, and the messy business of the surgery. It was much more private.

But if it was only Internet porn, Pa could have sat here all day and, well, self-medicated. Instead, he went out, prowling sex shops, where he'd met Hammett. Pa had wanted something more than pictures. But what? Why take the risk? What else had he been searching for?

An email pops up on Davis's screen.

Hi. My book says your appointment is now? C xx.

The sun splits the overcast sky and gilds the turf. The patchwork-mown oval glows, an oasis of geometry. The umpire rolls the scarlet ball, its gold lettering catching the sun, to Tom Pritchard. Applause shears the air for the Australian team springing onto the field, legs compressed beneath compact torsos and doorstopper cricketer butts.

Pritchard bends to the ball and in one motion flicks it behind him. The moment Pritchard touches the ball, cheers turn to boos – distinguishing him from his team. Morning talkback radio has condemned the captain for declaring and cutting Chris Brand short of the Australian record, the world record. Pritchard pulls down his mask of hat and sunglasses.

A standing ovation ripples around the stadium, following Chris as he rounds the boundary. He takes up a position near the fence, a proletarian position, normally a fast bowler's agistment, but he likes to field out there when his reflexes are too tired for close catching. Or when he doesn't want to be near his team-mates.

Children stumble over the plastic seats with their bats, programmes, autograph books, cardboard visors, pens. Chris signs autographs, his back to the game, sensing, the way a mother senses her child's next cry, the exact intervals between balls.

'You're a ledge, Brandy,' a nine-year-old boy says sternly. Chris returns his pen and magazine.

A legend. Well, he is, isn't he? He's built his monument. None of those fuckers will be able to forget him now. At last, the grudging admiration in today's press. Things that used to cause outrage are now endearing signs of his toughness. *The Australian* has a two-page Chris Brand extravaganza, recalling his quintessentially Australian ruthlessness. (They used to call it dourness.) His amusing idiosyncrasies, like soaking his socks in whiskey between sessions on long days. His cautious running between wickets, which once attracted accusations of selfishness, is now held up as the footprint of his determination. And then there are the anecdotes. The *Daily Telegraph* reported a conversation on the pitch between Chris and Nathan Such during their big partnership. After Chris had edged his way to twenty runs, the kid said: 'They're bowling well, aren't they?' To which Chris had apparently replied: 'Bullshit. Look how easy I'm playing them with the edges [of the bat]. Just wait till I start using the full face.'

Chris wonders where that came from. It's pure crap – or, more likely, a true story about some other cricketer that has now been transferred, like an inheritance, to him.

But he's engraved his 331 not out. Not even those pricks in the press box can rub that out. He can sleep with his record books for the rest of his days.

Australia take two quick wickets, and the South African captain comes in. The Australian bowlers pound his heart and throat. The captain counterattacks. Instead of ducking, he starts hooking and cutting. The brainless assault continues – against commonsense and order – as the bowlers are drawn into the pissing contest. The South African hooks two sixes and a four. He slices a six over third man. Simmo flings another ball at his face. The captain flashes and the ball skews off the shoulder of his bat and flies over the keeper's head. Arms go up to alert Chris at fine leg. He runs – was that an autograph book he let flutter to the ground? – towards the sightscreen. The ball may go over – no, will hit it. In an instant, Chris calculates the size of the parabola. Eyes on the ball, he looks as if he'll collide with the sightscreen. The ball descends. He has little chance of intercepting it and might as well save himself from injury, but at the last second he accelerates again, simultaneously avoiding impaling himself on the screen while catching the ball in his outthrust right hand. Breath is sucked out of the ground.

He is living in a dream of which he is not part. Mobbed by his team, he wishes they would go away. He spins with a sickening vertigo. Roar after roar accompanies the replays of his catch on the big screen. Pritchard calls Chris to field in close.

'Come on, on your toes, boys!' Pritchard says, winking at Chris.

The two South African batsmen are being sledged mercilessly by the fielders around Chris. One batsman, a left-hander, was touted as a future star but hasn't made many in this series. According to the press, he's been 'struggling with the psychological pressures of Australian conditions'.

Chris's only thought is that his ingrown toenail aches. He has a pain in his temple. Foreign to the applause surrounding his catch, indifferent to the course of the match, he goes into a crouch for the next ball. The left-hander pads it away.

'Ree-aw-ree-aw-ree-aw!'

Chris glances at the taunter. It's Nathan Such making an ambulance sound. Well, the kid's grown up fast. Emboldened, no doubt, by his strong batting.

As Nathan cackles across the pitch from Chris (who pulls his collar around his ears), the batsman takes strike. He's got a black father and a white mother – which brings him into the quota of 'black' players South Africa must choose. He's not really Test standard, which pisses off the other Yaapies. But he's not bad, Chris thinks: he's scored some pebble-in-our-shoe thirties and forties, hasn't been their worst by a long way.

From across the pitch, Chris hears: 'Ree-aw-ree-aw-ree-aw!'

After the over, the fielders around Chris laugh with an explosion like schoolboys escaping from class. Chris folds his arms and looks skywards. He doesn't even want to acknowledge the presence of his teammates, let alone Nathan Such, who's leading the choir.

A new over, another ball. 'Ree-aw-ree-aw-whoop-whoop-whoop!' Laughter.

The black batsman walks away from the wicket between balls, collecting himself, tapping down an irrelevant divot halfway to the square-leg umpire. Chris has no idea how he's handling this. Maybe he's batting with the determination of hatred. Maybe he's decided that when he goes home, he'll never play Test cricket again. Chris examines his face. It's so young, like Nathan Such's. These guys were playing under-tens when Chris first batted for Australia.

'Ree-aw-ree-aw-ree-aw!' Nathan Such again.

All right, the joke. The guy lost his parents in a highway pile-up on the Ciskei last winter. Four or five months ago. And these Australians – Chris sees the blood-bloated face and pig eyes of Nathan Such – these Australians, who three days ago were wearing black fucking armbands, can do this.

The batsman swings at a wide half-volley. Chris jumps in the air, spinning away in anticipation of the missile, his arse to the ball. But the batsman is beaten by a late dip. He mis-cues his shot, inside-edging it onto his pad. It pops up gently but Chris, leaping away for self-protection, is out of position. It falls harmlessly to the ground. When Chris regains his footing, his teammates are standing with their hands on their heads.

'Come on, let's finish him off!' Tom Pritchard urges. They're all afraid of having a go at me, Chris thinks. I'm a sacred cow. Well, it's only taken twelve years.

The South African batsmen stage a fightback, punching the ball into the gaps and seeing off both Australian bowlers. The advantage is still safely Australia's – thanks to Chris's innings, the South African pair would have to bat until this time tomorrow to have a hope of saving the match – but the weather forecasters are saying storms tomorrow, so a spike of anxiety injects itself into the Australians' demeanour.

A drinks break arrives. Chris stands apart from his teammates, queasily distant. Thoughts of his family press on him, like a cage of lunatics he can restrain no longer. Davis. And Hammett. Pa. Fucking bullshit, but – but . . . *WHAT THE FUCK AM I MEANT TO DO?*

He claps his hands, urging action.

He is called into a huddle. Tom Pritchard is telling the four close-in fielders: 'Okay – anything – they pad one down? Go up. Okay? Anything that goes to hand, any play and miss – we all go up. Right?'

Nathan Such nods and grins at Chris. It's a set-up. They're going to try to con the umpire into thinking the batsman is out when he's not. Chris has been involved in these before – or at least, he's been in teams that have done it. He's never falsely appealed in his life. He wants to push Pritchard's nose back into his brain. Cheats. Baggy green cheats.

Sure enough, the black South African swishes and misses a ball. The Australians go up – Pritchard, the wicketkeeper, the fielders around Chris – Nathan Such charging the umpire with his arms raised. A better impression of certainty you could never witness. It's too much for the umpire, who points his finger to heaven: out.

As the black guy departs with a rueful half-smile – but why should he expect them to observe the laws of the game when they ignore the laws of human decency? – Chris stands with hands on hips. His mates embrace, laughing. They've done the umpire a beauty. Test cricket is, after all, a man's game.

Chris drifts away into the outfield. Pritchard calls him. Chris doesn't even pause. He finds a wide open space for himself, where he can't hear a thing and won't have to pretend he is playing in a team.

Pritchard waves, but Chris lowers his face, intently scratching a mark on the ground. The wicketkeeper shouts. But the match has to go on. They give up trying to alert him. He moves in with the bowler; and now is when it hits him.

January 5

Davis and Claire walk down Liverpool Street from Darlinghurst into East Sydney, towards the cancer clinic. A soft after-rain breeze blows off Woolloomooloo Bay. Claire is talking about the studio she rents. 'Yeah, it has a harbour view, if you lean out of the kitchen window like this.' She motions giraffe-like, crooking her neck sideways and squinting. 'The advertising calls it "harbour innuendos".'

Conversation with her has an effortless familiarity. This, Davis thinks, is how you meet your soul mate in a dream: she knows you, and you know her. The only surprise is that you've taken all this time to acknowledge each other.

'You'll be all right.' She gives his hand a squeeze. She smiles with the corners of her mouth turned down. He returns her smile and stiffens himself to conceal his limp. His hip bears a single black cloud of a bruise, and his ribs sing out every third step.

She needn't have come with him. But it is her lunch break, she said, and she didn't trust him to find his way unsupervised. Davis replied, with a flirtatiousness that seemed risky up to the moment he opened his mouth, that she only wanted to come so that they could spend time together. Claire gave him her wry smile, and a nod, as if to acknowledge his gambit and say she'll think about it and get back to him.

He dares to think that whatever it is, she shares it.

A few blocks from the clinic, they pass the pink-doored brothels of Liverpool Street. Inside, plain hefty women sit in comfortable chairs with their legs crossed watching daytime soaps. Davis and Claire stop at a traffic crossing.

Claire ignites a tongue of burning gas under the tip of her cigarette, pops her lighter back into her pocket. The sound of a slightly unwound car window whistles down Bourke Street. Across the road, workmen gut a terrace. Davis notices the way men look at Claire: less than lust, more than idle speculation. At Lucy, men have always stared lubriciously, as if Davis weren't there. He yearned to lash out; whether to defend his wife's honour or simply to assert his own visibility. With Claire, he feels that whatever other men do, she can look after herself.

Claire stamps out her cigarette and they climb the clinic's stairs in silence. Within minutes, Davis is summoned to see Professor Birch, the founder of the clinic and a longstanding friend of his parents. Claire looks so unaccompanied, so spousely, in her waiting room chair that in a rush of affection and gratitude Davis lurches back across the floor and buries his face in her shoulder.

'I have to tell you something,' he whispers.

'Okay, just . . . after.' She pats his back.

'I miss him so much. I'm scared, I miss him and I don't know what to do.'

'I miss him too, Davis. But here, you have to go in. Go in, we'll talk later.'

She takes him back to the desk like a child on his first day of school. Davis gives her a forlorn look.

'I'm not myself,' he says. 'I'm sorry.'

Claire musters a smile and nods him in. 'I'll be here.'

Professor Birch seats Davis in a reclining chair and reads the referral. Professor Birch has a putty nose and a dry rash around the corners of his mouth, and pterygiums on both of his blue eyes.

He comes around to Davis and peers at his lip. The professor's suit trousers are pulled high over a pot belly.

'So, how's your mother then?'

Professor Birch's bare fingers stretch and palpate Davis's lower lip. Davis's tongue wags loosely in his mouth.

'John would be thrilled to see you taking his place at the surgery.' Professor Birch wipes his hands on a paper towel but continues looking at Davis's lip. 'Looks like a precancerous lesion there. How long have you had it?'

'Not sure. Year, eighteen months.'

The professor returns to his desk, knobbly fingers feeling his way around the edge like those of a blind man, and makes a note. He must be in his mid-seventies now; he has the same talcum smell as Pa, a generational smell.

'Yes, proud as punch.' Professor Birch leans back in his chair and steeples his fingers. 'I took a call from Jim Cobcroft this morning. He told me what's happened with John's share of the surgery. Can't say I approve. I'm sure, in the circumstances, he'll come around. You know, we've had terrible interference from council over our liquidambars.'

Apparently satisfied with his non sequitur, Professor Birch writes more notes. He stands, as if to usher Davis to the door, and Davis gets up too. Then, as if remembering something, the Professor embarks on a long tale about neighbourly disputes and council intransigence over trees. Davis checks his watch. He hopes Claire is still waiting.

Then, as suddenly as the Professor began, he interrupts himself: 'You will find a lot of ready-made friends in the community. They can look after you, you know. You only have to ask. Your parents have helped all sorts of people in all sorts of situations. Priceless bounty of goodwill, community capital. Best not to waste it.'

The Professor gives him a long, searching look. His irises are beginning to milk with cataract.

'Well,' Davis says.

'I think I might take it off right now,' Birch says.

'What – this?'

'Your complexion puts you in the danger zone. Not to mention the family history.'

'Now?'

Hustled from room to room like a remand prisoner, Davis is soon lying on his back inside the theatre. His ribs hurt and he wonders why he is having this done, here, now. But he's always had a weakness for decisive doctors. It was one of the reasons he tried to become one.

He concentrates on the nurse who prepares him for the procedure. Her smoker's lips are pinched, as if pulled overly tight by a drawstring.

'What time is it, Prof?' he asks when Professor Birch appears in his gown.

'Now what exactly is the law on these things?' the Professor says, checking his watch but not responding to Davis's question. 'Where do you stand vis-a-vis James Cobcroft? Do you have any friends we can talk to at the A.M.A.? Seems we could streamline the process, keep the question of . . . reputation . . . out of it.'

Professor Birch injects an anaesthetic into Davis's face and asks a string of questions, presumably rhetorical. He muses aloud on ways he might be able to corrupt various processes to help Davis keep his father's share of the practice. The professor seems to have taken his bedside sociability to the point where he has forgotten the procedure he is about to perform. Soon Davis has had enough.

'Look Prof, I've got to say I don't have time for all this,' he says thickly.

'. . . and the constitutional matters it raises are quite – what's that, boy?'

'Can you just, um, get on with it?' Davis tries to say it with a smile; but the anaesthetic robs him of a certain facial suppleness and the words come out more tersely than he intended.

Professor Birch looks at the nurse. It is impossible to assess his expression behind his mask and glasses. After a moment, he gives off a quiet sigh and puts out a hand for his scalpel.

He cuts, Davis senses, in silent anger. His blade hacks rather than strokes. Usually, Professor Birch has a registrar do his surgical work. His reputation was always for research rather than operating skills, and he does have a name as something of an abattoirist. Davis's eyes water as the scalpel gouges at his lip. Suddenly this feels like a very bad idea. Davis foresees the week ahead. Today his pulse will throb inside the scar; his lower lip will be swollen to the size of a chipolata. It will bleed through the dressing. He will become depressed with the administration of painkillers and the frustration of not being understood, and of eating through the gap on the other side of his mouth. Now the Professor is stitching it too tightly at the ends – stitching in anger – causing the lip to fold over and knot on itself. The swollen lip will turn leathery; he will mumble like Brando at Pa's funeral. There will be a referred pain through his mandible, and his tongue will grow so worn with working itself around his teeth that it will feel as if it has a hole bored through it. The scab will turn white and soft like tapioca. The referred pain will make his eyes water. Davis will notice a tendency of others to touch their lip while their eyes wander to his. His tongue will start worrying the scab and stitches. Then, on the fifth day, he will take out the stitches himself. Prematurely, drawing blood and pain out of his whole face, his whole body, he will snip the stitches. He won't want to come back to beastly Birch. The combination of his impatience and Birch's incompetence will leave unsightly lumps and holes. Operate in haste, repent at leisure.

'That should do it.' Professor Birch rips the thread tight on the last suture. 'Come back in five or six days and we'll take those stitches out and give you the path report.'

'Is Doctor Mullally still waiting?'

'Can't understand you.' Birch wipes his hands and turns away.

'Nobody will be able to make much of what you're saying for a day or two. It should improve after the anaesthetic wears off, but I'll give you a script for some codeine.'

'Is Claire still outside?'

'Can you understand any of this?' Birch asks the nurse.

'Something about Doctor Mullally.' The nurse dabs the corners of Davis's mouth.

'Oh, well,' Professor Birch removes his gown, 'if you don't want what your father has built up for you, then Doctor Mullally will be only too pleased to step in. It was my understanding, until the last couple of days, that it was yours if you wanted it. But it seems you don't, so why would we bother helping you? I was only trying to –'

'I want to know if Doctor Mullally's outside.'

'Can't understand a word. Perhaps that'll be better, eh?' Birch addresses the nurse. 'He can't say anything incriminating! I've done you a favour, Davis. Believe me. That lesion was nasty. And I suppose after your father, you felt it was urgent to come and have it looked at.'

The nurse hands Davis a mirror. One look is enough to know why Birch has regained his good humour. He's had his little revenge for Davis's cheekiness; he has confirmed his hard-won reputation as the butcher's butcher.

Davis cannot speak. He wants to go home. He gets sight of the professor's watch. Will Claire have waited an hour?

He inhales and says, slowly, as clearly as he can: 'What's it got to do with my father?'

Birch is at a desk writing, his back to Davis. For a few moments Davis thinks the old man is going to force him to repeat the question, but then Birch answers:

'Since you're the only one he told.'

'Told what?'

Birch spends some more time writing, then comes and squints at Davis's lip.

'Nurse?'

Something in his tone tells the nurse that she has vital business outside this room.

'Well,' Birch says, sitting down and swivelling his chair to face Davis. 'He told you, didn't he?'

Davis's lip is starting to throb. He closes his eyes.

'Told me what?'

'About the melanoma problem.'

Davis opens his eyes. Birch is sitting close to him, but the old man's eyes slide away. The Professor shakes his head at the memory.

'Poor bugger. More lumps than a nut loaf. I still can't understand why he left it so long. But then, that's the problem when you don't have any bleeding. Those flesh-coloured melanomas, he never suspected. I had the feeling he only came to me to confirm a theory of his. He wasn't interested in treatment. And it was a moot point, as it turns out. All too late. But of course, I'm not telling you anything you don't know, so . . .'

Davis's heart pounds. He can barely breathe.

'Why do you say I know?' he mumbles carefully.

'It was good that he told you, damn good show.' Birch looks up at him with a sad smile. 'The last time I saw him – we only had two appointments, and a couple of scans – the last time I saw him was a few days before Christmas. He was quite excited about showing you the scans. Kept saying, "My son and I are talking about everything, and I am going to show him all of this." Babbling on, really. Wasn't in the best shape. And I know how you and he used to discuss work. It seemed natural that he wanted to share these results with you, even though he was concealing them from your mother. I couldn't quite work out why he was so excited about it, almost as though he was happy to find out the awful truth. But it wasn't for me to ask questions. Poor bugger had enough on his plate.'

'How . . .' Davis tries to inhale to stop his voice trembling. 'How do you know he meant me?'

Birch gives him an indulgent smile. 'It wasn't going to be Chris, was it?'

Davis pushes himself upright. He steadies himself against a wave of dizziness. Birch shows him to the door.

'Well, my condolences to your mother. Funeral's Saturday, eh?'

Birch holds the door open. Davis stands, feet stapled to the floor.

'Melanoma?' he says.

'Like a nut loaf.'

'He died of heart failure.'

'Don't we all?'

Davis shakes his head, uncomprehending.

'Well.' Birch claps him on the back. An old man, still alive. Long may he be chipper. 'Think about what I said. Don't waste it, boy. Your father's reputation. Keep things quiet, play it straight with Jimmy Cobcroft, and everyone will only remember the good.'

In the waiting room, Claire Mullally's face scrunches up in an empathetic smile. Davis's stomach melts. The contradiction, he thinks: if Claire is my soul mate, my twin, my alter ego, then there's no way she can fall in love with me, because I could never love anyone so disgusting, gross, wounded, as Davis Brand.

'I've called the surgery to take the afternoon off,' Claire says.

'No need for that,' he mumbles through the bandage.

'You need looking after.'

'Jim will be pissed off.'

'As if I care.' Hard apostrophes form at the ends of Claire's mouth.

They walk up the hill, past the brothels, to Green Park.

'Let's go away,' Davis says, slowly, so she can't mishear. 'Let's go away together. Somewhere. And sort ourselves out.'

Claire trains her eyes straight ahead, as if avoiding meeting someone she knows.

'Let's just take it easy,' she says.

'I want you,' he mumbles through his dressing.

Claire stops, militarily, on the spot. There is a graffiti logo from a multinational corporation on the pavement. She glares at it, as if it has caused the offence.

'Davis.' She looks up at him. He sees himself in her eyes. Davis is sure now. He loves her. Fuck it all. He loves her. This is it. 'Before you start saying things like that, there's something else you should know.'

'Let me guess. You're taken.'

A half, a quarter, of a smile. 'I'm not some table at a restaurant that's either taken or not taken. This thing with Jim – I'm still pretty hurt over all that. It's going to take time. But that's not what I have to tell you.'

'Right.'

'You just seem to have made a lot of assumptions about me. Without asking.'

'I know.'

'And you're married.'

'That's what you had to tell me?'

'You are acting as if you need reminding.' She pauses, with a smile. 'Come on, let me take you home. We'll go to your place, and I'll make us something cold and wet. Okay? How does that sound?'

She links an arm through his. As they walk through Kings Cross, a gust hurtles up William Street. At a pedestrian crossing, Claire pauses to smooth down Davis's hair with a firmness that is (he hopes) too formal, too impersonal, not to be a disguise for affection.

'You know,' she says, 'I think you'd look really good if you shaved your head.'

'Claire.' His heart flaps like a pancake at the sound of her name on his lips. 'I've got some things to tell you too.' He looks at her nose, which has a lovable horizontal crease from where she's been wiping it.

'I can't understand what you're saying, Davis. But just . . .' She frowns intently at the Coke sign, her eyes filmy with sad red and white streaks. 'Just wait until I've told you what I have to say.'

Ninety-three times he's done this, in more than a decade, and a finite but countless number of times he's walked in with the bowler and tapped his bat and clapped his hands and appealed and shouted encouragement and thrown the ball; finite, but countless.

Nothing's ever hit him like this, though: uninvited.

Incinerating his guts, legs, hair, brain: *Oh Jesus oh Jesus. Too many.*

To rein in his stomach, he rams a finger into his mouth and bites down on it. His teeth grip on his fingernail and tear it back.

The next ball happens, and the next ball, and he's seen each one before. Australia press inexorably. Seen every moment. This one – and this one – they happened before, in a dream, was it? Last night? Did he dream this entire day last night?

And so many watching him. (Dreamt them too.)

The tears are streaming down his face, his stomach a ruffling flock. Hatless, he has no brim or peak to pull over his eyes. His finger bleeds brightly. The coppery taste, warm red juice rolling on his tongue: he dreamt that. His face rumples.

Cameras, cameras.

Bill Lawry will be up there, saying: 'It's all catching up with Chris Brand now, feeling the emotions, a very emotional week for all the Australians.'

There will be questions. What's happening to him? Do Test cricketers cry on the field? A new statistic – Test cricketers who cried: 1. Chris Brand, Sydney Cricket Ground, versus South Africa.

He's bawling now. A curtain of tears blurs the game like a stream down a window. Two wickets to victory. He'll win an award. He'll have to go on television. Someone will ask why he was crying, and he'll say: Sweat in my eyes. And someone will laugh, and someone else will say that Chris Brand's sense of humour has been hidden for too long. And someone will say: Maybe we should offer him a job in commentary.

He has to get off. He waits till the end of the over, then runs for the Members' Stand, a green blur. He hears Tom Pritchard distantly. Snot runs down the back of his throat. Hasn't cried since he was a kid. Fuck's going on? Off he runs, up the race, past the room attendant, past the fucking twelfth man, and locks himself into a toilet cubicle, bawls like a wounded bull in the Domestic Shithole.

Nervous breakdowns on a Test match field: 1. Chris Brand, Sydney, versus South Africa.

The Australians can't quite finish it off: Tom Pritchard plays all the cards in his deck, but to no avail. When bad light closes in, a dressing of thick cotton wool pressed down over a sore earth, the South Africans are able to walk off the field with one wicket still intact. Pritchard protests the umpires' decision to go off early. Hands on hips, he fears rain tomorrow might rob Australia of its certain win. The umpire nods amiably and replies that if Pritchard needs another day, or even another hour, to get rid of these two rabbits then maybe he doesn't deserve to win.

The SCG empties. In lieu of jeering the home bowlers for their inability to take the triumphant wicket, fans jeer Pritchard. The green and gold of the empty seating spreads on the grandstands like a stain.

Eve, the autograph-hunter, is sitting outside the dressing room. Chris finds her propped on the concrete, her back against the wall, scorebook against the lectern of her knees. She touches up the bowling figures, cross-checks her sums.

'Hi there,' he says flatly. He wears fawn chinos and a polo shirt. He looks around, as if to check that nobody in the team is watching.

'Why did you go off?'

'No reason.'

'No reason?'

'Well . . .' He glances around again. He lowers his voice and leans across the rail. He's only a few inches from Eve's cheek. 'Let you in on a secret.' He holds up the third finger of his right hand. It's capped in a white bandage. 'I was standing in the field, picking my fingernails, and . . . you know that bit of skin around the edge?'

'The cuticle?'

'Right, the cuticle. I was picking a bit off, and the whole thing just ripped away. Jeez, I've been hit in the groin by Curtly Ambrose, I've been sconed by Wasim Akram, I've had my arm nearly busted by Allan Donald, but nothing ever hurt as much as this. Nothing! So that's why I came off.'

Only the bottom half of his face smiles.

'I thought you'd come off because you'd decided to retire.'

'Retire?' He throws his head back and lets off a high feminine laugh, its loudness and high pitch somehow shocking. 'Why would I retire?'

'You said in your press conference last night that you'd play on for as long as you were enjoying the game. I've been watching you all season. You're not enjoying the game.'

'That's because I haven't been making runs. Until this week.'

'This week you've enjoyed it even less.'

'Shit, eh?' His eyes are studying her, or something through and behind the centre of her head, with deep sadness. He's about to say something else, but appears to change his mind.

'So,' Eve says. 'Are you?'

Chris nestles his sore finger into his other hand. He massages the tip. His mouth forms a tight white hyphen in the redness of his face.

'Don't wait around here,' he says in a softer tone. 'We're heading to the casino, the upstairs bar, can't remember the name – some kind of nautical theme. I'll make sure your name's left on the door.'

'You're going out tonight?'

'Tommy Pritchard reckons the game's over. We only need one wicket tomorrow, and it's always a bit of an anticlimax when a match ends before lunch. You've got to wait around all day before you can go out. So he's letting the boys party early.'

'I'll think about it.' She readjusts her string bag on her shoulder.

Chris and the Australian team are in the Landlubbers Lounge, along with a couple of Channel Nine commentators and a dozen sultana-textured women in black cocktail dresses. He sees Eve across the desert of carpet between the door and the bar. She is wearing jeans and a loose T-shirt. She hitches her string bag over her shoulder.

As she crosses the expanse, she looks like a batsman on his nervous walk to the centre wicket. The girlfriends, the groupies, dogs at a feeding frenzy, dart sidelong looks at her, but without judgment – their mouths and teeth are too busily engaged in the kill.

Chris is standing rather unsteadily in a group with three blonde women, Tom Pritchard, Nathan Such and one of the bowlers. Each of the Australian players, except Chris, is wearing a baggy green cap. It's a tradition: they wear their caps out when they're celebrating. Eve looks so excited to witness it first-hand, Chris doesn't know if she's going to be able to talk.

The conversation carries on as if Eve weren't there. Chris bellows drunkenly. He's smoking cigarettes. When he leans away from the circle to find an ashtray, Eve skirts around and brings one to him.

'Ta!' he says, acting, for the benefit of the others, as if he's surprised she's here. 'How are you?'

'I'm good. I didn't know you smoked.'

'I decided to take it up after the fifth beer,' he says. 'Then,' he raises his voice to include the group, 'I can score some bullshit Nicorette sponsorship so I can pretend to quit. Eh?'

His teammates laugh. The blondes give Eve a dogshit-sniffing glance.

The conversation continues around her like a stream washing around a rock. The men exchange stories among themselves, ignoring the blondes too, but every now and then pause to swap a quip with the girls. Nathan Such leans into a jewelled ear: 'It's amazing how good-looking you become when you're a Test cricketer.'

Eve stations herself beside Chris. After a while, she says: 'So, none of the wives here tonight?'

'Victory night is the boys' night out,' Chris says.

'And these girls are just . . .'

'They're one of the boys!'

He's very drunk. His elbow knocks a bowl of Bombay mix off the bar.

'Not got your autograph book?' Chris says.

'Everything I have, you've already signed. Thanks, by the way.'

'Ar, fuck it,' he says. 'I still got my shirt, in my room. The one I wore in this match. I can sign that for you.'

'Oh my God. Would you?'

'It's going to have historic value, y'know? Given I'm retiring!'

He says it loud enough to alert the others, but Pritchard and Simmo are swamping two of the blondes, and Nathan Such is putting his finishing touches on two others.

'So you are retiring?'

'Don't sound so surprised.' Chris's smile is wet and gummy, beer-sentimental. 'You're the one who guessed it. Like you said, I'm not enjoying it anymore. I can't stand these cunts. Oh, sorry, scuse my French.'

'Gosh.'

'Lemme tell you something.' Chris puts an arm around her birdlike shoulders. Her string bag falls to the floor. Chris turns her away, making a group of two. 'You know why I really came off today? We were fielding close-in, trying to get these last wickets. The boys were sledging for all they were worth. Now I've been in the Australian team for a few years now, so I'm not, like, a shrinking violet. It's a tough game. No probs. But some of these new boys, their sledging leaves us oldies for dead. Anyway. What happens after a while is, between overs the boys get together – the fielders, keeper, bowler and Pritchard. And Tommy boy says it's time to get serious. We're going to orchestrate an appeal. He says, next time the ball comes off the batsman's pad and any of us catches it, we're all gunna go up.'

'And it worked.'

'Yeah, well.'

'That's cheating.'

'Yep, your all-Australian heroes. Cheats to a man.'

'And that's why you're retiring?'

His eyes widen, as if she's said something he hadn't thought of.

'Nah, that's why I came off today. I didn't want to be playing with fucken cheating cunts anymore. Oh shit, I oughta wash my mouth out.'

The group re-forms around them and moves off to the tables. Eve stands with the other women behind the men, who flirt with the attractive croupier. Eve sits on her first beer while Chris works his way through the bar, gaining confidence with some rum-and-cokes, lashing out extravagantly with a Midori and lemonade, before digging in for the long haul on scotch-on-the-rocks. One of the blondes pinches Nathan Such's green cap and plants it on her head. Such tweaks the woman's breast, making her squeal, then fits the precious cap on Chris's head. Mired in blackjack, Chris doesn't look up.

They play for a couple of hours, the women disappearing periodically into the bathrooms. Eve's beer puddles brownly at the bottom of her glass. Suddenly the gang is piling into taxis. Chris drags her into a cab with Nathan Such and two blondes. The taxi driver doesn't know who Such is, not even with his cap, and Such shouts: 'Bloody rag-head, call yourshelf an Australian?' The blondes cackle like geese at a pond.

'Sho,' Such leans back between the seats, 'Shimmo got a pair last night – but you shee those bimbos on him? Going for a royal flush tonight – who the fuck are you?'

'She's just a fucking hanger-on,' says one of the girls.

Eve frowns for a few moments. 'I'd say the same for you but without the last four syllables,' she says, gathering her string bag around her knees. Chris's lips move, trying to work it out, but he can't concentrate and loses count.

'What'sh a shyllabubble again?' Such leers. Before Eve can say anything, the girls beside her are shrieking and pushing her into the door as the car rounds a corner. Such rams his hand between Eve's thighs and pinches her.

'Quite nishe and shlim, ishn't shhhhe?'

When they get to the hotel Chris slumps against a pillar, eyes drooping.

'Can I have that shirt?' Eve says. 'And I think you ought to go to bed.'

'Yeah, yeah,' he blinks. Confusion, then bemusement, cross his face. 'Why don't you head upstairs. I've just got to say a couple of things to a couple of people.'

'What's your room number?'

He fumbles a key card out of his pocket. 'Fourteen oh two. Make sure you wait.'

'You sure you're okay?'

He grins blearily and raises a thumb.

'Um.' Her blushing face is looping across the same point in his vision. She seems tortured by some kind of decision.

He is about to offer some genial assurance, some sloppy version of 'No worries!', when a familiar face materialises, grinning behind

Eve. She spins around. Under the warmth of his smile, some hardness inside her, some dry wall, melts away.

'Hey.' Tom Pritchard shows his famous teeth. 'How you doing?'

Chris never sleeps well after a blitz. The alcohol keeps working inside him, like an overnight staff readying the system to hit the morning at top pace, so that when he wakes he is both unrested and alert to the full diary of shame.

He is lying on a bed, in a hotel room. Not his. The window's on the wrong side. His arms and legs refuse to move. The light is dove-grey, dawn. It must be about six, but he cannot budge his head to look for a clock. He hears snoring. He shuts his eyes again.

It's there, waiting for him. But at first it doesn't seem too bad. He passed out in a chair against a pillar, in the foyer downstairs. His head was too heavy . . . He was unsure how much time had passed when he opened his eyes to find one of his teammates, the wicketkeeper, shaking him by the shoulders.

'C'mon, buddy, party's upstairs.'

Chris was helped into the lift, past the laughing security guards on the top floor and down the hall.

He was dragged into Tom Pritchard's suite.

Inside were drinks and music and laughter. He remembers collapsing into a corner chair. He wrenched his eyes open but only caught every fifth or sixth minute as they flew past. He remembers bodies going in and out of the bathrooms. He remembers the glittering views over the harbour, the bridge, the Opera House.

A memory: Tom Pritchard emerging from a bathroom wearing nothing but his pads, a thighpad, his cap and a box. Wielding his bat. Chris saw girls running around in underwear. He can recall, but cannot place in the chronology, the girl in her 'STUPID'S WITH ME' T-shirt sitting on the arm of his chair, smoothing down his rumpled hair.

'I didn't want to come here, I only wanted your shirt,' she kept saying, but Chris remembers not quite understanding, what the fuck, what's the shirt, what's she on about?

Sydney Harbour twinkled. He remembers that. Spots of rain against the glass. Cold Chisel on the stereo. Champagne spurting.

An image, but in no particular order: Simmo stalking out of a bedroom naked and ripping down a girl's underpants. Then, his arms in the air: 'Hazzat!'

He remembers some point of the night, before the sky lightened, himself and the autograph girl being the only people in the captain's suite who still had their clothes on.

Which must have been before Nathan Such and a couple of blondes dacked him. 'Hazzat!!!'

The autograph kid clinging to his neck. His neck not being strong enough.

Tom Pritchard, out of the bathroom with a rolled-up fifty-dollar note and a woody, asking the autograph girl to go into the bathroom with him. But she was trying to hold Chris upright and keep him from being stripped. He remembers thinking, or hearing someone say: *Good luck to her*.

Being picked up by his ankles and wrists, slung like a hammock onto a bed.

Being curled up like an anemone.

He remembers blinking in the dark at the fucking autograph-hunter, Eve, that's right, the shirt, his shirt, he was going to sign it for her, and she'd been stripped too, she was trying to cover him with the bedspread.

And Pritchard, and Such, on the bed. Chris remembers

thinking: *It would be worse, much worse, for her to fight this, and I'm getting out of it, this is some kind of hell all right, and now it's got to be clear why her hero's retiring, because this is what he's retiring from, and I'll fucken bet this is more and more and more of everything than she'd ever suspected, and now she's gibbering,* and, far off on the other side of his career, Tom Pritchard whispering to the autograph girl, *Roll over and take it like a man, yeah?*

He remembers Eve kissing him, Chris, all the way through, tear-greased kisses all over his mouth and his cheeks and his forehead and his ears and his hair, screaming her kisses, and though he couldn't kiss her back, in his dreams Chris knew he was being loved, and he was sick of it, sick of being someone's hero, just so fucking sick of being someone's hero, and then he heard Such, and Simmo, and Jimmy Dent, and then Pritchard back again, the laughter of these fucking pricks, sick of them, just sick.

He opens his eyes again. Peace has fallen on the captain's suite, the curtains grey. It feels like six still. Her head is on his chest and his breath is feathering the back of her neck, delicately.

He can think of only one person in the world he could look in the eye right now.

His finger throbs all the way up his arm.

December 31

John had always thought that if he were a visitor to Sydney, he'd have found this city more European than American, with its picturesque red-light district under the plane trees, neon girlies tacked onto art deco facades, the old quarter housing the oldest profession. But as he turned into the loading bay in the industrial area off the Hume Highway at 4.06 pm on the last day of the year, and parked on a sweeping asphalt plain shared by a self-storage warehouse, an auto wrecker and a hardware supplier, as well as being the temporary premises of the event to which he had come, he couldn't help concluding that his home city had a touch of America.

At a corner of the vast corrugated-iron hangar was a red banner flapping in the wind proclaiming the name of the show. Hammett waited at the entry, wearing a broad smile and a summer linen suit with bunched-up sleeves. He hugged John, but rather stiffly, as if straining to hold himself back from some expression of excessive gratitude and excitement that might embarrass the old man. As if presenting his father with an Olympic medal, Hammett looped a laminated card on a cord around John's neck.

In the area partitioned as a foyer, the late-afternoon emptiness of the outer-Sydney steppes was swallowed by the hum of a large crowd of men. At turnstiles, men queued in golf shirts and casual slacks, carrying showbags they had collected at the registration counter. To pass time in the slow-moving queue, many were reading glossy catalogues and box covers, the solitaries impassive, the pairs and groups splaying them showily and laughing too loudly. They were not the types of men John saw in the shops; these were suburban fathers catching a free hour between finishing off the mowing and picking up the kids from the train station.

'Here – no need to line up with the plebs,' said Hammett, guiding John by the elbow to a turnstile marked 'VIP'. A burly guard checked John's laminated pass, which gave him cause to examine it for the first time. It was marked with the red letters, 'VIP', and John's name.

'I – I'd rather not have this . . .' he said, thinking: *Evidence*.

'Yeah no, keep it as a souvenir!'

John turned its face against his chest. The pass trembled with the beat of John's heart, which was now aching constantly, a sharp muscular pain that kept him awake at night and weak and meek during the day, his spirit extinguished. He put one foot after the other, an inert trailer dragged along by the locomotive power of his son.

Inside, John kept his eyes angelically raised above the things that were happening. He wished to preserve his innocence – and it would hurt to look. Jagging up every so often out of the mass of male voices, like shoots of grass in a desert, were piercing female moans, video simpers. Overhead, he discovered a different version of the present: steel girders, corrugated-iron roofing – a reminder that this Disneyland of the flesh was an illusion projected onto moulded metal.

Hammett led him from display to display. John listened, nodding with stern concentration, like a member of a delegation from a very foreign and culturally conservative country. His pained nervous tautness stripped expression from his face. Hammett chatted with men, shook hands not only in conventional handshakes but in those other combinations of hand and wrist and percussion that John recognised as American codes of male acquaintance. Hammett also greeted some of the women – *girls*, John realised, in the flesh, in person, no older than girls – who were sitting at raised platforms signing autographs for long queues. The same men who had been queuing to get in now re-formed into lines to have their catalogues signed and their photos taken. Worshipping at the feet of these girl-children.

While Hammett touched knuckles with a middle-aged man whose cheeks and chin had been vandalised by a hairdresser, John slid into the background. When he let his eyes fall to the detail he felt dazzled, unable to fix himself against the tides of his nausea. He concentrated on the inanimate objects rather than the humans. Some stalls were little more than portable shops, partitioned by shelves of videotapes, magazines and DVDs. The bigger ones took up more space and displayed long vertical banners like the iconic May Day pictures of Communist leaders, bearing the images of the stars. One stall, bearing the name 'Wicked', was surrounded by a white veil-like curtain through which a long queue snaked. Another large stall, called 'RCA', was dominated by a giant video screen showing a scene starring three females and a squeezable bottle of baby oil. Below the screen at a high table, like a board of directors, three young girls – quite probably the same as on the projection, though John cringed from taking a second look – sat smiling regally, signing autographs and posing for happy snaps with their fans.

The conventioneers paled into a bland mass, a background neutral against which the girls were vivid paint. Each stall had three or four starlets serving the queues. The girls' features were scalpelled into their surgeons' idea of perfection: noses like thorns, chins tapered to round points like the tips of cones, cheek-bones fluted like cut glass. Their clothing gave them a reptilian slinkiness – skintight white lizardskin, scaly lamé, the shedding ruches of glomesh – and their chemically-white incisors glittered like fangs. John looked back at Hammett, who was absorbed in an uninhibited conversation with the facial-hair man.

Near John, a fellow was shouting into a mobile phone: 'I'm standing near Sidney Steele! She's signing autographs! Can you believe it! She's only . . . I can almost touch her, that's how close!'

John followed the man's eyes to the scalloped brunette in a fluffy red halter signing and posing. Like many of the models and actresses, she gave off a monarchical attitude, preserving her smile and poise above anything that could happen here as if her magic powers transported her to another universe, light-years above and beyond these men cuddling her shoulders in the camera-flash. Perhaps she, like John, sought a meditative stillness in the rafters.

At that moment, Sidney Steele noticed Hammett with the facial-hair man and gave him a demure wave. Hammett blew her a kiss and resumed his conversation. She shimmered back at him and went on to process her next fan.

Leaving Hammett, who seemed to have forgotten about him, John meandered from stall to stall. He breathed deeply, suppressing his pain. Women customers wandered the floor, though only a few. Some were in pairs, others dragged along by their men. Now and then he saw prostitutes and strippers he knew in Kings Cross as patients. He turned away if they came near. As mere customers, the local girls seemed to fit into the hierarchical nature of this place. The most beautiful women, the American visitors, were enthroned behind their autograph tables. The cheaper stalls were peopled by older, rougher models, such as the one who was road-testing some kind of athletic gyroscopic chair: clad in a red leatherette bikini, she had her ankles and wrists strapped into the contraption and was pivoted upside-down, for no purpose John could see. Other older models seemed freer in their ways, too. They flashed their leathery, scarred breasts and laughed more genuinely than the higher-priced versions.

John passed two men who were arguing.

'She's coming later today – tonight.'

'No, no,' the other shook his head. 'Asia and Christy are coming tonight, and she's coming tomorrow.'

'Everybody's coming! Hahaha!'

By the gusto of their discussion John guessed whom they were talking about. For a moment he almost went up to show off his inner-circle status, his VIP card, and settle the debate by telling them with a wise knowing wink that She would indeed be appearing tonight.

But they moved off, and John went to stand by another queue, watching another starlet sign and pose with plastic graciousness. He had been there a minute or two, taking in the scene, when an immense black-shirted security guard materialised beside him. The colossus folded his arms, puffing his biceps. He only unfolded himself when John moved off self-consciously.

Just then a commotion rose from behind a stall. John found himself quickening his step with the other men around him, racing – not quite running – to the source of the shouting. When he got there, a great crowd was gathered around a pair of models who were showering them with free X-rated tapes. Some men drifted off while others tussled for the giveaways. John backed away from the elbows, the open-palmed fends, the knees in the thigh.

He soon found himself near a stall where a comely young woman was 'reporting' for a television camera. She wore her hair in a high chignon and her body in a black sheath. Her microphone had 'X-TV' on the little display box around its neck. She was interviewing a man of indeterminate age who looked as if he'd given still more trade to those evidently very busy plastic surgeons.

'You know,' he said, 'I did you in your first movie.'

'I sure do remember that,' said the attractive interviewer, who quickly turned to the camera and assumed the role of talent: 'I came into the studio and was more nervous than I'd ever been in my life. I saw you, and you put me at ease right there. You said did I want a bottle of wine. I said I didn't need to get drunk to go to bed with a good-looking man. Do you remember that?'

'Sure, baby.' The man hooked an arm around her shoulders and grinned at, or just beyond, the camera.

'Can't take my eye off you for a second!' a voice said in John's ear.

He started. 'Oh, Hammett, I was just . . . er, looking for the exit.'

'The exit? You've got to be joking! This is the great show down under, the first time they've got so many big stars down here and –'

'I . . . I don't think . . . This is not my thing, son.' To reassure Hammett that he still appreciated the invitation, he added with a timid smile: 'This is your thing.'

'Yeah no, well, let me introduce you to some of the girls, Pa.'

Hammett tried to lead him, but John shook his hand free and raised it into a stop sign.

'This . . . this is your thing, not mine.'

As he said it, John realised that he was, in a difficult and not exactly proud and certainly not speakable way, envious of his son. He envied Hammett's youth and hope and comfort among his business associates. Even though this was a questionable pursuit, Hammett had made a go of it, and from all appearances was well respected and trusted. Yes, in his ill-fitting way, John was proud of the boy. But it was a pride that disgusted him too, because he couldn't convince himself completely and utterly that he wasn't just envying Hammett's connection with the girls, his proximity to the idol flesh, to Herself. So, unsure if he was envious or, more poisonously, jealous, John kept his mouth shut and hardened his mask.

'No.'

'Hey-ho, uh-huh, come on.'

Hammett grabbed the soft part of his father's arm forcefully enough to remind John of the boy's grip around his throat. John didn't want to make a scene. Hammett led him among the stalls and commenced a rapid patter.

'Yeah no, what they pay for is an autograph, uh-huh, have their photo taken, have their arm touched so they'll never fucking wash it again. It's the girls, Pa, the aura of the girls, you can come here and say you've met her, you've heard her voice. Look at them, Pa, grown men lining up at a circus for the fucking kissing booth. Only they're not getting a kiss. Ha!'

Hammett went on like this, sotto voce at John's shoulder like a diabolic familiar. They paused while another disturbance rose. This time it was the entry of a man John knew, in his head, as The Grub: an unlikely pornographic actor, a dishevelled, oily, overweight, stupendously ugly, self-satisfied would-be thespian whose presence in nearly every video John had seen attested to some unfathomable corruption in the film-making business. Men were mobbing him, deserting the starlets and begging for his autograph.

'Wow, Ron Jeremy,' Hammett murmured in John's ear. The Grub's appearance had awed even Hammett.

'They pay him more attention than they pay the girls,' John said.

Hammett shook his head and said softly: 'Yeah no, it's a mystery, Pa. This guy's a folk hero. Guys reckon – they genuinely reckon this – if a guy like Jeremy can do it, then it's not beyond the realm of possibility that they too can . . . uh-huh, you know.'

The Grub was swallowed by the crowd. As they stood watching, John was conscious of another security guard hovering by himself and Hammett.

'Oi,' Hammett winked at the guard. 'No worries, he's with me.'

The security guard twitched his eyebrows and moved off.

'You been causing trouble?' Hammett said to John.

'Not at all!' A nervous explosion escaped John. 'But . . . but I have noticed . . . they watch me very closely.'

'Yeah no, it's because you're a fucking freak, Pa, anyone can see that. Get into it, man!'

'I have no –'

'Yeah right, I know – you're just waiting for the great Kelli, Kelli's Komet, comes once a lifetime! Ha! Uh-huh, you know it and I know it.' Hammett pinched the skin between his eyes, onto his riff once more. 'But the guards don't know who you are, see? They think you're some fucking perv.'

'I'm a –'

'Yeah no, well, you stand out like a pimple on an arsehole. You stare up at the roof and pretend you're somewhere else – like you are now – stop fucking looking at the . . . thank you. You've come to a fucking porn expo, and you're embarrassed some girl might catch you staring at her tits! You're fucking priceless!'

'I think I'll just go . . .'

'You're not going anywhere. Don't bullshit me, Pa! Time for bullshit is long gone!'

Hammett leaned close, the overstimulated look in his eye, and hissed: '*We are trying to ascertain whether or not you are alive.*'

John hung in the air. The scene around him had dissolved. The burble of male voices retreated to synthetic distance, like the canned applause on a television comedy. *Canned*, yes: the air smelt of glue and tin, the interior of a disposable container. He and Hammett were alone in this vast tin. That was the only reality: a clanging demountable shed on a disused cow paddock one hour from town. A father and a son facing each other.

'We *are* alive, Hammett.'

'You don't know what the fuck you're talking about. If you were sure you were alive, you wouldn't be here.'

'I don't understand . . .'

'Yes you fucking . . .' Hammett pinched his forehead again, in that way that broke John's heart it so resembled Margaret, and seemed to reconsider. He took a breath and said: 'You're *here*, Pa – stop pretending you're not. Your name's on your fucking pass!' He waved the evidence in John's face before slapping it back down on his chest. 'You've come to see what's at the other end of this fucking idol stroke of yours, and you're not going to fucking leave, because here she is!'

John had, for some time, been primitively aware of a new stir behind Hammett. Camera flashes were filling the hall. The shouting grew more frantic, with a violent edge, and then a mass swelled like a rolling boulder from the far end of the hangar. Television cameras and fluffy boom mikes rose above the crowd. Whatever was at the centre of the commotion was attracting a great moving mass, like flies crowded onto a carcass so densely that the carcass itself disappears and becomes nothing but black flies. The fans, hundreds of men, even the women, the local prostitutes and strippers, were climbing over each other.

'Fucken nightmare,' Hammett said. 'Let's just take it all in.'

Hammett led John to a quiet corner, near the gyroscopic chair John had seen earlier. It too had been abandoned, its inhabitant rushing off to the fuss.

John, whose desire to catch sight of Her was outweighed by his shortness of breath and his claustrophobic fear of the crowd, shuffled towards the exit. Hammett moved with him, apparently wanting to get away from the clamour too. Soon they were both outside, in the loading bay.

'Well, that was . . . interesting, son. I'd better be off.'

'No way, no way!' Hammett grabbed John's arm and leered. He came close to his father's ear and whispered: 'It's not over yet – what, you reckon the best I can do is give you a glimpse of her in an expo? You didn't even see her! You can fucking *do* her, Pa – that's what I'm saying – I've fucking lined it up!'

'Please don't speak like that to me. And I'll never touch another . . .'

'Woman, yeah?' Hammett doubled over, laughing with a forced hilarity. 'Ah, fucking priceless!'

'I've never been unfaithful to your mother,' John said, jaw firming.

'You and your technicalities! Nah, you still don't believe me, do you, even after all I fucking showed you at my fucking house and you fucking have sex with whores and you're still too high and fucking mighty to –'

'I don't have . . . I don't have s-sex with anyone.' He tripped over it. The sound of the word in his mouth was wrong. But everything was wrong now. Or right.

'Oh sure, all you use is pornography, uh-huh. But see, who's paying the money? Who's the client?'

'There's a difference between this –'

'Yeah no, all you're doing is jerking off into your –'

'Please, Hammett.'

'Jerking off into your hand, Pa – shit, you can't kid me. No reason to hide it. Love's a miracle! Enjoy!'

'No . . .'

'Oh yeah, you want to keep your figleaf of fidelity to my mother. But think of your soul, Pa. Your *soul* travels wondrous distances. So, yeah no, you think because your body's here, you're still being faithful to Ma?'

'I want to go. And I'd like you to come with me. I want to take you to see –'

'Hypocritical horseshit.' Hammett shook his head as if stunned and appalled by the truth of his own reasoning. John was wondering if his son had heard him, so he repeated:

'I want to go. And I have something to . . .'

'But that's what I'm saying!' Hammett grabbed John's shoulders. 'You *don't*! If you wanted to *go*, you wouldn't have *come*! Gimme ten minutes, Pa. Ten! Okay?' Keeping one hand clamped on John's shoulders, he flashed five fingers of the other. Realising he was only halfway to making his point, he closed the hand to a fist and flashed another five. 'If I don't come out in ten, then go. I'll stop bothering you. But if you pike on me, if you piss off now, then we're back where we fucking started. Think, Pa – do you want to be back where we started? Before we met in that shop? Okay? Uh-huh? You just wait here, wait here, and I'll be right back.'

John watched Hammett skip inside. He heard the commotion die: She must have made her little appearance and vanished. Men filed out, past John, trailing their showbags. Some shook their

328

heads. He heard one shout into his mobile phone: 'Came in for two seconds . . . fucking riot . . . nah, never even saw her . . . only about five foot . . . someone said silver latex . . . but – nah, never saw her . . .'

John knew he was not leaving. Hammett was right: he didn't want to go back to where they'd started. It was beyond John's control. He could not deny Hammett's logic. John had come here. His body was here. His soul may have wished to travel to a plane of innocence, to deny, to provide an alibi, but this was where he was, out here on the fringe of the city, and he wasn't going back home.

December 31

It was 6.36 pm on the last day of the year, and John was playing truant again. Margaret and the family would be at Chris's hotel suite looking forward to the fireworks on the harbour. Chris would be greeting the important men who would oversee the rest of his life. There would be queries about John, but Chris and Margaret would shrug off his non-appearance with a family in-joke routine. 'That's Pa for you,' Chris would say, 'probably forgot it's New Year.' Margaret would add: 'No doubt he's at home wondering why I'm out.' Chris would say: 'If he's noticed.' Margaret would chuckle wryly, satisfied with their little show. The important men would nod their appreciation. My wife and sons are tolerant of me and my quirks, John thought. Or indifferent.

He had come here with a plan to spirit Hammett away, take him back. But as his plans always seemed to do now, it had melted under high heat. As he waited outside the hangar, a line of cars filed onto the access road up to the freeway. Her short appearance seemed to have punctured the event. The number of men leaving indicated how many had been waiting for Her.

When Hammett came out, he was silhouetted against the doorway of the hangar. He whispered to John to come to a back entrance. The boy showed neither acknowledgement nor surprise at John's having stayed. John nodded and followed him around to the auto wreckers' section, through a series of corridors, to a checkpoint where Hammett's raised thumb got them past two man-mountain security guards, and to another entrance guarded by two pock-marked girls at a desk. John had lost track of where in the maze of hangars they were now. From inside, a bass beat thumped.

'We've got a club set up in here,' Hammett said behind his hand. 'VIPs only.'

John nodded, swallowing drily. But he was feeling better. An infusion of some adrenal release – or perhaps just boyish excitement – subdued the sickness.

'Hey Shahnee,' Hammett said.

One of the girls pouted. 'How ya goin'?'

Hammett went through a curtain with the girl. John waited at the desk, hands behind his back. A statuesque model in a lime-green bikini came through another doorway. Her other clothes, diaphanous and white, were scrunched up in her right hand. She whispered to the girl at the counter, casting John a quick uninterested glance. Escorting his eyes anywhere but her – her perfect back, her perfect behind – John deflected his gaze over the counter, to a black-and-white security monitor divided into four quadrants. This he watched dully, not realising what he was looking at until the counter girl said:

'You mind?'

'Pardon? Oh, sorry, sorry.'

He'd been staring at hidden-camera pictures of what was happening in the bowels of this place. Hairy white torsos lying on tables, the screen decapitating and disembowelling them, while pairs of hands ran over them as if kneading dough. Now and then a female form glided across the screen.

Hammett, returning into the foyer, nudged him with an eye on the security monitors.

'Anyone you know?'

John coughed and said: 'Ah, son. I can't come in there. I have to get back, Chris is having a New Year's do at his hotel, and your mother will be expecting my, my –'

With an ironic grin – *yeah yeah, sure* – Hammett took John's arm firmly and led him through the curtain, following the lime-green bikini girl. John's protest petered out as his senses fought to adjust to the darkness and mayhem. The room heaved with smoky moisture and voices. Around the walls were dartboards and racing-car video games. Pool tables took up the margins inside the walls, where young men played raucously. A cumulo-nimbus front of cigarette smoke advanced over the tables. From one table a security guard, a Tongan in a black knit shirt, cleared the players away so he could lay down a big sheet of plywood, which he covered with a black cotton sheet, flicking it out and letting it float down as if spreading a tablecloth for dinner. Hammett led his father by the elbow to a bar, past a figure-eight-shaped stage, black with white concentric lines around it like the tracks on a child's slot-car set. Scalectric, John thought: We gave one to the boys one Christmas.

Smeary steel poles pierced the two bulges in the figure-eight stage. Hammett clutched two beers, which he appeared to have obtained for free. Customers ate from gashed packets of chips at the bar and tables. Topless waitresses hefted trays and screwed their faces up while trying to hear orders.

'Don't know about the hygiene situation.' John nodded towards a waitress struggling to keep her nipples out of a plate of fried calamari.

Hammett nodded, smiling. He tapped his ear and shook his head. He couldn't hear. An awesome thudding music and the release of smoke from a machine onto the figure-eight stage heralded a change in mood.

'Quick, show's starting. Let me take you to gyno row.' Hammett nudged him across the floor to two free seats between the pool tables and the stage.

The announcer heralded the first girl, 'Anna Nicole from the

US of A', who wore a stars-and-stripes bikini and danced to the song 'American Woman'. John sat up with a start. She was a fair facsimile of a so-called celebrity he knew from the Internet: same platinum hair, same trashy smile, same inflated breasts. He looked at Hammett, who was paying no attention, slurping his drink and laughing with a man sitting to his left.

John averted his face when Anna Nicole looked at him. She sang along with the words, danced with the poles, scissors-kicked, threw off her Stetson (the security guard caught it), and removed her bikini in a carefully planned sequence. 'American Woman' finished when she was down to a second bra and G-string she had been wearing beneath the star-spangled bikini. John sank his face into his beer, but perked up again when another song started: 'You Shook Me All Night Long'. It was so easy to know the names of these songs, once you heard them this way! Anna Nicole continued her dance, miming the words. When she removed her under-bra, coyly cuddling and hiding her breasts until the final moment, John nudged Hammett.

'Is that Anna Nicole Smith?'

His embarrassment, monumental, at asking the question was eased when Hammett put a hand to his ear, indicating that he hadn't heard.

'Don't worry, don't worry,' John waved his hands.

Anna Nicole dropped her face down between her thighs and winked back at gyno row. The men nodded, as if receiving tribute. John felt his head nodding too. She was gorgeous, this girl, yet there was something fugitive, elusive, about the dance. The way the lights skirted off her, the quickness of her movements, the flashes of different colour from the filters, frustrated him. He just wanted to *see* her. But the dance and the lighting, her choreographed flirtatiousness and her mouthing of the noise were themselves a form of clothing, a concealment. Why couldn't she stand still and simply allow him to admire her beauty? Why could he not behold her eyes?

The song and dance ended. John could have sworn she shot him a smile as she picked up her clothes and tottered off on her white stilettos, helped into a side room by the security guard.

'She likes you, uh-huh!' Hammett shouted into his father's ear. 'Yeah no, she does, ya sly fucken dog!'

Hammett was getting another round when the next dancer came up. She too appeared to give John a special smile. They liked older men. This one, 'Jaycee', was Thai and as lovely as Anna Nicole. Her moves were more supple and daring; indeed, by comparison, Anna Nicole now seemed rather wooden. Jaycee came off the stage and performed a little dance in the lap of a young man three seats from John. She climbed back to the stage, helped up by the guard, and John found that he had a fierce prong in his trousers. He crossed his legs to cover it. He looked around the room. Hammett returned with schooners and a handful of what looked like monopoly money.

'When they come close, slip this in their knickers.'

John clutched his monopoly cash. The third act was another blonde, slimmer than Anna Nicole but boasting breasts that she probably owed to her genes, not her doctor. John was transfixed by the way they swung with her dance, the way they lay back and spread over her ribcage when she arched herself and played with her nipples.

There was a fifteen-minute break after the three dancers, but, the announcer promised, 'They'll be back, bigger and better, with a special surprise, so don't go away.' Hammett encouraged John to 'register as a member' of the club, which meant signing his name to a clipboard a topless barmaid brought around.

'Yeah no, it means you can win a prize!' Hammett winked.

Something warned John against writing his name – and address – in such a place, but it was too late, he had already done it, and for god's sake, he was here with his son! What did any of it matter? For now, he was alive and alert, and he would never come to a place like this again. The announcer climbed onto the stage, dragging up a Big Wheel. The prizes were 'Cash' and 'Sex'. Hammett chatted with the men in gyno row and at the pool tables, while his father watched the wheel. A dumpy middle-aged woman won 'Sex' on the first spin. Her prize was a pair of erotic videos and a magazine. John smiled at the announcer's crack: 'You look like you'll need them too, Mrs Tran!' Everybody did seem to know each other. Hammett had friends at every table, and the prizewinners were greeted with cheers of familiarity. A Jack Skazich won free drinks and was Bronx-cheered – some old joke, apparently.

Hammett came back, hooked an arm around John's neck and shouted: 'C'mere, I want you to meet someone.'

He took him to a table where a man in his fifties stood surrounded by six or seven women. Hammett shook his hand and introduced John, who didn't catch the man's name.

'I'm sorry?' He shook hands and leaned closer.

'What you sorry about, fucking fag?' the man growled, his accent that of an eastern European taught English by Americans.

'I didn't catch your name,' John said.

'I have no name.' The man's hand was crunching John's to a pulp. 'You wanna fuck any girl at this table? You're a pal of Hammett's. You're a pal of mine.'

'Oh,' John nodded, dragging his hand clear. 'Well. Thank you. Good!'

Hammett stayed to talk with the man. John wrung his hand. One of the girls at the table blew him a sarcastic kiss. He wondered when Anna Nicole was coming back up.

The second act involved the three girls together. They feigned sex, snuggled, and performed sundry gymnastics to three jukebox songs.

Hammett was back beside him. 'Yeah no, that was the great Mike Oberman, uh-huh,' Hammett winked. 'My boss, ultimately. Kelli's boss, too. Out here from the States. Good man to have onside.'

There was another break after the second show, and once again the announcer, a chubby, weak-chinned lad who Hammett said was either a 'brat' or 'Brad', brought up his spinning wheel. This time the wheel spun onto 'Sex', and the Brad-brat drew a name from the barrel.

'Well,' he read, 'is there a John Brand here? John Brand? Marlon Brando?'

John couldn't resist his son's pushing. The men in gyno row were clapping and cheering him up to the stage. When he got there, John did not know what to do. He looked around the room. From the stage, with the hot lights beating down on him, he could not see faces, just smoke and darkness.

He was given a video and a magazine, and pushed back down. Hammett had moved off again. John sat alone with his video and magazine.

'You're in luck!'

He jumped. The lovely blonde girl, the third dancer, had slipped into Hammett's seat.

'Pardon?'

She nodded at his prizes.

'Who's a lucky boy then?'

'Ah. Yes. Well, I suppose I am lucky if you're sitting next to me.'

'Eh?' She craned her neck closer to hear.

'Never mind, never mind.'

'So what's your name then?'

'John. John Brand. Er – I mean, Ian. Ian, er, Bertrand.'

'Hello, John.' She looked at his hand, extended towards her. She frowned until she realised that all she was meant to do was shake it.

'Where do you come from then, Johnny?'

'Sydney. And it's Ian Bertrand.'

'That's nice.'

'Not from around here, but closer to the North –'

'Hey, John.' She leaned closer. He had never seen a woman this beautiful this close. His heart was surely going to give out. 'Why don't we take that fistful of dollars you've got,' she nodded to the monopoly money sweat-pasted to his hand, 'and get ourselves a bottle of champagne?'

'Champagne? Why, yes, yes, that would be lovely. But I have to say, my name is Ian. Ian Bertrand.'

'*Lovely*! Oh, you mature guys are so cute.'

He let her take his hand, and the monopoly money from it, and lead him to the bar, where she purchased a bottle of Great Western. Then she was taking him through a set of curtains into another bar. Booths around the perimeter of the room were occupied by half-naked women wiggling in the laps of concealed men. As his eyes adjusted, John made out a kind of reflexive writhing, as if he were watching a worm farm.

'Come take a seat, Ian.'

'Ah, I don't think so.' It was a Roman orgy. He didn't want this. He didn't want her. 'You're a nice girl, but I don't think . . .'

'Come on. You're a nice man too. Let's have some lovely bubbly.'

She really was a beautiful girl, but John was horrified by what was happening. Was he about to be unfaithful to Margaret? In a place like this? With a bottle of Great Western?

'Make yourself comfortable, Ian-boy.' She sat and patted an upholstered love seat.

'I'm sorry, I can't.'

'Course you can.'

People in the room were looking at them now.

'Oi!' a female voice miaowed.

'Sorry, sorry,' he backed away.

'Oh fuck off then, Ian.'

'Don't you speak to my dad like that.'

Hammett was beside him, standing threateningly over the girl.

337

'Fuck off, dudes!' another voice said from somewhere in the room.

Hammett guided his father out, back to the main bar. Without a word he sat him back down in gyno row.

'I'm sorry, I'm sorry,' John stammered.

'Yeah no, no worries, I shouldn't have left you alone. *Ian.*' Hammett chuckled.

'I couldn't do that to your mother.'

'You couldn't –' Hammett fixed him with a speculative smile. 'You couldn't do what to my mother?'

'Be . . . be unfaithful.'

'Unfaithful?' Hammett tried out the word as if it were an exotic dish, a delicacy in some parts of the world. 'Oh shit, Pa, you're totally fucked up.'

'Pardon?'

'No wonder we're all so fucked up. You're the worst of the lot.'

'I'm sorry, I can't hear you.'

'Jesus Christ, man. You . . . Ah shit, here, they're cranking it up again.'

For the third act, each of the girls came up separately and performed slower, more sensuous dances. They stripped naked. Anna Nicole arched herself back, but not in John's direction. Jaycee came up and threw herself onto the plywood-covered pool table. She affected to masturbate in front of the pool players, some of whom stubbornly refused to acknowledge her. She gave them a rude gesture and danced back up onto the stage. Finally the third girl, John's girl, whose name was 'Lucinda', flounced out and danced with a shining gold vibrator. Only – it wasn't her, was it? The girl who had dragged him away resembled the dancer, but, John realised, he had been confused into thinking they were one and the same. He blushed with embarrassment – a fool, again! – and concentrated on the dance, as if to restore self-respect. Anna Nicole and Jaycee returned and played at inserting the vibrator, but did not – for legal and/or health reasons, John supposed. This roused the pool players at last, who started a chant of 'Stick it in! Stick it in!' Hammett went to buy more beer. John's head was swimming, so he concentrated his mental powers on Anna Nicole. He looked for his son. Who was already laughing at him. *Unfaithful.* He was an anachronistic old man, clinging to the language of a bygone era.

Hammett shouted into his ear: 'Get ready, old man!'

The Brad-brat was trying to whip up a new frenzy, but the public address system was out of balance and his words were unclear. He seemed to be revving the crowd up for a new dancer. John strained to hear. The girls on the stage formed up in a kind of erotic honour guard. The announcer was screaming himself hoarse.

'I . . . I can't make out a word of it,' John said. Hammett winked and nodded towards the stage.

The black curtains at the bar parted, and there She was.

She wore a white cowboy hat, white fringed vest and white chaps. She twirled a silver pistol in each hand, firing caps into the smoke.

'Oh,' John swallowed. He reached across and clutched his son's hand.

Kelli Kittering danced and removed her costume to a song that sounded to John as if sung by monsters. The pool players stopped and watched. John knew every inch of this perfect body. But the jewels, the eyes, were shadowed by the brim of her hat.

Kelli broke from the stage and tiptoed down the steps. Her nipples were pierced with silver hoops. She moved along gyno row, mouthing the words of the song. She cradled her breasts and teased them before the men's faces. She made as if to sit in a lap, but pulled her silky rump away as the man reached out to touch it. Then she came to John. She disported in front of him. Out of the corner of his eye he could see Hammett laughing. John had no impulse to laugh. She was better, prettier, bouncier than he'd imagined. His face was parched, his throat a furnace. Her breasts, he noticed when she pressed them together and pushed one up to her mouth, were considerably softer than Anna Nicole's silicon spheroids. The desire to clamp his hands around them rose so swiftly that the need to suppress it choked him. Her eyes were impenetrable, smears of shadow. Her face jerked side to side, too fast for him to see the eyes. She licked a nipple, exposing a tongue pierced with a little silver barbell. It very nearly became entangled with the hoop. For a second, as he heard the metals clink, John imagined that they had locked up, and envisioned the emergency: Kelli, tongue stapled to her own nipple, hopping around like a hunchback, waving her arms to stop the music, the Tongan security man racing in and squaring off to smash the dirty old man until he was diverted by Kelli's muffled screams, and she would be carried away into the dressing room, doubled over onto herself, frozen in autoerotic contortion, and Dr John Brand would be shouting, 'I'm a doctor!' and saving the day, and her gratitude would be beyond measure . . . But the hoop did not catch the barbell, and Kelli skittered in the elusive light. She balanced on his lap for a second, but bounced up again. Mockingly, she placed a hand over her mouth and rolled her eyes for the crowd. In the next chair, Hammett was tearing himself apart with laughter, spilling his beer. Kelli bent down, dancing, and plucked rhythmically at John's trousers.

She closed her eyes, mouthing the words of the song.

She came close and shouted in his ear: 'I want to fuck you like an animal.'

He willed her to open her eyes, look at him. 'I'm . . . Hammett's father!'

'I want to feel you from the inside!'

Her pink strawberry perfume rushed up his nostrils. He threw his head back, spinning, willing himself not to faint. It was all so clear now. He just felt – stupid. *How stupid I have been. I should be at Chris's hotel. They're expecting me. How stupid, how idiotic, I have been.* Then, his eyes on the ceiling, he felt a hot breath on his groin, through his trousers. He jolted upright to look, but by the time he regained his focus Kelli had pulled her mouth away, pulled herself away, and was back up on the stage.

Her dance was a triumph. She finished and blew kisses to the cheering crowd.

John and Hammett stayed another hour. There were no more dancers. Hammett flirted with Mike Oberman's girls, and held incomprehensible conversations with Oberman himself. The four dancers had disappeared into the room behind the bar. John asked Oberman if Kelli was coming out for a drink, to which Oberman snarled: 'I got girls here. What, they not good enough for you?'

When it was time to leave, Hammett had to haul him out. John followed his son back up the maze of tin-shed corridors until they emerged into the night.

'Well,' John said. 'That was most . . . educational.'

Hammett was distracted, shifting from foot to foot.

'So,' John said, clearing his throat. 'Something I've been meaning to ask . . . Is there . . . is there a special la – is there someone special in your life, ah, these days?'

Hammett's distraction broke for an instant. Annoyance, puzzlement and sincerity flashed in rapid false starts across his features, before he clasped a hand around the nape of his father's neck and smiled.

'You're fucking priceless, Pa.'

'Well, I only –'

'Hey, Pa. Mike Oberman wants me to do him a favour. Or do Kelli a favour, really. Do you have to be home soon?'

'I have to go to Chris's hotel, in the quay. And I want to take you and show you . . .'

'Okay, okay,' Hammett interrupted. 'Can you bring the car round here? I've just got to go back inside. And, um, Pa?'

'I'll get the car. And bring it here.'

'Pa, I think . . . Yeah no, just bring the car round.'

December 31

At 9.12 pm on the last day of the year, John Brand sat at the wheel of his idling car. Hammett emerged from the back of the hangar with an arm around a short figure clad in a baseball cap, dark glasses and a shapeless tracksuit. The car bounced as they got into the back seat.

'The Cross, Pa.'

Obediently, John drove out of the carpark via a concealed back exit. He choked the steering wheel to stop his hands shaking. He swallowed back on the dryness in his throat.

'Yeah no,' Hammett said. 'Kelli would love it if we could go to your surgery.'

'The surgery? Is she sick?'

'Are you sick?' Hammett asked the mask of cap-and-sunglasses. John saw her in his rear-vision mirror. A white lollypop stick poked out of the corner of her mouth. She sniffed and looked out the window. She was very much younger than she had seemed: a child. She wore a child's perfume, a sweet pungent bubblegum smell that filled the car, less a scent than a flavour, and less a real flavour than a simulated one, a bubblegum strawberry, synthetically pink, the olfactory equivalent of 'Greensleeves' tinkling from a Mr Whippy van.

'I say we floor it,' Hammett said.

John pushed the Morris in silence towards the city. Finding Kelli's perfume a little cloying, he wound down his window. Brake lights of cars ahead blurred like Christmas tinsel on the streaky windscreen. Around Punchbowl, he tried to make conversation.

'So, er, ar, Kelli,' he swallowed, reddening at the sound of her name in his mouth, brushing a hand at his face as if to make it go away, 'ah, that was a very impressive show.'

No reply. Near Petersham, John tried again.

'Ah, is there anything specifically I can help you with?'

To which Kelli uttered her first words of the drive, looking at Hammett and saying, lollypop clacking against her teeth: 'How far?'

'Yeah no, how far, Pa?'

'Not far, not far at all.'

Finally they drove up William Street and turned into Kings Cross. John heard a murmur from the back seat. Hammett was peering out at the New Year's Eve scene, whispering to himself. Kelli's mask stared straight ahead. She chewed on the white stick.

John glanced helplessly at Hammett – was this how it was going to be, their meeting? Was she merely going to sit in the back like a hijacker? But Hammett offered no help. He was squinting through the window, brow knit, lips alive.

Without warning, Hammett's hand shot forward and gripped the headrest.

'Stop! Stop here!'

'No, it's just a bit further.'

'Stop, fuckya! *Stop!*'

John hit the brakes and Hammett leaped from the car. John reached for him, but Hammett threw the door shut and tripped on the kerb. Passers-by paused mid-stride. Hammett regained his footing and sprinted back the way they had come, in the direction of William Street.

'Oh, Lord,' John said. He looked for somewhere to pull over, but the traffic on Darlinghurst Road had banked up behind him, and someone shouted at him from the footpath. There was nowhere to park.

'Fucking come *on*!' Kelli waved her lollypop stick from the back seat.

John squealed into the underground carpark and reversed into his space so tremulously he scraped his rear bumper against a pillar. His heart felt like a pair of cats fighting. The pain had returned with new force. His breath came in short bursts, as if he could only breathe through a straw. A wet sheen covered his forehead. He turned off the ignition with the same feeling he'd had at Hammett's house, just before the boy attacked him: as if he were on a roller-coaster, his stomach floating in his throat, about to rush into a fearsome dive.

He was alone in his car with Her.

John looked at the mask in his rear-vision mirror. He felt dizzy, overwhelmed. He was here – with Her! Yet it was the banality, the effort he was having to make, that dizzied him. The over-strong perfume, the nocturnal sunglasses, the Cleveland Indians baseball cap, the formless tracksuit and sullen silence; and, outside the windows, the neon monochrome of the carpark where he came every day – all of it conspired to give her a certain elusiveness, as if reality were using its tricks to deny him. He wasn't so young or naive to expect the realisation of a hope to fulfill its anticipation. He wasn't surprised to be disappointed. That wasn't it. It was – well, when he'd been in the expo, watching her dance, he had been busily imprinting certain images on his mind, for later use, when he could reuse them at his own convenience. He wanted to do the same now, but she was frustratingly out of reach. What would he want to remember about the sight of her sulking behind her sunglasses in the carpark? Yet at the same time, her presence was such an overpoweringly real fact that he knew he would remember every useless detail, and this, here, in the car, the sweet strong perfume, all of it, was crowding into his mind like a computer virus filling his memory with useless, meaningless dots and dashes, spilling out of its assigned place, pushing every other recollection out, replacing them with a random infinity of Cleveland Indians baseball caps.

'Um,' he said. 'What is it exactly you want?'

'Jesus. Vi-co-din?' she said, as if she'd already told him a thousand times. Her voice gave the word the shape of a fish hook, a barb on the end. She shook her head out the window, as if at an audience sharing her impatience.

'Vicodin,' John repeated. 'Are you sure you want something like that?'

'Come on, man!' She rammed the heel of her hand into the window almost hard enough to shatter it. Simultaneously she kicked the back of John's seat, bumping him forward. His heart flurried.

'That's an American brand,' he said. 'I might have something similar. If that's all right.'

'Whatever.'

'Er, I mean, there are certain brand names and the pharmaceutical companies don't . . .'

'What-*ever?*'

'Well, yes, all right then.' In his day, the word *whatever* had had a single meaning: an indefinite relative pronoun shortening *any one thing*. But the young had made it capable of numerous meanings depending on arcane variations in tone and inflexion, like a Chinese word. It was the type of word his daughters-in-law used. Normally its many uses puzzled John, but Kelli Kittering's meaning was clear enough.

She didn't move, apparently intending to stay here while he went and got the drugs. Or perhaps, John thought, she was waiting for him to ask her if she'd like to come up to the su~
He should invite her. It would be the gentlemanly
turned in his seat.

'Would you like to . . .?'

'Oh fuck, guy, all right,' she huffed ~

cap and scratched her stiff, snarled blonde hair above the ears. It released a cloud of dried chemical gel. She placed her lollypop stick in the door-handle ashtray, shifted into the centre of the back seat and inclined forward, propping herself with her hands on the seat backs.

'Come on. Get it out.'

'Excuse me?'

'Why does this always . . .?' She turned her head to the side and grizzled to her invisible audience. She cut herself off and sighed. 'Okay, guy, I scratch your back, you scratch mine. It's all right, guy, you can just get it out here and I do you and then you go get the stuff.'

'I'm sorry, I don't think you under . . .'

'Fucking get it out?'

John's jaw flapped. Kelli Kittering was . . . *She* was offering here, in his car, to . . .

Yes.

But no.

He placed his hand, gently, on her forehead and tilted it upwards. He could not see her eyes, and it struck him then that he never would.

'I'll go and get what you want,' John said.

'Whatever.' She shifted back into her seat and found something interesting to look at out the window.

He trembled as he walked from the car. Had that really happened? Had Kelli Kittering just offered to? He must have been mistaken. That couldn't have been what she meant. He was frightfully glad he hadn't proceeded with the misunderstanding and unzipped himself. What kind of offensive presumption would she have made of that? His hands were shaking as he tried to unlock the surgery door. He fumbled with the keys and shouted at himself. He wiped the back of his neck.

Yet surely there was no misunderstanding. That was precisely that she had offered. In exchange for the pills: you scratch my back. But receiving such a favour from her, in such circumstances, constituted an imposition more than a fantasy. In his memory, he would have to exert himself to re-paint the background, re-shape the scenery, keep this kernel of fact – her offer – and put aside all the banality, all the disappointment, all the sullenness and shame. He would try to keep this one thing and transform it into something else, which would be infinitely more gratifying than anything that could have happened between the bucket seats of the Morris – but he would fail. He knew this much. He would fail.

'Hey, old man, you ought to see a doctor.'

Hammett's hand was on John's shoulder.

'Ah. Son. I was wondering where you'd –'

'Yeah no, I'm fucking over the moon, like *reborn*, uh-huh!'

Hammett wore a broad grin, calmer, more controlled than his usual amphetamines-but-not-amphetamines antic happiness. Hammett took John's keys and slid them into the lock.

Upstairs in the surgery, John got what Kelli had asked for plus, on Hammett's instructions, some prescription tranquillisers, anti-depressants and barbiturates 'to tide her over until she leaves the country'. John poured the bottles and packets into a plastic bag which Hammett twisted shut.

'Should I be hiding this?' Hammett said, stuffing the bag under his white jacket.

John nodded. He was locking the cabinet when his heart began to thunder, like a two-year-old child making itself known after a period of grace. He fell back into his chair.

'I can't do it anymore, son.'

'What's that?' Hammett was at the door.

'I'm finished.'

'Hey, Pa!' Hammett came back and knelt by his father. 'Yeah no, I know she's not a barrel of laughs, but – see, Pa, this is who she is. I thought you wanted to meet her. Get to know her. And later in the week, you can come out to where she's doing a show, a proper show, and watch her dance, and maybe . . .'

John held up a hand. The other was on his heart. He gulped air.

'Pa?'

'I have become . . . I despise myself.'

'Pa, nobody ever promised she'd be – I mean, what did you expect, like, Hillary Clinton?'

'It's not that. It's not that. I'm finished. Hammett, you won't have to put up with me for much longer, so . . .'

'Hey, old man – she's no Rhodes Scholar. She is what she is, uh-huh. Don't be disappointed, no disappointment will be allowed, no discussion or correspondence will be entered into.'

'I have to see your mother.' John was fighting back tears now, quaking. He doubled over. Hammett patted his back, like a football coach trying to pet a star player back onto the field. 'Oh Lord, what have I done? What have I done?'

'Yeah no, but see, there's always time.'

'There's no time.'

'Don't be a drama queen, old man, there's always –'

'There *isn't* time!' John was glaring wildly at his son. He got to his feet, pushing Hammett out of the way, and opened his desk drawer.

Hammett watched as John tore open a large mustard-coloured envelope.

'Let me show you *my* most . . . *pornographic* . . . pictures.'

John pulled out a set of ultrasound images. He handed them one by one to Hammett, who held them up to the light. He circulated the set twice.

'You're the doctor, Pa. I don't know what these are.'

John inserted a videotape into the player beside the computer. The tape showed another ultrasound record – a live, moving version of the still shots. Grey ghosts smacked spastically against a mottled, shadowy background. Things like jellyfish, like constellations in a night sky, shifted with their own alien choreography. A white whip-like form flicked and licked against a rigid bar.

A sound like crashing waves, sucking and rolling and thumping down, filled the room.

Hammett watched the monitor. John watched Hammett. The tape ran for three minutes.

'My heart,' John said.

'Your heart.'

John played the tape again, pausing when it came to the whip, or strand of seaweed, flowing out and rippling back with a noisy otherworldly whack against what John described as the mouth of the aorta. Normally, he said, the flap of flesh would close softly, but in his case the valve – for that was what it was, the door of a valve – was so ravaged as to be almost ineffective. Blood rushed back down into the heart. His blood pressure was dangerously low and his heart dangerously enlarged as it fought twice as hard to pump fresh supplies around his body. This failure, he said, had led to dizziness and breathlessness, palpitations and fainting. He pointed to the thickness of the heart muscle on the screen.

'Four times as big as it's meant to be. It chokes on its own dead muscle. I'm – as you would say, Hammett – I'm fucked.'

'But yeah no, I mean, you can have this fixed!'

'In normal circumstances, yes.'

'You're a normal sixty-fucking-seven-year-old. There's no reason not to . . .'

John was raising a hand to silence Hammett. Out of his envelope he took more images and passed them across the room.

'These pictures are my secrets.' He breathed. He was calm. 'This will explain why I have done what I have done.'

He didn't need to look at them with Hammett. The slides, the lurid blue and red tissue stains, the chromatin blurs, the rococo swirls of infiltrating carcinoma, he knew well enough. Hammett scanned them with a frown – John rejoiced, grimly, in seeing his son so absorbed.

Hammett went through his father's deceased serial-sected cells, fixed on the five-colour gloss printouts as if they were abstract art. The forty-times magnification of John's biopsy showed a carpet-bombing of mauve puffs, the aerial view of demolition. The 400-times magnifications got into the cells themselves, nuclei staring insolently with a blue eye, fried eggs surrounded by white cytoplasm. Hammett leaned over them, pored through them, contemplating the cellular beauty. And his father was beautiful, from the inside of his disease. His cellular disarray, his strobing sunsets, his science fiction octopus monsters with their pink tentacles and wobbly heads, all spoke of John Brand as lovingly as after-dinner speeches. Those rectangular mitochondria with fashionable-seeming cristae, the chubby secretory vacuoles, burst with new design principles, a journey into the outer stars, a side of his father he never knew.

'You talk about my *soul*. This is my soul.'

'I don't get it.' Hammett shook his head hard. He threw the pictures back across the desk. John noted that his son's eyes had filmed over.

'We are "visual" men, Hammett. Isn't that the word for it? The last few years have taught me that. I need to see. Look at my soul – pocked and chalky like chunks of pumice floating on a bath. Each facet of my soul is different, with a different aspect turned to the light, posing for the cameras.'

'This is not good, Pa.'

'We're all going to die, son. Why not sooner? What good would I be doing by hanging around? It is a busy world. It is full enough – overfull – as it is. In fact, life would run along more smoothly without me.'

'I don't understand these pic . . . This report says an "aggressive tumour". Pa? Please? What's this saying to me? What are you fucking going on about?'

'I'm an aggressive fellow, Hammett. It's something that's not widely understood about me.'

'I need to know what this means.'

'Death has whispered in my ear. At night, I hear it every moment: You're fucked you're fucked you're fucked you're fucked.' A grimly humorous noise effused through his nose.

'Why aren't you doing chemo?'

'Chemical warfare. Should be illegal. Chemotherapy would make me vomit in the middle of the night, and when I'm not vomiting I'd be seasick. Have you ever been seasick, my boy? They say don't carry guns on a yacht because somebody will use one to shoot himself. Nausea is worse than death. Chemotherapy would be worse than death. Every bone in my body would ache. Worse at night. In waves all through the night, coming, going, coming, going, and the going no relief because it only presages more coming. I would take my Cytoxan, my Adriamycin. They would destroy the new cancer cells, but they would also kill my hair cells, my bone marrow cells, the cells lining my gastro-intestinal tract. The cancer isn't hard to take – the drugs would be. And the full-time occupation of staving off death. Why should I, of all people, want to prolong life?'

Hammett looked at the pictures again, the paradox of these destructive cells that could destroy everything except themselves, these renegades, these mavericks, these rogues, these living-dead zombies who had forgotten what all other cells know by nature: forgotten how to die.

'That's what makes my enemies different,' John said. 'So full of the will to live – you have to admire them, don't you?'

'But . . . your heart, the ultrasound – what's that got to do with it – this cancer? I don't understand, Pa.'

'Don't cry for me, Hammett. Why would I have a new valve bunged in, a nice carbon fibre one? Just to give the cancer a good run at me? I'm diseased. My heart's shot, the cancer's swimming in lymph, and the brain – well, you know what the brain is. Disease has made me what I am. I lie in bed scared out of my wits. And you know . . . I was not going to come and join you tonight – I was determined not to. I only decided to come along at the last moment. Because, ultimately, I thought: I am going to die, so I might as well stop fighting my sons.'

'Fuck fuck fucking fuck!' Hammett got up and paced around the room. He stood at the window with a desperate, helpless look.

'It's not – I don't want anything from you, Hammett. I realised I should be blessing every day that I have with you. I thought I'd lost you, but you have come back. That is something, isn't it?'

Hammett turned around. Tears were streaming down his face.

'Pa, you fucking bastard, you fucking fucking arsehole . . .'

Hammett's face was on his father's lap. His tears soaked through John's trousers.

'All this – all that I have been doing – all this – can I say it? This masturbation, this obsession – this change that has come over me – it is death. This, this pornography, is an enactment of death. I am dead. It does not matter what I do, how I shame myself. I am already dead.'

'You need to talk to Ma.'

'I have such a short distance to travel.'

'Pa. Listen up. She's your wife, man. She's the mother of your children. Do you hear me? You have to talk to her, you know what I'm saying?'

John stood up and washed his hands in the basin. He dried them on a paper towel. He fussed about with the slides and X-rays. He packed up the videotape. Fastidiously, like a thief, he packed it all into the drawer the way he had found it, turning over the envelope so the torn edge wouldn't show.

Without looking at Hammett, he said: 'It's been a little anti-climactic for me. Er, Kelli. I don't know what I expected. But – well, now I know. I know what she is, and I know what I am. I'm sixty-seven years old. I've come to my own surgery and procured drugs illegally for a pornographic actress. I can look back proudly on my life, can't I?'

'Fuck!' Hammett bounced to his feet. His hand went up to his forehead, pinching. John saw Margaret. 'Fuck this, Pa! Nothing's over. Nothing's fucking dead until it's dead. Hey, yeah, uh-huh! Just fucking listen up, uh-huh?'

John sat behind his desk, an attentive doctor.

Hammett looked away, as if beholding his father squarely would break him. The boy snapped his fingers.

'Tonight. You asked me if I had anyone "special". Okay, I laughed at you. But – listen up. You know how I ran out of the car? Uh-huh? Well. I was looking for someone. There's someone around here – well, I thought she was dead. For the last five years, this person, it's a friend of mine – I thought she was dead. But we were driving into the Cross, you and me and Kelli, and I was looking for this friend, uh-huh. And I *saw* her! I saw her, Pa! This person! She's old now. I met her a long time ago.'

Hammett poured it out. He told his father about Old Faithful.

'I thought she was dead,' Hammett was on his knees. 'I thought I'd killed her.' He looked up, his forehead hot as flame. 'But she's not. See? She's not dead! I was . . . I was fucking . . . I thought I'd killed her! But – fuck, man, sometimes things aren't what you thought. They're not all bad. Sometimes things can be okay! And I went and I said hello to her, and she sort of remembered me! But that's not important! She's alive! Okay? I didn't kill her, that was all bullshit! And to see her, having thought what I thought – fuck, Pa! I'm alive too! Yeah no, it's not all bad!'

John and Hammett sat silently, holding each other's hands. Hammett buried his face on John's knee and did not raise his egg-plant-purple face until John's thigh was drenched with his tears.

John stroked Hammett's hair. Still a boy.

'You were wrong about something,' John said.

Hammett snivelled, his face averted.

'You said I do this – I force these risks upon myself – to assure myself that I'm alive. Well, that's not quite it, my boy. That may have been why I started, but the question is, why can't I stop? Why am I so gripped by this thing? And the answer is this. It helps me, even if for a few minutes, to forget that I am going to die.'

'You don't have to die so soon,' Hammett said sulkily, his eyes on the floor.

'Well, I have found that the more I do this thing that helps me forget about death, the more I am convinced that I have forsaken my right to live. I desperately want to escape the sickness, and equally desperately I want to escape the cure I have fashioned for it.'

From outside, the cheering of a crowd and the singing of a group of Christians filtered up through the surgery. The synthetic pink of Kelli Kittering's perfume was trapped in John's nostrils. Hammett shook his head and wiped his dripping nose on his forearm.

'Thank you, Pa.'

'No, son. Thank *you*. I suppose you should take her those now. She'll be getting impatient.'

'Sure. Okay then.' Hammett wiped his nose on his other arm. 'Let's go.'

'You take them down, Hammett. You're right, what you said about your mother. There is still time, and I want to take you to see her. We should both talk to her. I had this idea . . . tonight . . . that we'd do this. I didn't expect to get, er, waylaid for quite so long.'

'But, yeah no, what about Kelli?'

'Put her in a taxi.'

'Don't you want to see her when she's a bit happier?'

'I never want to see her again.'

'Pa,' Hammett wiped his face, 'she might not be what she's cracked up to be, but –'

'No. I've done wrong here, by giving her these drugs. I don't want to witness my wrongdoing any more than I have to. You go.'

The tears had dried on Hammett's face. His eye was caught by something on John's chest.

'I can't let you go to Ma with that.'

'What?' John looked down to see the incriminating laminated VIP pass.

'A week ago,' Hammett slipped the pass over his father's head, 'I'd have left you with it.'

'Thank you for reminding me.'

'Yeah no, I'd have got a buzz out of the idea of you having to explain that to the old lady. But I guess, you can deal with it at your own pace.'

'Son. I want you to come along. Your brothers are there. It's a new year. We can be together, we can ask each other for forgiveness.'

'Yeah no, but Kelli's gunna spew.'

'My son. May I . . . shake your hand?'

'You wanna . . .?' Hammett looked strangely at his father, then shrugged – 'Sure, why not?' – and offered his right hand, fingers to the ceiling, for an American grip.

'Please,' John shook his head. 'Like this.' He held out his hand formally, for a conventional handshake.

'Yeah no,' Hammett smiled. 'Whatever.'

They shook. Hammett's hand felt like heaven. The handshake dominoed into a hug. Hammett had caught John as he fell, freeing him to confess. The appalling thing was done. John no longer had to carry his secret on his own.

'Okay, okay,' Hammett said. They stepped into the reception of the surgery. 'Yeah no, we better get her these, and then pack her off back to . . . What's that?'

Hammett was staring at the front of his father's moleskins. John followed his eyes. Across his fly was the imprinted pucker of a large mouth in berry-pink lipstick.

'Kelli Kittering's lips,' Hammett said. 'You give those pants to me and I can auction them on the website for ten grand, no worries, uh-huh.'

'W-well!' John stammered. 'Well, I'd better change them before your mother sees them. I might have another pair in my cupboard here.'

John opened the door to the cupboard beside the light box. A pair of suit trousers was folded on the top shelf.

'Do you mind, er . . .?'

Hammett turned away while John put on the suit trousers.

'You know, son, that was a lot of fun. I mean, innocent fun.'

'I think Kelli wants you, Pa. Real bad. Real, real bad.'

'More than any other man?' John smiled, scrolling up the dirty pants.

'More than anyone in the world.'

'Then she'll be crippled with disappointment.'

John stuffed the lipsticked trousers onto the top shelf of his metal cupboard. Hammett chuckled and packed the bag of drugs more snugly under his jacket.

'I'll pop these down to the carpark,' he said.

They found themselves hugging again. John whispered into his son's ear.

'Your mother loves you, Hammett. That's the biggest secret. She loves all of us.'

Hammett put a hand on his father's shoulders, pinched his forehead with the other, as if summoning up a blessing. His neck rose and fell in a sigh.

'I've never been unfaithful to your mother, Hammett. I know you find that ridiculous. But I've always been an object of ridicule to you, so I suppose I needn't worry about justifying my position at this late date.'

At 11.07 pm on the last night of the year, John and his son walked out through the reception area. Hammett had grown taller, it seemed to John as he watched the boy pull the door open at the top of the staircase. Somewhere outside, down on Darlinghurst Road, a bus came to a sharp halt. The sound of its brakes shot like needles through John's skull. His hand went to his chest.

'Hammett.'

The gathering rumble in his head came in a wave, deep and disordered, plasticky and hollow, reminding him somehow of a thing rolling towards him down a hill. He felt he should move – jump out of its path – but was rooted to the spot. The feeling in his chest was like a stitch. He'd had this sensation before and been able to stay above it, as if treading the surface of rising waters. He still felt confident now. He reminded himself to breathe, but immediately forgot again, because he was thinking he looked ridiculous, standing with his right hand upon his heart as if swearing an oath, or listening to the national anthem, and now he was asking his son if he'd slow down a little, and surely he shouldn't have left Her in that carpark, what with so many shady types around.

'Pa, you right?'

The deep hollow thing rumbled deafeningly then began to decompose, as if collapsing into its single mechanical parts. The stitch braced across his ribs. He suffered a flash of panic as he felt himself losing purchase, as if those rising waters were assuming unnatural qualities, cheating on him, outwitting him, dragging him down, laughing at him. A thought came to his head: *Don't go swimming straight after lunch, you'll get a stitch.*

'Pa?'

John reached for his old notion of what should happen at this moment: his reckoning-up of decisions, his highlights tape. But it receded from his grasp like a neglected friend. *You didn't need me, I've moved on.* What was coming, in any case, would dwarf and obliterate his old morality like an eighteen-wheeler running through a wooden barrier. John thought, with a momentarily perplexing, momentarily soothing mixture of relief and panic: *I'll have to wing it.* A white ache exploded above his left ear, tugging up the side of his mouth. His fingers snaked, like a lover's, between his shirt buttons. For a second he was back with Hammett, the boy pinching the flesh between his eyes and blinking at him – or was it Margaret? – and it struck John that there was so much left to do, so much work, more to do, really, than the heart was built for.

It was 11.09 pm on the last night of the year.

'Oh, dear,' John mouthed, the air flowing not out but in. *Brand's sign.* 'Oh, dear.'

PART FIVE

PART FIVE

She is sleeping better. She does not know whether it is exhaustion, or the satisfaction of having smartened up the right-of-way and putting those townhouse renters to shame, or the uncharacteristically thorough cleaning Bonnie and Clyde gave the house yesterday, or the glee of having broken apart those floppy disks, right down to the last one, and piled them so neatly into shells, valves and flesh.

She finally got the blasted window shut last night. She couldn't keep on bundling herself up in blankets and rags like a derro. She climbed up on her chair and examined the window catch. It was jamming along the rail. She picked away at it, not caring about her fingernails because most had already broken in her endeavours with the floppy disks. Eventually she found something: a clump of wool, dark-red in colour, wound around the screw of the window latch. She balled it up in her fingers, recognising the colour: a jumper she'd knitted John, years ago. He must have been up there doing something, and his jumper caught on the latch. The wool in her fingers, she went to his drawer and found the jumper. Sure enough, a hole had been pulled out of the cuff.

After shutting the window, she took off her ski jumper and dressing gown, and slept in her nightie underneath a single sheet. She hasn't slept so well in years.

Around nine o'clock this morning, she is woken by the rain. She goes downstairs and stands at the back door, watching it with the wonder of a child standing on the underside of a waterfall. Thunder in the morning, such a tropical sound! The air smells of fizzling heat, of banana leaves and fresh mushrooms. Waves of vengeful thunder beat in from the south, as if the city is under attack. The garden shudders – in submission, in ecstasy? – under the weight of raindrops, heavy little clods of water, like an ocean picked up and shaken out from above. The Totem Tennis ball bounces under the onslaught, the dirt on Des's grave pocking and melting into mud. The swimming pool fills to the brim and masses on the pebbly decking. And still more thunder! In the morning, she thinks, thunder seems out of its time, like a theatre show before lunch.

As the morning goes on, the rain sets in. Even without the thunder, the downpour rattles so noisily on the aluminium porch roof that she has to turn the television volume to full. But what point is there? The match is as good as over. The pitch is covered, but the covers are invisible under a spreading lake. Australia have been cheated of their win. Tom Pritchard failed to get that final wicket yesterday afternoon, and they have paid the price. Margaret feels an unusual sense of vindication – as if Pritchard deserved this biblical punishment. The team did not deserve an achievement that might have overshadowed Chris's. This game will never be remembered as a great win. A footnote will record that a massive summertime downpour robbed Australia; but the headlines, the news, the memories will all orbit around her son's magnificent redemption.

At lunchtime Ian arrives and sets about cooking one of his Asian noodle dishes, with tender slices of beef. He's brought his spices with him.

'Pity they couldn't have finished the South Africans off,' he says, stirring.

For all her gratitude, for all her genuine love and affection for this man, nothing would please Margaret more than if he left. He can take his delicious food with him – she never asked for it – and jolly well get lost. She's sick of everyone, sick of the tiptoeing, sick of the kid gloves. Hammett wouldn't stand for this. He'd blurt something out, inappropriate but spot-on. He'd speak his appalling mind. He'd initiate something, disturb the festering inertia, exert a power which seems to have been denied everyone else in the family. Including herself. She wants Ian to go home, but can't raise a scene. She wanted to confront John, just have it all out with him, but never could. A paralysis of good form. Not just pretending it would go away – there was no pretending, she knew it wouldn't go away – but something more basic than that: just a paralysis, a simple fear of breaking the smooth surface.

The phone rings. Ian gets up.

'Chris! Good to hear from you . . . Congratul . . . Oh, sure, all right. I'll get her.'

Ian gives her the phone without looking at her. He finds something very urgent to toss around in his wok.

'Hey, Ma.'

'Where are you?' She clears her unused throat.

'Ah, in the dressing room. Forecast isn't good. We've blown it. So . . .' There is a silence as Chris waits for her to say something about the cricket. She has nothing to say. Chris coughs and says: 'So, how are you holding up?'

'Quite well.'

'Ian looking after you?'

'As always. We're – he's cooked me a lovely lunch.'

'That's great.'

'Yes.'

'Ma?'

'Oh, congratulations, dear. You've done it.'

'Done it? Oh, yeah, yeah, sure, thanks. Um. I might come up there later, as soon as the game's finished.'

'That would be lovely. But don't rush.'

'I'm bringing . . . Ma, have you spoken to Davis?'

'Davis? He came the other day. I haven't heard anything from him since.'

'He said he's been calling you.'

'Has he?' She looks at Ian, who remains riveted by his noodles.

'He said you weren't answering his calls.'

'I don't know about that.'

'He said Hammett's been calling too.'

'Oh, Chris.'

'Has he?'

'I don't . . . I've just been watching you. A proud mother.'

'Ma. You haven't heard from either of them?'

'No, I haven't.'

'Ma, I'm coming home later, and I'm bringing Davis.'

'Well.'

'And we're both bringing Hammett.'

'I'm sure you know what you're doing, Chris.'

'Ma, I . . . um.' Chris waits silently and she cannot speak. She wants to express her approval; she wants to say: *Yes, bring Davis, bring Hammett, I need my boys.* But it is too soon. She will have the words, in time, but not yet, not now. Finally Chris says: 'Can you put Ian back on?'

Ian takes the phone into the living room. Margaret can't be bothered eavesdropping. She unpacks the dishwasher, then stacks the plates. She is stretching her back when Ian comes in again, looking like a kicked dog. She waits, but no explanation is forthcoming. He fixes a dessert of fruit salad and yoghurt. She thinks of the chocolate thickshake she'll stir up for herself later, when she is alone.

So, she thinks: Davis has been calling, but Ian, interpreting what he thinks are my wishes, has not been allowing my son to talk to me.

And Hammett?

It defies belief, but there it is. Things have been running along for five days now, the world turning on its blind axis.

Her sons have questions about their father, do they? Well, why didn't they jolly well ask him when he was alive? That's what she wants to know: why did they have to wait until it's too late?

Suddenly she does something that shocks Ian to the core. She looks at him across the kitchen and asks: 'What are you thinking about?'

Ian springs away from the stove, embarrassed, as if she had uttered an obscenity. He collects his wits and retreats to the kitchen sink.

'I only asked you what you're thinking about . . .'

Ian rinses the plates angrily, bangs them into the dishwasher. It's as if she's insulted him in the worst possible way.

He looks in her direction. Her eyebrows arch question-marks.

'Come on, Margaret.'

'It's only a question, dear.'

He looks at her as if she's a raving lunatic.

'Do you know what I'm thinking about?' She flutters her eyelashes.

Ian shakes his head.

'I'm wondering if I should start returning some phone calls.'

'Margaret, there's no need . . .'

'No, there isn't any need, is there? Because no-one has called, isn't that right? None of my friends has called, nobody I know, of all the people who knew John, not a solitary one has called.'

Ian swallows, and pulls up the drawbridge of the dishwasher. It shuts with a loud click.

'Do you really want to know what I was thinking about, Margaret?'

'Only if I'm in a fit state to hear it, dear.'

'I was thinking . . .' Ian backs against the dishwasher, resting on his hands. 'I was thinking about all those years ago, I don't know if you remember, when I took a little break from . . . things.'

365

Margaret is smiling sociably, but a wasp of fear skitters across her face.

'I deemed it the only solution to my problem.' Ian fixes his eyes on the ceiling. 'And I did have a problem, a hopeless one, didn't I? I don't know if you knew this, or even suspected it, but when you – when your boys first came to the school, I was thirty-three years old and had never had relations with a woman. What a pathetic figure: an old maid, that's what I was. A dessicated old bachelor, married to his school. At thirty-three. And then I had the misfortune to fall disgracefully, without a shred of merit, in love with a married woman.'

Margaret steadies herself against the kitchen benchtop.

'I was obsessed with her, and tried to see her at every opportunity. I was sure that, given my, ah, my background, it would not bother me that there was no hope of advancing our friendship any further. I'd never had a great enough need for that type of contact in my life before, so why should I now?'

'Ian.'

'You asked for it, Margaret. You asked for it. So. It soon appeared I was mistaken. Now that I had fallen in love with someone, with a flesh-and-blood woman, of course I could think of nothing else but *that type of contact*. Every waking hour. I was half-mad with, with lust. No other word for it. So what could I do? I would withdraw with dignity. I would have to amputate this friendship to save my soul. And, I convinced myself, to save hers too. So I resolved never to have anything to do with this woman or her family again. I cut them off. I went off and sought other women, of a certain kind, who were available. I spent one glorious month in what they call the "mature singles scene". I advertised myself as a man who loves children, and would dearly like to find a ready-made family with whom to settle down. That, of course, brought me a certain degree of success, and I was quite the –'

'Ian, thank you, I get the picture.'

'Do you? Have you ever got the picture, Margaret?'

'More than you'd think.'

'I wonder if you have the slightest idea what I'd think. If what I'd think has ever exercised your mind for more than a –'

'Ian, stop it!'

'You asked for it.'

'For goodness' sake, Ian, I don't want to hear this! I only want to know why you've been stopping my sons, my friends, my family, from talking to me on the telephone! Why can't you tell me that?'

'I am.'

'Well, get on with it, and cut out this silly nonsense about the past.'

'That's just the thing, though. It's not the past.'

'Oh, Ian, please. Now's not the time.'

'Right, right. That's what I keep telling everyone else. Now's not the time. But I wonder if I'm correct in that. Perhaps now is the time. Perhaps there will never be another time.'

'You're embarrassing yourself.'

'Oh, Margaret, that's the least of my problems. Anyway, as you say, I'll get on with it. You know, when I got away from you, I felt I had to discover what it was I was missing out on. Love, sex, whatever people call it. And you know what? I could not drive you from my heart. I was, I am, utterly devoted to you, Margaret. But – just hear me out – I have enough respect for you, and enough natural pessimism, to know that this love will remain unrequited. This was what I realised all those years ago. I could not cut you out of my life without cutting out the best part of myself. My nose to spite my face, yes? So I came back. But I never lost hope. So, yes, I've been screening calls, turning off the phone, keeping you to myself. I wanted to clean out John's office as fast as I could. I felt, hoped, that this was my time. When I could prove myself to you. You would look up, in extremis, you would be seeking an answer, and finally you would see me, and me alone.'

'You have overstepped the line. I'm sorry.'

'I'm sorry too.'

He clears his throat and looks at her. She moves around to the pile of mail on the bench, and starts to sort through it. On top is a pamphlet that says: 'It's All Right To Cry'. She wants to ball it up and shove it in his poor silly face.

'I think I should go home now.'

'Yes,' she sighs, flipping through the envelopes. 'All right. You go home.'

She lets him go without another word. She wanders out onto the back patio, looks at the mud pooling around the Totem Tennis pole. What would old Des have made of all this?

Ian's gone, she thinks. Well, let him look after himself. For once. Let him look after himself.

They're coming. Davis, Chris and Hammett. Her sons are coming home.

They'll want to tell her things, as if she doesn't know already, as if she's a deaf, dumb, vegetal halfwit.

There was a night, Christmas Eve, their first get-together since he'd thrown his granddaughter against the kitchen drawers.

Margaret, John, Chris, Suzie, Davis, Lucy, Ian, Brooke, Emily.

Since his blow-up things were softer, more forgiving. She and Chris didn't pick on him. Chris had lost his form, and his cockiness had been replaced by a gentle consideration for his father.

As they ate, John grabbed Margaret's hand under the table. She gave him a surprised look. He leaned across and kissed her cheek. Her free hand reached furtively across and closed around his. He kissed her again. Her eyes were wet.

'I don't know what's come over you, you silly old goat.'

John's lower lip quivered.

'I've done something very stupid,' he whispered. 'You've no idea how stupid.'

Margaret's eyes narrowed, amused, chastising.

'Then you'd better undo it,' she said. 'You naughty boy.'

Later, when they were undressing for bed, John said: 'I've just got to do a few things in the study.'

'All right. Don't be up too late.'

He wasn't long in the study, for a change. He came in, switched off the light and turned to his side of the bed. Greyness fell over the room like a shroud. A dog barked distantly.

He spoke into the darkness.

'I have a surprise for you.'

'A surprise!' Margaret pushed herself upright and reached for a tissue on her bedside table. She blew her nose. 'Surprise,' she repeated. He might as well have said *lifestyle*, or *marijuana* (which she pronounced with a hard Y and five syllables).

She heard him swallow. She settled back into her space, without touching him.

'You've no idea how stupid I've been,' his voice said.

'You said that.'

'I have been worse than you could imagine.'

'John, nothing could be worse than I can imagine.'

He chuckled. 'Well, imagine your worst.'

There was a silence so impervious that she thought he had gone to sleep.

'John?'

'Yes.' His voice was strong, awake.

'I don't want to know.'

'I know you don't.'

'I have no interest, whatever it is.' She sighed. 'So perhaps you should spare me your surprises.'

She heard him scratch his chin. The mattress tilted as he rolled onto his back. He laced his fingers over his chest.

'It's not that,' he said. 'It's the New Year's Eve do. At Chris's hotel. I want to bring somebody along.'

Margaret did not need to think for too long. The thickness in John's voice told her enough.

'Are you sure, John?'

'It's about time, I think. What about you? How would you feel?'

She lay in the dark beside him. All things considered, he couldn't choose a more inopportune time. There would be school councillors, party executive members, significant people to whom their family name was hard currency.

'I know what you're thinking,' John said. 'But we've been finding fault for long enough. I don't think we have that luxury anymore.'

'We've done our best,' Margaret said. The sound of her own voice brought to mind a dead tooth: grey, empty of feeling, persistent but useless.

'We've raised them to be grateful to us,' John said. 'At this late date, it might be more important for them to enjoy spending time in our company. A little less duty, a little more cheer.'

Margaret could not find the words to oppose him. She too knew that it was time. She reached out and held his dry hand, and when she woke on Christmas morning she could not remember having let it go.

No let-up in the rain. It falls and falls, blotting out a world beyond the back fence. The darkness of the day feels perverse, as if the seasons have been inverted. She stands on the porch and reels in the garden hose, coiling it in big lasso-loops. She hauls it back and lifts it over the hook near the tap.

Inside, the cricket has been abandoned and Tony Greig is conducting the man-of-the-match interview. Margaret goes in and perches on the arm of her chair. Tony Greig presents Chris with a cheque and some kind of sponsorship logo masquerading as a trophy.

'So, Chris, pretty much a perfect end to the season.' Greig leans down to put the microphone before her son, whose skin is the colour of a sundried tomato.

'Yep, couldn't have finished it all off better,' Chris says. Greig waits for more. There is none.

'Um, yes. How was it, then, with all the emotion of it? And the events of earlier in the week – just tell us how hard it was for you.'

'It was hard, but I couldn't think of a better way to finish it all off, yeah.'

For all his courage and character on the field, Chris acts in interviews as if he barely gives cricket – his place in the game, its future, the sense of representing his nation – more than a passing thought.

'Aha,' Tony Greig says. 'Okay. Well, the boys must be happy and looking forward to the tour.'

'I s'pose they are. As for me, though, this was a great way to finish it all off.'

'Well, that's terrific. All the best, Chris, and well done.'

Greig turns back to the camera and begins his cross back to the central commentary position, but Chris stays and interrupts him.

'I don't think you were listening, Tony.'

'Eh?'

'I've just given you a scoop. Let me spell it out.' Chris looks directly at the camera, which closes in on him. 'I'm finishing up. That's it from me. Um, I'm retiring from cricket. All levels. I'd like to thank my supporters for everything they've given me over the years, and I'd like to thank my critics for the kicks up the bum. I've deserved it from time to time. But that's it from me. I've had enough. I'm pleased I made runs here, but to tell the truth I would have retired now either way. It's nice to go out with the selectors still wanting a bit more from me, rather than hoping I'd, you know, fall on my sword. But, as I say, that's that. I want to spend a bit more time with my family. A lot more time with my family. I've missed my kids growing up, you know, and there are a few other family matters to, you know, attend to.'

'Well!' The picture widens to show a flustered Tony Greig. 'Well! That's quite a, quite a bombshell. Uh, it's not often . . . Well! What's that, Richie?'

The picture splits to show Richie Benaud, smiling like a sunbathing lizard in the commentary booth.

'Tony, can you ask Chris what he's planning to do with his future? There has been talk of politics?'

'Ah, ah, yes, thanks, Richie. Ah, Chris, would you like to tell us what you're planning for the future, politics-wise? Or, ah, something involved with cricket?'

'I don't know if you or Richie were listening. I said I'm planning to spend more time with my family. Sure, every cricketer says that when he retires, and he goes off and spends five minutes with his wife before hopping back onto the caravan as a commentator or a coach or a selector. But you can't really see me doing that, can you, Richie?' (In the studio, Benaud's smile is a fixed quantity.) 'No, what I said was, I'm quitting the game because I want to spend more time with my family. My brothers, my mother, my wife, my kids. I don't think I've been attending to that very well for the last twelve years. You asked about politics. Well, I think I've answered that. I'm not ready for public life. I want to go home.'

'Well, that's . . .' Tony Greig is left flapping as Chris departs the press conference with his trophy and his cheque. 'That's quite a bombshell. Back to you, Richie.'

Margaret Brand's left hand twists the arm of her favourite chair. Her right hand goes up to her forehead and staples the skin between her eyebrows.

Funnily enough, as the television goes to a commercial break, Margaret imagines Ian Bertrand, her good friend, standing beside her. She knows that, in a silence like this, Ian could not help filling it with his chatter. 'Well, in the heat of the moment,' he'd say, flummoxed by Chris's surprise announcement. 'I don't know, really, if he knows what he's saying. He can't just . . . We're not ready for this. He's got at least another season in him, and it would have been better timing with the preselection if . . . Gee, I'm sure we'll be able to talk him out of . . .'

'Oh, shut up, Ian!'

She says it aloud. She blinks at the stupid television. Shaking her head, she points the remote control at it and turns it off.

'I said shut up!' she mutters, moving over to the kitchen to put the kettle on. 'Why don't you all just stop talking and listen for a moment?'

She goes through the biscuit tins and starts to lay out chocolate slices, Anzac cookies, shortbreads and peanut biscuits onto a plate. The boys will be here soon, she thinks, and we haven't done anything about the funeral.

January 6

The drive from Liverpool to the North Shore crosses every stratum of the city. It could take an hour and a half on the Hume Highway and Canterbury Road. But in the luxury of Davis's German pod, it is a mere zip down the rain-slicked chute between freeway noise barriers decorated attractively with moulded cockatoos and galahs.

'Pure driving pleasure,' Hammett says. 'Yeah no, you've really made good, Davo.'

'Goes fucken all right in the wet, eh,' Chris says.

Davis still has trouble looking at his youngest brother in the back seat. His swollen lip prevents him talking intelligibly. But this, he thinks, is a good thing. Unable to make himself heard, he can only watch and listen. His stomach knotted with the weight of this event – *three sons* – he doubts he could say much anyway. When they'd arrived at the big house with the fanlight window, Chris had done the talking, telling Hammett to go and get changed out of the fur-trimmed white leatherette overcoat he was, for his own reasons, wearing. He now wears a dark, sober suit.

'Make your point with your words,' Chris said, 'not your dress sense.'

The whole thing was Chris's initiative. He had called Davis at lunchtime, when the Noachian downpour signalled that Chris

374

would not be playing cricket today. It was the first time they had spoken since Chris had given Davis his kicking the other night. Without a word of apology or preamble, Chris suggested that Davis pick him up from the ground after the press conference, and that they drive together to Hammett's house and bring him home to Ma for afternoon tea.

'You sure?' Davis said, not quite trusting Chris.

'Look, I'll be upfront with you,' Chris said. 'If he says a word out of line, I'm going to kick him so hard he'll need to stick a brush up his arse to clean his teeth. But I want to give him a go.' As if it was his idea.

Davis drove to the ground in the early afternoon. On the radio he heard about Chris's retirement. He waited, as arranged, on the parking apron near the nets where Chris had beaten him up. Chris came out in casual clothes, without any cricket bags, and got into the passenger seat. When he saw Davis's lip, he said: 'Oh Jesus, brother. I'm fucking sorry.'

'Well,' Davis said, realising that Chris was thinking his bandaged lip was a result of their fight. Not wanting to let him off the hook, Davis played along: 'You don't know your own strength.' He nodded at Chris's bandaged finger.

'I can't really understand you,' Chris said, leaning close. 'But I'm one fucking cunt of a brother, that's all I can say.'

Davis shrugged, with a half-smile, as if to say: That's what I've been telling you for years.

'No, I mean it,' Chris said, leaning over to touch Davis's dressing, tenderly. 'I am a deadshit. Not a tough nut, not a ruthless bastard, not all those affectionate fucking cliches they've been serving up for me. I am just a deadshit, no excuses.'

Davis was sceptical about Chris's sudden rush of contrition and self-awareness, but Chris had continued in this vein during the trip to the McMansion near Liverpool and then, even more tellingly and surprisingly, had been bright and candid with Hammett.

Hammett, for his part, was cocky and self-possessed. Davis hadn't known what to expect and was clagged-up with tension when they'd arrived. But Hammett, having agreed to change his suit on Chris's advice, bounded into the car and broke the ice immediately, saying:

'What, Davo, you forget to duck?'

Davis shook his head. 'I walked into a door.'

Davis drives them back from the south-west, towards home. Rain drums on the roof and dances on the bonnet. Other cars edge along the freeway. Boldly, Davis weaves through the traffic, showing off.

Hammett scrunches up his jacket sleeves and asks Chris about his retirement.

'Wasn't enjoying it anymore,' Chris says.

'That takes guts,' Hammett said.

'To stop enjoying cricket?'

'To own up to it.'

After the initial pleasantries, Davis feels the well-intentioned joviality ebb. It seems to strike them all: where they're going, who they're with. The car grows quiet, and their exchanges, it seems to Davis, become post-apocalyptic, intermittent grabs out of the silence. Hammett stares out the window at the noise barriers. He'd have preferred the slow drive on Canterbury Road, but Davis wouldn't have it. Ma will be waiting.

'So you play for five days and it's a draw,' Hammett says to Chris. 'Fucken cricket, eh?'

'That's life,' Chris says. 'You expect someone'll end up the winner and someone else'll be the loser, but in the wash-up, everything's a draw and you've got to work it out yourself.'

'Shit, and you've become a philosopher in the last five years.'

Chris spins around. Hammett flinches, but maintains his challenging smirk, a hand half-raised protectively.

'How about,' Chris says, 'we call it a draw.'

As they approach their mother's address, the silences thicken and curdle. The rain stops and a light-grey dryness spreads across the roads. Chris turns on the radio and flicks from station to station. Davis's palms dampen.

They approach the street where the porch lights come on early, where the native flora is friendly, where the gutters are carved out of the earth in efficient vectors.

Davis comes to the crest of the hill. Hammett's eyes well up. But Davis is going too fast to make the right-hand turn. Chris and Hammett brace themselves against the door. *Solomon Grundy* . . .

'Whoa!'

Instead of turning in, Davis accelerates past the driveway and scoots down the hill past the house.

'Whoa, brother!'

He zooms down the valley, giving them a thrill and a fright. The tyres sing around a corner into a bush cul-de-sac. Davis pulls a handbrake turn, an authentic donut, bringing the car to a sighing standstill.

Hammett's heart pounds in his ears. Chris kneads his sore bandaged finger, still raw where he tore off the cuticle.

Davis stares out the window at the neat cul-de-sac houses. In the yellow-brick house directly facing the car, they used to know a kid whose parents were into wife-swapping.

Davis turns to his left and faces his brothers.

'It wasn't you,' he nods at Chris.

'Eh?'

'The lip. I had an operation.'

'Can't fucken understand a word.' Chris shakes his head.

'Yeah no, he says he had an operation. On the lip,' Hammett says. Davis nods agreement and switches off the engine.

'Ah, right,' Chris says. 'Collagen injection. Can't say I'm surprised, you always were a vain fucker.'

Hammett snickers in the back seat. Suddenly Davis remembers something of the dynamic between those two. When all else failed, they found common cause in picking on their eldest brother.

'So,' Hammett says. 'Who's going to be there?'

Chris says: 'Ma, probably Ian . . .'

'Mr Bertrand?'

'He'll behave. Ma wants you. He'll keep his trap shut. Anyway. Suzie and the kids will drop in later.'

'Lucy?' Hammett looks at Davis, who shakes his head.

Chris turns and gives Hammett his first smile of the day. 'Davo and Luce are no more.'

'Kidding.'

'Uh-uh. Finito.'

'What, Davo, you come out of the closet?'

Chris snorts and shakes his head. 'Not yet. He's got a new girlie. Doctor, locum at Pa's surgery. Davo's wrapped up in her like a kid on his first date.'

'Is she there?'

'Not today. Story is, Davo's been mooning around this bird for months. So yesterday he finally works up the guts to call Luce and says, you know, "Let's talk." And Luce says: "Davis, let me make it easy for you." Turns out she's been boffing some dickhead at work.'

'This family . . .'

'Yeah well, so it's like, the separation's mutual and amicable. The big Daily Double. Mutual and Amicable.'

'The locum, eh?' Hammett leans forward between the seats and grins at Davis.

'You'll meet her at the funeral tomorrow,' Chris says. 'Davo says she's a hottie.'

'I never said that,' Davis says.

'I can tell by the way you're smirking,' Chris says, shooting a wink at Hammett. 'Anyway, Pa told me she was a good sort. But if she's that tidy she won't be hanging out with a dork like Davo for long.'

'Yeah no,' Hammett says, 'I've always wondered why a cum-guzzling hornbag like Suzie's hung around with a dork like you.'

Chris shapes up to say something, but uncoils. Hammett falls back into his seat, cackling.

'Anyway, so I'm quitting,' Chris says, massaging his bandaged finger. 'Try and make up some lost ground.'

Chris considers telling Hammett what's uppermost in his mind. Waking up naked with that girl, that autograph-hunter, in a bed beside him. The state she was in. Putting together in his mind what must have happened when he passed out last night. His thoughts when he woke this morning: the clarification of what he must have been thinking for a long, long time: *Time I did something to make the family proud of me.* Hammett's one person who would be able to say something interesting about that. Hammett's the only one who wouldn't pass judgment.

But later. He'll tell Hammett later.

'Yeah no, I've met the locum,' Hammett says.

'Eh?' Chris looks at Davis, who nods. 'When?'

'That night.'

'So . . .' Chris swallows. 'You were with him.'

'That's why I'm here,' Hammett says. 'He had a message for you lot.'

'Fuck me,' Chris says, staring at the house across the road and flipping his armrest ashtray. Up, down, up, down. Davis wonders if now is the right time to tell Chris, whose behaviour has become so unpredictable, that it is as easy to imagine him responding calmly as flying into a temper and throwing Hammett out of the car. Davis is about to caution Hammett, but Chris says quietly: 'What happened?'

'What happened,' Hammett looks at Chris directly for the first time in five years, 'is he was sick. He was going to keel over any minute. And he'd really wanted to die, he hated himself so badly. But then he changed his mind. He wanted to make peace with all of us. He did. But it was too late.'

'Two days ago,' Chris says, 'I'd have beaten the shit out of you.'

'And now you like me again?'

'Enough not to beat you up, anyway.'

'Yeah no, Pa just wanted to talk to Ma. He wanted to clear things up. He just wanted us all to, you know . . .'

'Be back like we used to be?'

'We never were what we used to be. But he wanted us to be able to look each other in the eye and say the truth. Which would be something completely new.'

'So,' Chris says, 'you're going to say he keeled over on the job, he was out on the tool with some bird? What's the locum got to do with it? Is that what happened?'

'Tell him,' Davis says.

It is the first time Davis has spoken since stopping the car. He tilts the rear vision mirror and repeats, to Hammett: 'Tell him.'

Chris blinks at Davis, then Hammett.

'Yeah no, Davo's been a big detective,' Hammett says. 'He found it all out.'

'What?' Chris looks at Davis. Davis stares out through the window. There used to be a short cut between the two houses at the end of this cul-de-sac, cutting through a grevillea forest and coming out near home.

'Pa fainted three times in a week,' Hammett said. 'He was fucked, and he knew it. He came to see me on New Year's Eve, and we went to a show.'

'A show?'

'You don't want to go there.'

'What kind of show?'

'Fucken shut up, Chris. Just listen up for once. Pa and I went back to his surgery after the show, we were ready to leave, and he went down like a sack of spuds. Right in his own fucken reception.'

'He died at home,' Chris says.

'Oh yeah? Since when do you know jack-shit?'

'Jim Cobcroft signed his death certificate.'

'Well, no,' Hammett says. 'I was there. It happened in his

surgery. Cobcroft was the first person I called, but it turned out he was up in Noosa.'

Chris looks aghast at Davis, who nods.

'Jim Cobcroft,' Hammett continues, 'says to me, "Okay, call this number." So I call, and it's the locum. Who, like, I have no idea is Davo's girlie, but that's another story, right.'

'That's how you met her,' Chris says.

'Right. So Claire comes in, and she's all business, even though she's pretty cut-up. She goes through the old man's desk and finds this death certificate. It's all typed out, "heart failure" and that, and pre-signed by Jim Cobcroft. She just fills in the date and time and place. She looks at me and says, "Piss off." So I do what she says. She's on top of it all, totally. She arranges it so they take him up the North Shore so it all looks like he's kicked it at home.'

'This is bullshit, right?' Chris looks at Davis narrowly.

'All true,' Davis mutters through his bandaged mouth.

'Yeah, Davo worked it all out himself,' Hammett says. 'I mean, how the death certificate got signed and all that. A few weeks ago Pa found out from his skin cancer mate, old Birch, how far gone he was. He was totally fucked. So he got Claire and Jim Cobcroft to help him. He typed out his death certificate himself and got Jim to sign it, without a date. It was all fixed. He did it that way so Ma wouldn't be embarrassed. Just in case something happened at the wrong time. He didn't want an inquest.'

'He never told me.' Chris shakes his head.

'Why would he tell you?'

'Why wouldn't he?'

''Cause you're a fuckwit and, like, whatever else Pa had wrong with him, he still knew a prize fuckwit when he saw one.'

'Jesus.' Chris picks at the bandage on his wounded finger, lost in his thoughts. Minutes pass. Finally he says: 'We sort of patched things up a few weeks ago. Had a few laughs. He told me about Davo and the locum and that, but he never told me about this.'

'You're a fuckwit and a fuckhead,' Hammett pronounces.

'Anyway, but it didn't end there. Old Cobby had his own grubby little agenda. When Pa asked him to bodgy up the paperwork, Cobby got his fur up and said, "Okay, I'll sign your death certificate, but on one condition."'

'Which was?'

'If this death certificate had to be used, then Pa's share in the surgery would go to Cobcroft instead of Davo.'

'Shit, I thought I was the biggest cunt in this town.'

'Yeah no, and old Cobby would invite his little girl, Claire, in to take Davo's spot. But it didn't work out that way, see? Claire knew Cobcroft was a prize prick, and her loyalty was to Pa. So she and Davo put their heads together and worked out that they have big dirt on Cobcroft now – they could have his balls for brekky for signing a false death certificate. So as long as they've got that over him, he'll be a good boy.'

'Meaning what?'

'Meaning in three months' time, after Davo and Claire have taken a bit of a break, old Cobby will go out to pasture, and the surgery will go to them.'

'You're kidding.' Chris looks at Davis, who sits impassively in the driver's seat. It is a good thing not to be able to talk, he concludes. This tiny, hermetic space could not contain three voices. Very soon they will be home, with Ma; they can go out into the back garden and stretch their arms and breathe, run around even, smell the flowers and listen to the birds. Ma will have tea and biscuits, and they can all relax a little. Relax – at Warramunga Avenue! Davis catches himself smiling.

Chris is pinching the skin between his eyes.

'But this "show",' he says. 'There was some bird?'

Hammett chuckles. 'A platonic friendship, I swear.'

'So Pa wasn't actually . . .'

'Yeah no, course not. Pillar of the community, our Pa,' Hammett says. 'There was a certain pair of trousers, but Davo came in and did the right thing.'

'This fair dinkum, Davo?' Chris blinks at his elder brother.

Davis nods.

'Davo found it all out,' Hammett says, 'without any fucken assistance from you.'

'I was playing a Test,' Chris mumbles.

'And look where that's left you.'

Davis restarts the car. It gives off a satisfying hum. He throws it into gear, but doesn't release the brake.

'We'd better bite the bullet,' Chris says, almost to himself. He turns to Hammett. 'If you're going to say what I think you're going to say, then – then I hope you don't single the old man out.'

'Meaning?'

'Meaning he's not the only wanker in the family.'

Hammett drums his fingers on the leather upholstery. His mouth has gone white, just the way Chris's does. His brow is furrowed in the same twin vertical lines between the eyebrows where Pa's creased. He chews on the insides of his cheeks, just like Ma.

'I'll take it into account.'

'No,' Chris says. 'You won't take it into account. You'll go in there, and you'll be polite to her, and you'll be good as gold. We'll walk in the door and have a cup of tea and talk about the weather. We'll plan the funeral. Okay? And if you've got any gravel in your guts, which I believe, deep down, you do, you'll treat today as the first day of the rest of your life. You'll do what Ma wants for the funeral, like we all will. We'll make an effort to be nice to each other. Especially to Ma. Today and every day.'

'And if I don't?'

Davis sees Hammett in the mirror, and smiles. It's so easy to yank Chris's chain.

'If you don't,' Chris says, 'I'll go and get my cricket bat and I'll hit you for 331.'

'Not out!' Hammett grins.

'Not out,' Chris says, easing back into his seat and fastening his seatbelt.

Davis releases the handbrake and wheels the car out of the cul-de-sac.

'Jeez,' Hammett says. 'If we all know what'll happen in there, why are we all so shit-scared?'

The suburban canopy is unaltered, at peace, a monument to eternity as convincing as a canyon or a mausoleum. The storm has retreated and the sky has broken through. Sun slants through the trees, their summer greenness throwing a veil over the freshly washed houses. The lawns are spread out like green picnic rugs: every fairy-lit porch a family, arms out to shelter the guest.

'Leafy, isn't it,' Hammett says.

Davis gears down, double-shifting as he comes to the crest, finger flicking the indicator.

'Mm,' Chris's mouth twitches. 'Very fucking leafy.'

'It's not bad,' Hammett says, 'this time of day. You could be forgiven for thinking you could make some sort of a life here.'

They crest the hill to the driveway.

'You never asked why,' Hammett says.

'Why what?' Chris looks in the mirror.

'Why he was doing it. Why he was caught up in all that shit.'

Chris makes a sharp noise through his nose, but it is Davis who speaks, very slowly.

'We've lost Pa. Isn't that enough?'

Coming from the opposite direction, Davis doesn't have to pause at the top to watch for oncoming traffic. Solomon Grundy get fucked. He, Chris and Hammett are the oncoming traffic.

'Ready?' Davis says.

'Yeah no,' Hammett blows a whoosh between the front seats, 'now or never.'

The Cape Cod house presents the side of its face, crablike, implacable. His hand painting a sweaty polish on the steering wheel, Davis leaves his foot on the clutch and rolls the car down the driveway. He brings it to a halt in front of the open garage and pulls the handbrake. Bertrand's Camry is not here. Davis takes the keys from the ignition and looks up. The screen door connecting the laundry with the garage has opened. She works her way out towards them, angling her hips to slide between her car and Pa's. She is alone. She wears the same elegant navy-blue dress with the polka dots that she wore the last time Davis saw her, four days ago. Her white hair is pinned neatly into its bun, not a strand out of place. As she emerges from the garage into the white light she raises a hand to shade her eyes from the glare; but her guard of shadow cannot conceal the smile she has for her boys.

A NOTE ON THE TYPE

The text of this book is set in Linotype Sabon, named after the
type founder, Jacques Sabon. It was designed by Jan Tschichold
and jointly developed by Linotype, Monotype and Stempel,
in response to a need for a typeface to be available in identical
form for mechanical hot metal composition and hand
composition using foundry type.

Tschichold based his design for Sabon roman on a fount
engraved by Garamond, and Sabon italic on a fount by Granjon.
It was first used in 1966 and has proved an enduring modern classic.